PRAISE FOR *MUCH ADO ABOUT NADA*

"I'll read anything Uzma Jalaluddin writes. Her latest embroils a pair of stubborn ex-lovers in a Jane Austen mess à la *Persuasion*. . . . Warm, witty, and utterly charming."

—Kate Quinn, *New York Times* bestselling author of *The Rose Code*

"At once achingly romantic, wonderfully funny, and with a cast of characters that makes you want to move to Toronto immediately, *Much Ado About Nada* is a book you'll wish you could read again for the first time. Uzma Jalaluddin is one of the best writers in romance today—and this gorgeous book proves it."

—Sarah MacLean, *New York Times* bestselling author of *Heartbreaker*

"Uzma Jalaluddin has a remarkable gift for breathing new life into classic romantic plots. . . . Jalaluddin has created a pair of star-crossed lovers with deep history, crackling chemistry, and a secret that could change everything. . . . A genuine delight."

—Kate Hilton, bestselling author of *Better Luck Next Time*

"Tender, poignant, and fiercely original, this is Uzma Jalaluddin's best book yet. . . . If a slow-burn romance can break your heart while lifting you up to the clouds, Uzma Jalaluddin's *Much Ado About Nada* is that book." —Ausma Zehanat Khan, author of *Blackwater Falls*

"A love story that is both addictively tart and marvelously sweet told by a writer who has mastered the art of blending romance with laughter. . . . I didn't want it to end, and will have a hard time waiting patiently for another novel by this outstanding talent."

—Marissa Stapley, *New York Times* bestselling author of *Lucky*

BERKLEY BOOKS BY UZMA JALALUDDIN

Ayesha at Last
Hana Khan Carries On
Much Ado About Nada

Much Ado About Nada

Uzma Jalaluddin

BERKLEY ROMANCE
New York

BERKLEY ROMANCE
Published by Berkley
An imprint of Penguin Random House LLC
penguinrandomhouse.com

Copyright © 2023 by Uzma Jalaluddin
Penguin Random House supports copyright. Copyright fuels creativity, encourages diverse
voices, promotes free speech, and creates a vibrant culture. Thank you for buying an authorized
edition of this book and for complying with copyright laws by not reproducing, scanning, or
distributing any part of it in any form without permission. You are supporting writers and
allowing Penguin Random House to continue to publish books for every reader.

BERKLEY and the BERKLEY & B colophon are registered trademarks of
Penguin Random House LLC.

Library of Congress Cataloging-in-Publication Data

Names: Jalaluddin, Uzma, author.
Title: Much ado about nada / Uzma Jalaluddin.
Description: First Edition. | New York: Berkley Romance, 2023.
Identifiers: LCCN 2022058278 (print) | LCCN 2022058279 (ebook) |
ISBN 9780593336380 (trade paperback) | ISBN 9780593336397 (ebook)
Subjects: LCGFT: Novels. | Romance fiction.
Classification: LCC PR9199.4.J3515 M83 2023 (print) |
LCC PR9199.4.J3515 (ebook) | DDC 813/.6—dc23/eng/2022129
LC record available at https://lccn.loc.gov/2022058278
LC ebook record available at https://lccn.loc.gov/2022058279

First Edition: June 2023

Printed in the United States of America
10 9 8 7 6 5 4 3 2

TO IMTIAZ, FOR EVERYTHING

PART ONE

Once upon a time at a Muslim convention . . .

CHAPTER ONE

Present day

Nada Syed was no coward; at twenty-eight years old, she had simply learned that strategic retreat was the better part of valor.

Cell phone clutched in one hand, black ballet flats in the other, cream-colored hijab loosely draped over her short, dark hair, she tip-toed down the spiral oak staircase of the home she shared with her parents and two brothers. She crept toward the laundry room, which had a side entrance that led to the driveway, her car, and freedom. As she reached the door to the laundry room, her phone pinged with another message from her best friend, Haleema: I'll be there soon! We're going to have so much fun at the convention!

Nada shuddered. There were few things she could think of that would be worse than being forced to attend the Islamic convention over a hot July weekend. Perhaps skinny-dipping in the Arctic Ocean. Or being forced to eat her mother's offal-and-tongue *nihari* curry.

Her phone pinged again. Haleema really didn't give up; that persistence had fueled her rise to the top of her graduate engineering program, but right now, Nada wished her friend had the profile of a party-forward humanities major, because Nada needed to concentrate.

Coordinating a covert weekend outing was tricky. Her mother, Narjis Syed, guarded their front door more zealously than a nightclub bouncer and asked more questions. Nada glanced at her phone, reading her friend's messages quickly.

Aren't you excited? Girls' weekend! Then: Babe? Where's my sister from another mister? Nada? HELLOOOOOOO????

Haleema wasn't going to stop until Nada responded. Carefully dropping her shoes and slipping her feet into them, she texted her friend the perfect decoy message: Just getting ready. Big plans for the weekend! xxx.

Nada knew two things: 1) she couldn't attend the convention for reasons that couldn't be disclosed to anyone, especially not Haleema and 2) by the time her habitually late bff showed up at Nada's house, she would be long gone, snacking on a delicious latte and blueberry scone from her favorite café.

One might wonder why a twenty-eight-year-old woman didn't simply stroll out of her parents' house as if she owned the place, flip her busybody neighbors a flirty goodbye, and head to wherever the hell she wanted. That person was clearly not the daughter of traditional South Asian parents, nor did they live in the Golden Crescent neighborhood in the east end of Toronto, a.k.a. "the nosiest place on Earth." And they were particularly not the daughter of Narjis Syed, mother of three, interferer of all.

The side-door escape was the perfect plan, Nada thought, opening the door to the laundry room.

"*Beta*, what are you doing?" Narjis straightened in front of the washing machine, where she was sorting through a pile of clothing.

Busted.

"Answer your mom, Nada."

Framed in the doorway, her best friend, Haleema Olawi—pretty, perky, perfect—lifted one perfectly threaded eyebrow.

Double busted.

"Your friend has been waiting for you this last half-hour," her mother scolded, closing the washing machine door with a snap. She was a plump, diminutive woman, just barely five feet tall. Like Nada, she had full eyebrows and dark, knowing eyes. Her gray-streaked hair was gathered in its habitual braid. She and Haleema both stared at Nada, waiting for an explanation, but Nada's mind blanked.

Haleema had always possessed an innate ability to charm the aunties, and she used this superpower to full effect now, gracefully lifting her hands in frustration. "Honestly, Narjis Aunty, I don't know what to do with this one! Zayn got us free passes to the convention, plus a hotel room. I even have tickets to the matrimonial speed-dating event, and your daughter tries to back out at the last minute."

Narjis's eyes gleamed at the mention of matrimonial speed-dating, and Nada contemplated making a run for it. But Haleema had been on the track team at university and would hunt her down. Nada went with the snarky approach instead.

"When was the first minute?" she asked.

Haleema ignored her. Instead, Nada's soon-to-be-ex-friend widened her eyes. "Can you believe Nada hasn't even met my fiancé yet? Zayn's family runs Deen&Dunya, you know. Imagine, my best friend too busy to meet the man I'm about to marry!"

Deen&Dunya—Arabic for "faith and life"—was a massive Muslim convention held in downtown Toronto over a July weekend. It was like Comic-Con, except with hijabs, *jilbabs*, beards, and kufi skullcaps rather than intricate fan-created costumes. Nada had managed to avoid the convention since it first launched five years ago. This avoidance had little to do with Zayn, but Haleema refused to believe that, and now Nada was trapped between a long-held secret and her best friend's willful personality.

Haleema was the only daughter of wealthy entrepreneurs who lived in Dubai. It was true that she was a little bit spoiled and used to getting her own way, but she had always been a good friend to Nada. And it was also true that Nada had been ducking an introduction to Zayn for three months, the entire length of Haleema's whirlwind engagement. There was a certain inevitability to this moment, Nada realized, and as a good Muslim, she should know better than to keep fighting her fate.

"I was just on my way to pick up some coffee?" Nada tried, a last-ditch attempt at escape. She had never been one to give in quietly.

Her mother wrinkled her brow. "Waste of money. *Chalo*, I'll make you some chai while you pack for the convention. Make sure to bring a pretty dress." Narjis walked toward the large kitchen at the back of the house.

"And put on something cute," Haleema added. "You never know who you might meet."

Shooting her friend a "this isn't over" glare, Nada made her way to her bedroom. It was a good-sized room with two windows and an en suite bathroom. She had decorated in muted creams and beige. The bright, geometric cover on her Ikea Hemnes double bed was the only splash of color, the result of a failed attempt at reinvention years ago.

She hesitated at the door to her walk-in closet, her eyes drawn to the very back, where she had carefully hidden a large floral hatbox behind her overflow-hijab storage unit, beside her collection of salwar kameez. Inside the hatbox was . . . Nada shook her head. No time for that line of thinking. It was fine. The convention would be fine. It had been years and years and . . . everything was fine.

She threw a long dress, heels, and a matching hijab into a backpack, along with some toiletries, then changed into a navy-blue jumpsuit, an oversized blazer, and a pink hijab.

In the hallway, she bumped into her father.

Abbas Syed was a tall, thin man, an accountant by trade but a mediator by inclination. His thinning hair was streaked with gray, as was his carefully cultivated mustache. He looked at her from behind round glasses that magnified his large brown eyes, no doubt wondering why she was in a rush—and what he could do to help. Abbas was forever trailing after his enraged wife or irritated children, calming everyone down and smoothing the path back to grudging family tolerance. Her father had only ever wanted one thing: that his whole family live together under one roof forever. This wish had led him to buy a large house at the edge of the Golden Crescent, with enough bedrooms and bathrooms for everyone, and a driveway big enough to accommodate a fleet of cars. He had also encouraged his eldest son, Waqas, to move into the renovated basement apartment with his new bride when he had married ten years ago, when Nada was finishing high school.

Waqas still lived there. Unfortunately, his now ex-wife had moved out six years ago. They shared custody of their twin daughters.

As her father's large brown eyes peered at her, Nada explained her haste. "Haleema is here to pick me up. We're going to the convention downtown."

Her father frowned. "Downtown is not a safe place for young girls. Dangerous pedestrians, opportunistic parking lots, malicious puppies, and traffic is always bad on the highway. Maybe you should livestream instead?"

Her father's anxiety was legendary in the Syed family. Maybe she could use this to her advantage now.

"You should tell that to Mom and Haleema," she suggested. "They're both insisting I attend. You know I would much rather stay home with you, Waqas, and Jamal."

A look of alarm crossed her father's face at the mention of Haleema. "As long as your friend is driving," he said.

Drat. Everyone was afraid of Haleema.

"What about the opportunistic parking lots?" Nada asked. "The malicious puppies?"

He patted her hand absently and shuffled to the kitchen in search of chai. Reluctantly, Nada hefted her overnight bag and followed him.

Downstairs, Haleema and Narjis were enthusiastically discussing wedding details as Nada rejoined them. Haleema glanced approvingly at Nada's outfit change.

Although Nada knew that Zayn's family ran the largest Muslim convention in Canada, his role was a bit murky. Haleema had described him as the general manager and once as the CEO.

"Actually, Zayn is an artist," Haleema now confided to Narjis. A risky move, in Nada's opinion—her mother didn't approve of any profession she couldn't find on the Aunty Pyramid of Eligible Careers: doctor, lawyer, engineer, accountant, or IT professional, in descending order of respectability.

"He paints?" Narjis asked, smile fixed. "So good for men to have hobbies, *nah*? Otherwise, they are always hanging about."

Nada hid her smile behind a sip of the cardamom-spiced chai her mother had left for her at the wrought-iron kitchen table.

"No, he's the lead singer of The Companions," Haleema said proudly, but Narjis only looked blank. "They're a famous Muslim band? Their first album, *99 Ways to Love*, even got a write-up in the local paper, and their first tour a few years ago sold out."

Privately, Nada wondered if this was true. She had done some light snooping after Haleema had announced her engagement, and while Zayn had a professional-looking website and enthusiastic fans on social media, she doubted the market for Muslim spiritual music in North America was large. Her mother, despite her prejudice against any arts-adjacent career, likely had it right: Zayn worked with his parents running the convention, and made mildly popular music on the side.

"We're going to get stuck in traffic," Nada said, now anxious to get on the road. She was very aware that any conversation involving weddings and employed men would inevitably lead back to her lack of either. The other women ignored her. Haleema was busy snacking on samosas and Indian *mithai* arranged on her mother's good plates.

"In any event, I am glad you have convinced Nada to attend the matrimonial speed-dating event," Narjis said now. "She has put off marriage for too long. She is the last single woman among her friends and she is almost *thirty years old*."

"At which point I'll be voted off the island," Nada added agreeably, and shot Haleema another glare. This was the first time she was hearing about her alleged participation in the matrimonial speed-dating event.

Narjis ignored her daughter. "There is a time and a place for everything, don't you agree?" she said to Haleema. "You can't leave marriage too late. Otherwise, women grow set in their ways. The problem is that Nada is too picky."

Haleema, ever the loyal friend, interjected. "Nada will marry when she's ready, Aunty. She has excellent judgment and has never rushed into anything in her life. She has her engineering job, she has her family and friends, and for now, that's enough. When the time is right, she will find her match. Inshallah."

Nobody could argue against Inshallah—"God willing." Nada appreciated the subtle reminder that the future was out of their hands, but felt uneasy with the rest of her friend's pronouncement. Was this how Haleema saw her? A woman with no agency. A staid, timid singleton too set in her ways to ever take a chance. Someone who waited for the vagaries of fate or an unseen hand to land the perfect partner in her lap, or preferably, in her father's study, asking for his daughter's hand.

Even more appalling was that her mother and best friend seemed to think that Nada was content. She must be a better actor than she thought. Then again, as the middle child in her family, her role was clear: make no waves, cause no fuss. So what if her heart was filled with regret?

Seeking a distraction from these uncomfortable reminders, she spotted a felt box on the counter and reached for it. "What's this?" Nada asked.

Her mother glanced at her father while he refilled his mug with chai from the simmering pot on the stove, before shrugging. "Some of my old gold jewelry. I'm taking it to be cleaned, to have it ready for when you marry. I will expect a full report after the convention."

Nada carefully tipped the jewelry out into her hands. Looking over Nada's shoulder, Haleema cooed at the treasure trove of bright yellow gold. It seemed polished enough to Nada, but she didn't have her mother's exacting eye.

This wasn't a few odd items; it was the bulk of her mother's collection, gifted and curated from her days as a young bride nearly forty years ago: floral *jhumka* ear bobs, heavy gold bangles studded with semiprecious stones, long chains with pendants, and several bridal sets with precious stones. This box contained tens of thousands of dollars' worth of twenty-two karat gold. Narjis seemed wistful as she watched her daughter handle the pieces, and on impulse removed a small chain familiar to Nada. The pendant had her name in cursive.

"I had this made when you were born. You never wear it anymore," Narjis said, before tenderly packing up the jewelry.

Nada fastened the necklace around her neck and rose, quietly thanking her mother for the chai. Even though she usually preferred coffee, she was convinced that her mother's homemade chai had magical qualities. "I'll keep an eye out for any suitable, single Muslim men at the convention," she promised, not really meaning it but wanting to make her mother happy.

Narjis nodded but didn't say anything else. It was a veritable truce and a sign that it was time to go. They had collectively consumed a half-dozen samosas, three *chum chum*, and two *gulab jamun*, along with the cardamom chai. If they didn't leave now, her mother would pull out the lunch menu. As much as Nada dreaded Deen&Dunya, delaying the inevitable was worse.

As if reading Nada's mind, Haleema smiled prettily at Narjis and uttered the only sentence that could free them now: "Thank you so much for the delicious snacks and chai, Aunty. Did I mention that Zayn has a younger brother who is single? He will be at the convention too."

Even though Nada's stomach lurched at her friend's words, they were effective: the women were on the road and speeding toward the highway in five minutes flat.

In the car, Haleema broke the silence. "I know why you didn't want to come to the convention," she said, eyes fixed on the inevitable 401 traffic.

Beside her, Nada held her breath. Was this it? Would she finally be forced to come clean about her reluctance to meet Zayn?

"Why is that?" Nada asked casually.

"I saw the program. I know Sister Rusul is one of the speakers at the convention, and Haneef will be there too."

Now the lurching in her stomach became a wave of nausea. She hadn't experienced car sickness since she was a young girl. Nada closed her eyes. "Did you really sign me up for matrimonial speed-dating?" she asked, hoping to distract her friend.

"Nice try. Anything new with Ask Apa?" Haleema asked, and Nada's heart twisted painfully.

Ask Apa was Nada's first, and only, business—the culmination of her dream to become a techpreneur. A dream her mother's best friend, Sister Rusul, herself a business owner, had encouraged. *Apa* was Urdu for "big sister," and Nada had conceived of the idea in undergrad, when she had few mentors who understood her dreams and struggles as a second-generation South Asian Muslim woman. What she had needed was an *apa*, a wise older sister to give her good advice. Ask Apa was born—a community-focused app that would allow users to get advice from a culturally sensitive search engine. Nada had seen the potential in microtargeting years before it had become fashionable.

Except her app, and business, had failed spectacularly.

"Nothing is happening with it. The app was dead on arrival," Nada said, and she knew how bitter she sounded. She had invested nearly two years in the app. She had borrowed money, worked closely with Sister Rusul on her business plan, toiled day and night, right out of undergrad. She had even had business cards made up: *Nada Syed, Ask Apa CEO*. The thought of them neatly stacked inside her closet made her want to cry.

"I always thought it was a great idea," Haleema said, her tone firm. "If that jerk Haneef's Ukhti app hadn't launched six months before yours—"

"I don't want to talk about this," Nada said. Whenever she thought about the wildly successful Ukhti app—Arabic for "sister"—she was filled with shame. That chapter in her life had been devastating and was inexorably linked with Sister Rusul and her son, Haneef, Nada's forever-nemesis.

"You're in a rut, and you hate your job," Haleema said, interrupting Nada's gloomy thoughts with her characteristic bluntness.

"I'm a junior solutions architect," Nada said. "It pays well. I just got a promotion last month. It makes my parents happy."

"I think you're scared to move on from what happened," Haleema said. "But I got you. If we spot Sister Rusul or her slimy snake of a son, we'll throw halal gummy bears at them. Nobody hurts my girl and gets away with it."

Nada felt a sudden rush of affection for her friend. Haleema was half Pakistani, half Egyptian, and blessed with smooth tan skin and large hazel-green eyes that gave her small, triangular face an elfin look. She stood at a petite five foot two, and her hijab was always fashionably styled. They had first met at the Muslim Student Association during Nada's first year of university and had become fast friends, though Haleema was two years older. They were both studying engineering and spent a lot of time panicking over assignments and exams. Haleema in turn had introduced Nada to the group of Muslim women she still hung out with today. Since graduation, they had all gotten married; a few even had babies now.

When Haleema turned thirty last year, she started to panic at her single status, even going so far as to ask her estranged parents for help finding a husband. Her parents had worked their Canadian contacts, and by spring Haleema had been introduced to, fallen for, and agreed to marry Zayn Haq, convention entrepreneur and allegedly famous community musician.

Nada picked up her friend's phone and examined the picture that graced the home screen. Zayn was a good-looking man with deep-set hazel eyes, a square jaw dusted with stubble, and thick black hair that flopped attractively over his forehead. He smiled cockily at the camera, one eyebrow half-raised in challenge, a knowing look in his eye. He was a bit too pretty for her taste, but her friend seemed happy. He looked so different from his brother. She put the phone away and opened the windows to get some fresh air.

They zoomed past the familiar outlines of the CN Tower and the Rogers Centre stadium, where the Blue Jays played, the wind making Nada's hijab flap around wildly.

"Maybe I am a little nervous to attend the convention," Nada admitted in a small voice, her nerves playing an entire orchestra in her stomach.

Haleema threw her a wide smile. "You're going to love Zayn. And I can't wait to introduce you to his brother. Forget about everyone else. They don't matter."

Nada had tried forgetting. She had buried her secrets and regrets in a small bundle she kept hidden in a floral hatbox inside her closet. It hadn't helped; even years later, they kept bubbling to the surface, magma that threatened to erupt in a dramatic volcanic explosion, obscuring her emotional atmosphere and making progress impossible.

She had prayed for a sign. She had been patient. She had tried, again and again, to move on, to forget. Nothing had worked. Now fate had set its sights on her at last. In a way, this moment was inevitable. More importantly, Nada was tired of running.

They pulled up to the Metro Toronto Convention Centre, and Nada stepped out, ready for whatever came next.

CHAPTER TWO

Present day

As she stood outside the convention center entrance, Nada realized that she had spent so much time trying not to panic about who she might bump into at Deen&Dunya that she hadn't devoted any panic to the convention itself. Her eyes widened as she walked into the soaring entrance hall with Haleema. The space was already teeming with people. While she had known the Deen&Dunya convention was popular, she hadn't realized it had grown into such a massive success these last five years.

"Zayn told me over twenty thousand people registered this year, with people coming from all over the States and Canada," Haleema said, pride clear in her voice. No wonder she had insisted Nada dress up—this was clearly a place to see and be seen, if the fashion parade of attractive hijabi women everywhere was any indication. Haleema had chosen a pretty emerald dress that cinched at the waist and highlighted her hazel-green eyes, paired with a camel-colored hijab and matching heels. Nada was glad her friend had forced her to change. The elegant navy-blue jumpsuit and blazer with the sleeves rolled up to showcase her favorite bracelet was the right combination of effortless cute. She was also grateful that she had decided to stick with her black ballet flats; Haleema would be complaining about pinched toes within the hour, judging by the sheer sprawling size of the convention center.

Beside Nada, Haleema chattered on about the Islamic scholars and politicians who had traveled to be on the bill, as well as the gala dinner for VIP guests tomorrow—for which they had tickets, naturally. "Also we can't miss the concert tonight! Zayn will be performing. You're going to love it!"

As the women made their way through the entrance hall, Nada kept turning her head, trying to take everything in, from the banks of escalators transporting eager conventioneers, to the enormous bazaar with more booths than she could see from this angle, and was that a pop-up food court? Her head grew dizzy as she tried to absorb the scope of Deen&Dunya. Haleema's boasts about her fiancé now took on a new light, and she rapidly recalibrated her initial assumption. If Zayn was even partially responsible for this undertaking, she was impressed.

"See why I've been bugging you for years to attend?" Haleema said now. "You're going to meet so many boys!"

Nada laughed. Her friend was nothing if not focused, though it was true that Islamic conventions were notorious for meet-cutes—sanctioned, serendipitous, or more formally arranged.

But it was more than that, Nada thought as she looked around. There was a buzzing electricity in the air, the happy hum of thousands of people greeting, meeting, and reuniting. The only other times Nada had been surrounded by large numbers of Muslims were during Eid celebrations at her mosque, but this convention was on another level. An unexpected swell of joy replaced the butterflies in her stomach. It felt affirming to be part of the crowd, to watch her fellow Muslims take up space and center their stories, experiences, problems, and triumphs.

This feeling of belonging lasted until she spotted the snaking line in front of the registration tables by the escalators. Undaunted,

Haleema headed straight for the middle, where their friends Marya and Owais let them cut.

"My sisters," Marya explained to the older woman behind them, who rolled her eyes and muttered something insulting about their mothers in Urdu, before shifting to accommodate the interlopers. Cutting the line was a mostly tolerated tradition at these events.

Marya had been one of the first women Haleema had introduced Nada to in undergrad. She was a thickset woman with sharp eyes and a generous mouth, now a pediatrician and married to a tax attorney. They lived with Owais's parents in a massive house on posh Mississauga Road, in the west end of the city. Marya hugged Nada first before turning to Haleema, cooing over her friend's two-karat princess-cut diamond engagement ring, and peppering her with questions about Zayn. Owais held their two-year-old son, Ali, in his arms and listened with interest. Haleema's engagement had been quick even by the standards of their marriage-obsessed community; many of their mutual friends would meet the groom for the first time at the wedding.

"So where is Zayn?" Marya asked, scanning the crowd as if he would appear when summoned. "I thought you'd get the royal treatment, now that you're marrying into the Haq dynasty. Text your man and tell him you're here."

Haleema obliged, and her phone pinged back almost immediately. "We're supposed to go to the hospitality desk over . . . there." She pointed across the hall at a lone booth with no line. As they approached, Nada spied a tall man, his face in shadows. There was something familiar about the shape of his head, the breadth of his shoulders, and her steps faltered.

"Is that Zayn?" she asked Haleema hopefully.

Her friend shook her head. "His younger brother," she said with a mischievous smile. "Zayn is busy right now, but Baz will take care of us. I've been looking forward to introducing you."

Nada felt as if she were walking through soup as she approached the booth, each step a leaden weight. Blood rushed to her face as she made out familiar features: smooth brown skin, hair cut close to his head, deep-set eyes, full lips. Baz Haq, after all these years. She couldn't stop staring. Then Haleema greeted him and gestured to her friends to come forward. He caught sight of Nada, and his warm brown skin turned ashy. As if he had seen a ghost.

"Do you two know each other?" Haleema asked, pretty brow furrowed in confusion.

Nada said nothing, but Baz answered. "From a long time ago." His tone was clipped, discouraging further questions. His face shuttered tight, Baz kept his eyes trained on Haleema and ignored Nada entirely. Mortified, she joined Marya and Owais, who were fussing with Ali.

Haleema returned to the group and distributed cloth swag bags with the convention program, name tags on lanyards, complimentary meal coupons, and business cards.

"You never told me you knew Baz," she said. She seemed hurt, her grand gesture ruined.

"It was years ago. I barely recognized him," Nada said, trying to change the subject. She ducked her face, hoping her friends wouldn't notice her panic. Baz had been so cold. With shaking fingers, she rummaged inside her bag and pulled out a shiny, bright pink badge with the words *Happily Ever After Matrimonial Matchmaking* emblazoned across the front in silver. There was also a bright pink ticket to go with it. The speed-dating event. Baz had packed this bag for Nada. She put the badge and ticket back in the bag. *Breathe*, she instructed herself. *The worst is over. You've seen him, he still hates you, the world will continue to revolve.*

"He said the same thing," Haleema said. "He said you looked so different from the last time he saw you. I was hoping to set them up," she explained to Marya and Owais, who observed this exchange with more than a little curiosity. "But I don't think he's interested after all. Sorry, Nada. You'll have better luck at the speed-dating event, I'm sure."

"Maybe Nada should put on some more makeup and try again. If you can bag a Haq brother, you're set for life," Owais said.

Nada wanted to smack him. "What do you mean?" she said mildly instead, trying to buy time, to calm down. The instinct to feign ignorance kicked in, and her friends stared at her, confused.

"The Haq family is rich," Marya said simply. "Why else would Haleema want to marry Zayn?" She handed Nada a business card from the swag bag.

Haleema made a face, clearly offended. "My family has done well too. Zayn is a good guy."

"A good guy is a bonus. A big bank account from a successful business is the lure," Owais said.

Marya frowned. "Don't be crass," she scolded her husband. "Zayn's family took a chance putting this convention together five years ago. It was a big gamble, but it paid off because of their hard work. Actually, I heard Baz Haq is the real brains behind the operation. You need to think like him, Owais, and open your own practice. I keep telling you . . ."

Their voices descended into bickering, and Nada tuned them out. She still held the business card Marya had shoved into her hand a moment ago, and now she stared at the black type against the muted gray background: *Baz Haq, COO, Deen&Dunya Inc. Conventions and Event Planning.*

She looked over at the booth where Baz was finishing up helping a young family. He glanced back at her, and even from this distance, she caught the subtle narrowing of his eyes, the cold blankness of his expression. A sudden anger seized her. Nada plucked the pink badge and ticket from her bag and marched back to the booth.

Baz warily watched her approach. She slapped the badge and ticket on the counter.

"Do you need a few extra?" he asked flatly. "It was hard enough to get one. The event has been sold out for months."

"I don't need this. Take it back. With my thanks," Nada added. Now that they were face-to-face, her bravado vanished as she recalled Haleema's words. Did she really look so different? She knew the years had sharpened her features from their youthful roundness. Her one vanity was her clear, light brown skin, for which she had her mother's genes and a nightly application of expensive cold cream to thank. Still, Nada was well aware that her beauty was the sort that grew on a person rather than striking them at first glance. This had never bothered her; the gift of spectacular good looks seemed more trouble than it was worth. Her height was average at five foot five, and she had inherited her mother's curvy figure. She had always felt comfortable with her even, neat features—her small, round face, large brown eyes, full slanting eyebrows, and slightly-too-large lips.

In contrast, Baz had glowed up. He had always been tall, but he seemed to have grown taller still, and his frame had filled out in the years since their last meeting. Now his shoulders were so broad they made the booth feel cramped. His skin was a smooth brown, and while the dark brown, deep-set eyes fringed with outrageously thick lashes were now making a thorough inventory of her face, she knew they were as unpredictable as his mood: warm amber when he was happy, darker when upset. His hair was cut close to his skull, a neat fade with little ornamentation, and a short beard outlined a stubborn jaw.

"Are you sure?" Baz asked, still in that strangely impassive voice. "Haleema said you were looking to get married. She promised your mother she would find someone at the convention." His eyes bored into her. "You're lucky to have such a thoughtful and kind friend. And here I thought people always got what they deserved."

Nada's face heated. "Can we please be civil?" she said quietly, hoping her friends—who were no doubt straining to hear every word—were out of earshot.

Baz laid a single finger on the pink badge, the color stark against his skin. "I don't know what you're talking about," he said smoothly. "Thank you for returning the ticket. Enjoy your first time at Deen&Dunya."

How did he know she had never attended the convention before? Nada turned to go, then turned back. "Your brother is going to marry my best friend," she said.

"It would appear that way, yes."

"I'll be part of the wedding party, which means our paths will cross. We can be friendly, if only for their sake," she suggested, her thoughts whirling. Had he looked for her in years past?

Baz stared at her, seeming somehow taller still, an implacable ice giant. "We're not friends, Nada. Our circumstances make that impossible." The implication was clear: *And you are to blame for this situation.* There would be no give, no path forward here, and Nada had been foolish to try. Still, he wasn't the only stubborn one.

She lifted her jaw. "Will you perform at the wedding? Maybe you could play the *daf*," she said, hoping for a light chuckle or a smile.

Instead, his eyes flashed with hurt so sharp that she felt viscerally wounded and nearly took a step back.

"I don't play music or write songs anymore. I had to grow up. I suggest you do the same." He looked behind her to the next customer in line, a curt dismissal.

Humiliated, Nada walked back to Haleema, Marya, and Owais. Baby Ali had started to fuss, and they were crowded around the stroller, cooing at the toddler, when she rejoined them.

"All good?" Haleema asked with a tentative smile. Her friend would expect an explanation later. Nada had no idea what she would say.

"Perfect," she said, forcing herself to return the smile. "Let's go meet your mysterious fiancé."

They made their way to the bazaar, Owais and Marya clearing a path through the crowd, which seemed to have doubled in size.

Behind them, Haleema leaned close to Nada. "Where did you and Baz meet? You never mentioned him."

Nada shook her head, feeling even more foolish. By insisting on speaking with Baz to return the matrimonial speed-dating ticket, she had aroused Haleema's suspicion even further. She had never had to explain Baz to anyone before.

"Oh my God. Were you and Baz a thing?" Haleema asked, misinterpreting her silence.

"Did he behave as if he was my secret boyfriend?" Nada asked sharply.

"No . . . ," Haleema started, then brightened. "A secret love, long buried in the past. How romantic!"

Nada sighed. "I first met Baz at Sunday school when we were kids. He . . . we . . ."

"Childhood sweethearts?" Haleema asked hopefully.

"At one point, I was his bully," Nada said quietly. "He can't stand me." She prayed that this would satisfy her friend and she wouldn't ask any follow-up questions.

Thankfully, Haleema only cracked a smile, amusement crinkling her pretty eyes. "Really, Nada. His bully!" she repeated, laughing. "Wait until I tell Zayn."

CHAPTER THREE

Seventeen years ago

Nada was eleven years old when she became a bully.

Regular school was tough, a jungle of hormones and mean girls and meaner boys, but Sunday school was different. For three hours every Sunday morning at the Toronto Muslim Assembly mosque, a large white stucco building adorned with a giant copper dome and minaret tower in the heart of the Golden Crescent neighborhood, Nada reigned as undisputed queen. And she loved every second of it. For one, she was popular. Her parents were well-known community volunteers, which granted her status. For another, she had attended Sunday school since she was six years old and was considered an old-timer. She knew how to access the best bathrooms, which stairwell to use for confidential conversations, and which of the Sunday school teachers were the most strict and which were most likely to turn a blind eye to small mischief. As reigning queen among the younger set, she also ruled on who was acceptable and who was not.

When eleven-year-old Baz joined the class in October of her grade-six year, Nada decided he didn't make the cut. Baz was a scrawny boy and short for his age. His hair was thick and unruly, sticking out in wild tangles from beneath a tight-fitting white kufi skullcap. He was dressed in a blue salwar kameez that was too short in the arms and too long in the legs. Worse, he smiled at everyone, displaying large, uneven teeth. His face was a jumble of mismatched parts too, his nose too big, his eyes too deep-set, his ears sticking out, and his neck too skinny.

In short, for a young girl who was neither cool nor popular in regular life, who was instead a frequent target of schoolyard bullies, Baz was an easy mark. Within five minutes, she wiped the smile from his face. By recess, she had convinced the rest of the girls in the class that he was persona non grata.

That year, Nada's Sunday school teacher was Sister Huda, a cheerful young woman who had recently married and was training to be a kindergarten teacher. Nada thought she was nice, even if she treated her students like babies.

"Class, can we all say a big assalamu alaikum to our newest student, Ba-zil?" Sister Huda said, carefully enunciating his name.

"My name is Baz," the young boy corrected.

Nada laughed out loud. "Basil. He's named after a plant!"

The class laughed. In regular school, she was most often the butt of jokes. One boy in particular, Matt, had started to say unkind things in the schoolyard. Last week, after a seating plan change, Matt had joined her table group, and the first thing he did was make fun of her name. "Nada means nothing," he had said, lips curled in a sneer. "You're *nothing*."

"Not Basil. Baz," the boy corrected quietly now, before taking a seat across from the table she shared with two of her friends.

When Sister Huda's back was turned, Nada leaned over to the young boy. "Why is your kufi so tight? It makes your hair stick out, like a plant."

Her friends gasped with delight at her remark, which only encouraged her.

"No, wait," Nada said. "Your head looks like a dome. The SkyDome!" she said, referencing the white-domed stadium in downtown Toronto.

Baz gave his tormentor a pointed look. "You're mean," he said. He ignored her for the rest of the class.

I'm mean, Nada repeated to herself. She liked the sound of that. At regular school, Nada was just another kid who wasn't very good at sports or lessons. She wasn't part of the upper echelons of the playground social hierarchy, and now that Matt had decided to make her a target, her remaining friends had made themselves scarce. When she had tried to tell her parents, they dismissed her complaints and told her to tell the teacher. But the teacher never seemed to notice when Matt picked on her.

And now Baz thought she was mean.

How delicious.

During recess, Baz joined the other boys on the basketball court. The boys had little interest in or opinions about the new kid's clothing or hairstyle and were happy to let him join them, especially when he proved adept at three-pointers.

When class resumed after recess, Nada drew a picture of Baz's head and made it resemble the SkyDome, its retractable roof open to an angry-looking sun. Smaller stick figures sat inside the dome. Neatly below the drawing, she wrote, *The Adventures of Dome Head*. The cartoon was passed around among the girls, who thought it was hilarious, until it was confiscated by Sister Huda.

Nada was roundly scolded for her artistic efforts and told to stand in the corner. She had never been in trouble before. On her way to the corner, she brushed past the desk where Baz sat. "Dome head," she whispered.

Baz ducked his head, and Nada felt the first curl of malevolent hunger climb up her spine. She spent the next ten minutes in the time-out corner plotting how else she could torment her victim.

For the next few weeks, Nada carried out a systematic campaign to destroy Baz's Sunday school life. She waited with a sense of glee for him to arrive in the classroom every week. When he did, she made sure to make eye contact and then roll her eyes and snicker, or whisper something to one of her friends. She always made sure Baz saw; she lived for his flush of embarrassment. He continued to play with the boys and ignore the girls. The children were still young enough to separate into two distinct groups—the boys played sports, mostly hockey or basketball, while the girls chatted or walked around the building.

Nada plotted.

She spread a rumor that Baz smelled, and the girls spent a few Sundays holding their breath whenever he walked past. Matt had started a similar rumor about her. He had said she smelled like B.O., and she asked her older brother, Waqas, a freshman in university, to explain what that meant. He kindly bought her a deodorant stick, which she applied diligently every morning before school. Lately, she had taken to carrying it in her school bag to reapply after lunch.

In Sunday school, she started another rumor that Baz was an orphan sent to the school to learn how to behave, because the orphanage couldn't deal with him anymore. At home, her parents were still not listening to her complaints about what was happening at school. They told her to avoid her bully. "He's probably jealous of you," her mother had said to her the night before.

Her favorite trick, the one that got her a stern talking-to from Sister Huda as well as the frazzled principal of the Sunday school, was when she stole Baz's brand-new Nike basketball shoes during the prayer and hid them in the girls' bathroom. When the shoes were finally discovered an hour later, Baz's face had shut down entirely, but she could detect faint tears in his eyes. Matt had stolen her deodorant from her bag last Friday and taunted her on the playground with it. "It smells like your stinky farts," he said, which didn't even make sense, but everyone laughed anyway. She'd cried in the bathroom afterward.

"I don't know what has gotten into you, Nada," Sister Huda stormed. "You've always been such a quiet girl with excellent *adab*, 'manners.' I know your parents raised you better. Is this any way to behave toward your Muslim brother?"

He's not my brother, she thought, staring mutinously at the ground. *My brothers would have told on me by now.*

But Baz never did. He never complained throughout her torment of him. He stopped smiling during Sunday school and grimly ignored her. He continued to wear his too-tight kufi jammed over his unruly curls. He continued to show up to class in a series of pastel-colored, ill-fitting cotton salwar kameez. He continued to play basketball with the other boys and not make eye contact with any of the girls.

Nada had started to feel a tiny bit ashamed of herself by this point, but it was too late. The other girls looked up to her, and she needed the mix of awe and fear on their faces to get her through the school week. She needed Baz's sadness and somehow craved his hatred. It made her feel better about herself. Sometimes she wondered if this was why Matt bullied the other kids. At parents' night, his father had been stern and aloof, and openly scoffed at his son's work, loudly comparing it to others' in the class.

The school year dragged on until it was time for the Sunday school talent night.

Every year the Sunday school put on a performance for parents during the spring break. The younger grades were pressed to sing an Islamic *nasheed*. The older children would put on a funny skit poking fun at their teachers. Nada's class prepared a tableau based on a prophetic story, with the message to be kind to everyone. Sister Huda pointedly made Nada play the role of victim in the tableau.

On the day of the talent show, the small gym of the Toronto Muslim Assembly was decorated and set up with chairs for the parents. There were streamers and a balloon arch, and Nada sat in the crowd with her friends, watching as the other students performed to applause and shouts of *"Takbir!"* from the crowd of captive parents.

Nada was dressed in a salwar kameez for the occasion—a pink, slippery confection that her mother had picked out, and which she hated. She wondered what Matt would think of her dress. He would probably call her a FOB, a term she had recently learned meant "fresh off the boat," even though she had been born in Toronto. He had taken to calling her "small, smelly Nada." A few of the other kids had started calling her that too.

On stage, she played the part of the bullied victim. Baz was the narrator—the job that got most of the lines and all of the attention.

She felt like a fluorescent pink flower in the slippery, shiny outfit. Her hijab continually slid down her head and onto her shoulders. At one point during the performance, as she yanked at her hijab and the gauzy, useless *dupatta* her mother had pinned to her shoulder, she caught Baz looking at her with sympathy. She glared at him; she didn't want his pity.

After their performance, Nada went to rejoin her friends in the audience, but Sister Huda and Baz stayed back.

"We have a very special performance from Baz Haq, one of our most gifted grade six students at Sunday school!" Sister Huda announced brightly. "Baz has volunteered to play the *daf*. The *daf* is a large, circular frame drum commonly used in Persian, Kurdish, and South Asian cultures. It is also the national instrument of Pakistan!" The cheery tone and beaming expression on Sister Huda's face contrasted sharply with Baz's stoicism.

From her position in the audience, Nada leaned forward. Baz had clearly been pressed into this performance. Even better, the drum he was holding was nearly as tall as he was. Nada nudged her friends and they giggled loudly. From the stage, Baz glanced at them and flushed. He looked at Sister Huda, who nodded in encouragement. Nada saw him sigh, and then he began to play.

He was good. The beat was catchy, and though his fingers were not yet strong enough to make full use of the range of the *daf*, he had potential. He began to sing one of the most famous songs in the Muslim world, in a sweet tenor voice. Around her, parents perked up. The aunty sitting beside Nada even started to clap along to the familiar beat.

Tala'al-Badru 'alayna, min thaniyyatil-Wada' wajaba al-shukru 'alayna, ma da'a lillahi da'.

It was the song the children of Madinah sang when the Prophet Muhammad, peace be upon him, first entered the city as a refugee, fleeing the persecution and violence in his home city of Mecca. A song about friendship, loyalty, and generosity.

It made Nada unaccountably furious.

Afterward, she couldn't be sure how the idea came to her. A bolt of inspiration from a dark, angry part of her heart. Her older brother, Waqas, was a huge fan of *The Simpsons* and faithfully watched reruns. Since he controlled the remote, she was forced to watch the show alongside him. Waqas never wanted to watch *Lizzie McGuire* or *Sponge-Bob SquarePants*. One of her brother's favorite side characters was Duffman, the boozy, pelvis-thrusting mascot of Duff Beer. Now, Nada jumped up from her seat and yelled, "Duffman! Oh *yeah.*"

Her friends giggled, and some of the adults—*Simpsons* fans, no doubt—laughed out loud. A few of the boys joined in, and a chorus of "Oh *yeah!*" rippled through the audience.

Sister Huda marched up to Nada and removed her from the gym, but not before she saw Baz carefully lay his stupid *daf* on the floor and walk off the stage.

Baz didn't return to Sunday school after the talent show. Nada looked for him every week. One of the other boys said his family had moved to Mississauga, the sprawling suburb in the west end of the city.

Meanwhile, things improved in regular school. Matt moved on to other victims. Her friends drifted back to her.

As the months passed, a quiet, tiny part of her wished she could see Baz one more time. To apologize or to further crush his spirit, she wasn't entirely sure.

CHAPTER FOUR

Present day

Nada followed her friends up one of a series of escalators that led to the top floor of the convention center, a cavernous building in the shadow of the CN Tower in the middle of Toronto's financial district. The convention's main lectures and concert would be held there, in a large ballroom, while a secondary area was occupied by the bazaar and food court.

The Deen&Dunya bazaar was housed in a space the size of an airplane hangar, one half devoted to the food court featuring dozens of halal food stalls, the other half filled with blue-swagged booths set up in a grid pattern with a central circular stage. The bazaar, teeming with families, couples, teens, and children browsing and snacking, had the atmosphere of a souk market. Nada dodged a caravan of giggling teenage girls followed by a pack of teen boys, their boisterous laughter on full display.

Zayn was somewhere in the bazaar, but Haleema didn't seem to be in a rush to find him. Instead, the three women browsed, Owais following with Ali in the stroller. Their first stop was the halal candy stand, where they stocked up on gummy worms, peaches, and cola bottles, essential snacks for the weekend. Next up was "Hijab Street," a stretch of a dozen or so booths that sold scarves in every color,

texture, and pattern imaginable. They identified colors and patterns to buy on the last day of the bazaar, when vendors eager to
get rid of stock would slash prices in an end-of-convention fire sale.
Over Haleema's shoulder, Nada spotted a small crowd gathering. She
drifted closer.

A young man stood on the circular stage, holding a microphone
and smiling rakishly at the crowd. He was dressed in a tight white
T-shirt that showed off impressive biceps, dark jeans, and expensive
sneakers. His symmetrical features, slashing eyebrows and deep-set
hazel eyes scanned the mostly female audience with the practiced eye
of a performer, and Nada recognized him immediately. Zayn Haq
was exactly as he presented in his photographs, down to the overly
familiar grin.

"Oh my *God*, he's *so* hot," a young woman said.

"I know, right? Have you heard his latest song?" her friend asked.
"I think this new album will be even bigger than *99 Ways to Love*. I got
chills when I was listening. He just gets me. I can't believe he's still
single."

Nada leaned toward the young women. "Excuse me, sisters. I
heard he's engaged to be married."

The girls—they appeared to be teenagers—gaped in astonishment.
"Are you talking about Zayn? The lead singer of The Companions?"

Nada nodded, wondering how many hearts this news would break,
and why the lead singer hadn't announced it himself. Maybe he had
been too busy with convention organizing. She glanced at the stage,
where Zayn was signing autographs and posing for selfies. How big
was his music career? If the throng of admirers was anything to go
by, he had a loyal following at the convention. She wasn't sure what,
if anything, that translated to in the mainstream.

The girls meanwhile were searching on their phones and whispering to each other. One of them tugged on Nada's sleeve.

"Nothing's posted about an engagement on his website or social media," she said, accusation clear in her voice. "We've been Zaynimals since, like, the very beginning." Her friend nodded vigorously at her side. "Even before he broke out with 'Only Noor' four years ago. I know he's been linked to a lot of women, so your news might be out of date. I'm Sofia and I run his fan page."

Nada was tempted to tell Sofia that her best friend had a solitaire engagement ring that might suggest otherwise, but the young woman had such a proprietary air that she defaulted to a mild query instead. "Zaynimals?"

This time Sofia's defensive tone was clear. "What his fans call themselves. It's just some fun. The whole vibe of The Companions is, like, tongue-in-cheek humor. That means it's ironic, but not in a mean way."

"Thanks for the explanation," Nada said dryly. "Maybe I was mistaken about Zaynimal."

"*His* name is Zayn; *we're* the Zaynimals," Sofia's friend explained, not unkindly. "But don't worry, you're a little old for his music anyway."

"Very true," Nada agreed gravely, her lips twitching. She remembered being this age. There had been a different band, a different pretty boy, and she recalled how intense her devotion had been at the time. It would be cruel to make fun now. Part of her was touched that these young Muslim women had a performer who shared their beliefs, perhaps even reflected their reality. If it wasn't for the fact that Zayn hadn't bothered to inform his fans about his engagement, she might even venture to say that this felt wholesome.

The two women turned back to Zayn. Catching them staring, he turned the full force of his smile on them, revealing even white teeth. He ran a hand through his hair in an "Aw shucks, who, me?" gesture he probably practiced in the mirror. Beside Nada, both girls sighed.

Sofia leaned over to Nada. "Even if he is engaged, it's not the same thing as being married, right?" she said slyly.

Shaking her head, Nada made her way back to her friends.

"I think I found Zayn," she said.

"He said he had a session," Haleema said, nonplussed.

Marya followed Nada's gaze and her eyes widened. "*That's* your fiancé?" she asked, goggling. "Is he some sort of . . . Muslim rock star?" The note of envy in her voice made Nada uncomfortable, but Haleema seemed to enjoy it. She shrugged, a small smile playing about her mouth.

"He's the lead singer of The Companions, a band he started in undergrad. Have you heard of them? They've gotten very popular with the younger kids," Haleema explained. *Mostly young women*, she didn't need to add. "Actually, three songs on their last album broke a few million views each on YouTube and are a big hit on a few streaming sites. They're hoping to do a North American tour, maybe next year. For now, he's working on his latest album. Zayn takes his creative process so seriously, but it's hard when he's also running things here at the convention."

Nada glanced back at Zayn, now posing for a selfie with Sofia and her friend. "I can see that," she said. "Do you worry how his music career will affect you?"

"It's all part of the job. You've got to be nice to your fans, otherwise where would you be, right?" Haleema flipped through hijabs.

"Sure, but the fans don't know your man is taken," Nada said. "He hasn't announced your engagement publicly yet."

Haleema paused in her shopping, and Nada spotted the hint of a frown before her friend shrugged her shoulders once more. "I'm sure he'll post about it soon."

Marya was still staring at Zayn. "He's heading over," she hissed, digging frantically in her purse for lip gloss. She quickly applied some, then fixed her hijab.

Nada rolled her eyes. "You already have a husband."

"I'm married, not dead," Marya threw back.

Next to the glamorous Zayn, Owais looked like a short, middle-aged banker. After five years of marriage, he had already developed a slight paunch. In contrast, Zayn was tall—though not as tall as his brother, Nada noted—with broad shoulders and a trim waist.

The crowd seemed to literally part before him, fawning eyes lingering on his easy, long-limbed gait. *Sex on legs*, Nada thought, and wondered if Haleema had started on birth control yet.

Haleema broke into that secret smile again as Zayn eased beside her. Nada couldn't tell if she was pleased to see him or just happy to show him off.

"These are my friends, Z," Haleema said casually, introducing Nada, Marya, and Owais.

Zayn smiled brilliantly at them in turn, crinkling his eyes at Nada and Marya in particular. "Welcome to the Deen&Dunya convention, sisters. Haleema has told me so much about you both. Especially you, Nada. Have you met my brother yet?"

Nada ignored the comment. "I heard you're working on a new album."

Zayn looked modest. "*Alhamdulillah*," he said. "It's a hobby, really. I'm grateful a few people enjoy our songs."

Seriously, Haleema? Nada thought. "I met some of your fans. Did you know they call themselves Zaynimals?" she asked. "One of them claimed to manage your fan page. They didn't believe me when I told them you're engaged," she added mildly.

A flash of discomfort crossed Zayn's face, and Haleema shot her a look. He leaned close to Nada, and his cologne made her want to sneeze. "I wanted to keep the news quiet," he said, his voice low, intimate, eyes trained on her face. "Some of my fans can be quite . . . intrusive. I don't want to put Haleema through all that."

Beside them, Marya piped up. "That is so considerate. Most husbands wouldn't even think to spare their wives the hassle. You must have so many young women stalking you, waiting for you, wanting to talk to you. I bet it's exhausting." Before Zayn could respond, Marya leaned close and held out her arm to take a selfie. "Don't worry, I'll just describe you as the hot—I mean, the super-talented singer taking over D&D! #MuslimRockStar."

Nada rolled her eyes at Marya's transparent ogling, but she had to admit that Zayn's words might hold some truth. The young women she had spoken with did seem overly interested in his private life.

She glanced over at Haleema, whose casual browsing now seemed more like an act, particularly since she was holding a hijab in a virulent shade of orange. But now wasn't the time or place to voice her concerns. "*Mubarak* to you both," she said instead.

"Thank you," Zayn said. "I feel really lucky. I can't believe Haleema said yes." It was a nice moment, but he ruined it by smiling at Nada and saying, "I heard you're going to the matrimonial event."

Nada's fist clenched. When Zayn smiled at her like that, he looked so much like . . . "I'm not going."

Haleema dropped the orange hijab and turned to her friend. "Yes, you are. I got you a ticket, and believe me, it wasn't easy."

"I returned the ticket to Baz already," she said, baring her teeth in a smile.

"Baz won't mind giving it back to you," Haleema said. "Maybe you should ask him now, before he gives it to someone else."

"Baz can give that ticket to whoever he likes," Nada said, trying to keep a lid on her temper. "I'm not interested."

The two friends stared at each other.

"I better go. I've got to discuss some D&D business with my brother," Zayn said. He winked at Nada. "I'll tell Baz you said salams."

"Please don't . . . ," Nada called, but he was already gone, the crowded bazaar parting for him once more.

"We should go too. Ali needs a nap, and we need to find good seats in the lecture hall. Sheikh Ilyas is speaking soon," Marya said, referring to one of the most popular scholars at the convention.

Once they were gone, Nada turned to Haleema. "I thought you said that stuff to my mom to get her off my back. We're here to meet Zayn and hang out before you tie the knot. Girls' weekend, remember? Finding me a date to your wedding wasn't part of the plan."

Haleema fiddled with another hijab on the table, much to the annoyance of the proprietor of the booth, an older Arab woman who had enjoyed the brief novelty of having #MuslimRockStar Zayn idling nearby, but now seemed eager to make a sale.

"I have that in green too. It will match your dress beautifully," she said.

"No, thanks," Haleema said, not looking at the saleswoman. "Nada, can I be honest? I'm starting to get a little worried about you. You're twenty-eight, and it took me a really long time to find my match. I don't want you to go through what I did."

"I have it in beige too. Young girls can't get enough of the neutral colors. How about pastel pink?" the lady asked.

Nada handed the woman a twenty-dollar bill and accepted the bagged hijab in whatever color she had blindly pointed out.

"Your friend is right," the shopkeeper said as she handed back her change. "Girls should be married by twenty-four years at the latest. After that, the men will go looking for a younger model."

With a tight smile, Nada thanked her, then steered Haleema away, maneuvering neatly through the crowd and lowering her voice. "We don't want the same things. I'm happy for you. Can you please just believe me?"

"Can you please just listen?" Haleema countered, not bothering to keep her voice down. "Not to indulge in scarcity economics, but we're swimming in extremely shallow waters here. You want to stay in Toronto? You want to have kids? You want to marry a Muslim guy who is nice, employed, religious, and doesn't have a girlfriend he's hiding from his mother? Your options aren't exactly plentiful."

They weren't fighting, not really. Haleema punctuated her comment with a warm smile, which Nada returned, but there was an edge running beneath this conversation. This wasn't about being set up or returning the matrimonial ticket, or refusing to accept her friend's prerogative, as an affianced person, to set up her single friend. This not-fight was about something deeper, and Nada knew what was really bothering Haleema. On another day, in another mood, she would simply say it out loud so they could discuss it and move on. *You're angry at me for not telling you that I knew your fiancé's brother. You're hurt that I'm actively refusing your help with what you perceive as a fundamental personality lapse: my inability to see my single status as a problem to be fixed.* But after the shock of seeing Baz again, she couldn't seem to summon her usual conciliatory words. Instead, she went on the offensive.

"Says the girl who is literally engaged to marry a *Muslim rock star*," Nada said. "You don't need to pretend to be cool about his teen-age fans, you know. Maybe instead of insisting on setting me up, you should talk to your fiancé about what will happen to all the fawning girls after the wedding. Or whether you need to take over the fan page, because the Zaynimals seem pretty cozy with their idol."

Haleema bit her lip. "It's not the fans I'm worried about," she said, then shook her head impatiently. "Focus, Nada. You know Venn diagrams? Like with the two overlapping circles and the tiny space they share between? Eligible, single, good Muslim guys live in that space. *You* live in that space. And it gets smaller as you age. Go to the matrimonial. What's the worst that could happen?"

Nada knew the worst. She had seen it happen to almost every married woman she knew: they lost themselves. They didn't mean to, of course. They might not even realize it was happening, but after the *nikah*, their old life ended and a new one began. Every woman she knew who had married seemed . . . diminished, somehow. She thought about her mother, even her brother's ex-wife, Jameela. Nada wanted something different for herself, and damn the Muslim Venn diagram.

She needed a break from her friend. "I'm going to pray *Zuhr*," Nada said. "You should spend some time with Zayn. I'll catch up with you later." She didn't wait for Haleema's answer before turning away abruptly. Heedless of where she was headed, she hurried through the crowded bazaar . . . and ran straight into a brick wall.

Or rather, a hard, warm wall of muscle. She jerked back from the force of the impact, and firm hands gripped her arms, steadying her. Face burning, she met Baz's annoyed glare.

"Watch where you're going," he said gruffly, taking a step back after she steadied.

"Sorry," she said, mortified. "I was . . . I just met your . . . Zayn is looking for you," she finished weakly.

"No, he's not," Baz said, his voice a deep rumble Nada felt in the soles of her feet. He jerked his head behind him, and she saw that Zayn had once more mounted the stage and was busy entertaining a growing circle of adoring fans.

"Glad he found his happy place," she muttered, and Baz's frown deepened. Trying not to compare the two men was impossible. Zayn was prettier, but Baz had more physical presence. With his sharp cheekbones and defined jaw, he exuded a barely repressed masculinity that paired well with the severity of his features.

"He insisted we add the circular platform this year. He said it would be a good place for interviews and performances. Now I think he just wanted a personal stage for himself," Baz said, lips quirking in fond exasperation. "I suppose you're a fan?"

He had put on a navy suit jacket over his crisp, white shirt, leaving the top button undone. The suit was slightly rumpled, as if he had spent the past hour running around to put out innumerable fires, and Nada swallowed hard. If Zayn was swaggering sex on legs, Baz's attractiveness was something different, more primal. She flushed. "I'm not a Zaynimal, if that's what you mean," she said.

Baz's lips twitched with the hint of a smile. "Pretty sure he wants to be the next Zayn Malik."

"Good Muslim boy breaks bad on the pop scene?" Nada said, a teasing note in her voice. "At his age, the best he could hope for is a Muslim Mick Jagger."

This time, Baz's smile was wide—spectacular, but brief. "I forgot you were funny," he said, almost to himself.

Nada tried not to stare. His smile was devastating. She had forgotten that about him, and a flutter of electricity swept through her at his words. He must have felt it too, because he shifted and took another unsubtle step back, creating more space between them, and turned to go.

"I always thought you were the musical talent in the family," she said. Why was she still talking? He clearly didn't want to be there. Yet he turned back to her, as if pulled, and while his expression had reverted to severe, he couldn't seem to stop looking at her. His gaze rested first on her eyes, then her hijab, then dropped to her jumpsuit, her hands, before returning to her face.

"Zayn started The Companions in undergrad. I wrote a few songs for him, but it was always his thing more than mine."

He was lying, but she had no right to call him out on it, since they were both still pretending their shared history had been nasty, brutish, and short.

Not a complete mischaracterization, in hindsight.

"You were talented. That sort of thing doesn't just vanish," she said. Why was she pushing this?

"And talent always leads to a successful career, I suppose." Baz's half-smile faded as he focused on something behind her. Then his gaze sharpened on her face. "I heard you launched your little app," he said, his tone suddenly mocking. "Are you the desi Sheryl Sandberg yet?"

Nada froze. "Go to hell, Baz," she said quietly, and a flash of uncertainty crossed his face. "Haleema made me come to the convention to meet Zayn. I never would have otherwise."

Somehow, they had drifted closer to each other, and he loomed over her now. "Mission accomplished. Now feel free to leave. But maybe you want to catch up with your mentor first. She always did give you excellent advice." He lifted his chin before walking away, his broad shoulders easily parting the crowd, not through sheer charm like his brother, but by his dark, determined presence.

Nada turned around and met the gaze of an older, well-dressed woman in her mid-fifties. Her brown eyes were set in a round, unlined face, her gold-colored hijab pinned in elaborate flourishes that resembled a piled-on updo. Gold and diamond rings adorned her fingers, and her wrists were heavy with gold bangles. It was clear she was comfortable taking up space; that was one of the qualities Nada had always admired about Sister Rusul when growing up.

Nada had learned the hard way that it was better to be wary of your childhood heroes. The older woman raised a hand in greeting, but Nada turned away.

CHAPTER FIVE

Present day

Of all the people Nada had hoped to avoid at the D&D convention, Sister Rusul was at the top of the list.

Rusul Nasr had been an old family friend. Even after Rusul moved with her children to Vancouver fifteen years ago, following her divorce, their families had remained close. The older woman hadn't just been her mother's best friend, she had also been a mentor to Nada, having started a series of small businesses before launching her wildly successful Muslim lifestyle brand, Just Her Co. She had been so different from Narjis, a stay-at-home mother who never dreamed of anything beyond the domestic sphere. When Nada had developed an interest in entrepreneurship, Sister Rusul was the first person she told.

Then, when Nada began working on the Ask Apa app, Sister Rusul had been one of her first investors. The older woman had guided her through every step of the journey. But in the end, Sister Rusul let her down spectacularly.

Nada's phone vibrated now in her bag, next to the bag of gummy worms. It was Narjis, calling to check up on her. Nada ripped open the packet of halal candy and stuffed a half-dozen worms into her mouth before answering the phone.

"*Beta*, where are you?" her mother demanded.

"Phmf," she answered, her mouth full.

"You should have messaged when you arrived," Narjis said. "I've called several times. When you didn't pick up, I called Haleema. She said she didn't know where you were."

Nada chewed the candy and felt strangely soothed by her mother's predictable scolding. Baz's words still burned: *Are you the desi Sheryl Sandberg yet?* Her shoulders hunched in fury and embarrassment. But her mother's next words pushed these thoughts out of her mind.

"We will be arriving at the convention tomorrow."

Nada nearly choked on a jelly worm. "You hate conventions. So does Dad. Jamal can't stand them either, and Waqas hasn't left the house in months." Nada's mind worked furiously. "Did Haleema ask you to come? I'm not going to that matrimonial event, no matter how many Venn diagrams she draws!"

Instead of asking Nada what she was talking about, her mother was uncharacteristically quiet. "I'm worried about Waqas. Ever since the divorce . . . I thought a few days around his friends might help."

Nada paused, thinking. While coming to the convention might just be an excuse to check up on her daughter—Nada would never underestimate her mother's nosiness—Narjis was right to worry about her eldest child. Ever since his separation and divorce six years ago, Waqas had avoided everyone. He went to work and then came straight home. He ate whatever his mother put in front of him, before disappearing into his basement apartment. The only time he seemed to come to life was when the twins were staying with him. He had lost weight, and the shadows under his eyes betrayed sleepless nights. In short, he seemed entirely bowled over by grief still. If she was being honest, Nada hadn't known her older brother had loved his wife that much; they had seemed like a passionless couple when together. Yet Waqas seemed to lose the will to live when Jameela left him.

"I will text you when we arrive. Make sure to register and make accommodations for Jamal. I'm sure there are elevators, but perhaps we will need a special accessible pass. Oh, and I expect you to stay with us at the convention tomorrow, instead of running around with Haleema."

"I'll make all the arrangements and won't stray from your side all day, even to attend the matrimonial event. I'm willing to make that sacrifice," Nada promised.

Her mother squawked her displeasure and, with one final reprimand, disconnected. Nada sighed loudly. During the call, she had drifted to the edges of the hall, where volunteers stood at the entrance to the bazaar, armed with walkie-talkies. One of them, a pretty young woman in a blue patterned dress and bright purple hijab, smiled at her in sympathy.

"Brown parents?" she asked.

Nada smiled tightly. "How did you guess?"

"You should meet my mother-in-law. I find the key to dealing with overbearing desi parents is to firmly and politely tell them what you're going to do, and then do it."

Nada snorted. "If only."

"It takes a bit of practice, but it works. Khalid, my husband, has improved a lot. You just have to be confident. Don't leave any room for discussion." The young woman smiled, and Nada admired her sparkling brown eyes and high cheekbones.

"You sound as if you're speaking from experience."

The woman laughed. "It took me a long time to find what made me truly happy, but I did . . . at last." She handed her a flyer. "You might enjoy this lecture. The speaker is really inspiring, and it starts in five minutes. Good luck with your family." The woman turned away to help a group of young tweens.

Nada looked down at the flyer: *Islamic finance: Women in Business and Beyond, 1:30 pm, Seminar Room C. Sister Rusul Nasr, CEO of Just Her Co.*

She was about to crumple the flyer into a ball, but her hand stilled. So far today, she had managed to hurt her best friend, provoke Baz, annoy her mother, and run from Sister Rusul. She didn't feel particularly good about any of those actions. Maybe it was time to embrace her chaotic good energy and try direct confrontation instead. Besides, she was curious about the sort of advice that her former mentor was now peddling to young women.

The seminar room was packed. At the front, a large table covered with a white tablecloth was set up, two large vases filled with bright flowers on either end. Two men were already seated beside a lone female speaker. The men were almost interchangeable, though one was in a gray suit with a long black beard, and the other was in a black suit with a short gray beard. In contrast, Sister Rusul, in her usual bright jewel tones, was a purposeful peacock strutting among dour peahens.

The moderator—another man, Nada observed—started the session off with a short *dua* in Arabic, before describing the seminar as a "deep dive into female entrepreneurship in the Muslim market" and then introducing the male-heavy speaker lineup without even a hint of irony. Sister Rusul, who'd always had a healthy sense of humor, seemed to find the situation amusing. Gray beard, a financial adviser, spoke first, followed by black beard, the owner of a small manufacturing business.

When it was Sister Rusul's turn, Nada could practically feel the audience of mostly women sit up and take notice. A few opened notebooks and recorder apps on their phones, their pencils and thumbs ready to take notes.

"Assalamu alaikum, thank you for joining us today. While my fellow speakers represent a wealth of knowledge, I'd like to share the mindset necessary to reach your potential and stay true to your roots when launching a new business."

Nada scrutinized Sister Rusul. The older woman hadn't changed much; she was still attractive, her face alive and brimming with confidence and ambition, but Nada couldn't help but raise an eyebrow at the older woman's current manifestation as a #GetItGirl business guru. Sister Rusul continued, sharing a story Nada had heard many times before.

"When I was a young woman in Tanzania, my father was a tailor. He was busy every day, working hard to support us. My mother was busy taking care of the family—I have six brothers and sisters, and the money was never enough. My older sister, on top of attending school, began a side business of delivering weekly magazines to the neighborhood ladies. You see, we lived in an Indian area of the city, and the women read *Pakeeza* magazines in Urdu. My sister made a deal with the local newsstand to have these magazines ready and waiting at the start of every week for her to pick up and deliver to customers. She made enough to help out my mother, and eventually she saved up enough to pay for my plane ticket to come to Canada when I applied for university here."

Looking around, Nada saw how entranced the audience was by the bright, blooming flower that was Sister Rusul and her charismatic storytelling.

The older woman continued. "As Muslim women eager to start your own business, I urge you to look around. You are privy to information and a circle of people you know better than anyone else. If you truly want to launch a business, you must think big, but also small. Who are you targeting? What do they need? How can you meet this need and make the lives of your community members better, easier? Ask yourself that and you will be successful, Inshallah. And Allah knows best."

On the panel, the man in the gray suit—Brother Haroon—shifted, visibly annoyed. Sister Rusul glanced over, and even from her seat at the back of the room, Nada could see the older woman's lips twitch in amusement. Nada could guess what was coming next. She remembered Sister Rusul ranting about the latent patriarchy that often greeted her during speaking engagements.

"Was there something you wanted to add, Brother Haroon?" Sister Rusul asked sweetly.

He grasped his microphone and said gruffly, "Women and these silly magazines. This is not good advice. We must return to the prophetic traditions, not fill women's heads with silly stories and *gossip*."

Despite herself, Nada gasped at his rudeness. She wished Haleema was here to witness this delicious moment of friction. Islamic conventions were usually staid, well-mannered places.

Sister Rusul turned her attention to the audience. "As Muslims, part of our prophetic tradition is to not bad-mouth someone behind their back, so allow me to say this to your face, Brother Haroon. The interests of women are important and meaningful. Furthermore, everyone is entitled to entertainment and joy. My sister's customers were mostly housewives. Reading these magazines brought them relief and happiness. They traded them with their neighbors. They discussed them with their friends. Most importantly, they recognized that my sister was trying to establish herself, and they supported her. That's what women do in our community, Brother Haroon. They raise each other up. I am happy to share that my sister's delivery service has grown and expanded. She is sometimes referred to as the Amazon of Zanzibar. And it all started with those *silly stories*."

Brother Haroon turned bright red at her words—nearly as red as Sister Rusul's dress, Nada observed. Around her, the audience seemed to be similarly enjoying the public showdown. A few women had their phones out, recording. She was pretty sure this interaction would be making the social media rounds.

Then Nada's smile faded. Did Sister Rusul believe her own words? Or were they simply part of this new girl-power persona, one which had already burned Nada? She had known this woman her entire life. Sister Rusul had attended her birthday parties and her brother's wedding. She had always expressed an interest in Nada's hobbies and what was going on in her life. Perhaps a little too much interest.

Nada's mother didn't speak to her best friend anymore and rarely brought Sister Rusul up in conversation. Narjis didn't have a lot of close friends in Canada, but she had taken her daughter's side in the aftermath without question. Another thing for Nada to feel guilty about.

Sister Rusul, a polite smile pasted to her face, scanned the crowd. Nada knew the moment she recognized her. They stared at each other, and then Sister Rusul reached deliberately for the microphone.

"We have a wonderful example of an empowered Muslim woman in the room with us right now, *Alhamdulillah*," Sister Rusul said, and Nada froze. All praise be to God, indeed. "Nada Syed is the young designer behind the Ask Apa app, a community-centered search engine. I am happy to share that my company Just Her Co. was involved in the early development process for this pioneering business. We wish her every success moving forward."

The audience's curious gaze drifted to Nada, and she ducked her head low, face heating. She could hear people beside her murmuring. One young woman asked another if she had heard of Ask Apa.

"I think it's an Ukhti copycat," her friend answered, and something inside Nada snapped. She was on her feet before she knew what she was doing.

"Sister Rusul, I have a question for you," she said loudly, heedless of the stares and phones now pointed in her direction. If Haleema was here, she would have tugged Nada back into her seat, or more likely, she would have talked her out of attending entirely. *Nothing good will come of this*, she imagined her friend advising. *Let the courts decide, not the court of public opinion.* But Nada had never taken the issue to court or spoken of it publicly. Besides, her friend was likely flirting with her rock star fiancé, and somewhere out there Baz hated her, and her mother would be at the convention tomorrow with her own agenda, and suddenly Nada felt an anger she had managed to tamp down for years roar to life deep in her chest.

The moderator told Nada that it wasn't time for the Q&A, but Sister Rusul waved his objections away and gestured for her to continue.

"You spoke about the need for Muslim women to support each other and shared that inspiring story about your sister," Nada began. "Would you also be willing to share some of the ways that you have failed to help your fellow Muslim sisters? A particular example springs to mind." Nada scanned the crowd, eyes glittering. "For instance, I wonder how many of the people in this room have heard of my company, Ask Apa. A show of hands, please."

A few people tentatively raised their hands. Most looked bewildered. They weren't sure what was going on. Nada didn't know, either. She felt out of control in a way she hadn't in years. She was usually so calm, so measured. *This is Baz's fault,* a small part of her thought. Two conversations with him had loosened something inside her. Or perhaps her body simply remembered things her mind wanted to forget.

"What about Ukhti?" Nada continued. On stage, Sister Rusul's eyes closed briefly. "How many of you have heard of the famous Ukhti app? How many of you have that app on your phone right now?"

The hands raised were a forest in front of her, the audience engaged now. The women beside her beamed, perhaps expecting a gold star for answering this question correctly. After all, Ukhti was a well-known success, the shining, golden example of Muslim-centered ingenuity. Stone-faced, Nada stared at Sister Rusul, and something dark and wordless passed between them.

"Failure is a part of the process of creation," Sister Rusul said. "A regrettable, necessary part. I have always admired your tenacity, my dear Nada, and I will make *dua* that your next business idea is more fruitful. Please tell your mother I said salams."

A dismissal, neat and swift. But Nada was not going down without a fight. "Failure is a part of starting any business, of course, but in this case, it was not exactly necessary," Nada countered. "And not particularly regrettable, either. Not when there were others to reap the benefits of my failure. Why don't you tell the audience what really happened with the Ukhti app, Sister Rusul?"

The older woman's lips tightened, and she nodded at the moderator, who quickly took control of the session, thanking the speakers and the audience for their participation, before ending with a closing *dua*.

Nada sank into her seat as attendees began filing out of the room. She could have kept going with Rusul, but a sense of self-preservation kept her quiet. Her eyes roved over the remaining audience. The few men were either waiting for their wives or waiting for the next seminar to begin. She noticed a tall, slender man leaning arrogantly against the back wall of the room. He was dressed in an expensive-looking light gray suit paired with designer brown loafers, hair carelessly mussed in a way that Nada suspected took at least half an hour in front of the mirror. He was attracting a fair bit of female attention, but at the sight of him, Nada's blood ran cold.

Haneef El-Haad. Sister Rusul's son and the CEO of Ukhti, the rival app that had launched six months before Ask Apa. A suspiciously close timeline, considering that his mother had known intimate details of Nada's app and that Haneef had been her adviser. Haneef smiled lazily at her, a poisonous plant unfurling in the shadows, and mimed a slow clap. Face burning, Nada fled.

Nada still remembered when she had first come up with the idea for her app. She had been twenty years old, and her friends had started to receive rishta proposals. Their descriptions of how awkward it was to go on a blind date while your entire family watched were hilarious. Even though Nada knew her friends weren't having any fun during their rishtas, part of her wished she had her own funny proposal story to share, which was the only reason she agreed to meet Abid Patel, aged twenty-five, on a random Sunday afternoon, when her mother had tentatively broached the subject. Nada agreed readily, even though marriage was the furthest thing from her mind, and her mother was thrilled. Nada looked forward to the comedic gold she would wring from the experience.

Abid seemed nervous, and after he settled onto the couch and Narjis disappeared to the kitchen to prepare a snack, he pulled out a glossy, multipage brochure, which he passed to Nada. *Requirements for my wife. Do YOU fit the bill?* was written across the front in fancy font.

Nada hefted the weighty portfolio. He had sprung for quality paper, at least. Her friends were going to die of laughter when she told them this story.

"I'm a business analyst," Abid explained, clearly pleased with himself. "One day at work I thought, why not streamline the rishta process, you know? Really put my cards down on the table about what I'm looking for in a wife."

"Great idea," Nada said, lips twitching as she skimmed through the glossy pages. There were pictures of Abid posing in front of a fancy sports car, in front of a tidy suburban home, with a drink she hoped was a mocktail. Interspersed through it all were his "requirements."

Do you get along with your elders? Because my parents are awesome and can't wait to welcome their new daughter to our home!

I really value education and I hope you do too! Your schooling will be a great asset when you homeschool the five children we will have together!

My favorite place to travel is my own imagination. Why waste money on a beach or the Colosseum when you can just use Google Maps and your own creativity?

Nada carefully put the portfolio down and leveled a look at Abid. His nervousness told her that he likely hadn't dated too much, if at all. She hadn't either, and she wondered at his naivete. Surely, he didn't think this was a good way to entice a wife into his arms?

"Abid, can I be honest with you?" she said.

The young man seemed startled by her question. "Sure."

"This portfolio sucks."

He was shocked. "My mom and dad thought it was great."

"It's not," she assured him. "It's patronizing, condescending, sexist, and makes you look as appealing as an expired bottle of achar."

Abid turned bright red and balled his fists at his sides. "What do you know? I only agreed to meet you as a favor to Aunty Rehana."

Nada smiled. "You're right. You and I are never going to be a match, so why not do yourself a favor and listen to someone who has absolutely no interest in you at all? I have nothing to lose by telling you the truth, and you have plenty of other rishtas to alienate if you don't listen to me."

To her surprise, Abid seemed to consider her words. He nodded at her to proceed.

Nada spread her hands over his brochure. "Women want to know that the man they are considering spending the rest of their life with will respect them, and this brochure shows them you will not. Think about it: you're asking a stranger to move into your parents' house with you, to quit her job, and to never go on vacation. Do you see how that might sound . . . ," she trailed off. *Insane* seemed accurate, but he might not appreciate that. ". . . a little disrespectful?"

Points to Abid: instead of bristling, he actually seemed to be listening.

She pressed her advantage. "Have you shown this to a sister or female cousin?"

He shook his head. "I don't have a sister or any female cousins that I'm close to," he admitted.

Nada spent the remaining ten minutes of her first rishta proposal giving Abid advice on how to go about finding true halal love. He wasn't a terrible guy, she thought, after he drank her mom's chai and they waved goodbye, never to meet again. When he loosened up, he had some thoughtful things to say, and the fact that he listened at all spoke well of his potential. For some other girl.

At the door, when she had tried to give him his portfolio back, he shook his head. "Keep it," he'd said, smiling. "And thank you. No one has sat me down and told me any of these things. My parents are too embarrassed. I have an older brother who would just make fun of me. My friends are either players or have never had a girlfriend, and I don't have any female friends. You made me feel . . . well, stupid, but also . . . comfortable. Thanks, apa," he said, using the Urdu word for "sister," a term of respect.

Nada smiled as he walked out the door toward his car, but the smile faded as a light bulb went off in her head.

Apa. Ask Apa.

There were a lot of guys like Abid. Hell, there were a lot of girls like her who could use some culturally specific advice on occasion. In the old days, they would have had a community to rely on for that advice—a trusted aunt or older sister, a community elder, their father or an uncle. Who did they have now? Unless they were lucky enough to have an older sibling or cousin who had traveled the path before them, most people were stuck. And then they made dumb brochures that would only lead to toxic, harmful relationships.

What if there was a resource? A widely available resource that Nada could put together and market. Everybody needed a big sister to run things by. It would be like a community-specific search engine designed specifically for her people.

She never agreed to another rishta visit, much to her mother's despair. Instead, Nada spent years developing the Ask Apa search engine and mobile app. It had given her a dream to work toward, some hope for her future and a light at the end of the tunnel while she slogged through engineering school, and other challenging moments.

Until Haneef destroyed her hard work without a second thought.

Afterward, she had hidden herself away. She secured a junior-level engineering job, which was where she still worked. And she avoided large-scale Muslim events where she might run into Haneef or Sister Rusul or even Baz.

She had lived in self-imposed isolation for six years. She should take Baz's advice and leave, tell Haleema she wasn't feeling well. A flash of red in her peripheral view, and Nada had a moment to contemplate inevitability once more, before Sister Rusul tapped her on the shoulder.

"Can we talk?"

CHAPTER SIX

Present day

The women found a quiet spot behind two pillars. Sister Rusul took a seat on a couch and motioned for Nada to join her. She did, reluctantly, wondering why she had agreed to this conversation in the first place. Was she about to be scolded for making a scene? Now that she had calmed down somewhat, Nada knew direct confrontation hadn't been the smartest move. For one, her mother would hear about it, which meant Nada would never hear the end of it. For another, Haneef had witnessed her outburst and now knew to be on the defensive. But after fiddling with the sleeve of her red dress, Sister Rusul's opening gambit had nothing to do with her son, Ukhti, or Ask Apa at all.

"I saw you speaking with Baz Haq in the bazaar, before the seminar."

Surprise prompted Nada to speak. "His older brother is marrying my friend Haleema."

Sister Rusul nodded. No doubt she had heard something about the wedding; their community enjoyed nothing better than news about matching, hatching, divorcing, and dispatching. "I hope you are being careful, *habibti*."

The endearment made Nada's fingers curl. "I noticed most of the audience at your session were young women. Does Haneef need another idea to steal for his company?"

Sister Rusul didn't rise to the bait. "I truly wish you every happiness. Baz might have managed to turn his life around, but he is still highly unsuitable—"

Nada stood, and now her teeth were clenched as well as her fists. "Why did you want to talk to me?"

"I was surprised to see you here after so many years. I tried to reach out many times, but your mother stopped returning my calls . . . ," she trailed off. Then she rallied. "Can we not put this unpleasantness behind us and look to the future? Haneef has repeatedly assured me that it was all a coincidence, that he had been working on a similar idea." She was not meeting Nada's gaze. *She feels guilty*, Nada realized with a start. "I suppose a part of me thought that in working together, you and Haneef might see how well you both fit. He has a lot of respect for you."

This made Nada snort. "So much respect, he stole my idea."

"He promises there was no malicious intent."

"And you believe him."

Head still lowered, Sister Rusul answered in a quiet voice. "He's my son, and I have always thought of you as a daughter. It was my fondest wish that someday our families might be more closely united. Your mother spoke of it too. Perhaps under your influence, Haneef might even have been persuaded in a better direction."

Nada stared at Sister Rusul. Was the older woman implying that she had wanted Nada and Haneef to marry? That she hoped Nada would be a good influence on her son, the human embodiment of *Shaitaan*? She tried not to shudder.

"Nada, there you are. I've been looking everywhere for you." Haleema eased beside her, and in that moment, Nada had never felt so grateful for her best friend. "I got you some chicken biryani, your favorite. I hope you're done here." Haleema stared daggers at Sister Rusul.

Nada allowed herself to be led away. While she was disappointed with her former mentor, the real villain had always been Haneef. The idea that her mother and Sister Rusul might have at one point contemplated setting them up made the chicken biryani lose some of its appeal.

"What were you doing talking to *that woman* without a lawyer present?" Haleema hissed. "Did she corner you?"

"I went to her seminar—"

"Oh, honey. Everybody knows you went to her seminar. Honestly, I leave you alone for an hour and . . ."

Haleema's furious expression easily cleared a path through the crowd to their friends, who were camped out underneath the escalators. When Owais, Marya, and another couple she knew only slightly caught sight of them, they peppered Nada with questions: What had happened at the seminar? Why had she stood up and yelled at the speakers? Look at this funny meme someone made of her launching a rocket at Sister Rusul.

"Cut it out, guys," Haleema ordered, before shoving the biryani container and a fork at Nada and commanding her to eat.

Nada obediently opened the container overflowing with still-warm chicken and rice, while the rest of the group returned to their chatter. Both couples had young children, who crawled on the carpet around them while their parents drank cups of steaming tea from the most popular vendor in the bazaar, Chai-lo. When Haleema handed Nada a fragrant cup of *karak* saffron chai, heavily sweetened, she nearly cried. Nothing was as soothing to her turbulent heart as a strong cup of tea.

Only after Nada had eaten did Haleema fill her in on what had happened. Nada's outburst at the seminar with Sister Rusul had been recorded and posted, and was currently being debated. While the older woman's shutdown of Brother Haroon had been entertaining, the "intergenerational cat fight" (Haleema's words) had captured most of the attention. Owais helpfully shared another meme, this one with Nada's face photoshopped onto Kylo Ren putting an end to Han Solo photoshopped with Sister Rusul's face. Nice.

"Not sure why you made such a fuss in front of everyone, Nada. No point being loud and argumentative," Owais said, munching on his second falafel sandwich.

"Would you have the same comment if it was a brother being loud and opinionated?" Nada asked. The food and chai had settled her, but she felt defensive over her impulsive words during the seminar. She should never have come to the convention. Even worse, a part of her agreed with Owais. She had been raised to keep her head down, to stay out of trouble, to swallow injustice, and above all, to never make a scene. But another part of her, the part that had been rattled by her meeting with Baz and the reminder of all she had lost, had revived and refused to back down.

Owais was taken aback. "I'm not saying any of this because you're a woman. I just think everyone needs to observe Islamic *adab*."

Nada resisted the urge to roll her eyes. A woman's behavior was often tied to the way she was perceived by others—and what was considered appropriate behavior. Yet what was appropriate often shifted according to the whims of whoever got to set the rules in the first place. Mostly men, in her experience, and then mostly reinforced by women.

"That lady you were yelling at, wasn't her son the guy who launched Ukhti?" Marya asked. "My sister loves that app."

"Haneef El-Haad. The IPO was in the seven figures," Owais said, crumpling his sandwich wrapper. "I made a bundle on that investment."

Nada wanted to scream, but Haleema beat her to it. "Shut up, Owais," she said. "You know the idea was Nada's first, and that snake stole it."

"Allegedly," Owais muttered, but he had the grace to look embarrassed. "Sorry, Nada. It was just a good business decision. I mean, a Google for the Muslim community? What a great idea." He realized what he was saying and flushed. "Have you thought about suing him?"

Nada scowled. With what money? And if a minor outburst at D&D provoked this much speculation, imagine the scandal if she actually tried to sue Haneef and Sister Rusul.

"We better hurry if we want to nab seats for the concert," Marya said, to defuse the situation. The group rose to their feet. The women threw out the take-out containers, finished the last dregs of their tea, and corralled the strollers. The husbands remained oblivious, not even issuing a cursory offer to help.

"Don't worry, we got this," Nada said to Owais and the other man, who didn't notice. "And you wonder why I don't want to get married," Nada said to Haleema, reaching down to pick up somebody else's trash.

"They're not bad guys. Remember how they were raised, the mothers who spoiled them. Not every desi guy is the same."

"Don't blame their mothers," Nada said, more sharply than she'd intended. "It goes deeper than that and you know it."

South Asian culture was deeply patriarchal—or at least the version of desi culture they had been raised with in Canada. It was a culture frozen in time from the moment of their parents' migration. Many of their parents had only been able to focus on preserving as much of their home culture as possible, in an effort to stave off their children's full-scale assimilation into their adopted country. As a result, there hadn't been a lot of space, time, or energy to question some of the more toxic ideas they had imported alongside other traditions.

Ironically, those same ideas had not remained static in India, Pakistan, Sri Lanka, Bangladesh, or Canada. Culture changed everywhere, but many of their immigrant parents hadn't. Haleema was right; their friends' husbands were, on the whole, far better than their fathers had been. But that didn't mean there wasn't a long way to go.

"They're all going to want to sit in the back, in case their kids fall asleep and they have to leave early," Haleema said now, conciliatory. "Zayn got us seats up front."

Nada leaned close to her friend. "Admit it: you're sick of hearing about dinner menus, in-laws, and husband problems. You're not ready to join the married zombie horde just yet."

Haleema shook her head but smiled. "See you all tomorrow," she called brightly to the group.

Nada and Haleema made their way to the main stage, where the evening lecture and concert would close the first night of the convention. It was always the highlight of the day, according to Haleema.

Her fiancé waited for them at the entrance, while a grim-faced Baz held a clipboard a few steps away. Zayn grinned when he caught sight of Haleema, his smile more real than the swaggering one he bestowed on his fans.

"You brought a second hijab, right?" he asked the women.

"A second hijab?" Nada asked lightly. "I'm already wearing one."

Zayn and Haleema laughed. "I'll explain later," her friend said, and Nada felt a pang at her words. The inside jokes had started already.

Baz glanced over at the trio, nodded politely at Haleema, ignored Nada, and scowled at his brother. "You should be on stage now."

Zayn shrugged his brother off and continued to chat with the women. Baz came to stand beside him, irritation radiating from his broad shoulders like a heat wave.

"Zayn," Baz said firmly. "Ammi and Abba will be watching you closely tonight."

Zayn didn't answer. He reached across to snag the clipboard from Baz without a word.

Baz rolled his eyes and left them. It wasn't until he was out of ear-shot that Zayn smiled cheekily at the women. "He's been such a pest since our parents put him in charge of the entire convention. I decided to take a back seat this year and focus on my music career. Give my little brother a chance to make use of that pricey MBA. But I insisted on the concert and Baz agreed. It's going to become the showpiece of Deen&Dunya, though my parents think otherwise." Zayn and Haleema exchanged glances, and Nada wondered when Baz had gotten his MBA.

"Zayn's parents wanted to keep the convention an educational, inspirational event, with lectures only. Except Zayn is so creative, and his band is so good," she explained. "They'll be thrilled at your per-formance, honey," she soothed, and sent a worried look through the open doors of the hall. "But maybe Baz is right? You're the master of ceremonies. The concert can't get started without you."

"They can wait. I'm talking to my girl." Zayn reached out and squeezed Haleema's arm—a daring gesture considering half the crowd at the convention would look down on unmarried men and women touching, even if it was an affectionate squeeze between two engaged adults. Haleema, on the other hand, seemed thrilled.

Baz reappeared at his brother's elbow. "Zayn," he said sharply, and this time his words held a warning. It was hard to believe that Baz was the younger brother.

Zayn held up his hands, waving the clipboard. "I'm going, I'm going." He snapped his heels together and saluted. "See you in the trenches, my sweet," he said to Haleema, before disappearing inside the venue.

Baz turned to go, but Nada was gripped by a perverse desire to get him to acknowledge her existence, like a child poking at a loose tooth. "Will you perform too?"

When he turned back, she noticed that he had fastened the top button of his white shirt and added a tie. Every time she saw him today, he had added more layers of clothing, as if he were donning armor.

"No," he said shortly.

"Why not?" Nada asked, mostly just to annoy him. He had a deep crease between his brows that only became noticeable when he frowned. Her fingers tingled with the urge to smooth it away.

"I'm not the artist in the family, Nada."

She shivered at the way he said her name. Beside them, Haleema looked from Baz to Nada, confused but willing to play along.

"Zayn said you supported the concert idea," Haleema said.

Baz nodded slowly. "We made a lot of money selling the tickets separately."

Haleema shrugged. "Zayn says it's always about money with you." She was teasing, but something about her words must have struck a chord, because he stiffened.

"Not everyone can play in a band all day and not worry about the bills, or paying vendors and creditors," he said sharply.

"I think it's a shame you don't perform anymore," Nada said, unwilling to let it go. "Especially since you were so good."

Too late, she realized that this was the wrong thing to say. The look Baz shot her was crowded with anger and something else, but he only handed his future sister-in-law a program for the concert. "Enjoy the show. The Companions are right after the lecture, so you should probably get inside. Knowing this crowd, your VIP seats might already be claimed by one of the Zaynimals." He stepped into the crowd, his broad shoulders easily cutting through the throng like a bad-tempered shark gliding through congested waters.

"He's just jealous of Zayn's talent," Haleema said to Nada, almost as if she was trying to convince herself.

Nada said nothing. Somehow she doubted that Baz envied his brother's musical ability, or the relative glory of performing for their community. He was moving away from the venue, and Nada thought she knew why.

"I'll meet you inside," she said to Haleema, and then headed after Baz before her friend could protest.

Nada caught up with him outside the bazaar. His long legs had covered the distance across the convention rapidly, and she was breathing hard by the time she found him.

"I can't do anything if a Zaynimal took your seat," he said, not slowing down. "I'm not getting into another fight with a tween today."

She trailed after him. "Why don't you sing anymore?"

He stopped and turned to face her. "Why do you care?"

I don't was on the tip of her tongue, but she clearly did. Otherwise, why would she have chased after someone who clearly despised her? "Because I'm afraid I might be the reason you don't perform, and for that I'm sorry."

Baz's eyes flashed, and he stepped close, crowding her. "It's years too late for this apology," he growled. "Don't think for a moment that my decision to sing or not sing, or play the *daf*, or look over the convention accounts instead, has anything to do with you. Your presence or absence does not matter to me at all, Nada. Do us both a favor and leave me alone."

"Coward." The word slipped out and hung in the air between them, startling them both. Then Baz's brows crashed down, and with a final glower, he departed, leaving her somehow breathless.

Nada returned to the ballroom on shaky legs and slipped into her front row seat without a word, grateful the darkness concealed her flushed cheeks. The concert was about to begin.

CHAPTER SEVEN

Present day

The concert was packed, the audience divided into three sections—women seated on the left, men on the right, and the middle section reserved for families and couples. Two giant screens projected the Deen&Dunya logo—two hands clasped together, surrounded by a braid of rope. A transparent acrylic podium was set up at the center of the stage, and behind it was a bank of tables covered with white tablecloths and decorated with ornate flower arrangements. Giant planters filled with ferns sat at each corner of the massive stage.

Nada opened a packet of gummy peaches and settled in to watch.

"Assalamu alaikum *wa rahmatullahi wa barakatuhu*," Zayn, the MC for the night's events, said over the loudspeakers. "May the peace and blessing of Allah be upon you all. Welcome to the fifth annual Deen&Dunya convention."

The audience roared their approval, some shouting, *"Takbir!"* followed by the rallying cry of *"Allahu Akbar"* (God is great). Nada loved this aspect of large Muslim gatherings: the freedom to make noise, to represent, to shout *Allahu Akbar* without being worried that the phrase might be misconstrued or twisted into something it wasn't. Muslims owning their space, even as they celebrated their culture. It was a thrill, one that almost soothed the sting of Baz's words. *Do us both a favor and leave me alone.*

Nada shivered and stuffed more candy into her mouth.

"We have a powerhouse lineup of speakers for you this year," Zayn continued. "Some of you have participated in the smaller seminars this afternoon, with speakers from all across the globe—Sister Rusul Nasr, Brother Yusuf Qari, Sheikh Omar Idris, the Right Honorable Jerome Levin, and so many more!"

Mostly male speakers, Nada noted.

"And finally, we are happy to introduce our headline speaker, who took time out of his busy schedule to be with us tonight: Sheikh Ilyas Raoul!"

The crowd erupted in cheers and shouts of *"Takbir!"* before Zayn ran through a brief introduction of the sheikh. He needn't have bothered—this was home court, and most of the audience members knew all about the famous scholar.

Sheikh Ilyas Raoul had converted to Islam in the 1990s. His family hailed from Venezuela and were devout Catholics initially wary of their son's embrace of the Muslim faith. The young Ilyas spent years traveling around the world to learn at the feet of famous *shuyookh*, or Islamic scholars. He had married and returned to the United States after earning a doctorate in Islamic theology from the University of Oxford. Once stateside, he founded his own Islamic organization in Michigan, the Center for Islamic Sciences. A charismatic speaker, he appealed to both younger and older audiences, and he had the ear of politicians and thought leaders. His profile had risen very high in the past few years, and this appearance was a major "get" for the organizers.

"Zayn told me they paid him six figures to attend," Haleema whispered, and Nada raised her eyebrows, impressed, as the star speaker took the podium.

"My dear brothers and sisters, it is an honor to be here with you tonight, to welcome you to another convention," Sheikh Raoul began in his famously resonant voice. "How happy I felt, earlier today, as I browsed the bazaar. How at peace I feel, taking in the smiling faces of my fellow brothers and sisters, my *ummah*, my community, as we enjoy each other's company, as we feel safe and comfortable and relaxed in this space. But, my dear brothers and sisters, not everyone feels safe representing themselves. Our sisters do not always feel safe, dressed in their *jilbabs* and hijabs. Our brothers do not always feel safe, with their beards and kufis. We are sometimes made to feel as if we were strangers in a land where we all supposedly belong. We are sometimes made to feel like outsiders when others look upon us with suspicion. What a blessing, then, to be at the Deen&Dunya convention. I return here with a sigh of relief. Take a deep breath with me."

Haleema leaned in to Nada. "I bet his speaking fee will help him feel a lot more *safe*," she whispered, and the snarky comment made Nada snort-laugh, eliciting dirty looks from the people seated around them. Listening to lectures was way more fun with Haleema's commentary in her ear.

The speech was heavy with the oratorical flare that the sheikh was known for. There were many dramatic pauses, repetitions, and questions that unerringly struck at the heart of his topic: "Remain Steadfast in the Face of Difficulty." A suitably broad subject for the famously off-topic scholar. After thirty minutes, the speech concluded to raucous applause, and Zayn took the mic once more.

"Thank you, Sheikh Ilyas Raoul, for your inspiring words. Our Saturday night concert will start shortly."

A hum of excitement ran through the crowd as the stage was transformed. The tables and flowers were taken away, and a thrust stage was moved into place. Zayn returned a few minutes later: he had changed into a long white tunic, and oversize wooden prayer beads hung loose around his neck. Haleema whooped loudly, and he grinned rakishly at her.

Three other men joined Zayn on stage. A Black man with a tightly defined beard pulled a large drum kit with *The Companions* emblazoned across the front in bright green paint, while the other two men looked so alike they might have been twins. Both were light-skinned with blue eyes, carefully mussed brown hair, and the exact same amount of beard stubble. The band members were all dressed in white tunics with different flourishes. One wore a leather jacket over his, another a vest, and the third a black and white checked scarf knotted loosely around his neck.

"Assalamu alaikum, Deen&Dunya!" Zayn roared into the microphone.

An answering roar came from the crowd, and Nada settled back, eager and curious to hear the band play.

"Before we begin, I have an announcement. Tonight is a very special night for so many reasons."

In the first row, Nada and Haleema exchanged glances. Was he about to reveal his relationship status and cause a Zaynimal riot?

"When I first started The Companions years ago, I had some help. He was my first supporter, my first songwriter, my biggest fan. He's the reason this concert is happening in the first place, mostly because he's the most persuasive man I know. Brothers and sisters, please welcome, for one night only, the secret master of verse, the behind-the-scene maestro of sound, and my baby brother, Baz Haq!"

Haleema gripped Nada's arm. "I wonder what happened. Baz never sings in public. I didn't even know he wrote their songs until Zayn let it slip a few weeks ago."

Nada didn't respond, because Baz hopped onto the stage, a large drum dangling from his neck. He was still dressed in the suit jacket and tie, a stark contrast to the other bandmates. In the audience, the

crowd of mostly women roared their approval. Nada was stunned.
Daf Man had returned.

"Whooooooo!" yelled a woman from somewhere behind them.

"Bang that drum, Bazzzzz!" another voice hollered, and Haleema
laughed. Nada's thoughts were a whirl. Hadn't Baz said he never performed anymore? Maybe he had just been saying that to make her
feel guilty.

On stage, Baz adjusted his microphone, ignoring the catcalls from
the crowd—because that's what they were, Nada realized with a lurch.
The mostly female audience was trying to catch his attention. Nada
had very little knowledge of spiritual music and Muslim artists. She
knew that there were plenty of talented musicians in her community,
but she didn't know any and rarely went to concerts. Around her, the
hum and anticipation of the audience were palpable.

Lights illuminated Baz's clear brown skin, elongating the shadows
in the hollows of his cheeks and emphasizing his strong jawline. He
looked out into the crowd and, for a moment, it felt as if he was staring straight at her. Deliberately, he placed his *daf* to the side.

Haleema pulled Nada to her feet and led her to the foot of the
thrust stage, where a small crowd of women had already congregated.
Haleema's cheeks were flushed, her eyes sparkling. This close to the
stage, Nada felt a rising, crackling energy, a current of electricity as
real as the one that powered the bass receiver, which was plugged into
the guitar Baz picked up now.

He strummed a few chords of the electric guitar, and the crowd
went wild, ululating, raising hands in the air, screaming with approval.
Nada had never seen anything like this at a Muslim event, and she
wondered what Owais would make of such loud female antics. Definitely not appropriate Islamic *adab*. As she looked around, she spotted a few familiar faces, including Marya's; she waved. It was so tightly
packed, there was no turning back now.

Baz strummed a few more chords and, after a nod from Zayn, grabbed the microphone stand with one hand and raised the other in greeting.

"Assalamu alaikum, Deen&Dunya!" he bellowed, his voice clear, loud, sexy. As if he had been doing this for years and not just for tonight. "Toronto, are you ready for THE COMPANIONS?"

The low hum of energy swelled into a great roar of approval, followed by thunderous applause, a tidal wave of sound, and then Baz—grumpy, angry, serious Baz Haq, who only an hour ago had assured Nada he would rather look over accounts than attend his own brother's concert—threw himself into a boisterous, high-energy rock anthem, accompanied by his brother and the other band members.

Nada's mouth dropped open. Baz was talented. The song was funny and sweet. It was about a failed love story, and the beat was fast and furious, a total earworm Nada knew she would be humming for the next week.

Around her, women swayed and cheered to the music, their arms up. An object flew by Nada's head, and she watched the projectile's path to the stage.

The piece of colorful fabric now lay by Baz's feet. It was quickly followed by another.

Not fabric. Hijabs.

Women were throwing their hijabs at the stage. Not the hijabs they were wearing on their heads, of course, but secondary hijabs, ones they had brought specifically for this purpose. The inside joke between Haleema and Zayn before the concert now made sense.

Baz belted out the next verse, and Nada felt the timbre of his voice run through her body in a delightful wave, while another feeling settled low in her belly. The barest curl of *want* unfurled, like a long-dormant flower. His voice spun a seductive web around her and held her fast.

His eyes closed, Baz sang out more lyrics in a deep, raspy baritone, his brother and the other bandmates backing him up on guitar and drums. The intense, almost pained expression on his face felt too intimate, yet she couldn't look away.

I'll find another bride
Call the rishta aunties
But how to forget you?
Teach me how to do that
Oh my habib-ti
Always my habib-ti
Never my habib-ti

Baz opened his eyes at the last line and looked directly at Nada. He winked, and the small gesture hit her like a physical blow. Every single woman around her screamed, and she felt stupid. Of course, he hadn't winked at *her*.

At that exact moment the tall woman standing directly in front of Nada pulled a bright red hijab from her bag. Screwing up her arm like a baseball pitcher winding up for a curveball, she jerked back. Her sharp, bony elbow connected with Nada's left eye socket with an audible crack.

Nada went down hard, and the world went black.

CHAPTER EIGHT

Fourteen years ago

It was her parents' idea to send her to MYNA camp, the week-long sleepaway camp for Muslim youth in the wilds of Northern Ontario. Campers slept in log cabins, ate their meals together, went on long hikes, listened to Islamic lectures, and bonded.

Nada did not want to go. For one, she wouldn't know anyone at the camp. For another, her brothers weren't being forced to attend. So what if Waqas was twenty-two years old and had just gotten his first full-time job? Or that Jamal was only six and afraid of the dark? It wasn't fair, and she let her mother know.

"Your father thinks this is a good opportunity for you to make some Muslim friends and get out of the house."

"I thought you didn't believe in sleepaway camp," Nada said. "You've never let me go on a sleepover before."

"This is different. It's run by all the local Toronto masjids. There will be adult supervisors, including the imam's wife. You will be fine."

No, she wouldn't. She would be bored and lonely, and all the other girls would already have friends. Her parents were the worst.

Her parents dropped her off at the Toronto Muslim Assembly parking lot at eight in the morning, where two school buses sat idling, ready to ferry all the campers from the east end of the city. Another two buses would bring campers from the west end. She boarded the girls' bus for the two-hour journey north. Her seatmate barely gave her a glance and slept the entire ride.

When they arrived at Camp Kinark, the sun was high in the sky as they unloaded. The camp counselors, all university students, organized the campers into groups. Nada was assigned to a cabin with nine other girls, eight of whom were already fast friends.

The ninth girl didn't seem to know anyone either, and Nada took the opportunity to introduce herself as they trudged toward their cabin, dragging sleeping bags, suitcases, and knapsacks.

"I'm prisoner Nada, reporting for duty," she quipped.

Her fellow prisoner had a sense of humor, thankfully, and stuck out her hand for a friendly fist bump. "Bisma, your fellow inmate," the girl said, her smile bright against her dark brown skin. "My parents needed to get rid of me for a week. They're in Hawaii, and I'm stuck here."

Nada nodded at the girls chatting in front of them. "I thought I would be the only one who didn't know anyone."

Bisma threw a contemptuous glance at the girls. "Oh, I know everyone. We've gone to Islamic school in Mississauga since kindergarten. Just stick with me and you should be okay. Try not to piss that one off," she said, nodding at a chatty girl whose hijab was down around her neck. "Firdous Malik, a.k.a. Queen Bee of all she surveys."

The other girls ignored Nada. They were too busy settling in and chatting about people—especially boys—they knew at school. Nada took the bottom bunk in the corner, while Bisma claimed the top, and they helped each other unroll bedding and arrange their bags. Their counselor, Sister Amal, was a meek young woman who steadily avoided eye contact with her young charges, and flinched when they giggled too loudly. Nada didn't think she'd last the night.

After putting away their bags, the girls were sent to the main lodge at the camp. Bisma chatted genially as they walked, sharing that she had been attending the camp since she was ten years old.

"My uncle's the imam at the Ibadat center in Oakville, but he volunteers at the camp every year. I'm an only child. My parents stopped at one because, they said, I was such a handful."

Nada wasn't used to such candor from a stranger. It was quite thrilling. "I have two brothers, one way older, the other way younger. I sort of feel like an only child too," she confided.

Bisma nodded in understanding. "Brothers are annoying. I have a lot of boy cousins, so I know. We all attend the Islamic school, and my boy cousins are always telling on me. At least 50 percent of the campers come from my school. Most of the girls are all right, but there's a few who will stab you in the back and laugh while you bleed out."

Nada blinked at the disturbing imagery. "Why?" she asked. She attended public school and had always assumed that the private Islamic schools were more civilized.

"Mom says fourteen-year-old girls are little psychopaths," Bisma said cheerfully. "Most of the fights are about boys, actually. We haven't learned how to actualize our femininity and therefore lash out from a deeply ingrained misogyny," she said carefully, as if repeating something she had heard. She smiled at Nada. "That's what my therapist says, anyway. Do you have a therapist?"

Nada shook her head, fascinated.

"Mom makes me go. Doctors all stick together, you know? Anyways, I'm not sure what my therapist means half the time, but she's helped a lot with . . ." Bisma nodded toward the girls in front of them. Nada understood: the little psychopaths.

The main lodge was a large building constructed from heavy logs with large windows on all four sides of the structure. It had a peaked gabled roof with wood shingles and a large wraparound porch, where weathered Adirondack chairs were set up. A hand-painted wooden sign that adorned the main doors said *Willow Lodge*, and there was an etching of a small bird.

Inside, campers dressed in hijabs, jeans, sweatpants, and cotton shirts were seated cross-legged on the floor. Firdous glanced at Bisma and Nada, then whispered something to her entourage. Her friends looked over and smirked. Nada made sure to sit with her back firmly wedged against a wall and ignored them.

"Here comes the reason why Queen Bee has ants in her pants," Bisma whispered to Nada, motioning as a crowd of boys entered Willow Lodge, all loose limbs and easy athleticism. Bisma nodded at one of the boys in the very front, a serious young man with skinny legs, a prominent Adam's apple, and messy, long hair growing past his collar.

"His parents and my uncle are all colleagues at the various mosques. But no one else is allowed to talk to or look at the object of Queen Bee's affections. His name is—"

"Baz," Nada interrupted.

It was the boy she had spent three months terrorizing, nearly three years ago. She still thought about him. If fourteen-year-old girls were psychopaths, she must have been an early bloomer.

He was staring at her now too. He almost looked as if he had seen an unwelcome ghost.

Bisma studied her before looking over at Baz, catching his quick movement as he jerked his gaze away. "Baz Haq, actually," she said slowly, a knowing smile stealing across her face. "This should be interesting."

After the camp director, an amiable older woman named Sister Salama, went over the basic rules (listen to your counselor; no wandering around unsupervised; no cell phone usage and especially no video without permission), they were put into cohorts and sent on their first activity. Nada and Bisma were put into the same group and would be canoeing on the small lake.

"How do you know Baz?" Bisma asked, making sure to keep her voice down. "He's real shy. It drives her highness Firdous nuts that he won't even acknowledge her presence. Usually, the boys she likes follow her around like puppies until she gets bored of them, but not Baz. He only talks to me because we've known each other since we were babies."

While Bisma chatted amiably, Nada wrestled with her feelings. She was so ashamed of who she had been when she was eleven: bullied at school, a bully at Sunday school. She didn't want to relive that time. Still, Bisma had been nothing if not open from the moment they had met.

"I made him cry," Nada blurted.

"What?" Bisma asked.

"When we were eleven, he joined my Sunday school, and I was sort of the Firdous at that school, and I . . . made his life miserable. He lasted three months. I haven't seen him since."

Bisma looked at Nada carefully. "Things rough for you at regular school?" she guessed.

"There's no excuse," Nada said. "I've felt bad about it ever since."

"People are complicated," Bisma said magnanimously. "I'm sure he barely remembers."

"You said he doesn't even look at girls," Nada said. "What if that's my fault?"

Bisma poked her playfully on the shoulder. "Ego much?"

At the lake, a cheerful facilitator divided the group into pairs and handed out life jackets that smelled strongly of damp. Nada and Bisma picked out a canoe and lined up alongside the other campers. Firdous stood a few rows down, trying to make small talk with Baz and another boy in a gray hoodie, who responded to the questions that Firdous posed.

Firdous: "Have you been canoeing before, Baz?"

Baz: ———

Gray hoodie: "Yeah, we go every year. You were here last year too, right, Firdous?"

Firdous: "I'm really not very good at canoeing. Do you have any tips for me, Baz?"

Baz: ———

Gray hoodie: "I thought you won an award for best paddler last year."

Nada caught Baz staring at her. She gave him a tentative smile, which he didn't return. His mouth was fixed in a severe line.

Unfortunately, Firdous caught the silent exchange and sent Nada a filthy glare that plainly relayed her feelings: stay away.

The lake was beautiful and lined with weeping willows whose branches dipped into the water along the edges, like a lady's dress trailing in the water. Bullrushes sprung up in between the branches, and Nada spotted lily pads and other aquatic plants. Beneath the surface of the water, small fish swam alongside their canoe. Nada turned her face up to the sun, the warm rays comforting.

"This doesn't completely suck," Bisma said.

"I've had worse experiences," Nada agreed. She fumbled in her pocket for her phone and, after checking to make sure no one was nearby, leaned back to take a selfie. Bisma lifted her fingers in a peace sign.

Firdous's canoe floated alongside the girls. "Phones aren't allowed at camp," she called. Nada slipped the phone back into her pocket.

"Everyone knows you keep your phone in a waterproof case around your neck," Bisma said.

Firdous ignored her and kept her eyes trained on Nada. "How do you know Baz?" she asked abruptly.

Nada shrugged, and Firdous reached across and grabbed hold of their canoe. Her partner, a scowling, plain-faced girl, held fast to the other end of the canoe.

"I asked you a question," Firdous said.

"They used to date," Bisma answered, mischief shining in her eyes.

"No, we didn't!" Nada said hastily, but the damage had been done. An ugly look passed over Firdous, and with a strength belied by her petite figure, she rocked Nada and Bisma's canoe. Behind her, her friend did the same.

"What are you doing?" Nada said, grabbing hold of the sides.

"You're such a loser," Bisma taunted. "He won't look at you, even when you throw yourself at him."

"Bisma, *stop talking*," Nada hissed, but it was too late. With a cry of fury, Firdous took hold of their canoe with both hands, and with the help of her friend, rocked it with such violence that the small craft flipped over, dropping Bisma and Nada directly into the cold water.

By the time Nada and Bisma surfaced, Firdous and her friend were expertly paddling away without a backward glance. As a parting gift, they had pushed the flipped canoe so that it was being gently carried away by the current, away from the girls.

"Sorry," Bisma said, treading water in her life jacket. "I wasn't thinking. Oh shit, your phone."

Nada started swimming toward their canoe, and Bisma followed. After several attempts, the girls managed to flip the craft, and they clambered ungracefully inside. Shivering and uncomfortable, they returned to the dock and mumbled an excuse to the concerned facilitator, before heading back to their cabin for a shower and a change of clothes.

"I'll make this right," Bisma vowed on their way back to the main lodge. "Don't worry about your cell phone; my mom will buy you another one."

"Just keep me out of whatever stupid game you're playing with Firdous," Nada said. She didn't speak to Bisma again that night.

As for Nada's cell phone, the screen was cracked and it wouldn't turn on. She returned it to her bag and silently cursed her luck. It was only a few months old, and her parents had warned her not to bring it to camp in the first place. They wouldn't replace it, and her pride wouldn't allow her to accept Bisma's offer. A part of her figured she might have deserved this, that maybe this was karma having a laugh at her expense for the way she had treated Baz three years ago.

The next couple of days were filled with more team-building activities: hiking, swimming, pole jumping, nature walks, arts and crafts. Nada decided she was better off with Bisma rather than remaining entirely alone all week. She would do her time and then get the hell out of Camp Kinark for good.

The only problem was that Baz was everywhere she went. His eyes were on her during the nature hike, as they fashioned friendship bracelets, when she made her way back to her cabin. Each interaction was in turn observed by Firdous or her posse, or by Bisma. In the close confines of camp, Nada felt constantly surveilled. She had done nothing wrong, but the intimacy of camp magnified any hint of intrigue.

When Nada and Baz nearly collided on the way to make *wudu* for the afternoon *Zuhr* prayer on day three, Nada had finally had enough.

"Assalamu alaikum," she said, planting her feet firmly in front of him and refusing to let him pass until he acknowledged her.

Baz looked at her for a long minute, before replying, "*Walaikum assalam.*"

"We went to Sunday school together in Scarborough three years ago," Nada said, forcing herself to maintain eye contact. Baz was taller than her now, his eyes even more deep-set, his features sharply carved, but he hadn't grown into his lanky, long-limbed body.

"I remember," he said evenly.

Nada opened her mouth to say something, to apologize, to ask why he kept staring at her and did he hate her still, but she chickened out. Instead, she nodded abruptly and continued to the bathrooms to make *wudu*.

Naturally, this non-conversation was observed by a half-dozen people. Bisma asked her for details. Firdous accidentally-on-purpose shoved her during their nightly nature walk with a mumbled "Watch where you're going, bitch."

Two more days. Nada could make it. Her phone was still dead, so she couldn't even send her parents an SOS text without making a big deal of it or giving the still-jumpy Sister Amal a heart attack. She would come to regret this decision after the bonfire.

The last night at camp was always celebrated with a bonfire, story-telling, and skits performed by the campers. They would roast halal marshmallows and make s'mores, something Nada had never sampled before.

Sister Salama started off the night with the requisite spooky jinn stories, and then it was time for the campers to show off their talents. A few boys performed a hilarious skit about camp life. Baz was in the skit, playing the role of the cantankerous cook and hamming it up for the audience. Nada's laughter was noticed by Firdous.

Next, Bisma, Nada, and a few other girls got up for their performance. The girls had penned a camp anthem to sing in front of the small crowd.

"This song is an ode to our camp experience," Nada explained, trying not to look at Baz. "It's sung to the tune of 'Y.M.C.A.'"

Giggling, the girls lined up. Nada stood next to Bisma. Using their arms, they spelled out MYNA as they sang:

> *M-Y-N-A*
> *You know you'll love it at the*
> *M-Y-N-A*
> *They have everything that you need to enjoy*
> *You can look at the trees,*
> *But NOT AT THE BOYS!*

The girls shouted the last line together, and the audience went wild.

Then everything happened at once. Nada, grinning with the other girls, happy adrenaline roaring through her body, saw an arm reach out from the corner of her eye and then felt the night's chill on her neck. She felt for her hijab, but it was gone, torn off in front of everyone.

She had started to wear hijab that year. Her mother had wanted her to wait until she was ready for the commitment, but Nada had insisted, despite the curious stares of her classmates. All year the hijab had felt like a comfortable blanket, a public acknowledgment of her faith and her community. Now someone from a Muslim camp had ruthlessly exposed her. These thoughts flashed across her mind in an instant as she stood frozen in front of the audience, her hair a mess around her, before she ducked down with a cry, covering her head with her arms. She reached blindly for her hijab, but it was tangled and her fingers were numb.

Then Sister Salama was on her feet shouting, and even jumpy Sister Amal ran to help. In the chaos, the campers were dismissed, and Nada, hands still clamped over her head, was led inside the empty main lodge along with Bisma. Nada untangled her hijab and put it back on, tying it firmly. Someone passed her a napkin, and she wiped her eyes.

Sister Salama crouched at her feet, concern and worry on her face. "Who was it? I didn't see; there was a crowd and it happened so fast. Do you know who did this to you? A face, a name, the color of their clothing, anything. This act must not go unpunished."

Nada shook her head and buried her face in her arms. "I want to go home," she said, voice muffled. "Please, call my parents to come pick me up tonight."

Sister Salama went to make the call and to interrogate the campers, leaving Nada with Bisma. Silence stretched between them.

"Why?" she finally asked her new friend. She had known it was Bisma the moment it happened. Bisma had reached out, after the hilarious chorus of the song they had written together, to embrace her, Nada had thought at first, until she felt the tug on her headscarf.

Bisma looked away, a tinge of red warming her brown skin. "You don't know what it's like," she said slowly. "You don't have to go to school with them or deal with their cruelty. I thought if I humiliated you in public, it might make things . . . better for me, with Firdous. I'm sorry. Why didn't you tell on me?"

Nada shook her head, unable to answer. *This is what shock must feel like*, she thought. *I didn't rat her out because I deserve this.*

She walked outside, to the wraparound porch and fresh air.

Baz was seated on one of the Adirondack chairs. He jumped up when he spotted her. "Nobody saw, like, anything. You ducked down too fast."

"Liar," Nada said softly, startling a laugh from him. The night was clear, the stars bright, and the scent of pine and cedar perfumed the air.

"So you've got hair under your hijab. It would have been more surprising if you had horns," he said.

"Maybe not that surprising to you, right?" Nada asked. "I was a real *Shaitaan* to you three years ago."

Baz shrugged, looking down at his feet. "Was it . . . Firdous?" he asked tentatively.

"More like a direct result of Firdous. How bad was it, really?" she said.

"As someone who has experienced my share of stage humiliation, it was . . . ," he trailed off, thinking. "Well, it was a ten, actually."

A snort of laughter escaped Nada, surprising her, and Baz continued, warming to his theme. "You're going to be a legend at MYNA camp forever now. They'll be telling this story for years. No, generations. You'll become a cautionary tale to scare the young ones." Lowering his voice in a menacing hiss, Baz said, "*Always double pin your hijabs, girls.*"

Nada laughed out loud, and her eyes filled with tears—of hilarity or embarrassment, she wasn't sure. Maybe both.

"Too bad no one is allowed to use their cell phones at camp," Baz said thoughtfully. "No pictures, no video. Almost as if it never happened."

Nada straightened, feeling better. "Why are you being so nice to me after what I did to you?"

Baz shrugged. "We were kids. I forgot about it."

"I didn't," Nada said. "I'm sorry."

"It's years too late for this apology," Baz said, but he smiled. "See you around?"

Nada nodded and watched him walk toward the boys' cabins. He had been worried about her, she realized. He had wanted to make sure she was okay. Baz lived on the other side of the Greater Toronto Area from Nada. If it hadn't been for this camp, their paths would never have crossed. In a city of millions, she might never see him again.

Waqas picked her up a few hours later. Her older brother didn't say a word until they were on the highway. "I told Mom and Dad not to send you. I knew you wouldn't like it here. These camps are cliquey, and besides, you're a city girl. Maybe they'll listen to me now."

Nada looked out the window at the stars twinkling down brightly in the vast darkness of the night sky, so much brighter than at home. "Thanks for coming to pick me up."

Waqas threw her a concerned glance but smiled at her words. "Anytime."

CHAPTER NINE

Present day

Nada regained consciousness beneath a circle of concerned faces: Haleema, Baz, and the tall woman with the very sharp elbows. Her forehead and left cheekbone ached. Now that her eyes were open, Baz's worried expression was quickly replaced by one of annoyance, which seemed unfair. She had been knocked out by an errant elbow because of *his* singing.

She sat up abruptly and felt the world tilt. "Why do I always get hurt around you?"

"I could ask you the same question," he said quietly, then turned to the small crowd gathered around them. "Is there a doctor in the house?"

Instantly, a rush of people stepped forward.

"I'm a dermatologist."

"I'm in first year."

"I went to Harvard Medical School," another woman called, pushing to the front.

The dermatologist pushed her back. "Shut up, Batool. You're always going on about Harvard. We all know you barely graduated."

Baz rolled his eyes. "I should have known better than to ask for a doctor at a Muslim convention. Do you think you can stand?"

Haleema helped Nada up, and Baz gestured at someone on stage. The music started up again, and the bickering doctors instantly forgot about her. Baz murmured something to Haleema, who nodded and disappeared into the crowd after a quick squeeze of Nada's elbow. Baz indicated Nada should keep moving, and he followed closely. Nada wanted to tell him she was fine, but the truth was she felt light-headed. Besides, it wasn't every day that one was escorted by a rock star.

"You're a rock star," she said out loud. The lights felt too bright and her head was pounding.

Baz sighed. "Not a rock star," he said, using his impressive shoulders to create a shield between her and the crowd pressing close on either side. It felt like there were several thousand people between her and the exit.

"Where's Haleema?" Nada asked.

"I sent her ahead, to Command Central."

Nada didn't think to ask why he hadn't gone ahead instead. A part of her wondered if he hadn't wanted to leave her and Haleema to deal with the rowdy crowd on their own. She wasn't sure how she felt about that.

"Daf Man is a rock star," Nada said instead. She knew she wasn't making a lot of sense; the knock on the head seemed to have loosened her tongue. "But you play the *daf*. It's confusing."

"I think you have a concussion."

"Are you a doctor too?" Nada asked.

"Not a doctor. Not a rock star," Baz said patiently. "I'm the COO of Deen&Dunya. You saw my card."

Nada felt faint again as she tried to make sense of something. Her train of thought was distracted by the closeness of his body. The crowd inhibited their progress to a slow crawl, and Baz shifted once more so she was protected in the circle of his arms, though he managed not to touch her directly. If her head wasn't hurting so much, she would be impressed. Anyone watching them would take him for her bodyguard, not the put-upon organizer of D&D and occasional lead singer of The Companions.

"Those women were throwing their hijabs at you," she said, trying to make sense of what she had witnessed before she blacked out.

Baz's steps faltered and embarrassment tinted his cheeks pink. "I didn't ask them to," he said, defensive. "It's just something the fans do."

"Their *hijabs*," Nada repeated. "They had extra hijabs in their bags, and they *hurled* them at you on stage."

It seemed important, somehow, that Baz understand how ridiculous, how insane, this situation was to an outsider. Muslim women did not throw hijabs at random people. Hijabs were expensive, something to be hoarded, not discarded like a tissue or tomato or bra or . . .

"It's like they were throwing their underwear at you!" Nada said, and Baz winced. He reached for her elbow when a gang of teenage dude-bros brushed against her. *Is this what it feels like to be drunk?* she wondered, blinking owlishly at him. She didn't like it. "Are you embarrassed about the hijabs?" she asked kindly, only slightly distracted by the pressure of his large hand on her arm. "I bet the memes are really cruel, but that's the internet. Everyone has to be mean because they're all lonely and sad."

"They were throwing the scarves at my brother. You might have noticed him? He's the pretty boy with the good hair." Baz wouldn't look at her, but the tips of his ears were bright red now, to match the self-conscious blush on his face.

"They made memes about me today. Just because I caused a scene at Sister Rusul's seminar. You hate Sister Rusul. Why do you hate her again?"

"I don't hate her. Plus, I'm pretty sure there will be memes about what happened at the concert too. You might actually start trending."

Nada stopped, swaying. This next part felt important. "Yes, you do. You hate her, and you hate me."

Baz stopped too, his hand still firm under her elbow. As if realizing this, he let go, and Nada rubbed the spot absently. "I wish I hated you," he said, almost to himself. Then, rallying: "This is taking too much time. Can you walk a little faster?"

Nada picked up speed and nearly stumbled. Baz's arms were around her waist instantly, steadying her, and this time he wasn't the only one blushing. He released her and cleared his throat. "Zayn calls them the Double Hijabis. Because they wear one hijab on their head and pack another one to throw on stage. It's funny," he explained, smiling, and Nada nodded, unable to look away. He was beautiful when he smiled. He was devastating when he scowled, like he was right now. Maybe she really did have a concussion.

"Let's get you to the sick room," he said, his voice rough by her ear.

She shivered. "Lead the way, rock star."

"Not a rock star."

The sick room was inside Command Central, a large room bustling with volunteers and staff. Baz settled Nada on a chair by a desk in the corner and pushed a cold bottle of water to her elbow. They had somehow beaten Haleema here. "Don't move," he said, and disappeared.

Nada didn't protest. She glanced around the room at the volunteers. There were about a dozen of them. One group peered at an iPad while a few others clustered around the weekend schedule posted on a large whiteboard. Along the back wall, a banquet table was loaded with snacks—cookies, pastries, bottles of water, a percolator with coffee, a kettle for tea. A pretty young woman around Nada's age walked in, and she seemed remarkably familiar. It took Nada a moment to recognize her, and then her stomach dropped: Firdous Malik, Queen Bee from that long-ago MYNA camp. Their entire community really did attend this convention.

"Can I help you?" Firdous asked, and Nada tried not to flinch.

"A minor mishap at the concert," Baz said. He had returned with a capable-looking young woman in a black hijab carrying a doctor's bag. "Firdous, can you get Nada some Tylenol? We have a first-aid kit somewhere." He introduced Dr. Iqbal, then moved to the other side of the room, to give them some privacy.

The young doctor began a physical examination of Nada, taking her pulse and calmly asking questions: Was she dizzy? Nauseous? How long had she been unconscious? Had she ever had a concussion before?

Nada answered as best she could, and after a few minutes, Dr. Iqbal told her to make an appointment to see her family doctor, but it didn't appear as if she had suffered a concussion. She scribbled her number on a Post-it. "Call me if you start to feel worse. Rest for a few more minutes before you head out. No more Double Hijabis tonight," she said with a smile.

At her elbow, two painkillers and another glass of water appeared. "Do I know you from somewhere?" Firdous asked.

Nada examined the tablets, trying not to appear too suspicious. "We were at MYNA camp together years ago."

Firdous looked blank. "Sorry, I don't remember." She turned to Baz. "Do you remember this sister from camp?" she asked, but Baz was already deep in discussion with a gaggle of volunteers. Firdous shrugged. "We both went to that camp every summer. Thank God for good friends. Baz offered me a job right after my divorce. Aren't you going to take the medicine? Unless you're afraid I'm trying to poison you." She laughed musically.

Nada swallowed the pills and tried to stand. Her vision went blurry at the edges and she sat back down abruptly, wondering where Haleema was. Baz was instantly at her side.

"I told you not to move," he said sternly. He had a piece of paper in his hand, with *Liability Waiver* written across the front.

"Good idea, Bazzy," Firdous said. "Can't be too careful these days. So many people jealous of your success. No offense, Nadia."

"It's Nada. Can you get Haleema, *Bazzy*?" Nada said through gritted teeth.

"I saw her on my way back with Dr. Iqbal. She'll be here to take you to the hotel in a few minutes." Baz nodded at Firdous. "Are the flyers ready for tomorrow? They're in a pile by the door."

Firdous seemed reluctant to leave them alone. Once she had, Nada raised her eyebrows.

Baz shrugged. "Firdous is going through a lot."

"I didn't know you were friends."

"She knows a lot of people in the community and keeps her ear to the ground. In my line of work, that sort of insight is valuable."

"What line of work is that? Making sure your convention attendees don't sue you?" She nodded at the paper still clutched in Baz's hand.

His grip tightened on the form. "My job is to make sure everything runs smoothly and to deal with every problem that comes up, no matter how I feel personally."

They stared at each other. "I'm not signing a liability waiver. You'll just have to trust me," Nada said, mostly just to bother him.

Baz handed her a pen. *Rude.*

Nada crossed her arms over her chest and lifted her chin. "I don't take well to being told what to do."

"That's not what I remember," Baz said, and in that moment, Nada hated him. Their impasse was interrupted by the entrance of Haleema, Zayn, and an older woman in a lavender *abayah* dress and a white hijab pinned beneath her chin so the ends dangled nearly to her abdomen. From the resigned expression on Baz's face, Nada knew this must be his mother, Haleema's future mother-in-law, Arifa Haq.

"*Subhanallah!* Look what has happened. Baz, Zayn, I warned you the concert would lead to disaster. A young woman has been hurt, perhaps permanently. Sister, I am so sorry about this. In the future, we must return to our original model. I want the concert shut down immediately!"

Nada spoke without thinking. "That would be a terrible mistake. The Companions have a large fan base, and they would be really disappointed. You should be proud to encourage Muslim artists in the community; otherwise, they'll look elsewhere for validation and support." She blinked, surprised at her impassioned plea. From the looks on their faces, both Baz and Zayn were just as surprised. Haleema surreptitiously gave Nada a thumbs-up.

Arifa seemed dubious but mollified. She patted Nada on the shoulder and went to talk to Firdous. Nada stood up, more carefully this time, Haleema helping her. Baz fussed with the water bottle and tried to hand her the liability waiver again, but she stopped him with a dark look.

"Thanks for sticking up for the concert and my brother's band," he said stiffly. "My parents want the convention to stay a place for academic lectures about Islam. It's been hard to introduce new ideas. It helps when outsiders speak up."

Outsider. The word stung, more than it should have. It was time to leave. She should probably quit while she was ahead—before anything else happened.

Inside their hotel room, Haleema immediately reached for the pins holding her hijab in place and eased out of her heels with a groan. "Want to order food? There's a halal burger place nearby."

Nada rattled off her order—a cheeseburger with onions and hot peppers, plus a bucket of fries—and flopped on her bed. After inputting the order on the delivery app, Haleema did likewise on the other bed, flipping onto her side and slyly taking in her friend.

"So, you and Baz . . . ," she started.

"So, you and Zayn," Nada countered.

Haleema rolled onto her back and stretched out. "Isn't he amazing?"

He is certainly something, Nada thought. "I'm happy if you're happy," she said.

Haleema threw a pillow at her head. "He's the best. Don't be a hater."

Nada was silent, staring up at the green blinking light on the smoke detector. "Do you know who that girl Firdous is?"

Haleema sat up and cuddled her other pillow. "She just started hanging around before the convention. I think she's after Baz, and Zayn doesn't like her very much. Something about not letting Baz alone in high school. It was Zayn's idea to introduce you to Baz in the first place. He thought you might hit it off. But don't worry, I can take a hint." She started laughing. "Baz definitely doesn't like you. I've never seen him that annoyed. Then again, he stopped the show when you fainted."

"I was hit in the face; I didn't faint," Nada corrected.

"He got down from the stage so fast, I swear I thought he had a jet pack. Must have been scared you'd sue."

Their food arrived, and the girls dug in, trading fries for onion rings and eating contentedly while watching one of Haleema's favorite reality baking programs on her laptop.

"Do you think he'll get together with Firdous?" Nada asked, hating herself. Haleema shrugged.

"He's never settled on one person. Zayn thinks he's a bit of a player."

"Then why did you want to set us up?" Nada asked, trying to absorb this information. Baz didn't behave like a flirt; that honor belonged to Zayn.

Haleema leaned against her friend. "I told you, it was Zayn's idea, and besides, Baz is a good guy. I thought he'd take one look at my hot friend and immediately fall in love. I must be doing this aunty thing wrong, because I'm really bad at matchmaking." She laughed, then quickly sobered. "I bet you could get that matrimonial ticket back. Admit it: you're lonely."

Nada disposed of their garbage and opened the window to clear out the smell of salty, fried goodness. "Why did it take you so long to return to Command Central? Baz and I were there way before you, and we were walking so slowly."

Haleema seemed disconcerted by the abrupt change of topic. "When I couldn't find a doctor right away, I went back to look for Zayn. The Companions had finished playing, and my friend had posted that he was taking pictures with his fans."

"You wanted to check up on him," Nada said, and color washed over Haleema's pretty face.

"Maybe?" she said.

Nada sighed. "Are you sure about this guy?" She knew that Haleema had been desperate to marry, and she also understood why. The pressure to settle down, find a partner, have children, all before the age of thirty, was almost overwhelming to many women in their community. Even Nada wasn't immune. Her mother had been fretting about Nada's single status since she turned twenty, and lately her father had joined the questioning chorus. The only reason it hadn't become unbearable was that her parents had backed off after Waqas's divorce—once bitten, twice shy. Plus they were aware that the divorce had stained their reputation in the community—which was both a relief and a huge insult. Still, she was highly aware of the low hum of anxiety over the fact she wasn't married, even if she managed to mostly ignore it. For Haleema, the pressure must have felt overwhelming, since it mirrored her own dreams for herself.

Haleema picked at the duvet. "I like Zayn a lot," she started. "I understand him, and I like his family too. I even think he's a talented musician. It's just sometimes . . ."

"Sometimes?" Nada prompted.

"I guess I always thought I'd marry someone a bit more . . . conventional? Someone like Baz, maybe."

Nada's heart contracted at these words, but she said lightly, "Is it too late to trade one brother for the other?"

"Ew, Nada, gross! I chose Zayn for a reason. He's fun, smart, romantic. He makes me laugh. I just worry he's not ready for the way things change after marriage. He'll have to shift his priorities. I will too, and I hope you'll be okay with that."

"What do you mean?" Nada asked.

"You're getting more isolated as the years pass. I won't be there to kidnap you for an awesome girls' weekend anymore."

"Maybe I'll be the one who shows up at your house and kidnaps you," Nada joked, but Haleema's insight bothered her. Her father was the one who hated change, not Nada. Anything that might alter the status quo for the family—his son getting married, his daughter's wish to move out—had to be navigated through Abbas's deep dislike of change. Nada loved her father. She respected what he had accomplished as a new immigrant to this country. But she knew that while Narjis used outright guilt to get what she wanted, he was no less effective at managing his children. He didn't want anything to change, ever. And so nothing changed for anyone in her family. Ever.

Haleema used the bathroom and got ready for bed, while Nada lay on top of her bedspread, thinking. She had thought she was okay with change in a way that her parents simply weren't. Yet when confronted with the reality of shifting circumstances, she seemed to be reacting no better than Abbas.

When Haleema emerged from the bathroom, Nada went in to change into her cotton pajamas, brush her teeth, and make *wudu*. She contemplated her friend's words as she smoothed moisturizer over her face and brushed her hair.

As she sat cross-legged on her prayer mat after praying *Isha*, the night prayer, she repeated the *tasbih*: *subhanallah, alhamdulillah, allahu akbar*. "Glory be to God; all praise be to God; God is great." The soothing mantra rooted her in the present moment and centered her thoughts. She settled into bed, turned off the lights, and stared into the darkness. "Are you happy?"

On the neighboring bed, her friend turned over. "Yes," she said simply.

"I thought Waqas was happy too," Nada said. "When Jameela left, we were so shocked. I just worry."

"I'm not Jameela, and Zayn isn't like your brother. Despite everything, Zayn makes me feel . . . lucky."

There was more silence, the velvety darkness heavy between them. Nada remembered that long-ago week at MYNA camp and the confidences that were shared. She thought about the honesty of the dark, which had the power to conceal faces and open hearts.

"Did Sister Rusul talk to you about Ask Apa?" Haleema asked.

Nada sighed. "She tried. More lies and excuses for her son."

"You know I'm not her biggest fan, but maybe it's time to hear her out," Haleema suggested tentatively. "It's been so long. If you could move beyond what happened, it might help."

"What do you mean?" The smoke alarm's tiny green light winked at her from the ceiling again, and she concentrated on it now.

"You were different in undergrad. Before all the Ask Apa and Ukhti stuff happened. Afterward, you just sort of faded away. Zayn thinks—"

"You talked to Zayn about me?"

"We're getting married, and actually, he had some pretty great insights."

Hurt, Nada settled into her duvet. "I bet he did."

Haleema sat up, her profile clear against the dark. "What is that supposed to mean?"

"I don't understand why you would talk about my past with Zayn. He doesn't even know me." Nada couldn't keep the trace of hurt from her voice. Had Haleema told her flirty fiancé all of her secrets? It felt like a betrayal, though some part of her knew that she wasn't being fair. Her friend was entering into a serious, lifelong commitment. That person would naturally become her first confidant.

"Well, Zayn thinks you're still in mourning over what happened with your business, and you need to get over it, because it's holding you back," Haleema said.

Now Nada sat up. "*Get over it?*" she asked, incredulous. "I thought your fiancé was a wannabe pop star, not a pretty-boy Dr. Phil." The moment the words were out of her mouth, Nada wanted to grab them back. Haleema didn't respond for a long time.

"At least Zayn is doing what he loves. Or do you think running away from your dreams is more fashionable?"

Nada didn't respond, not wanting to make this impasse worse.

Haleema sighed, and her voice grew more gentle. "Sometimes I worry you've allowed your sadness to become the biggest part of you. Whatever happened in the past is why you're afraid to take any chances now. It's probably why you don't want to get married. You're full of regrets, but you won't talk about them. You deserve happiness, Nada."

Nada lay back down and turned away from her friend. "Tell Zayn Haq to mind his own business."

There was another awkward moment of silence. Then Haleema, sounding distant now, said, "I left the liability waiver on the dresser. I told Baz you would give it to him tomorrow."

Nada didn't answer.

In the morning when she woke up, her friend was already gone.

CHAPTER TEN

Present day

Nada and Haleema fought occasionally, but this time felt different. So far, the weekend felt like the beginning of the end of something, or maybe the end of the beginning. In any case, she felt guilty as she walked into the convention building the next morning. Haleema had texted that she had plans with Zayn for breakfast, and only responded yes when Nada asked if she would see her later that day.

It would be fine. Haleema needed to cool down, and maybe some time on her own would be good for Nada too. Besides, her presence was required at her mother's side today. Narjis had texted to let her know that they were on their way downtown. Nada took that for the warning it was and decided she was in dire need of coffee before she could face her mother and brothers.

She had been thinking about Baz as well. Last night she had gone to bed wondering about him, and she had woken up thinking about him again. She didn't like the space he was taking up in her mind, but memories of their past interactions kept intruding and making her anxious. Haleema was right: Baz clearly didn't like her. He had been borderline rude to her all day. Yet he had also been kind, instantly swinging into action when she was hurt. While his primary motivation was likely to salvage the convention's reputation, that didn't entirely explain his protective stance when he guided her to Command Central. Maybe memories of their relationship affected him the way they did her. She resolved to be easy today, breezy and light, and not take anything too seriously, especially if she happened to bump into Baz and he said something designed to get under her skin.

This attitude stood her in good stead when Baz pounced on Nada at the entrance to the bazaar. Without even a salams, he held out his hand for the waiver. "Haleema said you had something for me?" he asked, his voice a deep rumble.

Why did he have to look so alert when she hadn't even had time to drink coffee yet? She gave him a stinging high five and walked into the bazaar, making a beeline for the Chai-lo tea and coffee stand in the food court.

He followed. "That hurt."

"That was the point," she said.

He walked beside her, giving her a quick once-over.

Her headache was gone, but there was some light bruising around her left eye, which she had tried to cover up with concealer as best she could. Judging by his frown, she hadn't done a very good job. "Like what you see?" she asked.

His face shuttered. "Get that form to me as soon as you can."

"I need to find a lawyer first. Can you recommend a good litigator? I'm sure you've got a few attorneys on speed dial. You have a face that makes people want to sue."

Baz sighed. "Nada."

"Baz." Her determination to not let him get to her had a nice side benefit: she was enjoying herself. Needling this ice giant of a man helped take her mind off Haleema.

As if reading her mind, Baz made a show of looking around. "Where's your shadow?"

"Ask your brother. Haleema left this morning to meet him."

Baz shrugged. "They're getting married in a month. What did you expect?"

Nada kept silent. She hadn't expected anything else, of course. It was natural that her friend would be distracted. It just seemed a bit rich, considering how hard Haleema had worked to get her here, only to abandon Nada after their spat. But she wasn't going to think about that now.

Her phone pinged with a message, and Nada glanced at it, hopeful. When she caught sight of the text, she groaned.

"What's wrong?" Baz asked with fake concern. "Is it time for your daily dose of mood-stabilizing magic mushrooms?"

"My mom just arrived and she's causing a scene. Jamal sent the bat signal." Nada showed Baz the text: an emoji of a witch on a broom followed by the fire signal. It was sibling shorthand for *Drop whatever you're doing because Mom is on a rampage!*

Her mother had a tendency to make a big production wherever she went. It used to bother Nada when she was younger, but now she realized that it wasn't entirely Narjis's fault. The woman simply invited drama. Sometimes the drama was warranted, and other times it was not. Nada often stepped in to mediate when her mother lost it on recalcitrant customer service reps, belligerent fellow customers, and sometimes even her own friends. One thing Nada admired and hated about her mother was that she never backed down from a fight.

Nada found her mother at the registration desk, arguing with a terrified-looking young woman. Narjis was dressed in a long blue *abayah* with a black hijab pinned so the ends hung below her chin, and she was in the midst of a tirade.

"Why won't you speak to my son? Why didn't you make eye contact with him? I need to speak to the person in charge. I will call the press. I will *badnaam* you on Facebook. I will start a chain letter petition on WhatsApp!"

A few steps away, Waqas stood beside Jamal in his wheelchair; both pretended not to know their mother.

"Cowards," Nada muttered, before throwing herself into the fray. "What happened?" she asked, stopping her mother from launching into another rant.

"I told Jamal to register us since you were nowhere to be found, but this woman wouldn't even look at him," she announced. "She is clearly bigoted against the disabled. I will file a human rights complaint!"

Nada narrowed her eyes at the young girl, who had the grace to blush and stammer.

"I wasn't ignoring him because he's in a wheelchair," she explained. "He wasn't trying to register for the convention. He was trying to get my number."

The three women turned to look at Jamal. Waqas took a few steps to the left, putting some distance between him and his younger brother, the ever-hopeful Lothario. Jamal, tricked out head to toe in expensive athletic gear and sitting in his racing-red motorized wheelchair, made a "call me" gesture to the young woman.

"I'm married," the girl said, now almost in tears. "He seems really nice, and I'm sure he'll find the perfect girl who is really into, like, disabled people—" She clamped her hands over her mouth. Her eyes filled with tears and she started to wail. "I'm so sorry! Here, take my number. Your son and I can totally be friends."

Behind the women, Jamal tried to high-five Waqas, who was now studiously ignoring them all.

"My son is *twenty years old*, and he is not looking to get married," Narjis thundered.

"You can introduce me to your single friends," Jamal called.

Narjis whirled on him. "*Chup!*" she commanded. "I'll deal with you later. Trying to flirt with a married woman—have I taught you nothing?"

Jamal only grinned. He had inherited the drama gene from his mother.

"Please just give me the registration packages and we'll be out of here," Nada said to the young woman, who handed them tickets and convention bags in thirty seconds flat.

"What is wrong with the young girls? In my day, we would simply reach down to remove one of our *chappals*, and the boys would go running," Narjis grumbled.

Nada made a mental note to have a talk about consent and harassment with her mother later. Right now, she had bigger things to deal with, because for some unfathomable reason, Baz was deep in conversation with her brothers. Luckily, Narjis didn't seem to notice; she had bumped into friends.

Baz shook hands with Waqas and then fist-bumped Jamal before casually handing Nada a take-out cup from Chai-lo, as if he had merely been holding the life-giving brew for her. She took a cautious sip. The latte was hot and sweet, flavored with cardamom and rose water syrup. She took another large swallow, eyeing Baz over the rim as he chatted genially with Waqas and Jamal. It was almost as if they knew each other.

The Syed family wasn't particularly social and had grown less so over the years. Even her parents' volunteer work at the mosque had tapered off. Nada knew this was a result of the blow their social standing had taken after Waqas's divorce, and after Jamal's health issues had become more obvious.

Her brother had started to use a motorized wheelchair when he was fourteen years old, when his ataxia, a rare neurological and muscular condition that caused tremors in his limbs and made it difficult for him to walk, had grown progressively worse. He could still walk, but not without help, and there was always the fear of a fall. Over the years, Nada had noticed her parents becoming more sensitive and protective over Jamal, no doubt a reaction to the stares, comments, and nosy questions they fielded even from close friends. They'd had to navigate their younger son's progressive diagnosis with little support outside of the immediate family. While the Toronto Muslim Assembly mosque was wheelchair accessible, with a ramp, elevator, and wide hallways, these accommodations had been made with the elderly in mind, not for the wide variety of disability and mobility issues present in their growing community.

Jamal wasn't stoic like his older brother or quietly rebellious like Nada. Instead, he was frank, forthright, and a bit of a brat, challenging anyone who looked down on him or who treated him like a child. Which tended to be everyone.

"Where's *my* coffee, bro?" he asked Baz.

"Get your own," Baz said easily. "I'm tired, and you're on wheels."

Jamal cackled, and something inside Nada relaxed. She took another, more appreciative sip of her drink. Most people tended to either infantilize Jamal, treating him like a very young, very stupid child, or ignore him, sending all their comments and questions to the able-bodied around him rather than speaking to him directly. Baz didn't do either, and she felt absurdly grateful. But she wondered how they all seemed to know each other.

"When are you coming back to ball hockey?" Baz asked Waqas now. He looked at Jamal and said, "You're still banned for life."

Jamal flipped him off. "You suck, ref."

To Nada's astonishment, Baz laughed. It was almost as strange as watching him perform on stage.

"How do you all know each other?" Nada asked.

The men shrugged. Waqas said, "Ball hockey, and before that there was the charity run—"

"You mean when your idiot brother ran over my foot?" Baz interrupted.

"You were so busy flirting with the girl handing out water bottles that you didn't hear me politely ask you to move," Jamal threw back.

"Yes, so polite," Baz said. "I believe your exact words were 'Look at this asswipe thinking he got game. Move it!'" Baz mimicked Jamal's raspy voice, and they both chuckled.

"You came to the office last year too, for some accounting work," Waqas added.

Baz nodded, taking care to avoid Nada's incredulous expression. Baz knew her brothers, had sought them out in social situations, and had even worked with Waqas?

It was strange to watch aloof Baz easily carry a conversation with her two very different brothers. Waqas was much quieter, but he conversed easily, and even perked up when Baz inquired after the twins. Unlike so many of Waqas's friends and acquaintances, Baz didn't mention his divorce or ask probing questions about Jameela and her new husband. Again, Nada felt a wave of gratitude. She knew that part of the reason that her older brother had retreated following his divorce was because his failed marriage seemed to be the only subject his friends wanted to talk about. The last thing her reserved brother wanted to do was provide a public postmortem of his still-bleeding heart.

"This is boring. I'm going to find my boys," Jamal announced. "Tell Mom, okay?"

"Behave yourself," she called, and he saluted with one hand as the other nimbly maneuvered his wheelchair through the crowd. With a pang, Nada noticed how many people stared at her baby brother. She caught a group of teen girls in hijab nudging each other as he passed, whispering and giggling, and her grip on her cup tightened. She wasn't as sensitive as her parents, but it bothered her that people who themselves were stereotyped and looked down upon for their appearance so easily did the same to others.

Nada turned back to Waqas and Baz. Too late, she spotted her mother disengaging from her friends and heading toward them. She tried to signal to Baz that he should leave, but he calmly took a sip from his coffee cup and waited.

Waqas performed the introductions, oblivious to the tension. Nada waited for the light of recognition to dawn in her mother's eyes, and when it did, Narjis shot her daughter a fleeting, intense glance, before turning back to the taller man.

"Your family runs this convention?" Narjis asked, something more than mere nosiness in her voice.

Baz nodded, impassive.

"It must make a lot of money," Narjis commented.

Nada looked for a handy cliff she could throw herself off. "Mom," she hissed.

"*Alhamdulillah*," Baz said coolly. He turned to Nada and held his hand out once more. "I'll take that waiver before I go."

"What waiver?" Nada asked, opening her eyes wide. "I don't know what you're talking about."

He frowned. The friendliness he had shown her brothers clearly didn't extend to her. "Nice to see you again, Waqas," he said. "Enjoy the convention, Narjis Aunty." He walked away.

Waqas made his excuses and left for the prayer hall, leaving Nada alone with her mother.

"This convention is very successful. I'm surprised his family is behind it," Narjis said. "Come, Nada. I have a few boys lined up for you to meet. And what on earth have you been doing? Why are all my friends forwarding me cartoon images of you fighting with a flashlight sword?"

Nada dutifully followed her mother and tried not to be too impressed with the masterful way Baz had managed his second meeting with her mother.

CHAPTER ELEVEN

Ten years ago

It was Haleema's idea to attend the MSA Welcome Back dinner. As a junior, she felt it was her duty to introduce Nada, a freshman, to the joys of the Muslim Student Association, which had a strong presence at the University of Toronto campus.

"Free food, cute Muslim boys, let's go!" Haleema had urged after class on a Friday in October. "I know you don't have plans."

The food at the buffet was mediocre but plentiful. As Nada spooned meat curry and butter chicken onto her plate, and helped herself to two pieces of naan, she surreptitiously scoped out the male Muslim population on campus. She didn't know where all these guys had been hiding, but this was better than her usual Friday night plans, which consisted of reviewing her calculus notes and praying she wouldn't fail her next lab.

First-year engineering was nothing like she had expected. She had been an excellent student in high school, scoring high grades in math and science, but she was drowning in every class at university. Thank God for Haleema, who was two years her senior and had given her some key advice the first week, after Nada failed a physics test.

"Remember, all you have to do is pass. Nobody is expecting greatness. Just get through this and then start the rest of your life," Haleema said.

Easy for her, a resident genius, to say, but it helped that she accompanied the sage advice with her notes from first year.

The president of the MSA, a first-year master's student named Mohamed, introduced the MSA executive—all men, Nada noticed. When she pointed this out to Haleema, her friend shrugged. "No girls ran for any of the positions, I guess."

Nada examined the men. Six were strangers, but she hesitated on the seventh. He was a tall man with short, curly hair, deep-set eyes, and broad shoulders, dressed in a slouchy hoodie and sweatpants. Baz.

She had thought about him often over the years, and had even tried some light social media searching, but he only had one Instagram account and it was set to private. She realized she knew so little about him. He had briefly lived in Scarborough, had attended an Islamic high school in the west end of the city, had inspired teenage girls to acts of great cruelty, and was athletic. Her interest had waned as the years passed and she figured that their strange relationship was truly at an end. Yet here he was at her university. Still, the campus was huge and he was not in engineering, so it was unlikely that their paths would cross often, if at all.

Nada bumped into him again a few weeks later, while hiding in the stacks of E.J. Pratt Library on the other side of campus. Most engineering students didn't venture outside their enclave, but Nada liked that this library was full of arts and humanities students furiously typing essays. Baz was curled in the corner of a wide-open room, frowning down at what looked like a novel. He was dressed in another hoodie and sweatpants combination, his gym bag at his feet. She passed by, nearly brushing his feet, but he didn't look up. He only shifted politely to let her pass on her way to her hiding spot on the second floor.

A few hours later, he wandered upstairs in search of another book. He glanced at her across the wide space, before doing a double take.

She quickly looked down at the texts spread out around her, cheeks flaming. When she looked back up, he was gone.

Around *Zuhr* time, he passed by again, and this time he stopped.

"Assalamu alaikum, sister," he said quietly. The room was a silent study space, and an older male student threw them a dirty glance. Resting a folded prayer mat on her table, Baz lowered his voice further and said, "There are prayer facilities in this building, on the main floor. Just thought I'd let you know."

She nodded, and his gaze lingered, but he didn't say anything. The last time she had talked to Baz, he'd been a lanky teen at MYNA camp, handsome but still growing into his body. At eighteen, he was a much more serious man.

Nada returned to the library every day for the rest of the week but didn't see him again. Haleema teased her about her secret hiding spot, but everyone seemed to have one on the massive campus. It had probably been a fluke that Baz had even come to this library. If he was like the other Muslim guys she knew, he was studying science or technology.

Just as she was starting to doubt that she had met him at all, he reappeared. He was sitting at a table with a stack of books, his gym bag near his feet again. He looked up and kept his gaze on Nada as she took a seat at a neighboring table. He greeted her with salams before returning to his books. They studied in parallel for the better part of the morning, and when it was time to pray *Zuhr*, she accepted his offer to use his prayer mat. Inside the multiuse meditation room, she ran her fingers across the red and gold velvet rug. There was an embroidered picture of the *Kaaba* at the top, which was soft against her forehead when she knelt in prayer.

They met every day for the rest of the week, but did not speak other than to exchange greetings. On Friday afternoon, he packed up early for *Jumah* prayer at Hart House, the ivy-covered student activity center located at the heart of the main campus. Built in the gothic revival style of the other buildings on the main campus on King's College Circle, Hart House had a restaurant, gym, and meeting spaces, and had also hosted Friday *Jumah* prayers for the Muslim student body and staff for over fifty years.

Nada packed up too, and they walked out of the library together.

"What are you studying?" Nada asked as they strolled in the crisp fall air. He was so much taller than her, but he slowed so their strides matched.

"English and sociology," he said. "I love it. You?"

"Electrical engineering. I hate it."

He chuckled, and the sound sent a shiver down her spine. "Why don't you transfer to something you like more?"

Nada shook her head. "My parents are so proud of me. I can stick it out. I have no intention of working in engineering after. I just need to survive the next few years and graduate."

"Pay now or pay later," Baz said.

Nada wasn't sure what he meant and was too shy to ask. She still didn't know if he recognized her, or if he thought she was just another hijabi on campus. They walked across Queen's Park, a busy, oval-shaped park crisscrossed with paved paths and lined with statues facing a fountain in the center that separated the central campus from the outlying buildings. An elaborate building dubbed the "pink palace" served as the seat of the Ontario provincial government and was located on the southern end, while the main campus, and Hart House, lay to the west.

Nada's eyes were on her feet as they crunched through yellow, red, and brown leaves underfoot. "I didn't think you recognized me."

"I'm still not sure who you are, actually." He grinned at her.

She smiled back uncertainly. Surely he was joking?

They arrived at Hart House, where they followed a steady stream of Muslims to a large hall upstairs, where the prayer would be held.

Nada sat cross-legged on the floor in the women's section and waited for the service to begin. Soon, a young man made the melodious *adhan*, the call to prayer that signaled the start of the sermon. Baz stood up and walked to the pulpit to lead the prayer.

He spoke clearly and recited the Quranic verses with the simple elegance of long practice. It made her wonder about him in a way she never had before. Who was he? Who were his parents, and why was he studying the arts instead of Islamic studies or religion? She waited for him after prayer, but he only nodded at her before leaving with friends.

The following week was a repeat of the last. They studied at the library, shared the prayer mat, and walked to *Jumah* together on Friday, though another student led the prayer. Baz rarely offered personal information, but their silences were companionable. After a few weeks, Nada felt it would be too awkward to ask him if he'd recognized her. But she wondered. She casually asked her friends about him, but they knew nothing.

Nada could feel herself becoming a tiny bit obsessed. She watched him while they studied. She watched him at Friday prayers. She wondered if she was the only girl he talked to, and then worried about what, if anything, that meant. She was starting to feel creepy, but she couldn't stop. Baz didn't seem to notice her attention. He remained respectful but never overly friendly. He spent his time in the library reading, napping, or taking notes. During midterms she camped out at the engineering college for an entire week, pulling all-nighters alongside Haleema. When she returned to the library, light-headed from sleep deprivation, Baz seemed fresh and well-rested.

"How were midterms?" he asked.

"Terrible. You?"

He shrugged. "Three essays and a paper. Not a big deal."

Baz didn't seem to be struggling with school the way she was, and while it would have been easy to blame the difference on his field of study—what did humanities students even *do* all day?—she knew that was unfair. Did he simply not care about marks? Baz never seemed worried, and that made her obsession grow even deeper. Maybe he didn't care about school because he didn't have to. He didn't dress like a rich boy, but she didn't know him. Why didn't she know him? Why wasn't he more interested in her?

She started to make more of an effort with her outfits. Instead of just wearing her engineering uniform of comfy sweats, she experimented with hijab styles. She even started putting on makeup—lip gloss, eyeliner, mascara—but nothing made any difference. Baz remained unfailingly polite, but unequivocally distant.

"What is up with the Muslim guys on campus?" she asked her friends at one of their late-night study sessions. "Either they want to hook up right away with everyone in sight, or they've never talked to a girl before. The religious ones won't even look at me, while the non-religious ones won't look at me either, but for different reasons."

"We make the non-religious ones feel guilty," Haleema said, nodding in agreement. "We remind them of their mothers, their aunts, their sisters, and the other women in their life they're disappointing with their behavior. The religious ones are too busy being awkward to take a good look at us."

Marya stole a fry from Nada's plate and nibbled on it meditatively. "It's because our mosques are segregated, and they never learned how to talk to Muslim girls without being weird," she said. "I guess that's what the college years are for, right?"

Marya was still seeing her high school sweetheart, Owais, and they were planning to marry after they finished school. Haleema was single, and so was Nada.

Fall turned into winter, and she continued to watch Baz surreptitiously. He carried a notebook with him always, she noticed, a plain black Moleskine. He'd pull it out on occasion and write in it for ten to thirty minutes at a time. She noticed he was careful with it, making sure to return it to his bag after he was done.

It took her weeks to work up the courage to ask what the notebook was for.

"Just a place where I jot down a few ideas. You know," he answered vaguely.

"Are you a writer?" she asked, even more intrigued.

"No, no."

"Is that where you write down your nefarious plans for the MSA?" she pressed.

"You got me. It's my plotting planner." He turned to his books.

Nada returned to hers, unsatisfied.

What happened next wasn't her proudest moment. But really, it was all Baz's fault for remaining such an enigma. One day before the winter break, she waited until he went to pray *Zuhr*. It took him at least fifteen minutes to make *wudu* and pray, and he usually asked her to keep an eye on his bag while he was gone. This time she rifled through the front pocket, extracted the black Moleskine, and flipped through the pages.

It was filled with poetry.

She read a poem, skimming quickly:

> *At home*
> *A flower unfurls*
> *At school*
> *Desire, wrapped in dark leaves*
> *Death or Life*
> *Choose, or the choice will be made for you.*
> *Impossible dream*
> *Impossible life*
> *Blossom, I beg of you.*

In the margins, he had sketched flowers and intricate geometric patterns reminiscent of Turkish art. She flipped to another page and saw herself: a sketch of a girl in hijab, at the same desk where she sat every day. She traced her features with an index finger, the barest impression of cheek, nose, lips. It was obviously her. His pencil had been kind, his artist's eye gentle, affectionate even. Nada's heart started to beat faster. Baz had looked at her, after all. Enough to memorize the curve of her cheek, the habitual peak of her hijab, the flash of mischief in her dark eyes. It made her feel seen, in a way that felt intimate and gratifying. She wondered now if he had spent as much time watching her, when he thought she wasn't looking, as she had watched him.

"What are you doing?" Baz demanded.

Nada jumped, dropping the notebook. Snatching it away, he shoved it back into his bag, his movements jerky, before scooping up his gym bag and heading for the exit without another word. He had forgotten his *janamaz* and had returned for it, she realized. She would have made a terrible spy.

She hurried after him. "I'm so sorry, please stop, you barely talk to me, I've tried to ask you questions but you never really answer . . . ," she babbled, running to catch up with his long-legged stride. "Your poems are really good," she hurled as he shoved the library doors wide open and exited.

Whirling, he faced her in the chill December air. Embarrassment, hurt, vulnerability, and anger all shook hands and formed fast friendships as they passed across his face, but his words sliced her where she stood: "How would you know? You're just an engineer."

Baz stopped coming to the library. She looked for him at *Jumah* prayers, but he stopped attending the congregation at Hart House and didn't seem to be at any of the other sites on campus. She didn't dare mention him to her friends; she was too embarrassed at how she had behaved, like a little girl desperate for a boy to like her back.

She couldn't stop thinking about his poem. *Impossible dream.* What could it mean? *Blossom, I beg of you.* It must mean something. She wished she had paid more attention in high school English class. She was sure that the words were some sort of symbol or metaphor or something. Baz was correct: Nada hung out with engineering, science, and technology students, and there wasn't a lot of space for stories or art in her world. Not when there were classes to pass, projects to finish, exams to crush, and applications for summer jobs and internships to fill out.

The rest of the year passed. Her final exams came and went. This time it was Nada who dragged Haleema to the year-end MSA dinner, hoping to bump into Baz. Maybe she could apologize, or explain, or ask for forgiveness.

But he didn't show up to that, either. He had disappeared, again.

CHAPTER TWELVE

Present day

Nada was hiding from her mother. After the third introduction to another brother nearly indistinguishable from the first and second, Nada had begged off to look for Haleema on the pretence that her friend was having a wedding-related emergency. Now she made her way to the prayer area, a large, open space where white sheets were spread on the ground for ready use. In the men's section, her older brother sat cross-legged, his head lowered in *dua*, and she watched him for a few minutes. Waqas had a kind face with gentle brown eyes and thick, dark hair. He had the same mild manner as their father. With an eight-year age difference between them, her older brother had always felt more like a beloved uncle, one who lent her money whenever she asked.

Waqas suddenly stood up, and even from her position in the women's section, she could sense his nervous energy. Within a few seconds, she understood the reason: his twin daughters, Safa and Marwa, ran into the empty prayer hall and jumped into his arms, followed more sedately by his ex-wife, Jameela, and her new husband, Esa.

It was still strange to see Jameela. They had lived together for nearly three years, and in that time, Nada had thought she was close to her sister-in-law. Yet she'd had no idea how unhappy Jameela was.

She had been stunned when, seven years ago on a random Saturday in October, a cube van had backed into their driveway. While two burly men emptied the basement apartment of her sister-in-law's belongings, Waqas explained to his parents and siblings that his marriage was over.

Jameela had moved to a townhouse complex nearby and shared custody of the girls with her ex-husband. It was as amicable a separation as possible, considering the circumstances, and they were polite when they saw each other at drop-offs and pick-ups. When Nada watched her brother interact with his ex-wife, he mostly seemed embarrassed.

Jameela was a square-faced woman who was more attractive at thirty-seven than she had been as a young bride. Unlike Waqas, she had thrown herself into her new life with a vigor absent from her marriage. She took up new hobbies like hot yoga, bought a trendy wardrobe, and a year after the divorce was finalized, married Esa Patel, a childhood friend.

In contrast, Waqas had turned inward and grown more isolated. Looking at him now with his daughters, Nada acknowledged that her mother was right: her brother was drowning.

"I didn't know you'd be here," Jameela said to Waqas, as Nada approached. The words were mild, but there was a hint of reproach in the observation.

"My mom's idea. I'll stay out of your way," Waqas said. "Thanks for bringing the girls to see me."

Esa stood a respectful distance away, looking at his phone. Jameela's new husband was taller than her brother, with a classically handsome face. In contrast to Esa, Waqas was settling into comfortable middle age. He had been slender when he was younger, but his sedentary job was starting to catch up with him. Today he was dressed in dad gear: khakis and a collared shirt, both in nondescript shades of gray and navy blue. Even his shoes were unfashionable loafers. His round face was emphasized by his round wire-frame glasses, and the short hairstyle he favored aged him.

Waqas never mentioned Esa by name if he could help it. Nada had wondered on more than one occasion about the timing of her ex-sister-in-law's new relationship.

Jameela tried to gather up the girls to go, but Safa and Marwa didn't want to leave, especially when they spotted their Nada *Phuppo*.

"I can take them for lunch, if you like," Waqas offered.

Jameela's lips tightened, but Esa spoke up. "We can grab lunch too, babe. It'll be fine. Maybe a restaurant without the kids?"

Esa had been married too, Nada knew, but hadn't had any children. The sudden intrusion of two adorable but high-energy girls into his life must have taken some getting used to. After a brief hesitation, Jameela agreed to meet Waqas and Nada back in the prayer hall in an hour.

"Thank you," Waqas said to his ex-wife quietly. "I didn't do this on purpose, really."

Jameela hugged her girls. "I know, Waqas. You never do anything on purpose."

Nada saw her brother flinch at his ex-wife's dig, and wondered again how they had come to this, their words like tiny knives jabbed under each other's skin. She turned to her nieces with a big smile. "Who wants shawarma?"

The girls booed, and they argued as they walked to the bazaar in search of child-friendly sustenance: plain cheese pizza or a bucket of fries. Waqas trailed them, his head down.

Safa and Marwa were six years old, chatty and bright and the light of the Syed household. Their parents had separated when Jameela was seven months pregnant, and their family had stepped in to help Waqas deal with infant twins once they arrived, and the logistics of divorce in their community. When they were first born, Nada would help bathe the girls, put them down for naps, and watch them on weekends when Waqas had custody. The girls hadn't been born when their parents lived together, and they had adapted easily, but there were still moments, such as the scene just now, when a fresh wave of sadness would hit Nada. Her beautiful nieces would grow up in a community still coming to terms with the realities of modern marriage and relationships, where extended families now included second and third marriages and stepparents and stepsiblings. Normalizing this, especially in their South Asian community, where divorce was still spoken of in hushed tones, would take time.

Holding her nieces' hands, Nada strolled into the bazaar and headed toward the food court, stopping when something shiny or interesting caught the girls' eyes, which was approximately every six feet. Waqas went ahead to secure a table and purchase food. By the time they joined him fifteen minutes later, he had put together a feast: fruit smoothies, mini pizzas, meat samosas, and smoked meat sandwiches—enough food to feed four adults, not two little girls, Nada, and himself. The girls shared a pizza and sipped at their smoothies, while Nada helped herself to a few of the excellent samosas and watched her brother.

He was an attentive father, patient and kind, wiping at Marwa's face with a napkin while encouraging Safa to drink more of her fruit smoothie. When the girls were done eating, he didn't just give them his phone like most parents would, but instead took out a wooden puzzle and two books he had bought for them at the bazaar to entertain them. It wasn't until they were settled that he turned to his own food, which had grown cold.

"You're a good dad," Nada said impulsively.

Waqas smiled wryly. "Dads always get applauded for doing the bare minimum, while moms are vilified for not being superwomen, according to Jameela. Whenever I took the girls to a park or remembered to bring snacks, I'd get so many compliments. The one time she forgot to bring water for the girls when they were at the mall, a stranger yelled at her and called her a bad mother."

"Do you hate Jameela?" Nada asked. Though it had been years since the split, their family had initially been so shocked and Waqas so shattered, they hadn't probed too deeply into what had led to the breakdown of the marriage. Nada had never had a heart-to-heart discussion about it with her older brother.

He blinked at her question, and then shook his head. "No, no, of course not," he said. "I mean, I didn't like her for a long time, but I never hated her."

"Do you miss her?" Nada asked. She was curious. "You never really seemed to be in love with each other. I mean, you never held hands or even looked at each other too often."

"You're such a brat, Nada," he said fondly. "Of course I loved her. She was my wife. We planned to have kids together. We were our first . . . Well, anyway." His ears were turning red. "But I don't think I really . . . paid attention." Waqas smiled sadly, and the expression softened the fine lines on his forehead.

"What do you mean?" Nada asked, leaning forward. The girls were occupied with their gifts. Safa flipped through the pages of one of the books while Marwa methodically put together her puzzle.

Waqas had his head lowered, and he spoke into his half-finished smoked meat sandwich. "Mom and Jameela's mom, they were the ones who wanted us to get married, and we both just went along with the plan. I don't think we really talked about what our life would look like afterward. I had these expectations, and she had other expectations, and in the end, we just stopped . . . working toward the same goal, the same sort of life." He reached for his fountain drink and took a long sip.

Nada shifted in impatience. Her brother was being too vague. Jameela had walked out before the children were born, shocking their family and community; she had married Esa only a year after the divorce was finalized. There had been talk, but she had never asked her brother about it. She felt emboldened now.

"Was there someone else, for you or for her?" she asked boldly.

Waqas shook his head. "You're looking for the same thing as everyone else. You want me to blame her, or for her to blame me. You want someone to be wrong and the other person to be right, and marriage . . . my marriage, at least, it wasn't like that. We just fell apart, and then we had to pick up the pieces and move on." Waqas took a deep breath. "I didn't make her happy. That's it. By the time I realized she was unhappy, by the time I paid attention and took her seriously, it was too late. She didn't love me anymore." He shook his head. "It took me a year of therapy to realize that, and then a few more to say it out loud."

Nada had to look away. "I'm so sorry . . . ," she started. She had known he had gone for therapy, on the advice of his friends. She hadn't known that it had led him to this painful, necessary realization. Her brother stood abruptly, cutting their conversation short. He looked around vaguely at the half-filled food court.

"Now she has Esa. And I have . . . well, I've got you, Jamal, Mom and Dad. And Safa and Marwa too, thank God. They're all that's important right now. We should get going. Jameela will be waiting for us."

They put away the books and puzzle and got the girls ready to leave. Nada suddenly couldn't help it: she gave her brother a half hug. It was awkward because he was bent over the chair, gathering the twins' bags. He stiffened, and she wondered how long it had been since he had been cuddled. She held on for a few seconds, until she felt him relax.

"You deserve to have love in your life again," she said.

Waqas shook his head. "I know Mom and Dad are worried about me, but I'm okay. Actually, I was thinking about . . ." His face went red again. "Never mind. This is too weird."

The girls were getting up from their chairs, and Nada took advantage of their relative calm to pull on her brother's sleeve. "Tell me," she said. When he shook his head again, she said, "Tell me, tell me, tell me, tell me."

Safa and Marwa took up the chorus, delighted by this new game that made their father turn red and start to fidget.

"Okay, okay," he said, herding them all out of the food court. He leaned close to Nada so the girls wouldn't hear. "I was thinking about . . . going to the matrimonial event here. Just to check it out, to see if maybe . . ."

Nada was amused that her older brother, a once-married father of two, still stammered like a schoolboy when he talked about meeting girls.

"Anyways, it doesn't matter. The tickets have been sold out for a while, and I wouldn't want to go by myself anyway."

They returned to the still-empty prayer hall with five minutes to spare. The girls started to run down the rows, laughing and chasing each other, as Nada studied her older brother.

"You really would have gone?" she asked.

Waqas shrugged. "Next year, Inshallah. It's not a big deal. Maybe I'll try one of those Muslim dating apps."

Except he wouldn't. Her brother had never been active on social media. He would spend another year alone, mourning his mistakes, caring for everyone but himself.

But she could help him.

Shit.

She reached into her bag to make sure she still had Baz's stupid liability waiver.

"I can get tickets," Nada said. "Leave it with me."

Baz wasn't at Command Central or in the main lecture hall or in any of the smaller seminar rooms. By the time she had scoured the crowded food court, she was starting to wish she had added him to Find My Friends on her phone. Imagining the look of horror on his face if she had suggested such a thing kept Nada amused as she systematically made her way through the bazaar. She finally found him in front of a tiny stall tucked into a corner of the bazaar. A small sign above the stall read *Nanima's Chai Shop (coming soon to the Golden Crescent!)*

Baz stood chatting with an intense young man, presumably the proprietor. He didn't notice Nada's approach, but the young man watched hopefully.

"Can I interest you in a sample of authentic chai, my sister?" the young man, who looked to be in his early twenties, asked. He had a small build, long hair gathered in a man-bun, eyes magnified behind heavy hipster frames. *Keep Calm and Chai Peelo* was written across the front of his black T-shirt in bold white type, and it made her smile.

Nada checked out the booth before responding. A large copper pot filled with milky, golden-brown tea simmered over a burner, and the young man absent-mindedly stirred the brew with a flat metal ladle, wrist expertly flicking so the milk frothed. Aware of her curious gaze, he poured some of the chai into a small porcelain cup and presented it to her with a fluorish. "My nanima's recipe."

Her mother made excellent tea, and Nada was a chai snob, but her eyes widened in surprise after her first tentative sip—it was possibly the best chai she had ever tasted: strong, with a creamy taste, the masala bite of cardamom and cinnamon perfectly balanced by the right amount of fragrant black tea.

The young man's intense expression didn't waver, but his lips curled in an almost-smile at her enjoyment. "The secret is *khoya*," he confided—dried evaporated milk.

"Should you be telling people that?" Nada asked with a smile, before taking a longer, more appreciative sip. Over the rim of the cup, Nada met Baz's amused glance, and straightened. She was here on a mission, not to fall in love with a cup of tea.

Except the young man—Nada was starting to think of him as *Mr. Chai-Wallah*—wasn't eager to give up his captive audience of one. "It's not the only secret ingredient. Nanima made me promise not to share the rest. She and my nana used to own an Irani teashop in Hyderabad. Well, he worked in one, when they were first married," he amended. He passed her another cup, poured from a thermos on the table. "Try this one."

Nada obediently took the cup, and behind her, she could sense Baz shifting impatiently. He must be wondering what she was doing here, and part of her enjoyed keeping him waiting. This tea deserved to be savored. She sighed happily after drinking.

"I know this," Nada said. "Lasa Lamsa—"

The young man nodded, excitement shining in his eyes at finding a fellow chai enthusiast. "Specially picked Assam CTC tea, but flavored with Lamsa, a proprietary blend from Hyderabad, it has notes of chocolate and a distinct nutty taste—"

"Okay, Sufyan, I think that's enough tea talk for today," Baz cut in. He turned to glare at Nada. "Don't you have somewhere else to be?" he asked meaningfully. *Far away from me* was implied.

"Actually, I'd love to hear more from Sufyan about his chai. What's the perfect temperature for Lasa Lamsa? And please tell me you have more. My cup seems to be empty." Nada grinned at Mr. Chai-Wallah—Sufyan—and ignored Baz's glare.

"Are you here to finally hand over the signed liability waiver?" Baz asked. "Because I don't have time to fix any other problems you've caused in the hour since I last saw you. I do have a job, Nada."

"Go away, I'm drinking the best chai in the world," Nada said, and Sufyan's ears turned pink, even as Baz frowned. She smiled at the young man, and his blush deepened. "Baz gets cranky when he doesn't get his way," she said to the young man, leaning close. "But don't worry, I know how to handle him. Please pack up some of that Lasa Lamsa mix you have for sale, and I'll be right back. This negotiation might get . . . delicate."

Sufyan's eyes widened, and Nada led Baz a few feet away.

"Stop encouraging my nephew," Baz said, as soon as they were alone.

Nada blinked in surprise, looking from Baz to Sufyan, who was back to stirring his pot of simmering chai. There was only a slight resemblance.

"Sufyan is my cousin's kid," Baz explained gruffly. "He's twenty-one, wants to start his own business. School wasn't really for him, but his nani—my aunt—got him hooked on her chai recipes. I set him up with a booth at the conference."

"That was . . . nice of you," Nada said, trying out the word. Somehow it didn't really fit with Baz's stony features. He was still annoyed at her. The prudent thing to do would be to get straight to the point. He was a busy man, and she needed a favor.

She decided to tease him instead. "Do you come here often?" she asked. "Nice weather we're having. How are your parents? Please give them my salams."

Baz sighed deeply. "You are a very tiny, deeply irritating human being," he said.

Affronted, she put her hand on her heart. "You're too tall, and you frown too much."

"What do you want?" Baz asked.

"Frowning gives you wrinkles," she added helpfully, causing him to glower. Her heart gave a lurch. She had forgotten how easy it was to tease him. "You were such a happy child. What happened to you?"

"You happened," he said. "Get to the point."

She waited.

"Please," he said gruffly.

She removed the signed liability waiver from her bag and handed it to him. He lifted a single eyebrow. "And people don't believe in miracles anymore," he said, tucking the form into a folder under his arm.

"Now you're going to express your gratitude by granting me a favor back. I'll take my matrimonial speed-dating ticket back and would be much obliged if you threw in another one."

Baz threw back his head and laughed, startling her. His eyes crinkled in amusement. "That ticket was sold before I left the booth yesterday morning. For an intelligent woman, you're very delusional," he said, and started to walk away.

"For a business bro, you're very naive. You might want to take a closer look at that form," she called.

Baz stopped and reached for his folder. After giving the form a quick glance, he stalked back, brows thunderous.

"*Gullible Baz?*" he said, shaking the form in her face.

"Isn't that your name?" she asked innocently. She was enjoying this far too much.

"You were supposed to sign *your* name," he growled.

Nada tried to tamp down the shiver that ran down her back at the low rumble of his voice. "I definitely will, cross my heart, just as soon as you get me those tickets."

Baz threw her a hateful look before taking out his phone and tapping for a few seconds. "Why do you even need them? You're not looking to get married."

"How would you know?" Nada asked.

"If you were in the market for a husband, you would dress better," he said, flicking his eyes quickly over her pink floral, empire-waisted dress.

"My dress is pretty!"

"Your dress matches the sofa in my mother's living room. From 2003," Baz said. His lips quirked at her annoyed expression. Clearly, he had caught on to her game and was needling her in turn.

"Maybe you should get another ticket for yourself. At least then you'll be sure your dates won't run away after five minutes."

Baz smiled crookedly at her. "Don't worry about me, Nada. I've had no complaints so far."

Nada's cheeks heated. "Are you and Firdous . . . Are you seeing someone?"

"No," Baz said. Then, after a short pause: "I assume you're not in danger of summoning an imam any time soon?"

Nada shook her head. Their eyes locked, and his grip tightened on his phone, his knuckles turning white before relaxing.

"I suppose you're open to the concept if you're in need of tickets to the matrimonial event?" he asked casually, his fingers busy texting.

He had nice hands. Long fingers and large palms. He looked up and caught her staring. She looked away, swallowing hard. What game were they playing? Should she tell him the truth, that the tickets were for her lonely older brother, who required her support as wing-woman? Waqas would be embarrassed.

"I guess that depends on how successful the matrimonial turns out to be," she said lightly. "Few things at this convention have lived up to the hype so far."

Baz's lips tightened, and he shifted his attention back to his phone. "Masood will expect a favor in return," he muttered, acting as if he hadn't heard her last comment.

"Who's Masood?" Nada asked.

"You'll find out soon enough. Just don't get him started on kanga-roos. Or life coaching. Or wrestling." He read the answering text and showed it to her. "I've secured two tickets. With any luck, you'll meet someone just as annoying as you are. Now sign the damn paper."

He dug out another form from his bag and waited impatiently as she scrawled her signature—the real one this time. She resisted the urge to ask why he carried around so many liability waivers, and if it was because of his face.

"Thank you," he said, snapping the folder closed. "Enjoy the rest of the convention. I'll make *dua* I don't see you again this weekend. Feel free to take that very, very personally, Nada."

She let him have the last word because they both knew she had won this round, and he strode through the bazaar without a backward glance. A familiar figure detached himself from a nearby booth and tapped Baz on the shoulder, stopping his progress. The men shook hands, clasping each other's forearms in a friendly gesture. Nada nar-rowed her eyes. Why was Haneef talking to Baz?

A throat cleared behind her, and Nada noticed that Sufyan had moved closer, clearly eavesdropping. "I didn't know Baz *bhai* was see-ing someone. How long have you two been a couple?"

Nada frowned. "Your samples are being stolen."

Sufyan jerked back before realizing she was having him on. He gave her a sly smile, and suddenly Nada saw the family resemblance. He passed her a packet of Parle-G cookies and another cup of tea, this one a vibrant pink Kashmiri chai, the bright color a result of green tea leaves reacting to baking soda, boiled in milk, and topped with pistachios and almonds. It was a tricky recipe to get right, and Nada was impressed. She nibbled on a biscuit, before sampling the tea, which was almost too pretty to drink.

"Baz *bhai* told me I should mingle more, try to make a few friends at the conference," Sufyan said. He looked at her speculatively. "I'm opening up my chai shop next week. Maybe you could visit, if you wanted. And bring some friends?"

Nada drained her cup and handed it back to the chai-wallah, in exchange for a small packet of Lasa Lamsa, which she paid for, adding a hefty tip. "I'll be your best customer," she promised. "And you should meet my younger brother, Jamal. I have a feeling the two of you would get along like a house on fire. Keep an eye out for the loud-mouth in the bright red wheelchair. And Baz and I are not together. He should be so lucky." With a final wave, she headed back to the prayer hall in search of Waqas, happy to finally be the bearer of good news.

CHAPTER THIRTEEN

Present day

One of the larger seminar rooms was set up for the matrimonial event. There were two separate zones: The left side of the room, where the actual halal speed-dating would occur, had two dozen bistro tables, each supplied with note cards, pens, bottles of water, and a vase of pink flowers. The other side of the room had been set up with rows of chairs, as if for a lecture. Another table by the entrance overflowed with bright pink gift bags. When Nada and Waqas arrived, ten minutes early, they were greeted by a beautiful young woman in a bright pink dress who spoke entirely in exclamation marks.

"Assalamu alaikum! I'm Hafsa Shamsi! Welcome to Happily Ever After event planning and matrimonial services! This is my husband, Masood!" she said, introducing an earnest-looking young man dressed in a natty, light blue suit with a pink pocket square.

Nada explained to the excitable woman that they had been sent by Baz as a last-minute addition.

Masood nodded eagerly. "Of course, we are happy to provide Brother Baz with a favor. Once you experience our patent-pending mate-matching system, I am sure you will relate to him how impressive our work truly is. Last year we matched over twenty couples! Of course, our astounding success has not surprised anyone, as my wife is a world-renowned wedding planner, and I am a world-famous life coach for professional wrestlers." He paused. "Except for the Australians. They kicked me out from the caucus after the scandal, but they will soon learn they have made a terrible mistake."

Waqas and Nada exchanged glances. "I'm very sorry to hear that," Nada said.

"It's always the traditionalists who ruin it for everyone. What's wrong with a little modernity? Is kicking really that terrible? Anyway, that life is behind me now. I'm all about love, thanks to my beautiful wife, Hafsa. She has been my rock through everything—the humiliation of a trial, the paparazzi staking out our house, even when the Royal Family shunned us."

Nada blinked, remembering belatedly that Baz had warned her not to get Masood started on life coaching, wrestling, or—

"I still blame the kangaroos," Masood said bitterly. "They're not that cute when they kick you in the—"

Hafsa patted her husband on the arm. "Not in front of the customers, my *gulab jamun*," she said firmly, before turning to Nada and Waqas. "I'm going to make you both my special projects and help you find your soulmates! My cousin Ayesha didn't get married until she was, like, twenty-nine, so don't worry. There's hope for everyone, even you." Hafsa passed them clipboards with detailed questionnaires to fill out.

Along with the usual questions about age, education, and relationship status, the form included some oddball questions: What is your favorite wrestling move? What is your favorite color and why is it pink? If you were a cloud, how high would you float? List your most high-profile and well-connected friends or family members, along with their phone numbers and social media handles.

Nada filled in the form quickly and returned it to Hafsa, who gave her a bright pink gift bag in exchange. Nada spread the contents of the bag on the seat beside her while she waited for Waqas.

The room quickly filled with people of various ages and ethnicities. Some of the younger women were accompanied by a parent, whether for moral support, as a chaperone, or to prevent them from bolting, Nada wasn't sure. Masood stood at the small podium and addressed the room.

"Assalamu alaikum, everyone, and welcome to the Deen&Dunya matrimonial event! I know how difficult it can be to find the right partner in your life. My wife and I have been in the trenches, and our path to happily ever after was not without issues. Which is why we want to help you all find your own 'halal ever afters'!"

Hafsa put her arm through her husband's and chimed in: "Remember, there's a 10-percent-off coupon for my exclusive wedding planning services! When you think weddings, think Happily Ever After event planning!"

She went on to explain how the event would proceed. The participants would be paired with a small selection of candidates based on their unique, patent-pending system. "You'll have fifteen minutes to talk to each suitor. And please keep an open mind! My beloved husband and I fell in love unexpectedly. Don't be afraid to let love into your life. Have fun, everyone!"

From his seat in the front row, a suddenly pale Waqas turned to Nada. "Actually, I think I'm ready to leave now," he said.

"Nice try," Nada said, patting his arm. "I expect a full report at the end of the event. Your homework is to get at least two numbers. Come on, you can do this."

Waqas took a deep breath and set off in search of his table, while Nada did the same. A nervous-looking young man was waiting for her, and for the first time since she had finagled tickets from Baz, Nada realized she'd have to actually make small talk with random strangers. "Hi," she said, smiling and taking a seat.

The other man sat, nodding shyly. "Hi."

"Actually, I think this is my seat?" a smooth voice interrupted. The young man startled like a bunny and ran off without another word. Haneef slid into the seat across from Nada.

She stared at him stonily. "What are you doing here?"

"You weren't going to marry that guy. Might as well talk to me instead." He flashed her a winning smile.

"I'd rather talk to myself, the wall, a jinn, or ten other strangers rather than spend a single second talking to you."

"You just spent fifteen seconds monologuing at me, so joke's on you." His expression changed to one of fake contrition. "Come on, Nada. Fifteen minutes. There's literally a timer. Or do you want to cause another scene? I'm sure it was hard enough to get your lonely brother here in the first place. Imagine what would happen to his reputation if you started yelling and he had to escort you out."

Nada imagined dousing Haneef with gasoline and lighting a match. "I hate you," she said.

"I'm aware."

She hadn't always hated Haneef. There had been a time when they were friends, when she had actually looked up to him, admired him for his mind and occasionally for his face. Haneef El-Haad was good-looking. He was tall, with broad shoulders, curly hair framing his sharp cheekbones and square jaw, and attractive hazel-green eyes. Even now, his presence garnered a fair share of attention from the surrounding tables. Nada wished she could announce Haneef's general terribleness to the room, but unfortunately, he was right: one more scene from her and she might become a permanent addition to the convention's drama queen hall of fame.

She leaned back in her chair. "Let's get this over with. What do you want?"

Haneef smiled and laid his hands—and cards—on the table. "I didn't steal your idea for Ask Apa."

Nada snorted and looked away.

"But I admit that there are some similarities between our two plat-forms that might appear, to the casual observer, slightly suspicious. The truth is, both of our ideas were simply floating in the zeitgeist at the same time. Sort of like how two movie versions of Jane Austen's *Emma* were released in the same year."

"Let me get this straight," she started pleasantly. "You just hap-pened to think of the idea for a Muslim-specific search engine at the same time I did, and happened to name it Ukhti, which is Arabic for 'big sister,' the same meaning as *apa* in Urdu, and then you launched it six months before my go-live. All while you were helping me develop Ask Apa?"

Haneef shrugged. "I consulted on your plan and helped you source programmers and developers. I had no obligation to inform you of my own business ideas. Remember that the movies *A Bug's Life* and *Antz* were both in production at the same time."

"You stole my idea!" Nada said loudly. Around them, couples looked up, and she lowered her voice. "Then you sold it for millions—"

"Allegedly. No numbers were confirmed," he interrupted, smirking.

"—and now you're here to, what, gloat? I already told your mother: I want nothing to do with you or your family ever again."

"Care to put that in writing?" Haneef flicked at a small piece of dust on the table between them. "If you agree to sell me whatever remains of Ask Apa and sign an NDA, I could make it worth your while."

Nada sat back. "What are you playing at? You got everything you wanted. You're the big man at the convention. Even my friends invested in Ukhti."

Haneef looked steadily at her. "Maybe I want to make things right."

"That would imply you had a conscience," Nada said, thinking rapidly. "Tell me what's really going on."

"Our families used to be friends. My mother misses talking to your mom. Maybe I just want to extend an olive branch for their sake." Haneef sat back, comfortable now. "You know, my ommi didn't talk to me for an entire year after the launch."

This surprised her. His voice held what sounded, even to Nada's jaded ears, like sincere regret.

"She cut me out for your sake. Imagine. I had to beg my mother to give me a second chance. Whatever you might think of her, she does love you. Think about it. I doubt you'll get a better offer from anyone else."

Nada heard the timer go off faintly in the background. Her hands were gripped tightly around the water bottle on the table, and she fought the urge to throw it at Haneef. "I'd rather burn Ask Apa to the ground than sell it to you," she said.

Haneef's handsome face grew ugly as he sneered at her. "Still so stubborn. I hope your pride keeps you warm at night, Nada. Nobody else seems to want to."

She sucked in a breath, and Haneef's eyes noted the direct hit. He thought he was getting through to her, but he was wrong. The only thing Nada realized was her mistake in attending the convention. Coming here had been a risk, which was why she had avoided it for years. She'd known that attending Deen&Dunya would force her to come face-to-face with everything she had spent the past six years running from. The only way this situation could possibly get worse would be if Baz suddenly appeared.

As if summoned, Baz began to politely make the rounds at the matchmaking event. Nada deserved a medal for not screaming in frustration. He chatted with an enthusiastic Hafsa and Masood. The matrimonial hosts threw their hands wide, no doubt boasting about their success.

Haneef turned to follow her gaze. He raised an arm. "Baz!" he yelled.

Nada shrank down in her seat. Waqas would owe her big-time for this.

Baz was inscrutable when he walked over to them. He nodded at Nada, taking in Haneef with a polite nod. "How's it going?"

"Take a seat and see for yourself," Haneef said, faux-bro hearty. "Nada, have you met Baz? He's the guy in charge, no matter what anyone else says. I'm sure your employees would agree."

"Hafsa and Masood don't work for me," Baz said stiffly. "We're partners in this endeavor."

Haneef gave a knowing chuckle that grated on Nada's nerves. "Everyone knows who really runs this place, Baz. I hope we can talk further about some of my ideas, once you're done here." He stood up and gestured to his seat.

Baz wordlessly sat down.

Another fifteen minutes of hell starting . . . now. Nada mentally composed a review of the Happy Ever After matchmaking algorithm: *I was set up with a sociopath and an ice giant. Zero stars. Would not recommend.* Instead, she took a sip from the water bottle that had narrowly escaped being an accessory to assault and waited for Baz to make the first move.

He cleared his throat, ill at ease. "I didn't come here to check up on you," he started.

Nada rolled her eyes at this. "We both know you can't stay away," she said, and to her astonishment, he blushed. "I'm kidding, Baz," she said, more gently.

The wry smile on his face showed that he accepted her words, while acknowledging the awkwardness of the moment. "I can leave," he offered.

"No," she replied instantly. "As Haneef delightfully pointed out, I can't afford to cause another scene."

Baz nodded, and they both looked around at the other couples, each intent on their own conversations, each wondering if they had just met The One. "I've never done one of these before," he said.

Were they actually about to have a civilized conversation?

"Maybe Haneef is right, as much as I hate to admit it," Nada said cautiously. "A good boss should know what happens at the company." Was she actually urging Baz to stay?

"I have complete confidence in Hafsa and Masood," Baz said seriously. His lip twitched. "They're very . . . intense."

Nada smiled, before remembering she was here under duress. There was a moment of silence as they looked away from each other, then back again.

"Should we give this a try? For research purposes only." His serious expression belied his casual request. He was asking, not insisting on her attention and commandeering her time as Haneef had done only a few moments ago. "I've been told my socialization skills have grown rusty from misuse," he added. Those dark eyes tracked her, just as they had every time their paths crossed this weekend.

Nada's eyebrows rose. Ice giants rarely had this level of self-awareness.

"Why don't you tell me about yourself," he said, leaning back as if they had all the time in the world, and not—she checked the timer— twelve minutes.

Nada scoffed. "Stop."

"I'm serious. What have you been up to since . . ." He faltered. "Since," he said more firmly.

She looked around, wondering if she were stuck in some creative madman's idea of a torture chamber. Then again, talking to Baz was better than listening to Haneef. "What do you want to know?"

"What really happened with Ask Apa?"

She lifted her chin. "It launched six months after Ukhti came out. I missed the window, and Haneef got all the attention and money."

Baz frowned. "The Nada I knew would never have accepted that. She would have sacrificed everything for her business, for her dreams."

"You never liked that about me. You were more traditional back then."

Baz shrugged. "And you would have told me to take my macho male self straight to hell."

Nada smiled faintly. "I found a job. I work for a small engineering company now. I moved on with my life. It all worked out the way it was meant to be."

Baz shook his head slowly. "None of this is how things were meant to be," he said.

Was this what Haleema had meant, that she had given up? If that was the case, then Baz had done the same thing. They hadn't seen each other in years, but they both seemed . . . diminished somehow. On the cusp of thirty, they both had the outer trappings of a normal, stable adult life, and yet here they were, making awkward conversation during a speed-dating event neither of them had wanted to attend.

"My turn. Why are you friends with Haneef?" she asked.

Baz seemed surprised. "We're not friends."

"I saw him talking to you at the bazaar earlier. You did that handshake thing where you grip each other's forearms," she accused.

"I shake a lot of people's hands."

"I hope you washed after you shook hands with Haneef. Actually, maybe you should take a full shower."

Baz quirked his lips. "Is he your ex or something?"

Nada jerked as if she had been electrocuted. "Definitely not. Next question: Why don't you write songs and perform anymore? I remember a time when that was all you wanted to do, along with traveling the world."

Baz looked away, then back. His eyes were always drawn back to hers when they were in the same space, she realized. They had been staring at each other over the past two days, and people were starting to notice. Around her, other women glanced speculatively between her and Baz. She could imagine what they were wondering: What was Baz Haq doing at the matrimonial speed-dating event . . . and when would they get a turn with him? *Never*, a voice whispered in her head, and an answering possessiveness tugged low in her belly. She shook her head. This was getting out of hand. It always did when they were together.

His gaze flicked to her lips now, then settled on her face. "What was I going to do, become a singer-songwriter in the Muslim community?"

"Yes," Nada said simply.

Baz shook his head. "My parents would have been horrified. It was bad enough that Zayn was so keen."

"Since when do you care what other people think?"

"For about six years now," he answered.

Nada sat back. She deserved that. "You're really good on stage. I mean, usually you've got the face of an expressionless robot, but when you're in front of others, it's . . ."

"It's what?" he asked, leaning forward.

"Magical." Nada looked away. "Shut up. You know you're good." Even a smirk looked sexy on Baz's face. How annoying. "If you don't want to perform or write songs anymore, have you thought about doing this," she gestured around her, "for others?"

Baz frowned, not understanding. The idea had grown in Nada's mind since she had walked into D&D yesterday. She had been blown away by the organization and attention to detail at the convention, which was apparent in every aspect of the event. As the lead architect of D&D, along with his parents and whatever it was that Zayn contributed, Baz's accomplishment was seriously impressive. "Maybe you could start a talent management company, for Muslim artists," Nada said, thinking out loud. "Not just for singers, but actors, writers, visual artists. You have the contacts, and you know the industry, plus you're scary organized. It would be a way to stay in the creative industry while utilizing your more marketable skills."

Baz's eyes widened slightly, and he leaned back, thoughtful. "A talent agency for Muslim artists," he repeated, turning the idea over. She saw him dismiss it, saw robotic, ice giant Baz flicker on and take control. "Not possible. My parents need me to help with the convention. D&D has really taken off, and they have some other ideas to expand our brand."

"Your brand? Are you rich now?" Nada asked with a smile, trying to cover her disappointment.

Baz returned her smile. "Very." Then his smile faded. "It was never about the money. I grew up with nothing, and I don't need much now."

"What do you need?" Nada asked.

He paused as he looked at her. The moment grew long, and she fidgeted and glanced away. Finally he spoke: "Purpose. Focus. A goal. Just like you."

She drew circles on the table in front of them. "Sometimes I wonder how my life would have turned out if things had been different."

"Different outcomes only happen if you're a different person. As far as I can tell, you're the same as you always were," he said lightly, but the expression in his eyes had turned hard. "What's done is done. Any regrets you might have are just wishful thinking."

That word again: *regret*. Lately, Nada was starting to feel as if her regrets were piled in heaps, though the biggest one sat before her, and she couldn't stand it. "Baz," she started, but the timer went off, and he stood in one graceful, fluid motion. She craned her neck up to find his eyes focused on the next table, where an eager young woman waited for him.

Nada met a few men in quick succession: a baby lawyer who spent the entire fifteen minutes bragging about his slightly used Porsche

Cayenne, an accountant who had clearly been coerced to attend by his mother, and a shy dentist who barely made eye contact. She watched as Baz charmed one woman after another, no doubt collecting phone numbers at every table. So far, not a single one of her candidates had asked for her digits or even to follow her on Instagram. At least her brother was enjoying himself. She caught Waqas smile widely at his companion, a pretty Black woman in a royal blue hijab.

The event finally ended, and Hafsa wandered over to her table. "Did you enjoy yourself?" she asked.

Nada thought for a moment. "I'm sure a lot of people made some great connections," she said diplomatically.

"It was fun," Waqas said, joining them. There was a spring in his step, and he seemed to be standing up straighter. "I don't know how you scrounged up tickets for me last minute, Nada, but I'm glad I came."

Nada's tense smile loosened at her brother's evident happiness. Her smile faded when she spotted Baz standing within eavesdropping distance. His eyebrow rose at Waqas's comment. So now Baz knew the real reason that she had needed tickets, while his presence was still a mystery to her.

Masood joined his wife. "I hope you have realized the effectiveness of in-person experiences. Online dating has its place of course, but finding the perfect partner is an in-person process. Right, my little *ras malai?*" He brought his wife's hand to his lips, and Hafsa giggled.

Nada looked away. She had to admit that they were a cute couple. Behind them, Baz talked with an animated young woman with doe eyes and perfect eyebrows. Another woman joined in, and then Baz was surrounded by smiling, eager beauties. The sour feeling in Nada's stomach intensified. *Regrets, piled one on top of the other.*

"Now that Zayn is engaged, the other Haq brother won't last long," Masood observed, watching Baz. "We should secure that wedding planning contract before the other vultures circle." Smiling, Hafsa and Masood drifted off.

Nada hadn't known that the news about Haleema and Zayn was out, and she felt a twinge of guilt that she hadn't thought about her friend in several hours. With a final glance at Baz and his admirers, she followed her brother outside.

CHAPTER FOURTEEN

Present day

Back in the main hall, Nada high-fived Waqas, who shyly shared that he had managed to score four numbers. "They were probably just being polite," he said.

"You are awesome and they instantly knew it," she countered. "Have some fun with this. Just don't become one of those cocky Muslim dude-bros who think they're God's gift to women just because their mothers keep calling them handsome."

Her brother's face was glowing. Confidence looked good on him. Nada was glad she had blackmailed Baz to get the tickets, despite their weird conversation.

"Don't text anyone until the weekend is over," she advised. "You'll come across as thirsty."

Waqas furrowed his brow. "I could use some water," he said.

Nada shook her head fondly. He would learn. "Enjoy the rest of the convention. Talk to your friends. But no contact with these women until Monday. Okay?"

He nodded. Then, hesitating, he asked, "Is there something going on between you and—"

"Gotta go!" she said cheerily. It was one thing to give Waqas love advice, but another thing entirely to have her older brother take an interest in her life in return. She walked toward the bazaar, searching for Haleema. She found her friend hanging by the circular stage with Zayn. Haleema was happy to see her. There was no trace of peevishness and no explanation for her disappearance this morning. Taking her cue, Nada gave her a hug before informing the happy couple that news of their engagement was making the rounds at the convention.

"I might have let something slip on my social media," Haleema said.

Zayn frowned. "I thought we had agreed to keep things quiet until after the *nikah*?"

Haleema shrugged and quickly changed the topic. "Don't forget, Zayn got us tickets to the fundraising gala dinner tonight," she reminded Nada.

He still seemed confused and troubled about being unknowingly outed. Nada wondered if he was upset that Haleema had done so behind his back, or because of the impact of this news on the Zaynimals. The circular stage did seem strangely bereft of adoring female fans.

Haleema waved a hand in front of Nada's face. "Hello? Aren't you excited for the gala? They're raising money for a children's charity or something."

Nada had attended a few gala dinners in her time, and they mostly consisted of mediocre food and boring speeches. Plus, Haneef and Sister Rusul were sure to be there.

"Do I have to go?" Nada asked.

The smile slipped from her friend's face. Sensing another dustup, Zayn made his excuses and left the two women alone.

"The tickets are five hundred dollars a plate! It's invitation-only, open to the VIP guests and close family," Haleema said.

"Tell him to donate the money and I'll get some takeout," Nada said, trying to make a joke.

"Zayn knows how important you are to me, but you're not even trying. Is this about last night? I don't want to ruin our girls' weekend. Let's just put this all behind us."

Nada sighed. A dull headache was starting behind her left eye, and she rubbed at the tender spot. Her life was complicated enough without a prolonged fight with her friend. "Of course it's not about last night. We're good. I'm happy to attend the gala." She paused. "Except I didn't pack anything fancy to wear."

Haleema smiled, excited once more. "Don't worry, I've got you covered."

They ended up at a booth inside the bazaar run by a young designer named Nisa, who created modest fashions that looked more like hand-sewn works of art. Haleema picked out a black lace dress that gathered at the waist and flared out in a full skirt.

Nada looked at the price tag. "I can't afford this," she whispered.

Haleema shook her head. "My treat. Reparations for holding you hostage all weekend."

Later, they dressed in the hotel room together, sharing makeup and giggling like they used to in undergrad. Haleema carefully applied winged eyeliner and sparkly gold eye shadow on Nada, before picking out a neutral lipstick. She had brought a stunning cream and green chiffon dress for herself. It shimmered with crystals when she walked and was much fancier than Nada's elegant long black dress.

"You came prepared," Nada said.

Haleema shrugged. "I knew I needed to look good once news about the engagement was out." She applied bronzer to her cheekbones, highlighting her delicate features. "Or rather, after I dropped a picture of my ring on the socials and tagged Zayn, his band, and his head groupies," she said nonchalantly.

Nada laughed. "The Zaynimals finally get to you?"

Haleema shut her compact with a snap. "The wedding is in a month. It was the right time."

Nada resisted the urge to ask her friend why Zayn hadn't made the announcement himself. The wedding was a bit rushed, but they had already been engaged for three months.

As if anticipating the question, Haleema began to pack away her makeup and said, "He offered to make an announcement when we first got engaged, but I told him it was fine. Being single is part of his mystique."

Nada thought about his easy smiles and willingness to take selfies for hours on the specially constructed circular stage. Charisma was one thing Zayn had in spades, but he was the least mysterious person she had ever met. His brother on the other hand . . . Nada made a noncommittal noise.

"You think I'm overreacting, that I should have told Zayn before I posted?" Haleema said.

With a pang, Nada recalled her own instinctive reaction to Baz surrounded by the eligible beauties at the matrimonial and softened. "You're staking your claim. The Zaynimals better back off," she said firmly. "Nobody pushes a Golden Crescent girl around." Haleema had joined the club when she bought her condo in the neighborhood last year.

They posed in front of the full-length mirror by the door, hands on jutting hips, lips pouting, and took selfies. Haleema chose the best picture and, after applying a filter, posted it to Instagram before they set off. She had suddenly amassed hundreds of new followers, and the pictures had to be flattering.

The gala dinner was held on the main floor of the convention center in a formal dining hall that had been decorated tastefully. Each table seated ten and was covered with a white linen tablecloth and a giant vase of fresh flowers. The hall was already full of people when the women arrived at seven. Nada recognized some of the speakers, including Sheikh Ilyas Raoul. Baz's parents, Arifa and Ahmed Haq, greeted guests at the door while an usher discreetly checked their invitations before directing them toward the buffet appetizers: vegetarian cocktail samosas, tandoori shrimp on skewers, paneer with fire-roasted green and red peppers, juicy meat kebabs, and crispy fish pakoras. Plus salad, which Nada skipped entirely.

Zayn was already posing with fans. Haleema's lips tightened at the sight, but she busied herself with the food.

"Maybe you should flash that solitaire on that side of the room," Nada said, nodding to where Zayn was taking a picture with a trio of gorgeous fans. "A friendly reminder?"

Haleema looked from the appetizers to Zayn and back again. Steeling her spine, she put her plate down and stalked over to her fiancé. Nada smiled as she continued to load her plate with samosas, fish pakoras, and shrimp skewers.

"I see you're hitting the major desi food groups: oil, meat, and spice," Baz said over her shoulder. The ice giant had changed into a more formal gray suit for the gala, along with a crisp white shirt and simple blue tie. The outfit attracted appreciative glances from everyone who walked past, but Baz didn't seem to notice. He was too busy giving her black lace dress a slow perusal.

"You look . . . nice," he said, settling on the bland adjective with some effort.

"You could have made more of an effort," she said.

He huffed in amusement. "Did Waqas have fun at the matrimonial? You could have told me the tickets were for him. I wouldn't have given you a hard time." His plate was full of salad, without a fried item to be found.

"And ruin your fun? I know you live to judge me." Baz frowned at her, but she quickly went on. "Waqas did all right; he pulled four numbers."

"What a player."

"Takes one to know one. How many numbers did you get?" She was losing the battle to mind her own business.

"I lost track after the first dozen."

Annoyed, she transferred a few cocktail samosas from her plate to his. Baz put them back on her plate and added a few carrots. "So you don't get scurvy."

"Since when did you stop eating junk food?" she asked, putting two cocktail samosas back on his plate.

He sighed. "Since I decided to give up things that are bad for me."

"Bazzy, there you are!" Firdous practically ran up to Baz. She was wearing a form-fitting dress with gold sparkles and a short train that puddled by Nada's ballet flats. "You look amazing," she gushed up at him. "And you smell great. What is that cologne?"

Baz had the grace to blush. "Whatever Zayn had lying around."

"Mmmm," Firdous said, inhaling deeply.

Nada bit her tongue to keep from laughing.

Firdous turned to Nada now, only just noticing her presence. "Oh, Nora. I'm surprised you were invited. By the way, I remember you now," she said sweetly. "You're the girl who had her hijab pulled off in front of everyone at camp when we were fourteen. Bisma did it, right? What a psycho."

Beside the women, Baz went very still, but Nada could handle this on her own. "If Bisma behaved badly, she was provoked," she said calmly. "We're still friends."

"Oh, *are* you? Well, good for you. I always thought she was a little off. Bazzy, do you want to grab our seats? We're at the front, with your parents." Firdous tried to usher Baz away, but he popped a cocktail samosa in his mouth and refused to move. Put out, Firdous glanced around the room, nodding at people she knew and waving at others. It was clear that she was popular. It was also clear that she didn't want to relinquish her plum position next to Baz. Nada smiled to herself and nibbled on a tandoori shrimp skewer.

They stood in awkward silence for a moment, until finally Firdous turned back to Nada. "I heard you own that cute little app Ask Apa. So clever of you to try to build on the popularity of Ukhti. You're like Duplo to Ukhti's Lego."

Nada drowned her samosa in green chutney and said nothing.

"What are you doing now?" Firdous asked, determined to keep the conversation going.

"I'm taking some time and considering my options," Nada said with a straight face, though inwardly she seethed. *For instance, should I step on your fancy dress and make you trip, or should I be the bigger person? Decisions, decisions.*

Firdous laughed prettily. "I wish I could do that, but I'm such a decisive person. When I make up my mind, it's made up."

Baz looked at Firdous with interest for the first time since she'd arrived. "Do you think you were born like that, or was it something you were taught?"

She preened under his attention. "I've always known my own mind. My mom says I never wavered or second-guessed a decision, even as a child."

"That must be a relief to your friends and family," Baz said thoughtfully. "A person too indecisive can hardly be depended upon. You'd always worry anybody might sway them one way or another." His eyes met Nada's. "Let those who would be happy be firm."

Nada put her plate down. "Let me make sure I understand you, Firdous," she said pleasantly. "You think people should never be allowed to waver, to come to a different conclusion?"

Baz interrupted before Firdous could defend her reasoning. "I think she means she knows her own mind and can't be persuaded otherwise. An admirable quality, don't you think?"

Firdous looked from Baz to Nada, frowning. It was clear she didn't like being sidelined. Though she wasn't entirely following the conversation, she didn't like the direction it was taking: away from her. "I think—"

"No, I don't. Seeking *naseeha*, sincere advice, and listening to people you trust when you're unsure is natural," Nada interrupted, eyes pinned on Baz.

"Even when their advice is wrong?" Baz gripped his plate so hard Nada worried it would crack.

Blood pounded in her ears, and Nada felt a sick feeling of dread pool in her stomach. They had finally arrived at the crux of everything, the reason she had avoided this convention for years. Despite her best efforts, they were about to have the conversation they had so far avoided this weekend—and for the past six years.

"There's nothing more human than being wrong," she said quietly now. "Or being persuaded one way and then regretting your decision. I would argue that learning to live with that regret is the most human thing of all."

Firdous, nearly wriggling with the urge to be part of the conversation, piped up. "Doesn't it just come down to faith?" she asked. "When you make a decision and stick to it, you're showing that you have faith in yourself, in your path, or in someone else. Right?" She looked from one to the other like an eager puppy seeking validation, and Nada wanted to cry, because even a stopped clock is right twice a day; somehow Firdous had hit on the truth exactly.

Regrets, piled in heaps all around her. The biggest one standing tall before her, an unreachable ice giant.

Baz loosened his grip on his plate, and that cool look was back in his eyes. "We should take our seats."

To her credit, Firdous didn't throw a triumphant glance at Nada as she and Baz walked away, but Nada felt devastated nonetheless. She wanted to run after Baz, to continue the conversation now that they were finally having it. She wanted to ask: Was there no forgiveness to be had, no redemption after one wavered?

But she also understood him finally. He could not forgive her for the past, but at the same time he could not be cruel. It was a reminder of his former sentiment, a shadow of their past friendship, and proof of his own good character, which she could not now contemplate without an accompanying stab of pain.

Nada made her way to her seat on frozen limbs. Haleema was already seated. Judging by the stony expression on her friend's face, something was wrong, but Nada didn't ask for details. Her own mind was a buzzing swirl, yet she felt strangely detached from her body, as if she were observing herself from the outside. Thankfully, conversation was not necessary—the program was about to begin.

Arifa and Ahmed Haq welcomed the crowd of two hundred guests and spoke warmly about the origins of the Deen&Dunya convention, from their humble beginnings selling Islamic songs and lectures recorded on DVDs, to the launch of the convention, which had grown in success through the years and now attracted tens of thousands of people from across the continent. They introduced a few new initiatives, including various charitable endeavors, and shared plans to expand the D&D brand in the coming years, with Islamic finance products, as well as guided tours to the Muslim world. Baz was the master of ceremonies, and when he walked on stage, he was serious and purposeful, as if born for the role. He outlined the program for the night: dinner would be served shortly, but first there would be a special performance by The Companions. Was it her imagination, or did Baz carefully avoid looking at her table?

Zayn, dressed in the same long white tunic with prayer beads around his neck, walked onto the stage and grabbed the microphone with the confidence of a natural showman. Behind him, his fellow bandmates tuned their instruments.

"Assalamu alaikum, speakers and VIP guests! We are The Companions. This is a very special song about trusting in Allah's wisdom while enjoying one of His great mercies—love."

The song was a slow ballad, and Zayn crooned into the microphone. He was talented, but Nada couldn't help but compare his performance to his younger brother's. While Zayn had more natural stage presence, Baz edged him out with a deeper, more soulful voice. She wondered once again why Baz had given up on performing when he was clearly so talented. She leaned back and listened to the words.

Even when I think I know you
I wonder if I do
Meant to be
Meant for me
Oh please—
Be meant for me

The words of lost love and heartbreak hit Nada like a blow, and she stood up. The room was too hot. There were too many people. She needed to leave, to breathe fresh air that didn't smell like musky, spicy cologne, that wasn't filled with the presence of Baz. Whispering to Haleema that she would be right back, she fled to the empty hallway.

"Nada," Baz said. He was standing outside too, and Nada's heart started to pound. Had he followed her?

"Your brother is really talented," she said, trying to keep her voice from shaking. "I liked his song and . . ."

His hands were clenched, knuckles white. "I wrote it," Baz said. The words burst from him, a fracture in a concrete dam. He took a few steps toward her and stopped. "I wrote every song for you."

She took a step toward him, and with a strangled groan he was instantly by her side. His breathing was ragged, as if he had run there. As if he hadn't stopped running all weekend. His hands settled gently on her hips, as if she were delicate glass, as if she were indescribably precious, and then he pulled her close, until their bodies touched. His gaze was hot—the ice giant melted now—and he looked for something in her eyes: permission, acceptance, wonder. When he found it, he breathed a sigh of relief.

And then he kissed her.

CHAPTER FIFTEEN

Eight years ago

Nada was enjoying her lunch on the grassy field in the middle of the University of Toronto campus, when she spotted Baz walking across the quad, deep in conversation with a pretty Black woman in a light blue hijab and elegant *abayah* dress cinched at the waist. Nada hadn't seen Baz since he disappeared in freshman year. She was staring at him so intently she didn't notice when the young woman by his side stopped in her tracks.

"Nada?" the woman called. A smile split her face, and she rushed over. "It's Bisma! From MYNA camp!" She ran into Nada's arms just as she was getting up, nearly knocking her back to the ground. Bisma's shoulders shook with emotion. "I prayed I would see you again. I didn't have your number, and your profile is private on social media. I can't believe it's really you!" She drew back and her face was streaked with tears. "I'm so sorry for what I did to you; you didn't deserve that. I was in therapy for months trying to sort through it all. Firdous is a cow. She lives in Edmonton now and is married to a rich developer. Surely justice rests with Allah and not on this earth."

Nada looked from Bisma to Baz. He had grown his beard out, and his long, curly, dark hair reached his chin. He was dressed in a salwar kameez. The ghosts of the eleven-year-old, the fourteen-year-old, and the eighteen-year-old she had known were present in the grown man who stood gravely before her. He smiled slightly at the strange reunion between the two women.

"Bisma, you're frightening her," he said, his voice a deep rumble.

She remembered that voice from two years ago. The warmth and wariness in his face confirmed that he recognized her too.

"Assalamu alaikum, Baz," Nada said, suddenly shy.

He nodded and returned the greeting. Recognition, at least. She turned back to Bisma. "We were kids. Don't even mention it."

Bisma enveloped her in another hug. The scent of flowers and coconut was briefly overwhelming. "Come for lunch with us," she said.

"I'm sure Nada is busy," Baz answered.

"She's eating a sad sandwich all alone. I have to make amends. Let's go to the Hart House café. They make delicious avocado toast." Bisma grabbed hold of Nada's hand, then reached down to scoop up her bag. "I won't take no for an answer."

Baz contemplated the sky for a moment, as if making *dua* for patience, and then the trio walked toward the popular eatery across the quad, with Baz in the lead.

Hart House café was located in the same building where he and Nada had regularly attended Friday prayers years ago—before she had snooped through his bag and read his de facto diary. Nada's cheeks warmed at the memory of his anger.

Thankfully, Bisma kept up a steady stream of chatter and didn't seem to mind Nada's reserve. "I went to college in the States, but my family still lives in Toronto. Baz offered to take me around, and I should be grateful the great world traveler could spare the time while on a pit stop back home. He used to attend U of T too, but he dropped out halfway through first year."

"I didn't drop out. I took a leave," Baz called back.

"You hated it here. You spent the last two years finding yourself, like some white woman on a journey of self-discovery." Bisma laughed. She turned to Nada and said, "Can you imagine?"

"Shut up, Bisma," Baz said good-naturedly. "She doesn't care about any of that."

"Of course she does. She started uni the same time you did. Maybe she wondered what happened to the cute, mysterious boy she saw around campus." Bisma laughed, and Nada and Baz didn't look at each other.

Bisma picked out a table on the outdoor patio and then waved imperiously at Baz. "Two avocado toasts and two iced teas," she ordered, and he disappeared inside to get the food.

"I can't believe we bumped into each other like this. It's fate," Bisma said. "Come to my wedding."

Nada blinked. "Are you and Baz . . ."

Bisma laughed as if that was the funniest thing she had heard all day. "I told you at camp, Baz is like my brother. We grew up together, and our families are close. No, I'm marrying Waleed, my beloved. We met freshman year in Philly. Mom was so mad. She had a nice brother picked out for me back home in Nigeria, but Waleed is my soulmate. He gets me. His family is originally from Kenya, but we'll make it work. Please say you'll come. You can't refuse a bride's request, that's the law."

Baz returned with their order balanced on a tray, plus a mug of black coffee. He distributed the food and took a seat. "You have to stop bossing everyone around just because you're getting married," he said sternly. "Now eat your food. I promised I'd bring you home before five." He took a sip of his coffee. Baz still hadn't looked at Nada after their awkward reintroduction.

Bisma took a huge bite of toast and stared at Baz and Nada in turn. "Baz, give Nada your number," she ordered after finishing chewing.

"Ignore her," Baz said to Nada.

"Baz thinks he's cool because he drinks his coffee black," Bisma said. "Something he picked up in Istanbul. *So* pretentious."

"Please stop talking," Baz said.

"I have excellent intuition," Bisma said. "The way you're not looking at each other tells me there's a story here. You might as well spill. I'll just get it out of Baz later. He tells me everything. I have enough dirt to blackmail him for life."

Baz and Nada quickly glanced at each other.

"No story," Nada mumbled before taking a bite of her avocado toast and chasing it with a big swallow of iced tea, generously sweetened.

"Give me your phone," Bisma ordered Nada. "Now that we've reconnected, I'm not letting you go again."

Nada dutifully handed her phone to Bisma, who input her number.

Baz's phone pinged with a message, and Bisma cackled. "Now you've got each other's digits too. What you do next is up to you."

With a martyred sigh, Baz stood up. "Come on, bridezilla. The GO train leaves soon."

Bisma rose, waving Nada back in her seat. "My *nikah* is at the Toronto Muslim Assembly in the east end. A week from Saturday, after *Asr* prayer. Promise you'll come? Baz can bring you." Without waiting for either of them to reply, she floated to the sidewalk.

Nada's phone pinged with a message five minutes later.

Feel free to delete this number, Baz wrote.

Nada thought for a minute. After you drive me to the wedding, she wrote. You can't refuse bridal orders. Apparently, it's against the law.

The Toronto Muslim Assembly was so close to where she lived, she could just take the bus, but she wanted an excuse to talk to Baz again. The seven-minute drive to the mosque would be the perfect amount of time to say what she needed to say.

On the day of the *nikah*, Nada took care to dress in a flattering, butter yellow salwar kameez with silver *zari* embroidery at the sleeves and hem. She put on a white hijab, subtle makeup, and her heavy silver bangles and earrings.

Her mother was busy with Jamal these days. His official diagnosis had come through only a few months ago, and the family was still adjusting. She slipped out of the house and walked quickly to the corner, where she had told Baz to meet her.

He pulled up in a black Mercedes. He was dressed in a formal dark blue salwar suit with subtle white embroidery around the starched collar, hair neatly combed and beard trimmed. There was something grounded and calm in his air that had been missing the last time they met. Maybe he really had "found himself" during his travels.

"This seems to have become a habit with us," she said once he started driving. It was awkward to be in a car with Baz. Though they had technically known each other since they were eleven years old, the total amount of time they had spent in each other's company wouldn't fill a month.

"What do you mean?" he asked, his eyes on the road. He had only given her a cursory glance and quickly averted his gaze when she settled in the passenger seat.

"You disappeared from campus for two years," she said, trying not to sound accusatory. "I looked for you everywhere. Around campus, at MSA events, the library. You vanished."

"Why were you looking for me? We're not friends. We barely know each other," he said.

He was right. She sat up straight. Might as well get this part over and done with; it was the reason she had spent months looking for him in the first place.

"I shouldn't have read your poems," she said. "It was an invasion of your privacy, and it was a rotten thing to do."

Baz shook his head, his eyes pinned to the road. There wasn't a lot of traffic on the quiet residential streets of the Golden Crescent on a Saturday afternoon. "Song lyrics," he said. "Not poems."

"You're a singer?"

"I'm not anything," he said.

"*Impossible dream*," she recited quietly from memory. "*Blossom, I beg of you.* Your words stayed with me, even though I'm only an engineer. You're definitely something."

Baz sighed, turned his indicator on, and joined the line snaking into the Tim Hortons drive-through near the mosque.

"We're going to be late," Nada said.

Baz waved away her objections. "It's a Nigerian wedding. An hour late is starting on time."

They waited in silence for their turn to order.

"Did you leave school because of me?" Nada asked, her voice small. She felt stupid for even asking, but the thought had haunted her.

"I left because . . ." He stopped, considering. "I was eighteen years old, and the future felt like a tidal wave heading toward me. I don't know if that makes any sense."

"I'm an engineer," Nada said. "I know how tidal waves work."

There was a pause as they both looked at each other, and then they burst out laughing.

"You know how *tidal waves* work?" Baz said. "That's all you've got for me?"

"You're the wordsmith. I do things that actually matter."

"You hate engineering; you enrolled for your parents' sake."

"At least I finish what I started, dropout."

They smiled at each other. It felt good to be able to talk like this with someone who didn't immediately get offended or defensive,

Nada thought. Abruptly, Baz's smile dissolved, and Nada panicked. She had stuck her foot in her mouth again.

"I'm sorry," she said.

He shook his head again. "Stop apologizing." He ordered a black coffee for himself and an iced cappuccino for Nada.

"We should get going," he said, even though only a few minutes had passed. He paid at the next window and handed her the drink.

The mosque was up ahead. There were empty spots in the parking lot, but Baz drove toward the residential neighborhood a few blocks away from the white stucco building with its large copper dome. He eased the Mercedes into a small parkette and turned the car off.

This is it, Nada thought. *We're actually going to talk. He's going to tell me what's been going on, and we can move forward.*

"You should probably walk ahead," he said. "I don't want anyone to get the wrong idea about us."

Bisma was dressed in a white silk wedding dress with a skirt so wide she had to turn sideways to enter the narrow doorway inside the prayer hall, where the *nikah* ceremony would be conducted. Her makeup was subtle but expertly applied, highlighting beautiful features that had sharpened with age. She glowed from happiness, and squealed when she spotted Nada.

"You made it! Did Baz bring you?" Bisma asked eagerly. When Nada nodded, Bisma clapped and said, "Next *nikah* is yours. I bet you fifty bucks."

Nada didn't want to argue with the bride on her wedding day, so she hugged Bisma tightly and told her she looked stunning.

"Yes, I know. My cousins are so jealous. Wait until you see my beloved. Try not to fall in love, because he's all mine."

Nada couldn't help but smile. She wondered what Bisma and Baz could possibly talk about; they were so different.

The *nikah* was a small affair with around fifty guests, mostly family as well as a small group of Bisma's friends from school. Imam Abdul Bari presided over the ceremony, and his wedding sermon was short and sweet. Afterward, the couple cut a small two-tier cake, decorated with edible pearls and gold lace icing, at an intimate reception in the gymnasium of the mosque, where a boxed lunch of rice, meat curry, samosas, and salad was distributed to guests. Nada didn't know anyone at the wedding except for Baz. She watched him move among the crowd with ease.

Waleed, Bisma's beloved, was a tall, skinny man with rich brown skin and too-large glasses that suited him perfectly. He and Bisma made a handsome couple. It was obvious that this day was the culmination of many years of dreaming. Bisma's mother, dressed in dark green and a pinched smile, nodded tightly at Nada when they were introduced. Nada recalled Bisma saying that her mother had hoped for a different groom for her daughter, but she seemed to be taking this well overall.

Nada texted Baz after the young couple made their exit: I've got a ride back. Thanks again.

Baz replied almost immediately: See you around.

That was unlikely, Nada thought as she headed to the bus stop down the street from the Toronto Muslim Assembly. This time she was sure their paths would never cross again.

But on Monday he showed up at the same library he used to frequent. Since his disappearance, she had come to think of it as her own private study space.

"Shouldn't you sit behind me, in case someone gets the wrong idea?" Nada asked when he took a seat at the table beside her.

Baz huffed a laugh. "I deserved that. Do you have time for coffee?"

She contemplated refusing, but curiosity won out. Outside, it was overcast—Toronto's random weather machine was tuned to gray and windy. Shoulders hunched against the chill, they walked toward Grabba Jabba, a popular café off campus. Baz paid for the drinks—black coffee for him and another too-sweet concoction for her—and they took a seat by the door. Baz gripped his cup and stared moodily into its depths.

"Bisma was right," Nada commented. "You are a pretentious coffee drinker."

Baz cracked a smile, then leaned forward, grabbed a sugar packet, and dumped the contents into his coffee, stirring vigorously.

"That's better," Nada said. She took a sip of her own caramel toffee vanilla hot chocolate latte (the barista had not been amused) and nodded at several acquaintances. "Are you stalking me?"

"I'm stalking E.J. Pratt, not you. That library was the only thing I missed about this school."

She raised an eyebrow.

Baz shrugged. "I'm thinking about re-enrolling. My parents want me to finish my degree."

Nada smirked. "What is an arts education good for, anyway?"

"Build a bridge and jump, engineer," he said, smiling.

"Enjoy your life as a barista," she shot back. "I'll be sure to never tip you."

"And people say Brown women are passive and submissive. Way to push against the current."

"I'm only ever this way with you," Nada answered. It was true. Maybe it was the nature of their convoluted relationship, or the fact that they only seemed to see each other for a few weeks every few years, but she felt comfortable being her true self with him. No filters.

"It's settled, then. We'll both push against expectations. You'll continue to be a savage, self-hating engineer, and I'll . . ." He paused, thinking.

"Continue to disappoint your parents by becoming a famous singer-songwriter?" Nada suggested.

Baz leaned back in his chair and looked at her. "Nada Syed," he said softly, "why is it that only you can see into my whole damn heart."

It wasn't a question. She flushed with pleasurable embarrassment. A few students at a nearby table kept glancing over.

"Are you famous?" she asked. "Because those girls can't take their eyes off you. Wait, do you have a YouTube channel?"

Baz shook his head, but he finished his coffee quickly and motioned that they should leave.

"My parents don't know I'm still here," he said as they walked on the paved sidewalk of the main campus strip. "I think those girls know my family."

She wanted to ask why but didn't. The wind had died down and the sun made its appearance as they made their way toward St. George Street. They walked leisurely in the direction of Robarts Library, a massive structure that resembled a very ugly concrete peacock, the school's mascot. A campus myth asserted that the engineers who designed the classic example of brutalism forgot to account for the weight of the millions of books stored inside. As a result, the library was slowly sinking into the ground, a few millimeters every year. Nada related this story to Baz, who snorted.

"Typical engineers. Why think about books, when you can obsess over concrete?"

"Why didn't you tell your parents you're still in town?" she asked.

Baz shrugged. "They aren't happy with me right now. They're coming to the end of their patience."

"What do they want from you?"

Baz smiled ruefully, and his lips twisted. "Not much. Just the rest of my life."

Nada laughed. "Our parents must be reading from the same play-book."

"Oh, they're kind and supportive, don't get me wrong," Baz said. "It's just that they should have had two different kids from the ones they got. I think Allah tested them with us. My older brother is just as artistic as I am. He's already started a band."

Nada was intrigued. "What sort of band?"

"The kind designed to infuriate your extremely religious parents," Baz said wryly.

"Let me guess: you write all the songs."

He nodded, then shyly added, "The band is just good enough to have the barest bit of potential."

"Your poems—songs, I mean, were really good, Baz. Your brother is lucky to have your talent."

They walked quietly for a moment before Baz said, "There's no manual for this, you know. For how to live a creative life as a Muslim, Canadian, child of immigrants. My parents want to leave a legacy. We want to create our own. We're all just making it up as we go along."

This was the longest conversation they had ever had, and the most open. Nada wondered if he was lonely now that he was back in town. His friends were likely finishing up undergrad degrees and thinking about graduate school, internships, jobs, and maybe even marriage, just like her friends. Maybe he had returned to campus thinking that things would be the same, and he had discovered that nothing was. Except for Nada, studying in her same library bolt-hole, a familiar stranger willing to talk.

"You have big dreams for a college dropout," Nada teased now.

Baz laughed. "Look who's talking. An engineer who hates engi-neering. What are your plans for world domination?"

She liked it when he teased her. "I have some ideas." She had met Abid a few months prior and Ask Apa had been looping around her brain ever since. Unfortunately, school took up most of her time. She hadn't told anyone about her secret goal to develop Ask Apa into a business, because there were complications. For one, she wasn't a coder. For another, it sounded far-fetched, and she hadn't figured out the scope. She was afraid the tentative balloon of her idea would deflate in the atmosphere outside her mind.

He shook his head. "I told you mine, now tell me yours. I need details, my little friend."

"Who are you calling *little*?" Were they flirting?

His eyes glinted warm amber in the sunlight and fixed on her. "I remember when you were taller than me. A lot meaner too. But I grew, and you grew up. Lucky for both of us. Girls like tall men, right?"

Oh, God. They were definitely flirting. "I had this idea for a tech start-up. It's sort of like a social media/community hub. I keep thinking about it as a niche search engine for local Muslim communities. But it could be used for other communities too. I don't know, it's stupid."

"It sounds brilliant," he said seriously. "What are you calling it?"

"Ask Apa. For those times when you need a big sister."

His smile was encouraging. "Nada Syed, you really are going to take over the world."

His comment was over the top, but it loosened something in her heart. "Will you be back on campus tomorrow?" They were passing Sidney Smith Hall now, and Robarts was coming up.

"I'm catching a plane to Egypt in a few days. Mom has family there, so I thought, why not." Baz squinted in the sunshine. "I could write to you, if you'd like," he offered casually.

"Engineers construct sinking libraries, not sentences," she said.

He smiled. "I promise to write small, easily digestible paragraphs and use zero metaphors."

"I'll be sure to reciprocate with efficient emojis."

Asking permission with a lift of her eyebrows, Nada took the notebook from his hands and carefully wrote her email address on a clean page.

Outside the automatic doors of the university's largest library, they stood awkwardly, not knowing how to say goodbye. They didn't hug or even shake hands.

"Until next time. Inshallah," Baz finally said, and he disappeared inside the concrete peacock.

She recognized his words as both promise and prediction. God willing.

CHAPTER SIXTEEN

Present day

Baz's lips were as soft as she remembered, and then she was kissing him back, her hands looped around his neck, pulling him close, her fingers scraping against his fade. He gripped the back of her dress, fisting the fabric as if he would never let go. The gentle pressure of his lips became firm, then demanding, and his breaths grew ragged between each kiss.

"I missed you, *habibti*," he whispered.

Nada's initial shock at the kiss had given way to pleasure, and she felt as if she were in a languid dream. The scrape of his beard beneath her fingers was rough, and the blood in her veins filled with sparkly bubbles. Suddenly she was ravenous for him, her fingers grasping and needy for more, which only made him slow down as he teased her with his tongue. He trailed kisses along her jaw, nipping slightly before he returned to her lips for a more thorough exploration.

The feel of his crisp shirt and the warmth of his body hard against hers was overwhelming. She pulled him closer, and then closer still, until she wasn't sure where his body started and hers stopped, and what did it matter anyway? This was where she belonged. Where she had always belonged.

An alarm clanged in the back of her mind, trying to remind her about something, but she pushed it away. She was kissing Baz, and it felt so good, and it had been too long, and nothing existed beyond this moment, beyond them. Nada bit his lip, and he groaned into her mouth. His hand traced the delicate curve of her jaw before angling her face and deepening the kiss even more.

The slamming of a door behind them sounded like a thunderclap, shattering the moment. Nada's eyes fluttered open and met his. She pushed him away and he stumbled. His half-lidded eyes, heavy with desire, flew completely open with the growing realization of what had happened.

What had they been thinking? From the stunned expression on Baz's face, it was clear that neither of them had been thinking at all. She rearranged her hijab and reached with shaking hands to adjust her dress. Beside her, Baz straightened his shirt, his eyes trained on her face.

It had been so long since she had been touched like this. Nada pressed a finger to her lips, swollen and tender from his beard, and marveled at how quickly she had fallen into his arms the moment he'd reached for her, the sweet warmth of his breath mingling with hers. It had always been like this between them: bewildering, immediate, overpowering.

"Nada," he said. There was longing in that one word, but also anger, sadness, frustration. "Don't go. Please."

She couldn't stand it. This still hurt so much. More than it should after all this time.

Before she lost her nerve, she turned away and stumbled toward the main hall, half-hoping and half-dreading that Baz would try to stop her, but he didn't.

Nada texted Haleema while waiting for her Uber in front of their hotel. Migraine coming on. I need to go home.

Her friend answered immediately. Feel better, babe. Love you!

She settled into the back seat of a white Corolla and closed her eyes.

Her best friend was marrying into the Haq family. She would see Baz again and again—at the wedding, at Haleema's home. They would have to keep pretending they didn't like each other, that looking at each other didn't hurt, that there was nothing between them and never had been.

Or maybe he would simply disappear, as he had done so many times before. With any luck, she would only hear about him occasionally, or not at all. Her memory of him would fade, and she would finally be able to move on and find some peace. She tried to imagine that future, but it seemed just as bleak as the alternative. No matter which way she held her relationship with Baz up to the light, they still wound up unhappy, and alone.

The house was quiet when she returned. Her father was already tucked into bed. Her brothers and mother were still at the convention. Nada texted Waqas to tell him she had left.

After a quick shower, she changed into pajamas, prayed *Isha*, and got into bed. After fifteen minutes of staring at the ceiling, she threw off the duvet and padded to her closet. Overflowing with hijabs, sweaters, cardigans, jeans, and yoga pants, the closet also had an entire wall devoted to her collection of fancy desi clothing: salwar kameez, *lenghas*, and saris, most of which had only been worn a handful of times. Hidden behind the collection of bright, luxurious fabrics was a floral-patterned hatbox, which Nada reached for now. Her mother never came in here, and her brothers had long outgrown any interest in Nada's private life. She removed the lid and pulled out the old report cards and essays that formed the first layer of camouflage. Below, in a zippered plastic folder labeled *School Projects*, she pulled out a stack of printed paper.

Dear Nada was typed at the top of the first page, along with the date from seven years ago. She felt around the very bottom of the hatbox and found a small velvet drawstring pouch, from which she carefully drew out a plain gold band. Catching the dim light from the overhead fixture, she reread the inscription: *From Nothing to Nada.*

Baz always did have a strange sense of humor. The band slid onto her left ring finger perfectly.

Sitting down on the carpeted floor of the closet, she started to read the emailed letters, the ones that had started it all, as if she were Anne Elliot pining after her very own Captain Wentworth.

PART TWO

Back in the Golden Crescent . . .

CHAPTER SEVENTEEN

Seven (and a half) years ago

Dear Nada,

Don't make fun of me for using the proper salutation. I know you engineers are like deer caught in the headlights when it comes to the written word, which is why I'm trying to model proper letter-writing style. Always begin with a salutation. After you have finished a complete thought, place a period thusly. Commas are your friends but must be treated with respect and used to distinguish clauses separated by a conjunction. Remember that grammar is like a complicated math equation, except no one really understands the rules, because they were made up long ago by dead white dudes.

I'm in Cairo visiting family. It's beautiful and hot, and the people are so kind. I think I might move here, especially when I think about Canadian winters and shoveling three feet of snow. I always get stuck shoveling. My brother claims he has an old basketball injury, but he just knows I'll do it before Abba can get out there with the shovel.

Anyways, this letter-writing thing is sort of fun. Makes me miss school a little bit. Make sure your letter is full of complaints, or I might be tempted to fill out that re-enrollment form after all.

Your friend,
B

This is not a salutation,
First of all, I know what a comma is for. Second of all who uses commas anyway when they totally interfere with your flow. Third of all for someone as free-spirited as you claim to be you should be way more into throwing out old rules made by old dudes. Fourthly I am really enjoying listing things and I guess that's why I'm an engineer. Fifthly school is horrible and I am very stressed and have not slept in the past three days. So sixthly I am existing right now on Red Bull and triple shots of cold brew which I have been told is very bad for you. But seventhly I am not a life sciences student so I don't have to care about health stuff. Also eighthly is my lack of commas driving you crazy because if so then. Ninthly my random use of punctuation is hopefully also. Providing some;
    Amusement.

Your hilarious friend?
Nada

p.s. your brother is clearly a liar but you are a good son.
p.p.s. my older brother is always stuck with the shoveling because

I have an old injury too, it's called "taking advantage of the few gender stereotypes that work in my favor."

Dear Nada,

Sadly, not everyone is as brave or as bold with their grammatical anarchy as you. Some of us enjoy the order provided by rules, the sense of calm in a chaotic world.

I'm heading to Jordan next. Turns out the folks have some family there as well. As you can probably tell, my family is full of nomads and wanderers who happen to fall in love with people outside of their culture. Mom's Algerian, Dad's Pakistani. No sisters unfortunately, just one unfortunate older brother. We're not that close. Did you know that men who have sisters tend to be more well-adjusted and mentally healthy than those without? You're keeping your brothers healthy just by existing. Nice gig, if you can get it.

Yours in grammatical solidarity,
B

Hey B,

Well, well, well, so now it's MY job to keep my brothers well-adjusted mentally? This is an example of the not-fun gender stereotypes. Women always get stuck trying to socialize and tame the men around them and I'm not having it. Besides, from the way my mother sighs every time I enter the room and mutters about how hope-less a wife I will make some poor guy, I'm letting the side down. Which I'm thrilled about, tbh. In fact, your lazy brother sounds like my people. Do you have a picture? I bet he's cute. Is he single? 😈

Sincerely not like those other girls,
Nada

p.s. both my parents are Indian by way of Hyderabad, and me and little bro were born in Canada, big bro in India. Don't you hate being asked where you're from? Never know how to answer that question without pulling out a family tree. And since I'm Hyderabadi-Canadian, that tree is a massive oak with many, many, MANY branches.

Dear Nada,

Hands off my big brother. Even you have standards.

As for your mom, cheer up. It might never happen. That's what I'm trying to tell myself about school.

Thinking about going to school in the Middle East, actually. It doesn't really matter what I do in terms of school, because where I'll work is already set. There are worse things than having your mom mutter over you. At least she cares enough to worry. My life has been pretty much already decided for me. All I have to do is walk the path laid out.

Your expert (at feeling sorry for myself),
B

Yo Baz,

Pretty sure I just failed one of my engineering finals, so I could use someone to guarantee me a job right about now, but you go ahead and enjoy that existential crisis. Also, get over yourself. Double also, who is footing the bill for your travels again? But points to you for recognizing when you are wallowing in self-pity. Most people (read: most guys) have no idea, which is highly unattractive. Interpret that comment as you will.

If it doesn't matter where you go to school or what you study, then you should go exactly where you want and study exactly what you want, and worry about the future in the future. This is my very wise counsel to you. Can't believe I'm telling an artist to not worry about the future. Isn't not worrying sort of the whole point of being an artsy singer-songwriter type?

My older bro fulfilled his manifest destiny a few years ago and married this girl my mom picked out. The happy couple moved into our basement because my parents never want their eldest son to leave home. Not sure if my parents want any of us to move out, actually. I've brought it up a few times, but then Mom starts muttering again, and Dad looks like he's about to cry, so I just shut up and stay.

It's funny, but it feels like we're both stuck, in different ways. Are you going to tell me what this super-secret job is that your parents have lined up for you? If you're an assassin or a spy or something cool like that, you might go up in my estimation.

Curious but sure to be disappointed,
Nada

p.s. or are your parents rich in the old-fashioned way, by owning land back home? That's it, isn't it. You're an "ancestral lands" brat. It's always the quiet, nerdy ones.

Dear Nada,

No ancestral lands to sell. Not an assassin or a spy (or am I?). The parentals own a media business; they record and sell Islamic educational stuff. I know, boring. But they've got dreams and are hoping to expand, and that's where I come in. Business has been okay, and with me and my older brother helping out, they're sure it will do even better. No, they didn't ask if I wanted in. Yes, I am being a typical Brown son and outwardly going along with their plans while secretly resenting them. No, I have no plans to back out, and yes, this parental-funded traveling is my form of rebellion, thanks for pointing that out.

I guess you're right, we are both stuck. I'll throw your advice right back at you: you should do exactly what you want, and worry about the future in the future. I haven't known you for that long, but I can confidently say that your parents will be disappointed no matter what you do. You might as well make yourself happy. Isn't that what being twenty-one is all about?

As for your older bro, I've heard arranged marriages mostly work out. And if they don't, at least it will get your folks' attention off of you. Do you have a groom waiting in the wings too? I bet he's tall, handsome, and rich. I think I hate him.

Your friend with the golden handcuffs,
Baz

To Good Brown Son,

No arranged-marriage groom waiting in the wings. Mom knows she's got a tougher road with me. I assume you have a gorgeous, well-behaved, perfect little wifey waiting for when you finally stop traveling, get your life together, and take your rightful place at Baz's Parents' Educational Media Empire (I'm assuming that's the name of the family biz, very catchy). And if you hate my fake fiancé, I get to hate yours too.

Also, I resent hearing my own advice echoed back at me. Don't you know how this works? I get to tell you things I would never do for myself. Rule number one in the advice-givers playbook is to Embrace the Hypocrisy.

Sincerely The Best Advice-Giver Ever,
Nada

p.s. Run after your dreams! Shoot for the stars! Don't get a day job! Think outside the box! Be a leader not a follower! Chase your bliss!
p.p.s. Yes, I could do this all day.

Dear Nada,

Care for a meet-up? I'm back in town for a bit. We could celebrate carrying on a correspondence for an entire five months using actual sentences in the age of the poo emoji. Only if you're free. I know how busy you are, memorizing math equations you will never use and planning to make your parents proud at the expense of your own dreams.

Nope, no perfect future wifey waiting for me once I eventually settle down. I prefer to do things the old-fashioned way—meet someone I hate at eleven, watch their public humiliation at fourteen, realize they're stalking me at eighteen, then quietly pine after them before winning them over with my letter-writing prowess.

In case that wasn't clear, I'm asking you out.

Yours,
Baz

Dear Baz,

What took you so long?

Potentially yours,
Nada

CHAPTER EIGHTEEN

Present day

Nada heard the front door bang open, followed by children shrieking, signaling the return of the rest of her family from the convention. Nada quickly scooped up the letters strewn around her and shoved them back into the plastic folder, then back into the hatbox, before heading downstairs.

Narjis started a litany of complaints the moment she spotted her daughter. "I was looking for you. Where did you disappear? I found another two nice boys I wanted you to meet."

"Jameela asked if I could take the girls tonight to save her time dropping them off in the morning," Waqas explained, gesturing to his daughters as they launched themselves at Nada.

"The convention was getting boring anyway," Jamal added.

Waqas rolled his eyes. "You mean all the girls you were trying to talk to turned you and your friends down."

Jamal shrugged, unrepentant. "What else was I supposed to do at D&D?"

"Listen to lectures, become a better Muslim, make some *sidha sadha* friends instead of those hooligans you spend your time with," Narjis listed, but Jamal wasn't listening.

"Yo, I met your friend Sufyan. The guy obsessed with chai? Brother said he'd hook me up," Jamal said to his sister, grinning. Before Nada could ask what, exactly, Sufyan had offered to "hook up," the twins demanded her attention.

"We're not tired!" Safa said loudly, gripping Nada's right leg tightly. With a delighted squeal, Marwa grabbed on to Nada's left leg and squeezed.

"Daddy let us have ice cream!" Marwa announced.

"Chocolate espresso flavor. I didn't realize it had actual coffee in it until they finished. They've been like this for the past hour," Waqas explained, his shoulders drooping with weariness.

"Like what, Daddy? Like flying helicopters?" Safa let go of Nada's leg and started to zoom around the room. Marwa followed her sister, as she always did.

"I've got them," Nada said to her brother. "You should get to bed."

Waqas gave a token protest, but Nada insisted. He gave his daughters a kiss and retired to his basement apartment.

"Let's play submarine instead," Nada suggested to the girls. She grabbed their hands and headed to her en suite bathroom, which had an oversize soaker tub. The girls squealed in excitement. Their baths were usually efficient showers, so this was a treat. Nada added a generous amount of lavender-scented bubble bath to the water, as well as the bath toys she kept in one of the drawers for her nieces. Then she helped them into the bath.

Narjis joined Nada a few moments later. She watched her granddaughters with an indulgent smile. "Don't you want this?" she asked.

Being a single parent too tired to give my twin daughters a bath? Nada was tempted to ask. But it wasn't the truth, or at least not the whole truth.

"How was the speedy date party? If you wanted to meet strange men, you could have asked for my help, you know," Narjis said, referring to the matrimonial event.

Nada realized why her mother was grumpy: her pride had been wounded. "I was only there to keep Waqas company. I didn't talk to anyone interesting."

Narjis snagged on only one part of that sentence. "*Beta*, it takes time to find the right person, and if you keep saying no, no, no, your chances will pass you by."

Nada said nothing. This was a conversation they'd had too many times over the past years. If Narjis knew the real reason Nada refused to discuss marriage, it would cause a massive rift in her family, though the urge to come clean had nearly overcome her on many occasions. Nada was generally an honest person. The fact that she had managed to keep this enormous secret for over six years was the exception. Still, the time to confess was long past, especially since her secret relationship had, for all intents and purposes, died a sad and lonely death. No one else she had met in the years since had come close to breeching the fortifications around her heart.

But seeing Baz again—talking to him, teasing him, and then, in a moment of madness, reaching for him—had put paid to her neat ideas about moving on.

"You are twenty-eight years old. I was married for nearly seven years when I was your age," her mother said.

Narjis was a handsome woman still, with high cheekbones, smooth and unlined skin, and a soft figure. But the expression on her face was troubled. Even if her mother was occasionally intrusive and way too interested in Nada's love life, she always acted out of love. Maybe if Nada opened up, if she asked her mother the questions that had plagued her, Narjis might tell her something meaningful.

"Did you ever want . . . more?" Nada asked.

Seated by the tub, Narjis reached for the baby shampoo, poured some in her hands, and began rubbing Marwa's hair gently. "What more could I possibly want?" she murmured, tickling her grand-daughter as she rinsed her hair.

"Have you ever wished for something that was just yours? Your own work or your own friends?"

Narjis turned to her daughter with a hurt expression on her face. "I wanted this, *beta*. It was my choice to stay home and take care of my children, to manage the home."

"You went to university in Hyderabad," Nada said. She didn't know why she was pushing this now. In the past, she had tried to ask her mother about her life before she married, but Narjis never seemed too interested in revisiting those long-ago days.

"I was the first girl in my family to finish a university degree," Narjis said proudly, now massaging Safa's head with the shampoo, her hands moving deftly through the young girl's thick curls. "I wanted to be a lawyer, but then my abba and ammi received a good proposal from your father. A few years after Waqas was born, we moved to Canada."

Nada knew her mother had had to make difficult choices. She'd had to raise a family in a strange country; she'd had to learn its customs, language, and culture, and simultaneously try to guide her children through the same alien environment.

"We struggled in the beginning, like everyone, but *Alhamdulillah* your father did well, and we decided I should stay home and take care of the family," Narjis said.

"There are a lot of college courses you could take even now, or maybe just a certificate in something. Have you thought about training as a . . . chef?" Nada said, searching for something that might interest her mother.

Narjis laughed heartily at that. "I have cooked your meals for decades, and now you think I want to learn how to cook in school? What nonsense."

"It's not too late to do something, Mom." Too late, Nada realized she had said the wrong thing.

"I already do everything," Narjis said, wounded. "There is no need to do something." She leaned forward to stare at Nada's hand. "What is that?"

Nada looked down at her hand and saw the plain gold band. She had forgotten to put the ring away in her haste to come downstairs. "Costume jewelry. I bought it from one of the vendors at the bazaar."

Narjis came closer, squinting at the ring. "That doesn't look fake," she said. She reached out and clasped Nada's hand. "What store did you buy this ring from? How much did you pay? It looks like a wedding band—"

"I spoke to Sister Rusul at the convention," Nada said, desperate to change the subject. Her mother's face instantly shut down, and she dropped Nada's hand.

"What did she want?" her mother asked stiffly.

"She tried to explain what happened and to apologize again for her son."

Nada knew her mother hadn't made a lot of close friends in Canada, because she'd been too busy with her family. Sister Rusul was the exception. From their first meeting at a downtown mosque, the women had been inseparable, meeting frequently and talking nearly every day on the phone. When Nada had first started working with Sister Rusul, her parents had been thrilled. Sister Rusul's words at the convention came back to Nada now.

"Sister Rusul also hinted . . . She said that you both wanted something to happen between me and Haneef. Is that true?"

"Never," Narjis said firmly. "I was close with Rusul, and I know she loved you like her own daughter. But her son, Haneef, he was too much like her ex-husband: proud, arrogant, and never willing to do the hard work. There were incidents, even when he was younger.

He once spent two days in jail for stealing. Rusul would cry to me about him, but she always forgave him. But then what else could she do? He's her son. She chose to stand by him, and I stand by you. I should have told you all this before, but you seemed so excited to be working with Sister Rusul. I had no idea you would also be working with Haneef."

Nada felt a wave of helpless anger hit her. Part of her felt she was to blame for what had happened with Ask Apa. Yes, Haneef had been deceitful, but she had been naive. She should have talked to her parents and other people who knew Haneef. Instead, her excitement at seeing her dream project come to life had swept aside any caution. And, she had been particularly desperate for distraction during that time in her life. Afterward, when the project fell apart, she wondered if she deserved her misfortune.

"I'm sorry for what happened," Nada said. "I'm sorry you lost your closest friend."

"It is not for you to feel sorry," Narjis said firmly. "A world doesn't exist where I don't choose you, Nada *beta*, over everyone else. I will always choose you."

Blinking back tears, Nada reached into the tub and pulled the plug despite her nieces' protests. The warm water and lavender bubble bath had done their job. The twins yawned and rubbed their eyes even as they pleaded for five more minutes. Nada wrapped each one in a soft, fluffy towel before vigorously drying their hair with another towel until the hair stuck up from their heads like dandelion fluff.

After thinking over her mother's words, Nada said impulsively, "You should call her. I know Sister Rusul misses you."

"You should get to bed; you have work tomorrow," her mother said, sidestepping her question. "Check on Jamal for me?"

Narjis helped the twins into their pajamas and led them to the trundle bed set up in the master bedroom for the nights when the

girls had an impromptu sleepover with their grandparents. They settled under the covers with a copy of *Big Red Lollipop*. Nada impulsively hugged her mother and kissed the twins good night. Before
shutting the door, Nada caught a last look at her mom beside her
granddaughters, reading them a bedtime story.

Nada went down to Jamal's bedroom on the main floor, which
was just down the hall from the kitchen. He was still awake, and he
looked up briefly as she walked in. He had rolled his wheelchair to
the elaborate gaming system he had set up and was playing one of his
favorite RPGs.

"You'll rot your brain," she said, because she knew it would bug him.

He rolled his eyes, but he seemed happy to see her. "You know
how I'm your favorite brother?"

"You're one of my brothers," she amended.

"It's okay, you don't have to say it, Waqas is sensitive. Listen, can
you keep a secret?"

She nodded.

"Remember how I said your friend Sufyan said he'd hook me up?
He offered me a job at his chai shop. Mom and Dad won't approve,
so I'm not going to tell them until I get settled. I start next week."

Jamal had graduated from high school last year, after taking an
extra year to improve a few grades. She had expected him to apply
for community college or university, but instead Jamal had stayed at
home. She found out later that their father had promised to give his
youngest child a job at his accounting business, but the offer had yet
to materialize.

"You were supposed to work with Dad, right?"

Jamal looked at her. "Do you know what I've done for the past
year? Nothing. Do you know what Mom and Dad want me to do for
the next year? Nothing."

"I'm sure that's not true."

Jamal leaned in close and motioned for her to do likewise. "After I save up some cash, I'm moving out."

Nada reeled back in shock. Jamal was twenty years old, yet he had never spent a night elsewhere. "You can't!" she said without thinking.

Jamal frowned. "I thought you had my back. I thought you wanted me to be independent. You're just like everyone else. Forget about it."

"Maybe you should talk to Dad first, before you sign any leases or make a decision," Nada said, thinking quickly.

The look Jamal threw her now was laced with pity. "Don't you get it? They're never going to let any of us go. You've been trying to leave since undergrad. Waqas didn't even leave after he got married. I'm done waiting for one of you to make a move. You're too scared."

Nada thought about her mother reading the twins a bedtime story. She had a sudden vision of her parents from ten years ago, and then ten years in the future, and she knew her brother was right: nothing would change. Her parents had built this life to suit them, but it wasn't working out for their children. Jamal was restless, Waqas was depressed, and Nada was stuck. One weekend at the convention had revealed the cracks in their carefully constructed world, and she instinctively knew that things had reached a critical point: they could not return to how they were. She no longer wanted them to.

Her phone pinged with a message from Haleema: In the mood to go dress shopping on Friday after work? My wedding lengha is ready to pick up. Or are you sick of me already?

She texted back: Not a chance. We are on for Friday.

Nada headed back upstairs, leaving Jamal to his video game. Before getting into bed, she hid the thin gold band in her closet, with the rest of her secrets.

CHAPTER NINETEEN

Seven years ago

Baz and Nada decided to meet at the newly opened Aga Khan Museum for their first date. It was neutral territory, far enough away from their respective neighborhoods that the possibility of being spotted by a friend or acquaintance was low, especially on a weekday afternoon.

The museum, visible from the always jammed Don Valley Parkway, was a plain, rectangular building made of white granite and topped with an angular, jutting crown made of the same material, an intriguing architectural detail that lent the building a unique style, settled as it was amongst dreary glass condominium towers and commercial plazas. The museum was the crown jewel set on seventeen acres of land, with public gardens and the Ismaili Centre, whose distinctive glass roof reminded Nada of the Louvre Pyramid. The garden, designed by Lebanese landscape architect Vladimir Djurovic, contained five large reflecting pools, each lined with black granite, and a collection of mature trees and shrubs, neatly arranged in rows surrounded by white stonework.

Inside the museum, a soaring entryway rained light onto a registration area, where Baz and Nada paid for admission before entering the main exhibition hall. They lingered over fine ceramics and tapestries from various Muslim civilizations, and admired carefully preserved pages from gold filigree Qurans, making out the fine Arabic script of *surahs* they had memorized as children. They wandered into an opulent chamber whose walls were lined with cabinets containing ceramic plates and bowls. A round, upholstered divan and ottoman stools held pride of place in the center of the room, and the floor was covered with lush, bright red carpets.

Nada was overcome with a sense of wonder. Her Muslim-ness had always been a living, breathing spiritual soul, the lens through which she viewed the world. But as she wandered the halls of the museum entirely devoted to the art of the Muslim world, her understanding of community took on a bigger, sprawling, global definition.

She had visited India as a child. She had made *Umrah*, the lesser pilgrimage to the *Kaaba* in Mecca, with her family as a teenager and thought she had a sense of the global *ummah*, or Muslim community. But this museum was a testament to the enduring history of her people and the many civilizations they had founded, grown, destroyed, and contributed toward.

It was easy to forget, as a second-generation Canadian, that her heritage spanned millennia. Remnants of this heritage were visible in the fine weave of a precious carpet curated under glass, or in a carefully hand-painted Turkish tile, or even in the beautiful geometric mosaic flooring they stood on now as they lined up to order coffee. It made Nada feel small, somehow, but also filled with pride and wonder. Surrounded by artifacts that had existed for centuries, Nada felt every one of her brief twenty-one years. Would anything she did in her life survive the passage of time, the way that the carpet she had admired had done?

Baz was silent too, and she wondered what he was thinking. She could tell from the way his eyes lingered on various artwork and from the curious bent of his head as he read the descriptions that he was taking careful note. She imagined him in a corner of the museum, writing in the black notebook he used to carry with him everywhere, perhaps even composing a song inspired by this silent, beautiful space. This reminder that Muslims made art, decorated their holy books with gold and jewels, designed beautiful clothing, wove luxurious carpets, celebrated life.

Or maybe he felt awkward, now that they were both here, in the same room. His email invitation had been an admission, and perhaps he wondered how she felt about him.

I like you, she wanted to tell him while they stood in line at the tiny café. *Do you like me too?*

Her heart constricted as she thought these words, even as the more logical part of her mind—her engineering brain, Baz would have teased—was impatient. He had written her jokey, flirty letters and had asked her out. Obviously, he liked her. That wasn't the real question. *How much do you like me?* was what she truly wanted to know. For that matter, what were her own feelings about him? But such a question couldn't be resolved on a first date.

Baz paid for their drinks and pastries, and they settled into a cozy corner table with a view of the patio.

"Do you wish you had brought a notebook?" she asked impulsively.

He seemed startled by her question, but then smiled warmly. "I don't need a notebook to remember. I doubt I'll ever forget being here with you."

Nada flushed. So far today, their casual conversation had made no allusions to the purpose of this trip, no indication that they were anything other than friends. With these words, Nada felt the tension that had been simmering below the surface ease slightly.

"How long are you in town this time?" she asked, tentative. *Will we see each other again?*

"I'm not sure. Maybe a few weeks, or a few months. I'll see how things go." *I don't tend to make plans.*

It felt like their conversation was happening on two levels. She wondered if he felt this too. What was happening between them felt like more than the usual shifting currents of a fledgling friendship. That was likely because this wasn't a friendship, but a possible relationship being navigated by two observant Muslims who had been told all their life that romantic interludes were something that happened after marriage, not before.

Nobody had really explained how marriage happened in the first place, though.

Nada shook her head. "Not knowing would drive me crazy." *I'm the sort of person who needs certainty in her life.*

Baz shrugged. "This is home and I'll always end up back here. But in the meantime, I'm enjoying figuring things out." *I like to wander, and that is unlikely to change.*

"It's different for me. I want to move out. I want to travel. But my parents wouldn't be okay with that, not until I'm married." She froze, hoping he didn't think she was implying anything.

"What are they going to do if you just leave?" he asked, smiling. "Disown you?"

Nada was annoyed at his flippant remark. Did he have to be such a Muslim guy about this? Then she remembered that he didn't have any sisters. "That's not the way it works for me. Or for you, either. You said that you knew your wandering had a time limit, that you'd have to eventually return home to take your rightful place in the family empire."

"You're right," he said easily.

She liked that he hadn't gotten defensive or doubled down on his stance. Most guys would have hastened to assure her she was wrong and then insisted on giving a detailed lecture outlining the errors in her argument.

"I just meant, why wait until you're married? Isn't the whole point of being young and unattached that you can just . . . explore?"

Nada's breath hitched at his last word. Did he know that having the freedom to explore was what she wanted more than anything?

"My parents won't let me . . ." She paused. That wasn't true, not entirely. "I'm scared," she said instead. That was the truth. "I want to do so much, but I'm scared I'll fail. I don't have a safety net."

"Your parents can pay for a trip though, right? Maybe you could take someone with you, if they insist on company or a chaperone," Baz suggested.

"Middle class isn't rich, especially not when your parents are immigrants with family to support back home," she said, more sharply than she had intended.

Impulsively, Baz reached across the table and squeezed her hand. They both froze. He had never touched her before, and they had both grown up in a culture that discouraged casual touch between unrelated men and women.

"Sorry," he muttered, letting go of her hand.

She wanted to reach out and intertwine their fingers. Their brief contact had felt like the touch of a live wire—shocking, energizing. *This is why Muslims believe that when men and women are alone together, the third person is Satan*, she thought.

Baz raised his eyes and looked at her again, his lips twisting in a grudging smile. "I didn't mean to sound dismissive," he said.

Again she felt a wave of liking wash over her. He apologized when he was wrong. He knew the rules of their interactions. More importantly, he accepted those limits because he understood on an instinctive level that they were also the parameters of her own comfort. In that moment, Nada knew she could trust Baz—with her reputation, with her person, maybe even with her heart.

"Are you hungry?" he asked. Their mugs had long been empty and nothing was left of the pastries except crumbs.

She nodded, and they walked to the exit together. Neither wanted the date to end.

Outside, Baz shifted from foot to foot. "We could grab a bite at one of the restaurants nearby," he said. His ears were pink, and Nada realized he was blushing. "Or . . ."

"Or?" she prompted.

"I brought a few things we could eat. If you like."

Nada was delighted. "You packed a picnic?"

Baz was embarrassed. "Just some snacks."

But it was more than that. He unearthed a flannel blanket from the trunk of his car, along with a small blue cooler. Amused, Nada followed him to the public garden. He picked a spot behind the cedar trees, unfurling the blanket in an inconspicuous corner, and began pulling items out of the cooler: wrapped sandwiches, cut-up fruit, two juice boxes, and a sleeve of chocolate chip cookies for dessert. She sipped from one of the juice boxes and accepted a cheese sandwich. The tomato made the sandwich soggy, but she was too hungry to care. Baz kept looking around as they ate.

"When I was a kid, my parents were always working, trying to get their business off the ground. My brother and I were left at home alone. I learned how to cook when I was ten, and started making dinner for the family at twelve." He wrinkled his nose. "We ate a lot of pasta and sauce."

Baz's voice was low and soothing. They had lucked out with the weather today; the air was fresh and there was a warm breeze. She could take a nap here, surrounded by all this greenery.

"Once the business was going, things changed. But the expectations were still there. They got worse, actually. By the time I got to university, I just needed it to stop. Leaving school was the best, and the hardest, decision I ever made. I had some money saved up, so I did it, without telling anyone my plans."

"Were your parents mad when you left?" Nada knew her parents would have freaked out. All of their dreams for their children revolved around university degrees and respectable employment.

"I broke their hearts," Baz said matter-of-factly. "I told them I'd return to school eventually, but now I'm not sure."

They had finished their sandwiches and the drink boxes. Nada leaned forward and pulled the sleeve of cookies toward her, just as Baz scrambled up. A security guard was walking swiftly toward them, and he did not look happy.

"We have to go. We're not really supposed to eat on the grounds," Baz said, swiftly gathering their garbage and rolling up the blanket. Giggling, Nada grabbed the cooler, and they set off for the parking lot. Baz waved apologetically at the annoyed guard. They stashed the remnants of their picnic in Baz's car. "Worst date ever?" he asked, grinning at her.

"Unclear. Maybe we should try again? Just so we have two data sets, for comparison."

Reluctant to leave, he walked her to the car she had borrowed from her mother. "I looked forward to every one of your emails," he said quietly. "I used to save them, to have something to read at the end of the day."

"Same," she said, ducking her face.

"I haven't told anyone about this. Have you?"

She shook her head. "It felt . . ."

"Too soon," he finished. "But I'd like to see you again."

"I'd like that too," she said, smiling up at him.

Baz texted Nada every day after their first date. She would wake up for *Fajr*, and a late-night text would be waiting for her, followed by an early-morning text.

Do you think it's too late to eat Frosted Flakes?

I'm reading Rumi again, this translation is great, it actually left the Muslim parts in, unlike that Orientalist Rumi-lite trash.

Check out this clip from this guy on Insta, it is hilarious, part of a series called "Muslims be like" 😂

And then there were the random texts, the ones that made her heart jolt every time she got one: Thinking of you.

Nada's texts were just as random.

Fell asleep laughing at that Insta account. Our people are so funny.

Final exams coming up. What if I fail? Did I just spend years doing something I hate only to not even get the stupid piece of paper that will make my suffering worth it?

At noon, Nada received a picture of Baz's lunch, with the caption Sad Sandwich. That afternoon, Nada countered with a picture of her afternoon chai, a recent addiction she blamed on her parents. He countered with a funny selfie.

On campus, she found herself storing up stories to share later, like when she sent a pic of a half-eaten bag of halal gummies. Break in case of emergency.

Two weeks after their first date, Baz asked if he could call her.

Do people even do that anymore? she texted back.

I won't tell if you won't, he replied.

I sense a theme, she typed before she could help herself.

The dots appeared and disappeared on her phone, and Nada felt foolish. What was her problem?

I'll call you tonight, he responded.

Nada turned her phone off and went back to studying.

He called that night after *Maghrib* and greeted her with salams, which she returned with a certain wariness. He picked up on her tone right away.

"I really like you, Nada, but I haven't done this before," Baz announced abruptly, the words hanging in the air between them.

"Neither have I," she said.

Something eased between them. "I want to tell everyone about you. But I also want to figure out what this is first, before I bring anyone else into it," Baz said.

Nada wanted to jump in with reassurances, but she also really wanted him to tell her what he was thinking, and so she forced herself to listen, to not fill up the silences after each sentence with *It's okay* or *Me too*. She felt the same way he did—conflicted. While keeping her blossoming relationship secret made her uneasy, she also wasn't sure she wanted to deal with the consequences of telling her parents or her friends. She knew they would ask questions she wasn't ready to answer yet.

"My parents expect a lot from me and my brother," Baz said. "I've already disappointed them once. They will only be patient with me for so long. I have responsibilities, and whoever I end up with will have to understand that."

He was being honest, and it was time for her to open up as well. "I like you too, but I agree we should take things slow. What if we just keep seeing each other over the summer, to make sure this is something we both want? Assuming you plan to stick around."

"Right now, I don't want to be anywhere else," he said, and her heart lifted. "My dad just announced I'm his unpaid summer intern, so don't think you're the only reason, okay?"

"If you bore me, I'll dump you at the end of August."

Baz huffed out a laugh. "Deal."

She didn't keep her end of the bargain, not entirely. It felt wrong somehow to not at least hint that she was seeing someone. One evening, while her mother cleaned up the kitchen and her father drank his bedtime chai and read the *Toronto Star*, Nada tentatively broached the subject.

"I made a new friend," she started.

Her mother looked up from rinsing plates, but her father didn't pay any attention. "New friends can be a good thing, so long as they are serious."

Her sharp-eyed gaze had Nada coloring. She had suspected that Narjis had noticed her frequent texting and moony behavior these past few weeks, and this confirmed it.

"I hope your new friend understands this too?" her mother said.

Abbas looked up from his newspaper now, and a knowing glance passed between him and his wife. He returned to his paper, disappearing behind the front page, but Nada knew he had understood the subtext.

Her mother was energetically wiping the countertop now, not looking at her daughter. "Make sure you meet your friend in a public space, and be careful," she said. "Perhaps you can bring your friend to see us, once you are better acquainted, and if you think we will like him."

Nada nodded, and her mother's tacit consent loosened something within her. Her parents trusted her to make the right decision. This thing with Baz had become very real, very fast, the result of years of pent-up feelings rising up all at once. She was sure he felt the same. Nada was on the cusp of a roller-coaster ride, bracing with white knuckles for that weightless, delirious, uncontrollable fall. They both were.

CHAPTER TWENTY

Present day

After the excitement and drama of the convention, it was almost a relief to go back to work, where Nada had her own cubicle and was mostly left alone to sort through files and write her reports. There were no meetings, because everyone seemed to be taking time off for summer vacation, and she was grateful. It left her time to think about what had happened at D&D, and with Baz.

He hadn't reached out after she fled the convention. She kept waiting for him to, and then she'd berate herself for not reaching out to him. What would she say? The truth was, she was afraid. Now that Nada was back in the real world, the convention was starting to feel like a long-ago, slightly muddled dream. She had lost her head and leapt for a brief moment back into the romance of her youth, but it wasn't real, and she couldn't jeopardize her hard-won prudence now.

Yet Nada also couldn't help obsessively checking her phone every five minutes. Her number hadn't changed in the years since she and Baz had been together, but the only texts she'd received since the convention were from Haleema and her mother. He hadn't messaged her on social media, either, though she doubted he used Instagram much or at all. She knew this because she had looked him up, and aside from

LinkedIn, he had no public social media handles. The social account for Deen&Dunya was blandly professional, the work of a publicist.

By Friday, Nada was itching for something, anything. A door had been opened in her mind, and her past had nudged into the present, blurring the lines between what was and what could have been. She practically flew to her car and drove too fast to the desi bridal shop where she was supposed to meet Haleema after work.

Located in the heart of the Golden Crescent, the bridal shop was one of the new storefronts built recently, a welcome addition to the business community. The name of the shop was Dulhaniya, Urdu for "bride" and also "bridegroom," and catered to the growing number of South Asian customers who wanted to buy their wedding outfits locally rather than have them shipped from overseas. It was a modern boutique, with a seamstress on site for bespoke fittings. The store sold outfits for the entire wedding party, including *shervani* suits for men. Nada figured she might as well see if she liked something; Haleema had been bugging her for a while to purchase a new dress. It would be Haleema's treat, of course. She loved desi clothes.

Inside the shop, a woman in her late thirties greeted them before disappearing to fetch the bridal outfits Haleema had ordered weeks ago.

"Is your head better?" her friend asked idly, examining the elaborate jewelry sets displayed behind glass. The ornate *jarawi lacha* necklace with matching *karan phool* earrings were exquisite pieces of art made with gold-plated filigree and set with semiprecious stones.

Nada thought fast, remembering her excuse of a migraine at the gala dinner. "I took my medicine once I got home and slept it off. Did you have fun at the dinner? Zayn was great on stage." She hoped her friend didn't notice the flush that crept over Nada's cheeks at the real reason she had bailed.

"He's so talented, and he looked so hot," Haleema agreed. "He had a lot of fans at the dinner. They all wanted to talk to him, take pictures, get his autograph." Her tone was carefully neutral, but Nada could read between the lines.

"But he sat with you, after his performance?"

Haleema didn't answer right away. Instead, she pointed to a gold choker necklace lined with pearls and unpolished emeralds in the display case. "Do you think this set would look good on me?" she asked.

"Everything looks good on you," Nada said. "The key is to match the jewelry to your outfit. What happened with Zayn?"

Haleema shrugged. "He ended up eating with a few of his fans, but it was cool. I had some interesting people at my table too."

Nada closed her eyes. She had abandoned her friend, even though Haleema had begged her to attend the event and stay by her side. *Tell her the truth*, a voice whispered in her head. *Tell her now.*

Nada opened her mouth, but no words came out.

Haleema stooped to look at the earrings and *tika* ornaments in another case. "Baz disappeared around the same time you did," she said.

"Oh?" Nada asked. Her voice sounded unnaturally high to her ears.

"He came back halfway through dinner. He said he had a headache too. Must have been something in the air."

"Must be," Nada agreed. If Haleema ever found out that Nada had hidden an entire relationship—her only relationship—from her for years, she would never forgive her. Haleema told her everything. Another reason to stay silent.

The shopkeeper returned with an assistant bearing armfuls of luxurious, opulent dresses. They motioned for the women to follow them into a large private space at the back of the store, which was decorated with crystal chandeliers and a tufted pink sofa inlaid with mother-of-pearl buttons. Large mirrors took up the back wall. Nada took a seat as Haleema disappeared into a dressing room.

"Mango lassi? Masala chai?" the owner asked. She was wearing a name tag that said *Anisa*. Nada gladly accepted the offer of tea, and settled in for Haleema's fashion show.

The first outfit was deep green, a traditional *lengha* dress consisting of a tight-fitting bodice with full sleeves, a high scalloped neck, and a large skirt in alternating light green and cream. The *dupatta* was heavy with embroidery and an overlay of gold tulle. It suited Haleema's pale complexion and hazel-green eyes. The dress was for the rehearsal dinner. Since neither Haleema nor Zayn were especially cultural, they had opted for a formal sit-down dinner for the wedding party and a few close friends, instead of the usual *mehndi* dance party. Haleema had decided to wear the traditional green color as a nod to her South Asian heritage.

The next dress she tried on was for the *nikah* ceremony. It was an exquisite full-length gown, fitted through the bust and waist, delicate rose-gold satin overlaid with soft pink netting with gold and silver *zari* embroidery. Beneath the heavy pink net *dupatta* draped over her head, Haleema's face glowed.

The pink dress looked so much like . . . *Don't think about it*, Nada thought. "You look stunning," she said.

Haleema grinned. "I know, right?" She gathered the voluminous skirt in her arms before twirling. Beside her, Anisa and her assistant clapped.

The next outfit was a cream sari with dark red embroidery for the *walima* wedding reception, but Haleema wasn't quite sure if it was the right choice. Should she wear the next outfit, a mauve *gharara* with intricate silver and gold *zari* work, instead? Nada preferred the sari, but Haleema decided to take both and decide closer to the date.

Haleema tried on a dozen more dresses in various shades of pink, beige, blue, purple, and green, and after another two hours, two cups of masala chai, and one mango lassi, Nada begged for a break. She couldn't keep track of the outfits anymore, and she was hungry.

Haleema relented with good grace. It was time to pray *Asr* anyway. Anisa provided the prayer rugs and a quiet corner in the store, and after praying, they drove to Kamran's Superior Sweets, a favorite restaurant nearby.

An older man, dressed in a black apron and white shirt, took their order without a flicker of recognition, though they had eaten here plenty of times before. "Thank you, Kamran Uncle," Nada couldn't resist adding, hoping to prod a reaction from the owner, but he only raised an eyebrow.

The women sat at a table; it was late afternoon and the restaurant was nearly empty between the lunch and dinner rush. Besides, everyone knew Kamran's Superior Sweets drew most of their business from catering for the many community events and functions, rather than their sit-down service. Nada asked about the wedding arrangements, and Haleema launched into an update on the catering and floral centerpieces. "I decided to hire a wedding planner. They're local, and they were really persuasive."

"Happily Ever After? Hafsa and Masood?" Nada guessed.

Haleema nodded through a mouthful of fries. "Zayn insisted. They work together at the convention, and I think he got a discount. They're handling the rehearsal dinner in a few weeks, and I'm so relieved. Especially now with this whole Baz thing."

Nada tried not to perk up at the mention of his name. Ever since Haleema had talked about Baz having a headache at the gala dinner, Nada had been wondering how to turn the conversation back to him. "What Baz thing?"

Kamran returned with their food before Haleema could reply, and Nada noticed he had added an extra dish, *shahi paneer*—rich tomato and cream curry, from which plump pieces of *paneer* cheese peeked through, her childhood favorite—but he disappeared before Nada could thank him. She spooned some onto her plate, pairing it with fragrant basmati rice and fresh tandoori naan, and then turned her attention back to her friend. She had a feeling she would need all the comfort food in front of her to hear the rest of this story.

Haleema sighed dramatically. "He wants to invite Firdous, and I don't know how to say no." She lowered her voice, though there was no one in the restaurant. "I think something happened at the end of the gala dinner."

Nada's heart pounded and her hands fiddled with her napkin. "What do you mean?"

Haleema spooned chicken *karahi*, a curry made in a shallow pot with garam masala, yogurt, tomato, garlic-ginger, green pepper, and onion, before reaching for the rice. "I think he might be getting serious about her. You know how boys are—once they start to see people close to them getting married, they need to join in the fun. But I'm like, stop stealing the spotlight from me and Zayn; you can announce your engagement later. And Firdous has been married before, so it's not like she needs to make a big deal about things." Haleema took a large spoonful of the rice and curry and moaned. "So good, right?"

Nada mechanically put naan in her mouth, but didn't taste anything. "What happened at the end of the gala dinner?" she asked. Her mind was still trying to process what her friend had said. Baz had reached for her at the gala dinner. He had kissed her like a drowning man. He had told her he missed her, and asked her not to go.

Her mind skidded: he had asked her not to go, but she had turned around and left. Again.

Haleema, mouth full, shook her head. She chewed and took a long swallow of her mango lassi before answering. "He left the dinner with Firdous, before dessert. She posted about it later. Take a look." She pulled up Firdous's handle: @ForRealFirdouz. She had posted a selfie with Baz seated across from her. Nada's heart clenched at the sight of those impenetrable dark eyes staring into the camera. She

read the post quickly, trying to calm her breathing: *#LateNightSnack*
#blessed #OldFriendsNewDreams.

Haleema rolled her eyes. "Trying too hard, right? Not that I blame
her. He's so aloof a girl would have to throw herself into his arms to
get his attention. Anyways, it's a good thing you and Baz didn't hit it
off at the convention, otherwise I might have had to cut a—hey, are
you okay?" Haleema peered at Nada's ashen face. "Headache back?
You might want to go to the doctor, babe. I'm getting married in a
few weeks, and you need to be on your game for all the fun events."

Nada smiled wanly and assured Haleema she was fine. She drank
some water and finished the *shahi paneer*, which now tasted like ash in
her mouth. "Tell me more about all the wedding drama. I need details."

Haleema happily obliged.

The moment Nada returned home, she went straight to her room and
FaceTimed the one person who would know everything and tell her
the truth: Bisma.

Nada's friend had moved permanently to Philadelphia after her
wedding eight years ago. Without the burden of a secret failed relationship and the semipublic failure of her business like Nada, she had
settled into happily wedded bliss. She and Waleed had two children—
Maymoona was four years old, and Saleem was two—and a third was
on the way. Bisma was currently sporting the most adorable baby
bump, and she glowed as she showed it off to Nada over the screen.
Waleed was a local imam and community activist, while Bisma ran
the outreach center at the same mosque, working alongside her husband—which was where she was currently, pulling another late night.
Bisma and Waleed had become quite the power couple as Waleed's
star rose steadily. He had been invited to speak at Deen&Dunya this

year, but the dates had clashed with interfaith meetings at the White House. Bisma imparted this news casually during the first few minutes of their catch-up.

"Making friends in high places," Nada observed.

"More like pissing off people wherever he goes. He nearly got escorted out by the Secret Service when he demanded more action on police brutality in the city."

"Things aren't much better here," Nada reminded Bisma.

"Things are always better in the Golden Crescent. Waleed and I are thinking of moving back to Canada."

Nada decided not to share what had happened last year, when a hate-motivated attack had devastated local businesses in the neighborhood. Her friend was right: sadness and tragedy existed in the world, and while it was important to always agitate for justice and change, it was also important to seek joy where you could. However, Bisma announced her imminent return to Canada every time they talked. Nada would believe it when her friend pulled up in a moving van and a red-and-white maple leaf hijab.

Nada knew she should get to the point. It was late, and Bisma had kids and a busy life. Instead, they continued to update each other. Nada talked about her job, Haleema's wedding, her mother's matchmaking machinations, but compared to her friend, she felt like a lazy bum.

"How do you do it all?" Nada asked, genuinely curious. "We're the same age and your husband works all the time, you work all the time, you live far away from your parents, and you have two kids under the age of five, with another on the way. I'm tired just thinking about it all."

Bisma laughed. "You know how they say that when you do something you love, you never work a day in your life?"

Nada groaned. Not this bullshit, not from Bisma.

"Well, it's not like that at all," she said. "I'm tired all the time. Sometimes I fantasize about packing a suitcase and running away.

Just leaving the kids and Waleed—the people I love most in the world—and making a break for it. Then I make *wudu* and pray, or I read Quran, or I go for a walk, or call my mom, or text my friends. It helps to have . . . purpose. I know why I get up in the morning." Bisma had always been an optimist, someone who worked hard and prayed harder.

"You're my shero."

"Yuck," Bisma scoffed. After a beat of silence, she looked directly into the camera. "Are you going to get to the real reason you're calling me this late?"

"I'm sorry," Nada said automatically.

"Stop being so Canadian and apologizing. I know you saw Baz at the convention."

"How?" Nada asked, startled.

"You think you're my only Canadian friend?" she teased. "He called me."

"How . . . is he?"

"I'm not doing this with you. Not again," Bisma said more sharply. "I was at your *nikah*, for God's sake."

"Haleema wanted me to meet Zayn. She dragged me to the convention."

"Does Haleema still not know who Baz is to you?"

"No one knows."

Bisma was silent, thinking. Her expression softened. "You carry your burdens so close to your hearts, both of you. It hurts to watch. Are you together again?"

"No." Nada's heart started to pound. She knew what Bisma was going to say next.

"But you're still married," she said.

Nada sat very still. "For now."

Bisma was quiet, thinking. "I think he's finally ready to move on," she said gently. "He told me that seeing you again after all these years made him realize he's been holding on to something that doesn't exist anymore."

The words felt like a dagger to her chest, through bone, and straight into her heart. "Okay," she said. *Alone, alone, alone.*

"He's been talking to Firdous." Bisma rolled her eyes. "I told him I don't approve, but . . ."

Nada knew what she wasn't saying, what she had been not-saying from the start of this call, and maybe for the past six years: Nada and Baz had had their shot, and she had walked away—twice. It wasn't fair to either of them to keep this sham of a marriage going when it had no future and only caused exquisite pain.

"I love you both," Bisma said quietly. "I wish things were different, but he's still so angry and resentful. That's no way to continue a marriage. I think it's best if you end things and move on, for real this time. I'm coming to Zayn's wedding in a few weeks. Let's talk more then."

Nada thanked her friend and ended the call.

Bisma had been the one to give Nada and Baz a final nudge into each other's life on that sunny day at Hart House. If their mutual confidante and well-wisher truly believed all hope was lost, then maybe it really was over.

Bisma had been married to Waleed for eight years now and had much to show for it: kids, a home, a life built with the person she loved. Nada had been married for almost the same amount of time, but had nothing except a relationship barely anyone knew about, not even her parents or her best friend.

Her thoughts drifted to Abbas and Narjis. Her parents had married when they were in their early twenties. They had been matched by a second cousin who knew them both well. Their courtship had been brief, weeks only. They declared themselves satisfied with each other following a handful of brief encounters and decided to take the plunge. The wedding, swiftly arranged, was attended by five hundred of their nearest and dearest. When Abbas immigrated to Canada shortly after the birth of Waqas, Narjis stayed behind for a few years while he established himself. She moved to Canada when her eldest son was five years old. She had not been happy to move, but she knew it was her duty to stay by her husband's side, even if the side he had chosen was thousands of miles away from everything and everyone she had known and loved, in a country full of cold people and even colder weather.

Maternal and paternal grandparents had come to visit at various times during Nada's childhood, for a few months at a time, but they always returned to Hyderabad. When Narjis and Abbas made trips back, they never stayed long. They had changed too much to return to their remembered versions of themselves in a country that had grown and developed without them.

Nada knew that her marriage was a failure compared to the steadfast devotion of her own parents. They had taken a chance, first by marrying, and then by staying together and raising a family. In contrast, she had fallen deeply in love at twenty-one, but hadn't managed to grow that relationship from early infatuation into the warm and tender affection she witnessed daily between her own parents.

Still, she couldn't help but mourn this last sputtering candle of hope, the flame so tiny she hadn't even realized it was there until she came face-to-face with Baz at D&D. That last vestige of hope hadn't been enough to stop her from running away after they kissed, and it hadn't been enough to make him run after her, either. It was time to extinguish the candle.

She got into bed and cried. In the morning, she sent a text. It was time to fix the rest of her life.

CHAPTER TWENTY-ONE

Seven years ago

Nada was in the first rush of love—an intoxicating, brain-fogging state. Her entire world was taken up by Baz, and based on the frequency of his texts and calls, he felt the same. The summer had been a blur of laughter and meals that tasted more delicious because he was there to share them. But now it was September, and the guilt of keeping him from her parents was eating away at her. She was sure they would love him. How could anyone not?

Her mother had been dropping broad hints about meeting her "new friend," so Nada and Baz decided to arrange an introduction on neutral territory—a midtown coffee shop. Baz was nervous when he walked up to the table where Nada and her parents were sitting. She had arrived with them five minutes early, and Baz was fifteen minutes late. Traffic, he had texted, and she wondered briefly why he hadn't left extra early, as she had done, to make a better first impression. Her father had already finished his tea, and her mother had ripped two napkins to shreds while they waited for him.

At the sight of Baz, Nada's heart caught in her throat as it always did when she looked at his beautiful face. He apologized for his tardiness with a smile and offered to fetch more drinks, which her father refused with a grunt and her mother with a nervous smile. Nada suddenly became aware that this meeting must be strange for her parents as well. With Waqas, the entire marriage had been arranged "in-house," as her brother joked. They'd had their first meeting in Jameela's parents' living room. Nada had accompanied her parents and made awkward, stilted conversation with the family while Waqas and Jameela talked quietly at the dining table a few feet away. A few weeks later was the *baat pakki*, the official engagement, followed by an elaborate wedding six months later. This coffee shop meeting was something different, a hybrid of cultural expectations and modern sensibilities.

"Tell me about yourself, Baz," her father rumbled, pinning him with a sharp look. "You are both so young, and Nada has not yet finished her engineering degree. I heard you are no longer in school?"

Nada groaned inwardly at the question. Her father hadn't been enthused about this meeting. Initially, he had been open to Baz, but after she'd admitted that he'd dropped out of university in his first year, and moreover that he had been studying English and sociology when he had been enrolled, her father's eyebrows had drawn together in a disbelieving frown. "And how does this *Baz* person expect to support a wife as a college dropout?" he had asked.

"Don't be so old-fashioned," Nada had teased. "He's an artist. Most likely, I'll be the one supporting *him*." Abbas had not liked that joke, but he hadn't said anything. Clearly, her father had been saving up his more pointed questions for the man of the hour.

Now Baz visibly swallowed. "I've been traveling these past few years. Right now, I am helping my father with his business."

"He's also been helping with his brother's band," Nada piped up. "Baz is a talented writer and musician." From the sour expression on her father's face, she would have done better to keep silent.

Abbas turned back to Baz. "What does your father do?" he asked. The underlying question was clear: *What does your father think of his loaf-about son?*

"My parents run a shop. They sell Islamic videos and lectures, mostly over the internet, but they have hopes of expanding into a bigger venture. I've been helping them set up the logistics this summer."

Narjis and Abbas looked at each other. With a sinking feeling in her stomach, Nada realized that this long-anticipated meeting was not going well.

"Baz is very talented, smart, and hard-working. He'll be successful at whatever he puts his mind to," she said loyally.

Abbas didn't even look at his daughter. "And in what direction do you plan to turn your talented, smart, and hard-working mind, Baz? Or do you plan to stay at your father's shop indefinitely?"

Baz squirmed under her father's intense gaze. "My current role is only temporary. I have some plans to continue my travels and see the Muslim world in the fall. Sir," he added, and then seemed slightly appalled at the honorific.

Beside her, Narjis reached for her now-cold cup of tea. "If you plan to travel, what is the rush? Perhaps in a few years, once Nada has finished school and started working and you sort yourself out, we can revisit this discussion. Right now, I see no point in continuing this relationship, if it will not lead anywhere."

Nada and Baz looked at each other, dismayed. To Nada, it was inconceivable that her parents were not impressed by Baz. Under their intense scrutiny, she felt a flare of stubbornness ignite, but it tussled with another part of her that wondered if her parents were asking the questions she should have asked herself. She and Baz were young, only twenty-one, and still figuring things out. They had no money or assets or even their own cars. What were they doing?

I love him, she thought, her feelings coming into crystal-clear focus. *I'm pretty sure he loves me too. Can't they see how rare that is?* Her parents simply didn't understand; that was all. She would make them understand.

"Baz is the best person I know," she said, and across from her, he flushed in embarrassment. "We want to be together. You let Waqas get engaged to Jameela after a month."

"Both Waqas and Jameela were in their late twenties when they married, both university graduates, and both had jobs," Abbas said. "Even with all the advantages of a stable foundation, they are not . . ."

Narjis reached out to squeeze his arm. Nada didn't know what he was implying. Were stolid, plodding Waqas and quiet, demure Jameela having problems? During their three years of marriage, Nada had never even heard them raise their voices at each other.

Abbas turned to Baz. "She is my only daughter," he said, and his voice caught. "Nada has called me old-fashioned, and perhaps I am. But I am old enough to know that there are few decisions in life more important than the one you both seem intent on making at such a young age. The person you spend your life with, raise children with, this decision will impact everything else for the rest of your life."

Baz squared his shoulders, and Nada felt a thrill at the steely look in his eyes. "I know I don't have much to offer right now, but I promise to do everything in my power to be worthy of your daughter. *Wallahi*, I will," he vowed.

The ride home was quiet. Nada sat in the back and leaned her head against the window, watching the traffic zoom past. In the rearview mirror, her father caught her eye. "Your young man has plenty of confidence," he remarked. It wasn't a compliment.

"And he is certainly good-looking," Narjis added. She had been lost in thought since they left the coffee shop. "I hope that is not the only reason you like him, Nada. Looks fade all too quickly, and then you're left with the person beneath."

Nada knew not to push her parents too hard. They might not have liked Baz at first sight, but then neither had she. She had grown up, and her parents would grow to love him as much as she did.

On the phone that night, Baz was less confident. "Pretty sure your parents hate me. I had to change my shirt when I got home, I was sweating so badly. Your dad is terrifying."

Nada laughed. "They just need some time."

Baz was quiet for a moment. "Do you still want to do this?"

She didn't hesitate. "I'm with you until the end."

Now that her cards were on the table, it felt easier for Nada to see Baz. Her parents hadn't banned their relationship outright. Surely they knew that when she stayed late on campus or slipped away on the weekends, she was spending time with him. Nada and Baz still observed the rules of "halal" dating, only seeing each other in public places and never physically touching, but it was getting difficult for both of them. At night, she had started to dream about him, and sometimes the urge to hold his hand, run her fingers through his hair, or kiss him when he smiled at her was overwhelming. For two observant Muslims, this was the equivalent of a serious relationship, the first one either of them had ever had.

Nada's parents seemed preoccupied, and there never seemed to be a good opportunity to continue her campaign. Jamal was thirteen years old now, and a few months ago he had held up his right hand at the kitchen table after dinner to show his family the tremor that had started and that he couldn't control. Her parents were busy with doctor's visits, their worry and distraction understandable. Waqas and Jameela were expecting twins. After what Abbas had hinted at in the coffee shop, Nada watched carefully for signs that something was amiss in her brother's marriage, but they seemed as blandly happy as usual. Still, it felt as if the house were holding its breath—or maybe that was just her.

In late October, the other shoe dropped. Just after midterms, a moving van pulled up to their driveway. A stone-faced Waqas retired to the backyard after breaking the news that his marriage was over. Only Nada and Jamal seemed truly shocked. Jameela, heavily pregnant, directed the movers, while her parents drank tea in the kitchen in silence.

Nada cried as she related all this to Baz later that night, and he listened patiently.

"Your family will need you more than ever now," he predicted.

"And I need you," she said between tears.

Fall passed slowly as a deep sadness lingered in Nada's home. Waqas was grim-faced as he moved through his days, and it became clear that mediation wouldn't save his marriage. The twins were born—joyful news tinged with sadness. Waqas attended the birth, but when he came home, he locked himself in the basement for two days, while Jameela recovered at her parents' home. The news about their split spread, the story gaining traction because of the circumstances. Though divorce had become more common in their community, it still caused a scandal and was met with many nosy questions. Nada escaped from home as often as she could.

When she tried to bring up Baz again in December, Narjis seemed surprised. "Are you still seeing that boy? I thought we had decided you would wait until after your graduation and he has figured himself out. How can you think about marriage while your older brother is looking for a divorce lawyer, and Jamal's condition grows worse?"

Nada knew what her mother really meant: *How can you ask me to think about this while our lives are falling apart?* She didn't blame her mother. Nada's plan to wait her parents out might have suffered a slight delay, but she and Baz were meant to be.

Meanwhile, Baz was busy with his parents' business. They were grooming him to take on a bigger role, and his travel plans had been put on hold, which Baz was not happy about. Privately, Nada thought that his parents had unwittingly done them a favor. Abbas and Narjis would be more amenable to their marriage if Baz demonstrated a willingness to stay in one place for longer than six months.

Baz was so busy now, it was becoming difficult to find time to spend together. In addition to helping his parents, he was playing in his brother's band on the weekends, and writing songs and managing bookings. The band was starting to develop a following online too. Plus, his family was starting work on their new venture, and from what he had shared about the business plan, Nada thought it had potential. She believed in him. She believed in them.

Christmas came and went, and the grassy quad where Nada had rekindled her relationship with Baz was covered in snow. She broached the topic of marriage with her parents once more, but they again put her off: "It's not the right time. We will talk about this later. Waqas needs our full attention. Jamal needs our full support. You're the stable one. Be patient."

But Nada was the opposite of patient. She didn't want to defer her plans any longer. School was hard, but it was nearly over. She missed seeing Baz more regularly. Her ideas for Ask Apa were still percolating. She knew that her family expected her to immediately join the workforce after graduation, but the idea of settling for an engineering job gave her no joy. The only person who made her life make sense was Baz.

"You're the only thing keeping me sane right now," she told him one day in January. They spent a precious afternoon walking around campus, bundled tight against the cold. She needed to walk and walk, and Baz didn't complain once. "I want to see you every day."

"I want that too," Baz said. He reached out with his gloved hand and squeezed her hand before letting go.

Impulsively, Nada stopped walking and turned to face him. A few pedestrians had to walk around them, but she didn't see them, her heart was pounding so hard. A certainty had settled over her. For a second, an instant, she teetered on the precipice of two realities. Then she jumped. "I love you, Baz. Marry me."

Baz laughed. "I love you too, Nada. Sure, I'll marry you." Then, realizing she was serious, he said, "You mean now?"

Nada looked at him with steady eyes even as her heart beat wildly, even as a single voice of self-preservation screamed at her to take a step back from the ledge. "What are you doing Wednesday?"

"You're serious," Baz said, and he looked at her in silence for a long moment. Nada waited: he had to want this too. Then a smile broke across his face, and she knew they would be okay. "This Wednesday? Well, I was planning to marry the woman of my dreams," Baz answered. He stepped closer to her, and their breaths mingled in the cold. "Nada Syed," he said formally, his dark eyes shining, filled with everything he wanted to say, "I've been in love with you since before I knew what that word meant. I want to be with you always. You fill my heart with joy, and I can't wait to build a life together. Will you marry me?"

Overcome by emotion, she could only nod. Baz gripped her hand in his, and they grinned at each other in excitement, giddy at their beautiful, spontaneous plan.

Despite everything that came next, Nada would always feel grateful for this moment, when everything felt perfect and possible. They had chosen—perhaps foolishly, definitely impulsively—but the choice had been theirs to make. What happened next was meant to be. Nada would keep a picture of this moment framed in her heart, a talisman against the creeping dark, for the rest of her life.

Bisma tried to talk sense into Nada after learning the news from Baz. Their lone confidante, she called Nada that night with cautious congratulations. "I always knew you two were meant to be. I just don't understand why you won't tell your parents."

"My parents will give in eventually. They already told me they would in a few years. I'm just borrowing against their future acceptance, that's all."

Even over the phone, Nada could hear Bisma frown. "Marriage is hard, in ways you never anticipate while you're in the love-drunk phase. It can be lonely, and it complicates your life. Your life is already complicated. Why do this to yourself now?"

"Because as practicing Muslims, getting married to someone you love and respect is simply what one does," Nada joked.

Bisma didn't laugh. "Baz will wait for you. Delay this marriage by another six months, a year. See how it feels to be together in the real world. You haven't even met his parents or his brother."

Nada knew that Bisma was right, that every word was sincere *naseeha*. She also didn't want to hear any of it.

"What if you get pregnant?" Bisma asked bluntly.

"I'll go on birth control."

"That takes a month to kick in at least, and you're getting married on Wednesday. Are you ready to be a mother?"

"Aren't you happy for me? For us?"

Her friend only sighed. "Promise me you'll use condoms. Be careful, friend. Now there are two hearts on the line."

The wedding was held in a small *musallah* inside a Scarborough strip mall. Nada wore a pink and gold *Anarkali* dress with tiny pearl buttons down the back, an outfit she had been saving for a special occasion.

She knew she had chosen right when Baz stumbled when he first caught sight of her waiting outside the imam's office. His dark blue salwar kameez was simple, but he had never looked more handsome to her, his eyes glowing with love and wonder as he took her in.

The imam, a kindly older man, didn't ask a lot of questions, but made sure they were both over eighteen, present of their own free will, and had a legal marriage certificate. The ceremony took place in the prayer hall, and Baz presented a plain gold band to Nada as his *mehr*, or bride gift. They asked two men who had arrived for prayer to serve as witnesses in addition to Bisma, who had driven up for the occasion. Nada had been more touched by her friend's arrival than she could express. Afterwards, Bisma pressed a flower bouquet into Nada's hands, kissed her on the cheek, and told her she would pray for them. The only hiccup came after the ceremony, when the new couple signed their marriage license.

He scrawled his signature under *Spouse*, and Nada peered at it doubtfully.

"Your full name is . . . Bazilry?" she asked, trying to make out his handwriting. He laughed and kissed her on the nose.

Blushing, she swatted him away, looking uneasily at the imam. She hadn't grown up around public displays of affection and had spent most of her life being told not to even look at a boy, let alone be kissed by one in public.

"My full name is Bazlur Rahman Haq," he said.

Nada feigned a look of horror. "Is that the real reason we didn't have a big wedding?"

He laughed again and squeezed her hand. Ever since the imam had pronounced them officially *nikah*-fied, Baz hadn't stopped touching her. His warm fingers had rested on the small of her back as they'd walked out of the prayer room where they'd confirmed the *ijaz* and *kubool* of the wedding ceremony, and he'd placed his hand under her elbow as they sat down to sign the paperwork.

She noticed his careful attention as she looped her own signature onto the piece of paper that would bind them together, both in the eyes of God and according to Canadian law.

"Nada Maisara Syed," he repeated softly to himself. "My wife has a middle name."

And I didn't know my husband's full name, she thought to herself. But then he squeezed her hand and whispered that he had never been happier, and she promptly forgot her momentary misgiving.

The imam and witnesses offered congratulations, while Bisma took pictures. They ate store-bought strawberry shortcake, and Nada fed Baz. Then, he cupped her chin with one hand before spooning a small bite of cake into her mouth, his dark eyes never leaving her face. It was the most sensual moment of her life, despite the presence of the imam and their witnesses. The tart taste of strawberries lingered on her tongue.

The entire ceremony lasted thirty minutes, and then it was just Nada, Baz, and Bisma alone together in the snow-covered parking lot. Bisma, bundled against the January chill, hugged Nada, shot Baz a warning look, and got into her car. Baz reached for Nada's ungloved hand as they watched their friend drive away, and Nada blushed with pleasure at the feel of his skin against hers, his fingers caressing the band on her ring finger. He leaned in close, and she shivered at this intimacy. "Thank you," he breathed.

Her heart thudded against her chest. "For what?" she whispered.

"For trusting me. For taking a chance on us. I promise I'll be faithful and try to make you happy until the day I die. I love you, Nada."

He pulled back to look at her with a serious expression on his face. There was a lump in her throat now, rendering her mute. His hands settled at her waist, and he pulled her in close, until their bodies touched. Then he leaned down and gently kissed her. Nada closed her eyes, reveling in the moment. *Finally*, she thought.

Followed swiftly by: *What have I done?*

CHAPTER TWENTY-TWO

Present day

Nada waited impatiently outside Nanima's Chai Shop in the Golden Crescent. He was late, and it looked like it was about to rain. Just as a few droplets landed on her least flattering navy-blue hijab, Haneef arrived, dressed in a camel-colored coat despite the mid-July heat, with a Tumi messenger bag strapped across his chest. Underneath, he wore slim-fit chinos and a dark, collared shirt. In contrast, she had deliberately dressed down in jogging pants, a faded shirt, and scruffy sandals, with no makeup. This was a business meeting, but she hated him and he didn't deserve her best.

"Thanks for meeting me," he said genially.

Nada opened the restaurant door and walked in, where she was greeted by her brother Jamal. *Shit.* She had forgotten he worked here.

"Welcome to Nanima's Chai Shop, home of authentic Indian chai and snacks. Will it be just one unsupportive sister and one slimy snake for dinner?" he asked with a bright smile.

Nada hoped she could brazen through this awkward encounter. "What are you doing here?"

"You truly don't listen to me. Sufyan hired me to be the charming, sexy host who makes everyone feel welcome, even if we are currently feuding. I also serve when they're short-staffed. I've gotten pretty good at balancing dishes on my lap." Jamal led them to a booth in front of the bathrooms. "I hope you hate your seats."

"I'm not tipping," Nada said as she sat down.

"Sufyan believes in paying his employees a living wage, so joke's on you," Jamal said, before wheeling back to his post by the door.

Haneef removed his coat. "I'll just be a minute. I'm going to wash my hands and complain to the manager."

"Won't work. Sufyan hates your guts too," Jamal called. Haneef ignored him.

Alone, Nada had time to look around the café. It was a good fit for the neighborhood—there probably wasn't another corner of the city where a traditional chai shop would flourish better. The space was tiny, just enough to squeeze a half-dozen tables, with a small counter up front where snacks like *pav bhaji*, *kheema pav*, samosas, and specially imported, melt-in-your-mouth Osmania biscuits were sold alongside a dozen types of tea, including Kashmiri, saffron-ginger, Lasa Lamsa, and Irani *dum chai*. Twinkly lights decorated the front counter and adorned the large window at the front, and prints of the old Irani chai cafés from Mumbai and Hyderabad decorated the walls. It was a homey, comfortable space, and Nada looked forward to returning often—once this unpleasant business was concluded.

Haneef returned just as a waiter—not Jamal, thankfully—came by to deliver water and take their order.

"I'm really glad you called. Should we split an appetizer?" Haneef said, rubbing his hands.

"I'm not eating with you," Nada said coldly. She ordered Lasa Lamsa chai, in a to-go cup.

Haneef turned guileless eyes on her after the waiter left. "Then why did you text and ask to meet?"

"You can drop the innocent act. Nobody is watching, and I know you don't care what I think," she said.

A shadow slid behind her nemesis's eyes. "What do you want?" he asked flatly, all trace of friendliness gone.

"I want to know how much you're willing to pay to buy what's left of Ask Apa," she said.

He blinked in surprise. "You said, and I quote, 'I'd rather burn Ask Apa to the ground than sell it to you,'" he said, smirking. "You always were feisty. I like that about you."

"Gross. How much?"

Haneef thought about it and named a figure. It wasn't generous, but it wasn't an insult, either.

"Try again," she said.

He added 20 percent, and she shook her head.

"Once more like you mean it," she said impatiently.

Haneef paused, considering her face carefully. "What are you playing at? Why now?"

Nada debated answering, then decided to flip the coin. "I want to move on with my life, but to do that, I have to make sure my family moves on too. You saw the way Jamal spoke to you, and he's currently on the outs with me. We're a loyal bunch, the Syeds. My mom misses Sister Rusul, but she'll never talk to her again until I put this behind me. So, try again, pretty boy, and this time put some wind behind that money sail."

The number he wrote down on a napkin and passed to Nada was more than she had expected, enough for a nest egg. It proved that Haneef was willing to pay for peace between their mothers. Nada could take some time off work, maybe consider another start-up idea, this time with a partner who wasn't an ass.

"Done," she said, and stood up. Her chai was still hot, so this hadn't been a total waste. She took a sip, preparing to leave, and met Baz's shocked stare. He was at the counter, picking up drinks, and Nada nearly dropped her cup.

Haneef rose with a big smile, hand out to shake Baz's. "Nada and I were just finishing up," he said. "What are you doing so far from your hood?"

It took Baz a moment to notice Haneef's hand, and he shook it warily. "I had a meeting in the area. Sufyan asked me to stop by next time I was in the Golden Crescent." His eyes slid past Haneef to Nada. "How are you?" he asked softly.

She ducked her head. "I've been better," she admitted.

"Nada's fine. She's about to come into an unexpected windfall," Haneef said, chuckling. "We're old friends, did you know? At one point, we worked *very* closely together. I look forward to working closely again soon."

Baz turned to the cashier to pick up his order, paying with jerky movements. But Haneef wasn't done.

"You're no stranger to reviving old friendships, right, Baz?" he asked. "Please give Firdous my salams. She came to me recently, looking for some advice on a very interesting business idea, and of course I was happy to offer my expertise."

Haneef's smile stayed bright until Baz left. Nada stared at his hateful face, her mind working furiously. "Are you actually talking to Firdous, or were you just trying to mess with Baz?"

Haneef seemed surprised at her question. "What's it to you? You don't know Firdous."

Nada closed her eyes. She had been so close to ending this chapter of her life. "It will always be someone else. You'll never stop. Will you?"

He seemed surprised. "Stop what?"

Nada shook her head, not bothering to answer. "The deal's off,

Haneef. You can keep your money." Then she ran after Baz. She caught up with him halfway down the street, his long legs swallowing the sidewalk.

"Baz! Wait up!"

He slowed. "Aren't you going to continue your date with that guy? Sister Rusul always did want you to get together."

She blinked, surprised he had picked up on that. "You never called me."

"Neither did you."

"You blocked my number years ago. Remember?" she said.

"Yet you still can't take a hint."

She stopped walking. "Haneef ruined my life. He stole my idea for Ask Apa and started his own company."

Baz stood impatiently. "I know. I connected those dots soon after Ukhti launched."

"I offered to let him buy me out, like he always wanted. But if he's talking to Firdous about another business, he's up to his old tricks. I can't be part of that, even though what I want more than anything is to be done being angry. I can't keep carrying this feeling around. It's destroying me."

He looked away, and his eyes shone in the dark. "For once, we agree on something. Goodbye, Nada."

Baz took a few steps away from her, and the urge to reach for his arm was overwhelming. "I called Bisma," she said instead. "She thinks we're done."

"We've been done for a while," Baz said, his back to her. "Ever since you broke my heart six years ago."

"We broke each other's hearts," Nada reminded him.

He turned to face her, and the hurt, sadness, and vulnerability in his eyes was painful to witness. "You broke mine first."

Nada walked back to Nanima's Chai Shop, where her car was parked. She saw Jamal waiting on the curb, his lunch bag neatly perched on his lap.

"How about you drive me home and we call it even? I can't kick you when you're down," he said.

Jamal had been training at the café all week, he told Nada as they drove home. Sufyan was happy with his work, and her brother boasted that he would be promoted to manager within a year.

"Did you tell Mom about the job yet?" Nada asked. Her parents had certain ideas about their children, and working in the service sector did not jibe with their image of middle-class respectability.

Jamal snorted. "Maybe in six months. If she asks, I'm out with my boys, or chasing girls. Okay?"

Nada warned him that she wouldn't lie for him.

"Why not? You've had plenty of practice. How long were you and Baz together?"

Nada nearly swerved into oncoming traffic. "Who told you?"

Jamal laughed. "Even Waqas has a better game face. Seriously, Nada. Do you know how many of my desi friends have girlfriends or boyfriends they're hiding from their parents? My boy Idris has been with his girl for five years. His family has no idea. You and Baz, you're the same game, just an older model."

"Gee, thanks," she said wryly. "Six years or four months, depending on how you look at things."

Jamal shook his head. "Four months? Even my first relationship lasted longer than that."

"What?"

He laughed, but then grew serious. "Remember right after Jameela left, when things were really bad?" His voice was tentative. They were parked in the driveway now, but neither made a move to go inside the house.

She nodded. Those first years after Jameela had left, when Nada had been secretly nursing a broken heart and dealing with the fallout of Haneef's duplicity, not to mention her brother's rapidly worsening condition, had been the hardest of her life.

"I was so scared all the time. Mom and Dad were always worried. Waqas was sad, and you were distant and I knew you were going through your own stuff. It eventually hit me: I couldn't live my life like that, always scared and worried, or I'd never make it. So I just decided to stop being afraid. Or maybe to pretend like I wasn't. I forced myself to make jokes, to laugh when people were being shitty to me, to speak up and get loud."

Nada remembered the change. Her brother had donned a swaggering persona in his early teens. He had been hell on wheels for a few years. In some ways, he still was.

"I had to pretend. I had to do it," he said quietly. "I wish I hadn't, now."

"Why not?" she asked. Jamal was always the life of the party, the joker of his friend group. He seemed happy, despite his challenges.

"It's all the same, right? You kept Baz a secret for years. Waqas kept his problems with his wife on the down-low the entire time they were married. I hid behind jokes. It didn't do any of us any good in the end. The truth is, we're all so afraid of being judged—by Mom and Dad, or by the aunties, or some other community bogeyman—we don't say anything at all. It only ends up hurting us anyway, you know?"

"Look at you, all grown up and thinking deep thoughts," Nada said, impressed.

Jamal grinned at her. "Mostly I think about girls."

"Of course." She paused. "Are you still hurting?"

Jamal avoided the question by changing the topic. "Did you know Waqas is talking to someone? One of the women he met at the matrimonial thing you dragged him to. He wants her to come to Haleema's wedding. I told him he should keep playing the field, now that he's finally out there, but he's not listening to me. What a waste."

Nada laughed but appreciated being kept in the loop. She had no idea who Waqas was talking to, but she was happy that he was finally ready to move on. "He can't bring a date to Haleema's wedding; he doesn't have a plus-one," she said.

Jamal opened the door to the car, illuminating his mischievous smile. "It's a massive desi wedding, Nada. Everyone's invited. Grab my wheels from the trunk?"

As she helped her brother maneuver into his chair, she thought about the price she had paid for her secret relationship. If her brother was right, her secrecy had all been for nothing.

CHAPTER TWENTY-THREE

Six years ago

Having a secret husband was more complicated than Nada had anticipated.

While she had felt guilty for keeping Baz a secret when they were first getting to know each other, it was nothing to the guilt she felt now. The moment the *nikah* was done, a hundred more worries moved in and set up shop: How would they break the news to their parents? What would his parents think of her? How would she manage her near-obsessive feelings for Baz while finishing her final year of engineering? What did Baz plan to do with his future, continue to work for his parents, return to school, or begin touring with his brother's band? Everything felt up in the air.

Then there was the issue of sex. While they had agreed to take the physical part of their relationship slow, they also couldn't keep their hands off each other and ended up kissing in every secluded part of campus. Sex went from being a future dream to an imminent inevitability. But when to have it, where, and how? Teenagers managed to figure this out under their parents' noses. Why was it so difficult for two (secretly) married adults?

She tried to talk to Baz about it a few weeks after their *nikah*. They were cuddled on a couch at the E.J. Pratt Library. She had a test the next day, but Baz had abandoned any pretence of reading a book and was nuzzling her neck, distracting her. Her turban-style hijab made this easy, which he seemed to appreciate.

"Stop it," she said, though she shifted so he would have easier access to the sensitive spot near her shoulder. His musky aftershave enveloped her in a pleasant cloud, and the nearness of his body warmed her. He lifted her into his lap and she shrieked, attracting scowls from the other students.

"Sorry," she whispered to a nearby study group.

"Not sorry," Baz murmured, trailing a line of kisses from her jaw to her ear.

"We'll get kicked out in a minute," Nada whispered.

"Can't a man kiss his wife in peace?" Baz asked, his voice husky with desire. She pushed him away, took a seat at the other end of the couch, and reached for her notes and textbook.

"I have to get through these notes. Behave yourself, and I'll let you take me out for dinner," she promised.

He stretched his legs out in front of him and picked up his novel. "Are you dessert?"

Nada shivered. Even his cheesy lines were doing it for her. She tried to concentrate on studying, but she could feel his eyes intent on her.

"Stop staring at me," she whispered.

"Stop being so beautiful," he countered. "Can't a man stare at his wife while she studies for a test?"

It had been like this for weeks. She couldn't concentrate on anything except Baz. It was even worse than when they first started dating. This was on a whole other level. She wore her wedding ring on a chain under her shirt, and she reached for it now, the metal cold against her fingers.

"You need to take a long, long walk," she ordered. Then with a hint of desperation: "Please?"

He kissed her and obediently removed his distracting presence from her vicinity. A girl sitting across from them smiled when Nada met her eye.

"It's always crazy when you first start seeing each other. New boyfriend?" the girl asked.

New husband was on the tip of her tongue, but she only nodded and resumed studying, her mind a whirl. She couldn't even tell this random stranger who Baz was to her.

A few hours later, Nada and Baz went to get chicken shawarma sandwiches from a restaurant near campus. Sitting on bar stools, they ate and talked.

"I was thinking," Baz said, while she finished her sandwich. He had already eaten his first shawarma and was unwrapping his second. She would have to get used to spending time with an ever-hungry boy. "You're spending all this time studying, when you could be kissing me." Nada poked him, and he grabbed her hand, bringing it to his lips before continuing. "I know you hate engineering. Why don't we just leave?"

She paused, sandwich midway to her mouth. "Leave? What do you mean?"

"I was thinking about this during that long walk in the snow," he said, warming to his argument. "I want to see the pyramids with you. I want to kiss you while cruising the Nile. Let's eat at a Michelin-starred food stall in Singapore, and haggle for souvenirs in the Spice Bazaar in Istanbul."

"I'm in school until May," she reminded him. "Only a few months away. I need to see this through."

He shrugged and started to inhale his second sandwich. "Seems like a waste of time. You said you didn't plan to work as an engineer anyway. Why not chase your dreams right now? I want to go on an adventure with my wife." He grinned at the word, and she softened.

"I want to go on an adventure with my husband too," she said. Her shawarma was half-finished, and he eyed it hungrily. "But I need to see this degree through. My parents will already be mad when they find out about us. I have to show them I haven't completely lost my mind."

Baz leaned back, hurt. "You think getting married was crazy?"

Nada laughed out loud. "Of course it was crazy. I just couldn't resist putting a ring on it."

He looked down at his hands. Unlike her, he wore a silver band on his ring finger, for all to see. "You wanted this," he reminded her. "This was your idea. I've been so happy."

"Me too," Nada reassured him. "It's just been . . . different than how I imagined."

Baz stole a few of her fries, then hopped off the stool. He returned a few minutes later with two pieces of honey-soaked baklava. "Even better than I imagined," he said, passing her one of the pieces. "We don't have to make any decisions right now. We have the rest of our lives to talk and plan. I love you. The rest is just details."

Nada melted. "I love you too." He was right. Every couple had issues, and if their only problem was that their marriage was a temporary secret, well, nobody was perfect. There was no point in worrying about a negotiated future when she could enjoy the present. *Later*, she thought to herself. *We can figure this out later.*

For the next month, Baz haunted her engineering college, showing up every evening to surprise her with dinner, dessert, flowers. They would steal away to a quiet corner of campus or a nearby park and eat, kiss, laugh. He celebrated her birthday in February with a special dinner and gifted her a delicate bracelet. Nada began making excuses with her friends so she could spend more time with Baz, and she started skipping classes. Her grades dipped, but she couldn't help herself. Bisma had described this feeling as "love-drunk." Nada had never been drunk, had never even tried alcohol in her life, but she imagined that this was what it felt like—this falling, this dazed feeling, this giddy happiness. The world seemed brighter, she laughed more readily, and she felt as if she could burst into song for no reason. But the lows were just as dark—the moments she worried about what they were doing, about the secrecy and her web of lies.

Baz brought up their future travel plans a few more times, until she finally snapped at him to stop. The bigger issue, for her, was how to come clean with their family. Somehow it felt even more difficult to break the news now. Nada kept picturing the disappointment and hurt on her parents' faces, the worry she would add to the ongoing drama with Waqas, all while Jamal's symptoms worsened and they desperately sought treatment.

And how would she break this news to her friends? Everyone would assume the worst, that she was pregnant, that she and Baz had been secretly dating for years. They would be hurt at the deception and judge her choices. Her family name would be dragged through the mud once more, and they were still reeling from the scandal of Waqas's divorce.

She didn't know how to bring up these thoughts with Baz. He was so obviously enraptured with their coupledom, so sure that they would weather every crisis, even though they had yet to agree on the simple question of what they wanted to do next, or where they would live, or even if they would both stay in the country together. Nada worried enough for the both of them. The constant lying and dissembling was exhausting. She lied to her parents about spending late nights on campus studying. She lied to her friends about spending time with her family during this difficult time. She loved being with Baz, but guilt was her near-constant companion these days. Yet it was all worth it. They were deeply in love.

When Baz suggested they spend their first night together, it was Nada who booked the reasonably priced hotel room. They were both inexperienced, more enthusiastic than skilled.

"I don't know what I'm doing," Baz said when they were alone in the room. "I'm happy to cuddle."

Nada shook her head. They had both been looking forward to this. "Let's cuddle afterward," she said, and started to undress. She pushed away any feelings of guilt, at least for the night. She wanted Baz too badly to stop now.

The first time was clumsy, uncomfortable, and painful, but by now they had an easy intimacy that served them well. They laughed just as often as they made each other gasp with pleasure, and when morning dawned and Baz sleepily kissed her bare shoulder before ordering room service, she wanted to bottle this feeling of bliss.

"I don't want to leave this room," Nada said, stretching luxuriously before reaching for the caramel vanilla latte with extra syrup he had ordered.

Baz sipped his black coffee, watching her sprawling limbs with hungry eyes, even though they had been active all night. "We could have this every day. Waking up together. Sleeping in the same bed every night. No one to answer to except each other. Run away with me?"

Not wanting to burst the cozy, intimate mood, Nada agreed, though they both knew she didn't really mean it. She was starting to suspect that she had used up all her impulsivity by marrying him. It took the rest of her mental energy to keep her lies straight in her head. Baz didn't seem to have the same restrictions. His family never questioned where he spent his time or with whom. When she pointed out this dichotomy, Baz shrugged it off, but Nada knew the truth: in her community and beyond, there were different expectations for women and men, and she was carrying the brunt of that burden. As much as she enjoyed every moment with Baz, a small part of her was starting to resent him.

February rolled into March, and then Nada and Baz had been married for two months. They booked weekends away, and every night they spent together was charged with more and more passion. Yet every Monday morning, Nada worried about where they were headed. Her parents were asking more questions, and the constant lying, covering her tracks, and keeping track of each lie was a drain on her energy. She was barely passing her classes now. Sometimes it was hard to look at herself in the mirror.

Waqas noticed that she wasn't her usual self and cornered her when they were alone together at home. "Are you all right?"

"What do you mean?"

"I thought it was school, all your late nights and weekend study sessions, but there's something off about you. I know things have been tough here at home, and I'm sorry to burden you with my problems."

Nada felt stricken. Self-loathing rose at her older brother's words. He was always thinking about everyone else. She couldn't burden him with her problems too. Nada took shallow breaths and worried that she was about to have a panic attack. To divert his attention, she blurted out, "Did you and Jameela have the big conversation before you married?"

"About what?" he asked.

"Was she really okay with moving into our basement forever?"

Waqas shrugged. "I'm the oldest son. She knew how this worked. Why are you asking?"

Nada shrugged, unsure how to put her feelings into words. "Did she want to change things and you didn't?"

Waqas shook his head. "I'm asking about you, Nada. Are you all right?"

She lied, of course. These days, her lies and excuses flowed off her tongue so easily she didn't even think about them anymore—which made her feel even worse. "Just tired," she tried to reassure him, but Waqas didn't seem convinced. A part of her wanted him to push, to demand that she tell him the truth, but he took her at her word.

Bisma had tried to warn her, she realized now. Marriage—any long-term intimate relationship, really—complicated things in ways one couldn't anticipate. There were days she felt isolated by her secret, even though being with Baz still filled her with joy.

She was also starting to wonder about Baz's future plans. Aside from travel dreams, he seemed content to help his parents with their business and his brother with the band. When she broached the idea of him returning to school, he only laughed, joked about being a trophy husband, and distracted her with kisses.

His songwriting was taking off. He claimed that she was his muse and the song lyrics poured out of him easily, especially after the nights they spent together. His brother liked his new work, and together they were putting the words to music. When Baz spoke about his songs, about the band, his face came alive in a way it never did when he spoke about his job or his parents' plans. Even though Nada encouraged him to pursue his music, she secretly wondered if she even wanted to be a musician's wife. There were days when she felt very far away from Baz, consumed by guilt. Sometimes she felt trapped, and she'd be hit with a panic attack. Once, she even had one in the middle of class.

Nada wondered uneasily if her parents had been right after all: maybe they should have waited. Her restlessness calmed when she was in Baz's arms, but it returned with a vengeance every time she was alone. She worried about Waqas, the twins, Jamal, her parents, her future. She still hadn't done anything about Ask Apa, and she had no idea what to do after graduation. And now she had to take into account Baz's plans too.

Nearly three months after their spontaneous wedding, Nada couldn't take it anymore; she had to tell her parents, and there was only one person who might be able to help smooth the way.

She told Baz about her plan to ask Sister Rusul for help as they lay in another reasonably priced hotel room, legs intertwined. His fingers sifted through her long hair and twirled a strand absently. He thought it was a bad idea.

"Sister Rusul is my mother's best friend. She knows me and my family, and I trust her. She'll be on our side," she assured Baz. "I need to tell my parents. We need to move on with our lives."

He kissed the side of her head, then shifted to balance on his elbows over her, his arms cradling her close. They stared at each other for a long moment. "Mine," he growled, and kissed her deeply. They didn't talk anymore after that.

***

Sister Rusul listened carefully to Nada's story over the phone and didn't interrupt, save for a sharp intake of breath when Nada told her about the secret *nikah* and the relationship she had sustained for months. When Nada finished, she waited for the older woman to process the information, congratulating herself on her good sense to confide in her. It felt so good to finally unburden herself. Sister Rusul was like a mother, but not as demanding or judgmental. She might even offer to break the news to her parents and help ease the way.

"I don't know what to say," Sister Rusul said. "I am shocked and disappointed by this, Nada. You married a stranger with little thought of the consequences. What were you thinking?"

Her words were like an ice bath thrown in Nada's face. She stammered out a reply: "Baz loves me. He's a good person. I told you because I need some advice, not blame."

Another long moment passed, and Nada imagined Sister Rusul trying to calm herself down, taking deep breaths. "*Habibti*, I will do you a favor and treat you like an adult, as you are clearly capable of making adult decisions. This relationship is not good for you. If you say Baz is a good man, I believe you, because I know you are a smart girl. However, the way you started this relationship will taint it for the future. He might be a fine young man, but he is clearly not ready for everything a marriage will bring. Don't throw your future away on sex and a foolish first love."

"You think I should get divorced?" Nada asked, appalled. She wasn't sure what she had expected from Sister Rusul, but it wasn't this.

"Yes," Sister Rusul said firmly. "It would be the best, kindest decision for both of you. A secret divorce, following a secret marriage. You are not ready for this, Nada. I have known you since you were a baby, and I have known your family since before you were born. Don't do this to your parents, not right now. They are already going through so much with Waqas, with Jamal. This will break them."

"I can't leave Baz," Nada said. Not see her husband again? Cut off all access to his support, to his lips, to his embrace, to the way he made her laugh? The idea was inconceivable.

"What you are feeling for him, it won't last," Sister Rusul said. There was another note in her voice now, dark and bitter. "I was married for fifteen years, *habibti*. My husband was not a bad man, but he never wanted me to pursue anything for myself. He only wanted me to remain an accessory to his own life. When I started Just Her Co., he was never supportive. In our community, the men are learning, but the change has been slow."

"Baz isn't like that," Nada said, loyal still, even as her mind buzzed.

"Isn't he? You said he suggested you drop out of school and travel the world with him. He has no education, no training. He has not introduced you to his parents, his brother. These are not the actions of a man who is ready to embrace his responsibilities as a husband. Tell me, if he is not willing to support your ambitions now, how will he nurture your dreams in the future?"

Nada shook her head, rejecting these words. Sister Rusul didn't know what she was talking about. She was too old, too jaded by her own divorce to understand what Baz meant to her.

As if sensing Nada's emotions, Sister Rusul's voice softened. "It is your life, Nada. You only get one. I told my son, Haneef, about your idea for the Ask Apa app, and he thought it was a good one. He is a programmer and also has connections with VC investors on the West Coast. I meant to call you, to invite you to come to Vancouver to speak with him. It would be my privilege to invest in the daughter of my closest friend."

"You think Ask Apa has promise?" Nada asked, grasping at the only part of this conversation that was good, like a drowning person scrabbling for driftwood.

"I think you are brilliant, and I could never forgive myself if you threw it all away to become an unambitious man's wife," Sister Rusul said. The words hit Nada like an arrow slamming into the bull's-eye. "You are both so young, only twenty-two years old. We make mistakes when we are young, but then we learn from them. What happens if you have children? A child is the one thing you cannot undo. I know this is not what you wanted to hear, but a part of you knows I am right."

When Nada hung up, Sister Rusul's words continued to echo in her head. She started to count backward, trying to remember the date of her last period. She was two weeks late.

CHAPTER TWENTY-FOUR

Present day

After their conversation outside Nanima's Chai Shop, Nada couldn't stop thinking about Baz and everything she had lost. Seeing him again at the convention, talking to him, being kissed by him, had resurrected the ghosts of her past, and she could feel herself sink once more into a deep gloom.

During those first few weeks after she broke up with Baz, she had marveled at her ability to hide devastation in plain sight. Worse, no one seemed to notice that the real Nada had disappeared, replaced by an animated husk who sounded like her, worked like her, smiled like her, but who was dead inside. *So this is what depression feels like*, she had thought to herself. After a month, she went to her doctor and was referred to a therapist. She ended up taking antidepressants for a year.

Now Nada wondered if maybe her family had noticed at the time, but had chalked up her sadness to school burnout. She hadn't confided in them before taking the biggest plunge of her life, so she couldn't be upset when they had no context for her sadness.

She thought she had dealt with her feelings of guilt, shame, and regret, yet a few interactions with Baz over the course of one weekend six years later had shaken them loose once more. If that had been their second chance, she had blown it.

Jamal was right; keeping secrets was toxic, and silence only made things worse. Perhaps the cruelest part of all was the legacy of that silence: she had no one to confide in about her resurrected feelings for Baz, except maybe Bisma, who, as a mother with multiple responsibilities, didn't have time to console her heartsick friend.

Regrets, piled in growing heaps all around me. Regrets, authored by my own hand.

It was hard to get out of bed, but she forced herself to. It was difficult to pretend to be normal at work, but she smiled at her colleagues and attended the meetings that were back on again, now that her boss had returned from summer vacation. She filed reports, worked on a side project her supervisor assigned, was praised for her work during a performance review. Her parents went about their jobs and chores, and Waqas was absent in the evenings when he didn't have the twins. Even her little brother had a job.

Nada couldn't stop herself from creeping on Firdous's social media accounts. While the former Queen Bee of MYNA camp was a frequent poster, there was nothing further about Baz. She read the comments under the picture of him and Firdous from two weeks ago over and over:

> omg you're so gorg, stahpit!
> Who's the cutie?
> #NewFriend alert!
> I sense the start of a love story!
> Is that hottie Baz Haq?? Love #DDCon

Nada was alone and quietly drowning, and the hand that held her under was her own. She had realized a long time ago that she had been raised with a set of particular expectations, the same that so many of her friends had come to terms with in their own way: to refrain from physical or emotional intimacy until they became adults, capable of making mature decisions; to expect and encourage familial input into their choice of partner; to enter their first adult romantic relationship with the belief in marriage first, with love and intimacy to follow. This meant that their first relationships would inevitably carry more weight than the first relationships of their non-Muslim or less traditional friends who dated casually.

She had accepted it all, even as some of her friends and acquaintances chose a different path, because living this way felt normal, necessary, and right for who she was. But now, for the first time in her life, she was reckoning with the impact of these lifelong expectations. Not because she rejected their premise, but because she was capable of understanding the consequences of her decisions, even when those decisions disappointed her, even when she made them willingly and with eyes wide open. She had been trained to expect that her first love, her first relationship, would last forever. Baz had shared this belief, except he had the guts to finally call time of death on their shared dream.

It would be hard seeing him again at Haleema's wedding, which was only three weeks away now. Especially if Firdous was there, insinuating herself into Baz's life. But Nada knew she would survive. She had done it before.

At least the rest of her family seemed to be hitting their stride. Over dinner that Friday night, with only Nada and her parents present to enjoy her mother's excellent chapatis and *kheema* with green bean curry, they made casual conversation about their week and the upcoming wedding.

"I've been thinking it might be time to look for a bigger house," Abbas announced, once they had finished the chapatis. Across from him, her mother rolled her eyes but didn't say anything.

"Why?" Nada asked. Their home was large, with plenty of space for everyone.

"Your brothers think they are being sneaky, but I know what is going on. Waqas might finally be thinking of getting married again, and Jamal is up to something. I plan to follow him when he leaves tomorrow morning."

Nada and her mother exchanged amused glances.

"Or you could talk to him," Nada suggested.

Abbas shook his head. "He will only lie to my face. You know how he can be. Would you like to come to the new home presentation center with me?"

Nada appealed to her mother. "You don't want to move, right?"

Narjis shrugged. When it came to financial decisions, her parents enjoyed a traditional relationship. Unless home renovations, food, or their social calendar was involved, her mother would leave the decisions to Abbas. "Your father thinks this is a good idea. That way, when Waqas gets married again, his new wife will be comfortable in a larger space in the basement. Particularly if she has children of her own."

Nada stared at her parents. "If Waqas marries again, he will move out."

Abbas seemed startled by the suggestion. "Nobody will move anywhere if we make the proper plans. I will make sure the new house has a larger accessible space for Jamal as well. I think he might be getting restless, which is why he is always out with his friends. Of course, you will get your own suite, Nada, which you can use until you marry."

Many of her friends had lived with their parents until they married, and then with in-laws for the first few years of their marriage, before striking out on their own. It was the natural order of things in South Asian families, but her father had not reconciled himself to the moving-out part yet.

Until the age of twelve, Abbas had grown up in a sprawling family compound in Hyderabad. An only child, he never missed the loss of siblings because he was always surrounded by dozens of cousins.

The compound belonged to his dada and dadi, paternal grandparents, who had added extensions to their modest home as their family grew. After each of their four sons married, they added on: a second story, followed by a backyard extension, and then a third story. When Nada was younger, she had loved hearing her father's reminiscences about his childhood. It wasn't until she was an adult that she realized the stories stopped abruptly when he was twelve, when he had moved to Mumbai with his parents after his father got a job. In those days, the only way her father could communicate with his family in Hyder-abad was through expensive phone calls or letters, and he only vis-ited during school holidays. Eventually, her father lost touch with his cousins and extended family.

Nada realized that her mother understood that the decisions Abbas made as an adult were motivated by the deep loneliness he had felt after he moved away from his boisterous Hyderabadi family. So she said nothing to her father's suggestion, though she knew that this time, Abbas wouldn't get his way.

After helping to clean the kitchen and load the dishwasher, Nada stepped outside for some fresh air. It was mid-July, and the days were hot and sticky in Toronto, but the evening was cool. Headlights beamed as a car approached and then turned into the driveway. Waqas hopped out of the silver Lexus and then leaned down to the window to talk to the driver. Nada could see that it was the same Black woman from the matrimonial event, now in a pretty mauve hijab. The woman waved to Nada, and she waved back as the Lexus reversed out of the driveway. Waqas ambled over to her.

"You're too old to be spying on your big brother," he said.

"As if you'd ever do anything worth spying on," Nada scoffed, and they grinned at each other. "One of your new friends? Jamal ratted you out."

Waqas's smile suffused his face with a happy glow that made him look years younger. "The only friend I contacted after the matrimonial event," he corrected. "Khadijah works as an insurance investigator. She's been divorced for four years, and her son is nine. We're taking things slow, so don't tell Mom yet."

"They already know. I'm starting to think they notice everything. Dad has started talking about buying a bigger house, for when your new wife and stepkid move in," Nada said, watching her brother carefully.

A shadow moved behind his eyes and he sighed.

"Not part of your grand plan?" she asked lightly.

"To be forty years old and live in my parents' basement, even though I have a job and kids? No, not part of the plan. I'll talk to him."

"He won't be happy."

"I made that mistake when I was married to Jameela. I put Dad's comfort and insecurities above what my wife wanted, and I won't let that happen again." His gaze narrowed on her. "What about you?"

"What about me?" Nada asked, stalling.

"Any past mistakes you're learning from this second time around?"

She suddenly realized that Waqas knew about Baz. Maybe not the entire story, but enough. She hadn't given her family enough credit in the past, but she could do something about that now. She playfully nudged Waqas with her shoulder. "I have a few tricks up my sleeve, but a magician never reveals her secrets."

Waqas raised an eyebrow and nodded at her to go on. Nada opened her mouth to speak and surprised them both with her response: "I'm going to go public about what Haneef did to me. I think I'm ready to look into my legal options." They both blinked, and then her brother grinned.

"Took you long enough. My friend is a commercial litigator. I'll put you in touch tonight."

Something inside Nada eased at her brother's words, and she realized that on some level, she had been thinking about this for a while.

Likely since her confrontation with Haneef at Nanima's Chai Shop, when she realized that even if she let him buy Ask Apa, and even if their mothers reconciled, he wouldn't magically reform. Haneef would continue to take advantage of others, because he was a financial predator. If she were to let this go, it would be with the tacit understanding that because he had faced no consequences for his behavior, he would continue to hurt others in her community. She felt better having her older brother's approval. "You don't think it's a bad idea?" she asked.

He shook his head. "I'm sorry I didn't speak up when it all first went down, but life was pretty crazy back then, with Jameela and the twins. This has gone on for long enough. It's time to sue Haneef's ass back to undergrad."

Nada liked this confident swagger from her brother. It was refreshing and boded well for his future. She told him so, and he laughed.

"My little sister, the family Wonder Woman. I hope my daughters grow up to be just like you."

"An imminent disaster?"

"An evolving masterpiece," Waqas countered.

She liked the sound of that. They walked back into the house together.

CHAPTER TWENTY-FIVE

Six years ago

N ada bought the pregnancy test before she texted Baz. They made plans to meet at their campus library. She didn't tell him about her late period, because she was too busy freaking out. Sister Rusul had been right: Nada wasn't ready for everything that marriage involved, especially not this part. When she tried to picture Baz as a father, she knew he would do his best, that he would be fun and kind. But she couldn't imagine raising a child with him right now, at the age of twenty-two. How would she finish engineering while battling morning sickness and doctor's appointments? She would have to defer or drop out. A potential child made their secret marriage real in a way nothing else had done before, and as she frantically read the instructions for the pregnancy test in her en suite bathroom, she was overcome with a feeling of helplessness, shame, and disgust. What had she been thinking when she asked Baz to marry her in secret? Nada had prided herself on being a sensible, rational person, not prone to dramatic or impulsive behavior. Yet she had allowed herself to be swept away by her feelings for Baz, and the secrecy had led to this moment of sheer panic. Sister Rusul's words kept running through her mind: *We make mistakes when we are young . . . A child is the one thing you cannot undo. I know this is not what you wanted to hear, but a part of you knows I am right.*

While she waited for the two blue lines that would decide her future, Nada vowed to make the hard choice, no matter the outcome.

Baz was waiting at their designated meeting spot in the library when she arrived. His face lit up when he saw her. He wrapped his arms around her and inhaled deeply. "Did I tell you I love you today?"

Nada closed her eyes and tried to memorize this moment, before she set it on fire. She stepped back. "I'm late," she said flatly.

Baz looked confused. "No, we agreed to meet at four . . . ," he trailed off, comprehension dawning on his face. "You're pregnant? But we used protection." A delighted smile stole over his face. "We're going to have a baby?"

Nada shook her head and tears filled her eyes. He reached for her again, wrapping her in his warm embrace, her source of refuge and peace these last few months.

"Hey, it's okay. I know this wasn't what we planned, but I love you. Whatever happens, I'm here for you. I'll stay home and watch the baby, and once you're finished with school, we can travel. What's more portable than an infant, right? We'll have an adventure, the three of us. It will be amazing, just you wait."

Nada's initial reaction to a baby had been instant panic and dread at the thought of sleepless nights, the pain of labor, breastfeeding, the expense of diapers, an entire tiny wardrobe to buy when they didn't even have a place of their own. In contrast, Baz saw an infant as a minor inconvenience, something to work around as he made plans to leave the country. More than anything else, their different reactions told Nada everything.

"I took the test already. I'm not pregnant," she said.

Baz slumped. "Okay," he said. "I guess it wasn't the right time for us."

Nada closed her eyes and a tear seeped out. "Not the right time," she echoed, and he caught something in her tone. "Baz," she said, her voice breaking. "We have to talk. This . . . this isn't working. When I spoke to Sister Rusul—"

"I knew it," he said, his jaw tense. "You shouldn't have talked to her. I knew she would fill your ear with poison. Nada, please, it's us. We can make this work." Baz's voice was shaking.

It was that note of vulnerability in his voice, more than anything else, that cemented her resolve. That told her she was doing the right thing, the necessary thing. "Maybe we could," she said. It was time to be honest now, time to be brave. "I could finish school and start working on my start-up, and you would stay here and support me, but a part of you would die because you weren't doing the thing you want most— to explore the world, to work on your music." Baz started to protest, but she lifted a hand and he grew silent. She continued, "Or I could leave everything here and travel with you. I could leave school, leave the opportunity to build something of my own, leave my family. Right now, we both want things the other doesn't want. If we did have a child together now, it would be so special, because it would have us as its parents, but we wouldn't be happy, Baz. Maybe if we had met later—"

"We met at the perfect time," Baz said hoarsely. "I don't regret a thing." He held her gaze, and the hurt was unbearable, but she held his. She owed him that much. "We could compromise. Travel half the year, work half the year." He was pleading, trying to avoid what Nada realized now had always been inevitable.

"There isn't anyone else involved right now, Baz," Nada said softly. "Don't you see? The fact that there isn't and we still aren't on the same page on what to do next tells you everything. We're not ready for this. We're not ready to take this relationship public. We can barely manage without the pressures of our families' opinions, without everyone else's ideas about what we should be doing or how we should be living. I love you so much . . ." Her voice broke and she looked down at her hands, trying to regain control. Baz's warm hand reached for hers and held tightly. She clung to him as if she were drowning. "Divorce me. Travel. Live your life. Fall in love with someone else."

"You don't mean that," Baz said, and he removed his hand and took a step back. "You don't have faith in us. You don't have faith in what we could be. Marriages are built, not born. You let someone who doesn't know us get to you. Or maybe she just confirmed your own feelings?" His voice grew hard and suspicious. "If you were really in this with me, nothing could sway you. Nothing."

"That's not fair. I've loved every moment together, but aren't you worried about the future? I spend my nights wondering what will happen when other people find out, or what our life together will look like, but nothing seems to bother you. You haven't finished school, and you're unhappy working with your parents, but you won't do anything about it. I have dreams for myself . . ."

Baz folded his arms and stared at his feet. Silence stretched between them, a tense coil, and her heart thumped in her chest. The relief she had felt when the pregnancy test came back negative had been palpable, but it was quickly followed by panic about what to do next. She loved Baz, but it wasn't enough to vanquish her fear that she was throwing her life away on a dream.

"My parents always pitted me and Zayn against each other," Baz said quietly. "I never told you that because I was ashamed. They favored him until I worked harder. Then they favored me, and I could see it drove my brother crazy. I left school, I left home, to get away from that for a while. I needed to clear my head. When I came back and you and I started to get serious, it was the first time I knew what I wanted: you." He looked at her, and the intensity in his gaze made her shiver.

"For the first time in my life, I wanted something that was only mine. You make me so happy . . ." His throat moved with emotion.

He took a deep breath and continued as Nada's eyes welled with tears. "I wanted you for myself, but I can't be with someone who doesn't choose me as I am today, not the man I might be tomorrow. I won't fight for a phantom future. I love you, Nada. I've only ever loved you. But I won't live a conditional life, not even for you." He reached for his bag and turned to leave. "If you want this marriage to be over, you can divorce me yourself."

Ask him to stay, a voice screamed inside her. *Let him go*, another voice urged. Nada said nothing and let Baz walk out of her life.

She didn't see him again for six years, not until Haleema dragged her to the Deen&Dunya convention to meet her fiancé, Zayn. Haleema never suspected that Nada was meeting her own brother-in-law for the first time.

For the next year, Nada worked constantly. She managed to pass her courses and found a job working as a junior solutions architect at an engineering company that specialized in industrial solutions for small-scale manufacturing. She picked it from the handful of job offers she received after interviewing for over twenty positions. Though it paid the least, the job allowed for the most flexibility. She spent her workday building models, testing equipment, and doing field work. Her mostly white, middle-aged colleagues liked her because she never complained about even the most menial task and always handed in her work on time. Every moment she wasn't at work was devoted to Ask Apa.

True to her word, Sister Rusul put her in touch with her son, Haneef, who was finishing his graduate studies in computer science. She also invested a small amount of capital to get Nada started, which was matched with a loan from Abbas. Since Haneef was on the West Coast, they held standing meetings a few times a week, along with conference calls with Sister Rusul. With the design specs Nada put together and back-end coding provided by Haneef, they had a demo to share within twelve months. The app was simple, the target market receptive, and Ask Apa 1.0 was born. When Nada typed in her first query, she felt the faint stirrings of happiness, an emotion that had all but vanished since her breakup with Baz.

When should I get married?

The powered software responded in seconds: The average age of marriage in Canada is 27 for women, 31 for men, but this varies widely among demographics. As life span increases in the developed nations, the reasons for marriage have changed. This is an intensely personal decision. Bottom line: there's no rush.

The answer delighted Nada, and over Skype, Haneef smiled at this first test result.

"I've filtered for porn," he said. His words made her blink. "The internet is powered by porn," he explained matter-of-factly. "That's not our target market. I coded to stay PG as much as possible."

Nada felt foolish for not even considering the ways that her app might be used for something other than its intended use. "Thanks. I never thought about that."

"I figured. Here, let me try another question." He typed, and then the app spat out an answer on his screen, which he showed her.

Q: What is the best partnership?

A: A successful partnership, whether romantic, business, or collegial, is always based on trust and respect. To ensure success, it helps to have a common goal, and to keep talking about what you both want. Good luck!

Nada laughed. "This advice sounds a bit like a horoscope."

Haneef made a note of her comment. "We can tweak, but unless we want to turn this into a more personal experience, hire therapists and counselors, it will have to stay at this level. For now."

They discussed expanding the app to provide cost-effective mental health services that were culture, region, and faith specific. Nada's heart grew ten times inside her chest as she contemplated the future. Her little idea had come so far already.

"Thank you," she said impulsively. "You took a chance on me. You have no idea how much I needed this distraction."

So far, their beta testers' early feedback was positive, according to Haneef. The next step was to secure more funding and plan the business model.

"You've worked just as hard as me," he said. "Most people with a good idea have no follow-through, but not you." He looked straight into the camera. Across the country, in her bedroom in Scarborough, Nada felt the intensity of that steady, unblinking gaze. "You're not like most people."

Despite their increasingly close working relationship, Nada felt nothing more than fondness for Haneef. Theirs was a business partnership and nothing more. Besides, though he never discussed his personal life, she was sure he had someone special. It was there in the subtext, in the way he was careful not to share personal details about his day. He never talked about the other meetings he was no doubt taking, or the other apps and start-up ideas he was likely working on. Nada didn't care. She assumed that Ask Apa was a side project for him. For her, it had become more than that: it was a personal mission to prove she could launch her own business and run after her dreams—the ones that didn't include Baz.

Just before their call ended, Nada brought up their partnership agreement again, which would nail down the roles they would both play in Ask Apa, as well as the details on the sharing of profits, if there were any. They had both been slow to move on this. Nada had known Haneef her entire life, and Sister Rusul was a trusted family friend. When she first broached the subject of signing a partnership agreement, Haneef had agreed readily, but then he had stalled. First, there were delays with his family lawyer, who always seemed to be swamped and was slow to reply to email. Then Nada kept forgetting to ask about it. Juggling her day job and the demands of trying to launch a start-up meant that she was usually up before *Fajr* and not in bed until past midnight. She was sleeping only four or five hours a night.

Nada didn't mind her hectic schedule, because any sleep she did get was punctuated by dreams, and sometimes nightmares, of Baz. At first, she dreamed about their brief life together—sneaking out, late-night meals, his touch at her waist, the feel of his lips on her throat. As the months passed, he started to retreat. Now she only caught glimpses of him in a crowd, or she spent the entirety of the dream trying to find him. Her heart would be hammering when she woke up soaked in sweat.

Two months after ending the relationship, Nada had finally broken down and called Bisma. She said that Baz had left for Cairo almost immediately after the breakup. He was practicing his Arabic and had even tuned in to the local artist scene. Nada didn't ask if he seemed happy or if he had posted pictures with any women; she didn't want to know the answers to those questions.

"I finally heard back from my lawyer," Haneef said, breaking into her thoughts now. "He's done the contract, and I told him to have it couriered to you. Sign it and send it back. Maybe get your dad or one of his company's lawyers to look it over. We can discuss the split of profits too."

They had a few ideas on how to monetize the app. Nada was firmly against advertising, while Haneef was open to the idea. This had led to their biggest argument to date. The Ask Apa IP belonged to her, and while Haneef had put in work to turn her dreams into reality, she wanted to remain faithful to her initial vision for the service as a nonprofit application free to her whole community. They could find sponsors, but they would not prey on their clients for their personal information, or use shady biometrics to track their users' habits and sell that knowledge to the highest bidder. She wanted to make something that would bring good into the world.

Nada said she would look out for the contract, and after signing off, prepared for bed. As usual, sleep was elusive. She tossed and turned, changed into a different cotton T-shirt, then gave up entirely after another hour. She padded downstairs in search of warm milk or maybe herbal tea.

At work the next day, Nada's phone pinged with a Google alert. A few months ago, she had self-consciously set up alerts for her name, Ask Apa, and Haneef, and then promptly forgot about it. Now she swiped on the app with a smile, wondering if her name had been picked up in some community newspaper, or perhaps Haneef had been put on some random "Top 30 Under 30" list. He would love that.

But it wasn't clickbait or community gossip that greeted her swiping fingers. She stared at the headline in her email browser, puzzled: Canadian techpreneur does good with community-engagement app Ukhti.

Haneef had never mentioned another community-centered app he was involved with, but she knew he was busy during the day. She would have to send him a message to congratulate him on his achievement. Thinking nothing of it, Nada clicked on the link.

Haneef El-Haad, 27, alum of UBC's prestigious incubator start-up lab, is set to launch his first IPO with a revolutionary new idea: to make community wisdom accessible to everyone. His new app, Ukhti—Arabic for "big sister"—has been heralded as a game-changer in the world of edutainment apps aimed at niche markets with global appeal. The Ukhti app is being billed as the next Google, but for Muslims, offering real-time advice to users, the sort that a wiser, older sister might provide. While the app will remain free to use, it will also offer in-app purchases and upgrades, and make use of ad revenue. Initial investment has been enthusiastic, with a Series A funding rumored to be in the seven figures—an impressive feat for the brand-new CEO, and one that bodes well for the emerging social-capital market of apps that provide return on investment as well as socially responsible services.

Nada's mind raced. Haneef had worked with her for the past year. Surely this article wasn't talking about *her* Haneef. Then again, what were the odds that there was another Haneef El-Haad who was also an alum of UBC on the brink of launching an app aimed at a diverse young market?

Heart pounding, she typed in the website address for Ask Apa. It was gone.

She called Haneef, standing up to pace. The phone went straight to voice mail.

Cursing now, she looked him up on Twitter, the only social media app he used regularly, but he had vanished from her contacts. He had blocked her.

What was going on?

Fingers shaking, she dialed Sister Rusul, who picked up on the first ring, her voice warm as she greeted Nada.

"Did we have a conference call I missed? Let me check my calendar to make sure I haven't anything else before we talk."

"Sister Rusul, wait," Nada said, but she was put on hold. Sister Rusul sounded clueless. Nada wondered if this was all a misunderstanding.

Sister Rusul returned, chirping that she had fifteen minutes before her next meeting, and that she had been delighted to watch the first trial run of the app.

"You must be excited. I hope this will lead to many good things for you, Nada. And maybe even one good thing for you and Haneef? I know I sound like a matchmaking aunty, but I can dream."

"Where is your son right now?" Nada said.

Sister Rusul paused. "He said he would be coming in to see me this afternoon. Is something the matter? I hope you have not argued again about the advertising revenue. He did say he had a few large backers he wanted to run past me, but . . ." Sister Rusul's voice trailed off, as if sensing something over the phone line. "What has happened?" she asked, a note of alarm creeping into her voice.

Nada quickly told her about the Google alert and then sent her the link to the article. She waited on the line as Sister Rusul read. After a moment, the older woman gasped, clearly in shock. "*Astaghfirullah*," she breathed.

"Did you know about this?" Nada asked quietly.

"No. No. I knew nothing, *wallahi*," Sister Rusul said, her voice wild. "There must be an explanation. Nada, I will call you right back."

But she didn't call her right back. Nada informed her supervisor that she wasn't feeling well, and drove home. Making excuses to her mother, Nada headed upstairs to her room and tumbled into bed. She willed her phone to ring, while she read and reread the article.

Sister Rusul finally called her back three hours later. Her voice was muted and raspy, as if she had spent the entire time since their earlier call alternately crying and screaming. She broke the news swiftly. "My son has done a terrible thing. He has been planning this for months. I am so sorry, Nada."

"No," Nada said, willing this all to be a bad dream. She had hoped Sister Rusul would say it had all been a misunderstanding, a mistake the three of them could laugh about.

"He had investors lined up and a DevOps team hired. He denies that he stole your idea, but the facts speak for themselves. This is all my fault," she said, and quietly started to cry on the other end of the line.

Nada, feeling numb, tried to comfort the older woman as best she could, even as her world crumbled around her. She had lost Ask Apa, just as she had lost Baz. There was nothing left now.

"He said you did not have a partnership agreement in place. Is that true, Nada?" Sister Rusul asked, when she was in control once more.

"I trusted him," Nada said quietly. "I've known him my entire life."

"He has had . . . issues in the past, *habibti*, but he promised he had changed."

Nada closed her eyes and was instantly subsumed by deep shame as the enormity of what had happened hit her. How could she have been so stupid? She had foolishly accepted Sister Rusul's words. The excitement of watching her dream come to life before her eyes had been too tempting.

I deserve this, Nada thought. The idea settled into the very marrow of her bones and made itself part of her core. *I brought this on myself. This is my fault, my fault, my fault. God is punishing me for marrying Baz, for reaching for joy when I should have waited, and then for breaking his heart. This is what I deserve.*

Sister Rusul was still speaking, and Nada struggled to focus on her words.

"I accept full responsibility. Just Her Co. will pay for the start-up capital in its entirety, with no ROI expected. But please, Nada, for the sake of our friendship, let us try to resolve this between family. You are like a daughter to me."

She was talking about a few thousand dollars when Haneef already had investors on board for millions, according to the news report. Sister Rusul's money was a small drop in the bucket. It was more than she deserved. The thought of fighting in court for what was hers exhausted her. "I won't sue," Nada said dully.

"I will make this right," Sister Rusul said, and she sounded more steady, now that she had a plan. "I will make sure Ask Apa becomes a reality, just as you dreamed. It is the least I can do."

Except her app would be far behind Ukhti. If it did come out, it would be considered nothing more than a dupe, a copycat.

"You can still do so much good with your idea, Nada. This is simply a bump in the road."

Nada had dared to want more. She had banished Baz, had allowed fear to overtake her. And she had listened to Sister Rusul's advice to focus on her own dreams instead of trying to build a life with the man she was still dreaming about nightly.

"You will rebuild. I will have my lawyer—*not* the one who helped my son, he is fired—draft an agreement between us. This is a stumble only. Trust me."

But Nada didn't. She wasn't sure she would trust anyone—even herself—ever again. Maybe a larger, more ambitious life was not in the cards for her. Maybe it would be better to dream smaller, more manageable dreams.

That night, she broke the news to her family. After a tearful phone call between her mother and Sister Rusul, an almost thirty-year friendship lay in tatters. Nada's family took her side, but they were also barely staying afloat, with Waqas's impending divorce proceedings and Jamal's deteriorating physical health. They hugged Nada and told her they would support her, but she could tell they were relieved when she dropped it. After two days, Nada returned to work.

Six months later, she launched Ask Apa on her own, because she couldn't stand to ask Sister Rusul or her father for more help. It was a stripped-down version of her initial dream and made barely a ripple in the start-up world. The article that called it the "knockoff Ukhti for South Asians" particularly stung.

When Sister Rusul quietly offered to buy the Ask Apa business a few years later for a respectable sum, she refused. Instead, she went to work every day, bickered with her mother, hung out with her friends, teased her brothers, gave up on finding love, and saved money. She opened an RRSP and savings account, and invested in sensible index funds like the rational, low-risk person she resolved to be from now on. As she settled into her new, quiet life with her new, smaller dreams, she told herself that she was happy—and nearly believed it.

CHAPTER TWENTY-SIX

Present day

The litigator Waqas put Nada in touch with was an old university friend of his named Qamar, who was now a junior partner at a large downtown firm that specialized in commercial law. Her specialty was IP litigation. She called promptly at six and listened patiently as Nada related the entire story. Nada knew she came across as incredibly naive, but Qamar was warm and encouraging on the phone, and only interrupted to ask insightful questions.

"This definitely sounds like theft of intellectual property and breach of copyright, both of which are actionable wrongdoings," Qamar said once Nada finished explaining the situation. "Before we go any further, I have to ask: What is your ideal outcome? I suspect that Mr. El-Haad would prefer to settle, provided you have proof of wrongdoing. Is that what you'd like, money for lost income? If you know what you want, it will be easier to plan strategy."

Nada thought about this question. She had been so nervous when they first started talking, but as she relived the events from five years ago, she grew angry all over again. "His entire career is based on something he stole from me," she said. "I tried to put it behind me, but I can't. Especially because I've come to suspect he is a serial offender who has stolen other people's work as well."

"That's usually the case in these situations." Qamar dropped her professional mask for a moment and her voice warmed. "Your brother asked my advice about this a few years ago, you know," she said, taking Nada off-guard. "I told him you had to have proof, otherwise it would lead to an expensive forensic examination of computer code and a battle that would come down to character, which could be invasive and humiliating for everyone. The best thing you can hope for, in my opinion, is a settlement."

"I have proof," Nada said. "I made copies of my original code, and I have the texts and emails Haneef sent me from when we first started working together. I never pursued it for a variety of reasons."

Nada could hear the scratching of a pen on paper as the lawyer took notes. "It can take a while to process trauma. Some people react immediately, but oftentimes there are intense personal relationships at stake, which complicate matters. I understand why you waited. Mr. El-Haad was a close family friend who took advantage of your inexperience."

Nada gripped the phone tightly in her hand at these words. Qamar was right; Haneef had exploited her.

"While Ukhti is well known, it has not done as well as people have been led to believe," the lawyer said thoughtfully. "A colleague of mine, his firm handled the deal when it went public, and there were rumors of some security irregularities. I think your friend Haneef has been lining his own pockets in addition to engaging in predatory behavior. But I need to warn you that once news of your suit gets out, you won't be able to discuss this with anyone."

"Only my close friends and family know the real story," Nada said.

Qamar paused meaningfully. "No, I mean that if we decide to move forward and I file the paperwork, it will be in the system. Before that happens, however, sometimes it doesn't hurt to get your story out there in other ways. A young woman with an idealistic business

plan she dreamed up to help her Muslim community, taken advantage
of by a family friend with a history of shady business practices? The
court of public opinion can be a powerful ally in these situations. Not
that I'm suggesting anything, of course."

After they hung up, Nada thought about Qamar's non-suggestion.
The reason that Haneef had managed to achieve success in the first
place was because she hadn't said anything, both out of respect for
Sister Rusul and from a deep sense of shame. She had been embarrassed at how willing she had been to believe Haneef's lies, how
eager she had been to jump into business without any due diligence.

There was a deeper reason too. Because Ukhti had come so close
on the heels of what had happened with Baz, a part of her believed
she didn't deserve any better. She had caused inexplicable pain to the
love of her life; it made sense that her other dream, to launch Ask
Apa into the stratosphere, should meet a similar fate. It was karma. It
was what she deserved.

Misplaced guilt, her therapist called it years later. Nada had somehow convinced herself that she needed to be held accountable and
punished for one set of behaviors by being taken advantage of in
other ways. What she really needed was to be more kind and empa-
thetic to who she had been at twenty-two and twenty-three.

In any case, the facts remained: because she hadn't said anything,
Ask Apa had been declared an Ukhti copycat, and she a wannabe
techpreneur who simply didn't have the experience, knowledge,
and wisdom that her older, wiser male counterpart did. She was
just a girl who should be happy with the foam from other people's
waves.

She opened Twitter and started drafting a thread. It was time to
tell the truth.

Bismillah. This story will name names. Haneef El-Haad, community golden boy and CEO of beloved #UkhtiApp, is a fraud. He stole the idea from me. I finally feel brave enough to share this story. Oh, and I kept receipts.

Eight years ago, I had a bad rishta. My fellow #desi sisters, you know what I mean. He was clueless. He handed me a brochure of the ideal qualities he was looking for. Wife-shopping, the fav Brown pastime. I set him straight. Here's where the story gets strange: he thanked me. Never had a sister do that for him, give him some good advice. He called me "apa." Sister.

A light bulb went off in my mind.

Most people don't have that same community anymore in their daily lives. Sure, some of us find community through friends, mosque, temple, church, synagogue. Most of us just get by. But everyone needs a wise sister to set them straight sometimes.

What if I made a community-specific app that could provide guidance, advice, resources targeted for the clueless #Muslim boys and #Muslim women?

I started to work on @AskApa a few years later. Haneef El-Haad, a close family friend with a #tech background, joined as a consultant, then as a collaborator. He said he had access to VC funding. He said we were a team. I believed him.

We worked on code, design, marketing together. He wanted to monetize through advertising. I wanted to keep it free, a resource for my community and other communities like mine. I was 23 and naive.

Right before launch, he stole my idea, my code, and launched #Ukhti. His name, my idea, tweaked so he could turn a profit for investors.

He got all the attention, fame, money. He stole my future from me. I suspect he's done this to others. Reach out if this happened to you. Haneef is a predator. Spread the word by retweeting and using the hashtag #CrookedUkhti.

She read it over a few dozen times, and then hit "Tweet all." She took screenshots and posted on her Instagram. Next, she texted her parents and brothers to give them a heads-up about what she had done. Afterward, she forced herself to go outside for some fresh air and drank a cup of chai before checking her accounts.

The reaction was overwhelming. Her Twitter thread had been retweeted, quote-tweeted, and screenshot. The comments started piling up, many commiserating with what happened and applauding her for speaking out, standing up. There was a fair bit of shock sprinkled within the reactions.

I use Ukhti. I can't believe this.

I've never even heard of Ask Apa. Is this for real?

El-Haad is a crook. He did the same thing to my cousin's friend. DM me for details.

The trolls found her that evening, and they came clutching pitch-forks, flaming torches, bigotry, and misogyny.

> Sister, this is a private matter, you should have followed prophetic tradition and remained patient and prayed about it instead.

> Girls can't code. You're a jealous bitch.

> Haneef El-Haad is another victim of #MeToo #CancelCulture. Never heard of Ask Apa, never heard of Nada Syed. This is #fakenews and she's a liar. #BelieveHim.

There was more, but Nada's head was spinning. In her DMs, friends and acquaintances reached out, asking if it was true, how they could help, or for more information. A few people she knew accused her of making the story up because Ask Apa had failed and she was bitter. She was pretty sure they had been early investors in Ukhti.

There were a few more posts claiming that Haneef had done the same thing to them, and Nada responded to those first. One was a young woman who had been in undergrad with Haneef. He had ripped off her idea for a culturally specific financial adviser bot, though her idea had only been in the early stages. Another claimed that her cousin's friend had actually partnered with Haneef on a grocery app, and after they had designed the platform together, he ghosted her. Nada suspected there might be a few more. Qamar texted her a thumbs-up emoji and promised to call in a few days to plan their approach.

Neither Ukhti nor Haneef had issued a formal response yet. She had tagged both accounts in her original tweet. A part of her hoped that Haneef was panic-dialing his lawyer right now. She was glad that she had sought out legal advice before opening the floodgates. If he tried to countersue, she would be ready.

She made *wudu*, and prayed *Isha*. When she checked her tweet one last time before bed, it had already been liked nearly ten thousand times and retweeted by several thousand people. Nada had anticipated her father's reaction to be instant anxiety, but he had surprised her by sending an encouraging text and even offered to pay for her lawyer. Narjis sent a text that let Nada know that the Twitter thread had even breached the WhatsApp aunty circles. Narjis had yet to complain about the dent to the family's reputation Nada's new notoriety would likely bring. Overall, it was a more positive outcome than Nada had anticipated. Her family really hated Haneef, and the thought gratified her.

When Nada woke up the next morning, her first thought was about Baz. She wondered if he had seen her tweet somehow, and whether he cared.

The second thought she had was for another business idea. It was the first time she had thought about starting a business since Ask Apa. Reaching for her phone, she started making notes.

CHAPTER TWENTY-SEVEN

Present day

Haleema insisted that Nada dress up for the rehearsal dinner. Her friend dropped off an exquisite teal blue salwar kameez that had a shimmery net overlay and two-inch-wide gold embroidery running down the front.

"I'm so proud of you," Haleema said as she handed Nada the garment bag a week after she'd publicly called out Haneef.

"Thanks, but it's nothing to be proud of. I should have done it years ago." Nada shifted warily and scanned the sidewalk in front of the house. The day before, Waqas claimed to have spotted a few people loitering, and she was starting to get paranoid. She hadn't bothered hiding her identity when she tweeted, or taking any steps to protect her privacy, and in addition to the usual mean comments, she had received a few threats of violence.

"You did it now, and I know how hard it was," Haleema said firmly. "When you show up to the rehearsal dinner, you're going to look so hot and show all the haters what's up."

Nada startled. "What haters?"

Haleema waved her hand as if swatting a fly. "People are always haters when you speak the truth. Don't worry, Zayn and I have your back."

"What about Baz?" Nada blurted before she could stop herself. She had thought about him constantly this past week. Finally revealing the truth about Ukhti and Ask Apa had caused a dam to burst within her, and now thoughts of Baz dominated her mind. Well, him and her new business ideas. She had half-filled a notebook, and though on social media her actions were alternately lauded and condemned, for the first time in years she felt . . . free. Lighter. Happy?

"Who knows what Baz thinks. I barely see him these days. He's been helping Zayn with some top-secret project, while I've been running around doing wedding stuff. Did I tell you the latest update? The drummers we hired for our entrance, a bhangra troupe called Desi Beat, had to cancel because, get this, they made it onto *Canada's Got Talent*!"

Nada nodded and smiled as her friend rambled about the wedding details. Haleema confided that the guest list had spiraled out of control and now approached a thousand people. The caterer, Kamran, had to subcontract to a few other vendors to handle the number.

"It will be the event of the season," Nada said.

Haleema smiled, her cheeks rosy with excitement. "I'm so happy. And now that Haneef is finally getting the hate he deserves, life is perfect."

Nada was touched by her loyalty. Haleema was outspoken and never shied away from running after what she wanted, or backed away from a fight. It must have been difficult for her to sit back and watch Nada embrace passivity in the face of Haneef's betrayal. Nada was impressed, actually, that her friend had managed to contain herself from seeking bloody vengeance for five whole years.

She invited Haleema to stay for dinner, but she checked the time on her phone and started bouncing on her feet. "Too much nervous tension," she explained. "I can't sleep; there's so much to do and the wedding is in one week! Okay, quick, distract me. I don't want to become one of those women obsessed with their wedding."

"Yes, you do," Nada said fondly. "You've dreamt about becoming one of those women your entire life."

Haleema scowled playfully. "Tell me what's going on with you. Have you sued the Evil One yet?"

Nada and Qamar were still gathering evidence to support her claims, which had led to a lot of digging through old paperwork, looking for emails with dates and time stamps, sifting through code and plans and her earliest ideas for Ask Apa. It was exhausting, and Nada felt like she was working just as hard to prove Haneef's guilt as she had to launch Ask Apa in the first place. A few more people had reached out and shared stories about his deceit, and Qamar agreed with Nada's assessment that Haneef had gotten bolder and less ethical as time passed. Mostly because he kept getting away with his shady actions, with zero consequences.

Nada updated Haleema on her progress and shared the recent news that Ukhti had formally responded, first with a cease-and-desist letter, and just yesterday with a countersuit. Nothing Qamar hadn't anticipated, of course, so Nada was trying not to worry about it too much. Outraged, Haleema offered to hire someone to "take care of the situation" and save everyone a lot of money. Nada smiled and changed the subject.

"Any tips for the rehearsal dinner? I've never been to one before," Nada said.

Haleema shrugged. "It's just a party to kick-start the wedding. Zayn has been so busy it will be good to have fun with our best friends and close family. Don't be late, and make sure you look hot." She winked, and Nada was instantly suspicious.

"Are you trying to set me up with someone again? I told you, I'm not interested."

Haleema laughed and danced away. "I make no promises," she called, trotting toward her Mercedes G-Wagon. "Except that he's cute and you deserve to have some fun. Love you!"

Nada waved until her friend drove away. Then she caught the eye of someone standing across the street, and her heart started to race until she recognized the teenage daughter of her neighbor from a few doors down. Nada went back to her room to continue working on her case.

Haleema had rented an elegant party hall at the city's botanical garden for the rehearsal dinner. The Friday night event would kick off an entire weekend of celebration: Saturday afternoon was the *nikah* wedding, which would be followed by the *walima* reception, and brunch for family on Sunday. Unlike the *nikah* and *walima*, the rehearsal dinner guest list remained small, about fifty people.

Nada dressed carefully, mindful that this would be the first time she would see Baz since that awful night in front of Nanima's Chai Shop. The outfit Haleema had chosen was flattering, and Nada accessorized it with a chunky turquoise necklace, a muted gold–colored hijab, and a large gold bangle on her arm. Her mother joined her in the foyer as she slipped into nude heels and secured her hijab.

"You look pretty," Narjis said, and Nada flashed her a smile.

Her parents hadn't been angry with her for publicly calling out Haneef. While they weren't eager for a fight or the public scrutiny that a lawsuit would bring, they appreciated the change in their daughter. Already Nada was thinking about her future with hope and optimism, and her parents had noticed. They had always noticed, she realized. That was probably why her mother had cut off Sister Rusul in the first place. She knew how deeply her daughter had been hurt by Haneef's actions.

Narjis held out her phone to show Nada a text. The message was long; the sender was Sister Rusul. Nada read quickly, first with alarm and then with the faint stirrings of hope.

My dearest Narjis, I have nothing to offer other than another apology. I read Nada's account of Haneef's actions online, and I was horrified and grieved once more. As a mother yourself, I am sure you understand the great pain my son's actions have caused me, both regarding Nada and his other past behavior. It was not until I read her story that I fully understood that Haneef has not made sincere attempts to change and repent, as he promised me on numerous occasions. I have told him that while I will always love him as my son, I will no longer look away from the actions of the man he has become, or the harm he has caused others. I severed ties, and it has taken me until today to find the courage to reach out to you. You have always been my dearest friend. I will be in Toronto in a few months' time. Could we perhaps meet for coffee or a meal? Please pass along my regards to your entire family, and let Nada know that if she requires a witness for her lawsuit, I am willing.

All my love,
Rusul

Nada stared at her mother. "I don't know what to say. Did you respond?"

Narjis wiped a tear from her eye. "Not yet, but I will. My friend will need support after this. Her daughter doesn't live in the country anymore, and she has no other family in Vancouver. Haneef was a support to her, but she couldn't lie to herself about the truth of who he had become anymore. May Allah guide him."

"*Ameen*," Nada said. She meant it. The text made her sad, and furious. In order to benefit himself, Haneef had made decisions that hurt her and others, including his mother, the only person he actually cared about. She hated him.

"Have fun tonight," Narjis said, opening the door while Nada grabbed her purse, phone, and black ballet flats, in case her heels grew uncomfortable later. "Make sure Haleema enjoys herself. She was so jumpy when she dropped off the dress for you. She nearly started crying when I asked her about the wedding plans."

The party hall featured a solarium that looked out on beds of blooming florals, arranged in a spiral pattern. Inside, half a dozen tables had been set up family-style, and serving staff circulated with platters of appetizers: chicken puff pastries, juicy tandoori shrimp, tiny pitas with a dollop of creamy hummus in the center, falafel balls garnished with parsley, fizzy passion-fruit and mango mocktails. Guests mingled, and Nada recognized Haleema's parents, Noor and Hassan, holding court. They had flown in a few days ago and, according to Haleema, had found fault with every decision she had made about the wedding. No wonder she was near the breaking point.

Nada tried to locate her friend or Zayn, but neither could be found. His parents hadn't shown up yet, either. Nada noticed that the other guests, even the familiar faces, avoided her or stared. She smiled back at a few acquaintances, but they didn't return her friendly gesture. Most averted their eyes or leaned over to whisper into friends' ears. Awkwardness prickled the back of her neck. She was used to being an unnoticed wallflower at events, and she did not enjoy her internet infamy. Ukhti had been popular, especially among the younger set.

She filled her hands with a drink and three paneer pakoras in an effort to distract herself. She wondered where Haleema could be—likely getting dressed or putting the last touches on her makeup. But all thoughts of her friend disappeared when she recognized a familiar set of broad shoulders.

Baz stood with his back to her, wearing the same gray suit he had worn to the gala at Deen&Dunya, and she admired his well-shaped form. As if he could feel the heat of her wistful stare, Baz turned around, revealing a woman perched on her tiptoes beside him. Firdous was whispering into Baz's ear. Something dark slithered into Nada's veins, and she was by his side before she realized her purpose.

His polite, inscrutable face looked down at her.

"Hi," she said.

"Assalamu alaikum, Nayla," Firdous chirped. She was dressed in a tight white dress that hugged her curves and skimmed her ankles, adorned with beadwork at the hem and neck. Her hijab, also white, was pinned back from her face, and her makeup was heavy on the glam. One could easily mistake them for the bride and groom, Nada thought grimly.

"You know my name is Nada. Drop the act," she said, without removing her eyes from Baz's face. He took a sip of his drink—plain water, of course.

Firdous bristled. "If you're here to cause trouble, you might as well leave now. We've got enough on our hands already."

Baz silenced her with a warning glance, and the darkness in Nada's veins gathered. This woman knew something that she didn't. Was it about Haleema, Zayn, or Baz?

Before Nada could strike back, Baz intercepted, finally addressing Nada directly. "Let me get you a few more of those pakoras. Coming, Firdous?"

The young woman hesitated over whether to trot after Baz or stay put. In the end, her instinct for chaos won out, and she waved him away with a request for falafel balls.

"Healthier than fried paneer," she simpered.

"Deep-fried chickpeas? Hardly," Nada retorted.

With a faint smile, Baz drifted away, leaving the women to it. Nada willed herself to remain calm. Whether Haleema was currently present or not, she wouldn't appreciate a scene at her rehearsal dinner.

"I read your little Twitter thread. You're lucky Haneef hasn't shared his version of events," Firdous said, and Nada's internal promise not to start trouble took a running leap out the window.

"He mentioned he was 'helping' you with a business idea," Nada said. "Just a friendly warning: Haneef has a history of stealing other people's work. If you don't believe me, just look up #CrookedUkhti."

Uncertainty flickered in Firdous's eyes, but she settled on mulish resistance. "Haneef told me you had a thing for him, and when he turned you down, you started to spread nasty rumors."

Nada laughed out loud, which only seemed to irritate Firdous further.

"I think it's pathetic when a woman is so spiteful," she said. "You're ruining his life, you know. Ukhti is really important to the Muslim community, so why are you trying to destroy it? Did you know that over two million people downloaded the app in the first six months, from all around the world?"

A pang went through Nada. Her work had had an impact, after all. "He's not a good guy, Firdous," she said quietly. "He stole from me and others, and he'll do the same to you. We might not like each other, but I don't want anything bad to happen to you."

Firdous lifted her chin. "I'm not as stupid as you were," she taunted. "I won't let my personal feelings get in my way, and I'll make sure to sign a partnership agreement."

Nada blinked. "How did you know about that? I didn't mention it in my post."

Firdous shrugged. "Haneef told me. He's being really honest and up front."

"Wait, so was I stupid because I didn't make him sign a partnership agreement, or was I spiteful because he rejected my advances? I'm confused. It's almost as if the person trying to sell these theories is trying to cover something up," Nada said pleasantly.

Baz returned with a selection of appetizers. "What theories?" he asked.

"Nothing, Bazzy," Firdous said. "Just girl talk. You like Haneef, right?"

Baz looked at Nada. "Absolutely not."

Firdous seemed taken aback by his vehemence. "You just haven't heard his side," she started.

"He doesn't have a side. I believe Nada," Baz said firmly.

Firdous pouted and excused herself, ignoring the falafel balls. Nada helped herself to Firdous's plate and stood beside Baz in comfortable silence.

"Haleema told me you've been helping your brother with a top-secret project," she said, reaching for a neutral topic.

Baz took another sip of his water. "I'm producing Zayn's latest album." Nada stared at him in surprise. "Someone told me I was too talented to give up on music." He smiled slightly at his plate. "I'm thinking of starting that talent agency for Muslim artists you suggested."

"That's brilliant, Baz!" Nada said, more loudly than she intended.

He shrugged, but the tips of his ears were red with embarrassment. "Might as well put that MBA to good use. I could use another project, now that D&D is a phenomenal success."

"Your modesty will take you far," she teased, and the glint in his eye warmed her. "When did you get your MBA?"

"I finished my undergrad two years after we . . . ," he trailed off. "My parents suggested I get an MBA. You know, to turn my arts degree into something useful."

Nada laughed. He had always been able to make her laugh. They looked around at the other guests, and their silence took on a weighted meaning.

Baz shifted subtly toward her. "How are you doing?" he asked.

Nada, chewing on a chicken puff, thought about his question. "I wish I had gone public with what Haneef did years ago. But I'm glad I spoke up now."

Baz nodded. "Haneef tried to get in with D&D. My dad was impressed with his spiel. He's a big talker, and he knows the right things to say, but I never trusted him."

"Why not?" Nada asked.

"You told me about Ask Apa before. I knew he was Sister Rusul's son. That family is bad news."

Even though she agreed, Nada had to stick up for her mother's friend. "Sister Rusul isn't responsible for her son's behavior."

"You're right. If you take bad advice, or follow a bad example, there's only one person at fault," Baz said evenly.

Nada flushed. He was still angry; he hadn't forgiven her. Most likely, he never would. "I'm going to find Haleema," she said in an overly bright tone. "This is late, even for her." She walked away quickly and texted her friend.

Haleema replied immediately: I'm in the gardens outside.

When Nada approached her friend, she noticed that Haleema's eyes were red-rimmed. "What's going on? Where's Zayn?" Nada asked, suddenly alarmed. A feeling of foreboding trickled along her arm. Something wasn't right.

Haleema pasted a brilliant smile on her face. She was resplendent in the green *lengha* she had picked out at Dulhaniya, with a twinkly diamond *tika* ornament on her forehead and a matching necklace that gleamed against the folds of her dark green hijab. "Just having a mini meltdown. It's fine."

"Can I help?" Nada asked.

Haleema shook her head, dislodging the *tika*. She fixed it with trembling fingers. "Wedding nerves. How is it going inside? Are my parents doing a good job hosting?"

"Definitely," Nada lied. "We're all waiting for the stars of the show to make their entrance."

Haleema giggled, a high-pitched noise that rang hollow to Nada's ears. "Just me for now. Zayn is running late."

"For his own rehearsal dinner?"

"He's working on that project I told you about."

"But Baz is already here," Nada said, confused. "He told me they're working on it together. Haleema, what's going on?"

Her friend swept past her, face set. "Nothing. Let's go inside."

Haleema wrenched the doors open, framing herself in the entranceway. The guests stopped their conversations to stare at the bride, and then a muted cheer went up among the crowd. Nada noticed that Noor and Hassan only briefly looked at their daughter before resuming their conversation with friends.

Firdous hurried to Haleema. "How *are* you?" she asked, fake sympathy oozing from her pores. "I think what you're doing is really brave."

Nada wanted to scream. What was going on? A grim-faced Baz approached, took Firdous's arm, and steered her away.

Haleema began to mingle with her guests, that weird smile firmly affixed to her face. Nada was about to drag her friend to a corner and demand to know whose legs she would be breaking tonight, when a familiar voice sent a chill down her spine.

"Glad to see you're having fun after setting my career on fire." Haneef was dressed in a black suit, but his disheveled hair and the dark circles under his eyes gave her some satisfaction.

"You look terrible. What are you doing here?" Nada asked.

"Firdous told me you'd be here," Haneef said, taking a step closer. "She's been a really useful friend to me. She thought it would be good if you and I talked. Apparently, you've been filling her ears with more lies."

Nada silently cursed Firdous. "There's no way Haleema or Zayn invited you. This is a private event. Leave."

"Not until we talk. Because of you, my mother cut me off. Does that make you happy?" Haneef's face was filled with anger, but his voice remained calm. He hadn't come here to start a scene, and he was aware that he had a limited amount of time before his presence was noted.

"You stole my idea," Nada shot back. "You broke your promise to Sister Rusul about trying to change and make amends."

Haneef shook his head. "You thoughtless bitch. She promised to lend me money. Ukhti is sunk without it."

Nada narrowed her eyes at him and was about to retort, when a streak of green and gold passed in front of her.

"Get away from my friend!" Haleema seethed. Her eyes were wide and filled with rage.

Haneef, startled, put his hands up. "I'm leaving. Hope you have a really great wedding. Once the groom shows up," he added, smirking.

With a cry, Haleema attacked. Haneef danced back, and she tripped over the long skirt of her *lengha*. There was a sickening crack as the back of her head connected with the sturdy travertine tile. Haleema lay sprawled on the ground. She tried to sit up, then moaned, holding her right ankle, her skirts splayed about her.

Horrified, Nada sprang into action. "Give us some space," she ordered, and the circle of shocked guests obediently took a step back. She looked for Baz. "Call an ambulance, and then wait for them outside. She might have a concussion, and I think she broke her ankle."

Baz nodded, reaching for his phone.

"Firdous, get some ice from the servers," Nada said. "Where is Noor Aunty?"

Haleema's mother appeared at their side, looking faintly nauseous.

"What did Haleema do now?" Kneeling beside her dazed daughter, Noor said, "Darling, sit up, people are watching."

Exasperated, Nada explained that Haleema wasn't pulling a stunt. She asked Noor to make sure the guests were taken care of. The older woman hurried off, relieved to be given a manageable task. Firdous delivered the ice and then disappeared. Haneef had presumably slithered back into the primordial ooze.

The paramedics arrived and were directed inside by a grim-looking Baz. Haleema was carefully loaded onto a stretcher. There was a flash as someone took a picture, and Nada rounded on the perpetrator, furious.

"Delete that right now," she commanded. She glared at the onlookers. "If I see a single picture or video of this uploaded anywhere, I will come for you." Abashed, the culprit deleted the picture and slunk away.

Nada climbed inside the ambulance with her friend. Baz promised to make sure the rest of the party was taken care of.

"Tell Zayn," she urged. "Haleema said he's working late on his project. He'll want to come to the hospital."

Baz's face tightened, but he nodded, and said he would be in touch.

Inside the ambulance, the paramedic adjusted the ice around Haleema's ankle and then examined her head, her hijab loosened around her. "Nasty bump," she said. "We'll let the doctor decide if it's anything more. What's your name?"

Haleema readily answered the paramedic's series of questions until she asked, "What event were you at?" Then Haleema's lip quivered, and she looked beyond the paramedic's kind face to Nada's worried one. "I was at my rehearsal dinner," she said in a low voice. "Except there isn't going to be a wedding. Zayn called it off two days ago."

CHAPTER TWENTY-EIGHT

Present day

'll kill him," Nada said, pacing.

Haleema was settled in a curtained-off bed while they waited for the emergency room physician to see them. They were lucky: the ER wasn't that busy, and they'd made it through triage quickly. Haleema was still in a lot of pain; her ankle was puffed up and starting to turn purple, and she seemed disoriented.

"Does he think he can do better than you? I'm going to hunt that pretty boy down and make his face a lot more interesting," Nada said.

Haleema smiled weakly. "Stop trying to make me laugh. They only gave me regular Tylenol and it hasn't kicked in yet."

"Fine. I'll wait until they give you something stronger, and *then* I'll find your ex-fiancé." Nada slowed her pacing to look at her friend. Tears ran silently down Haleema's face, and it was this more than anything that nearly broke Nada. Her friend never cried. She screamed, fought, nagged, and cajoled. She never backed down, and she never let go.

"Why doesn't anybody want me?" Haleema asked in a small voice.

Nada was at her side in an instant. "That's not true. I can tell you one thing: whatever this is, it's not about you." She gently asked what had happened, and Haleema explained.

Zayn had called her two days ago, and he had seemed out of sorts. While Haleema was filling him in on the itinerary for their honeymoon, he had abruptly interrupted and said that he was starting to have doubts.

"I told him, 'Okay, if you don't want to go to the French Riviera for our honeymoon, we can book something else last minute. Jamaica is really nice, or maybe the Maldives?' I feel like such an idiot. I had no idea." Haleema's lip started trembling.

Nada resisted the urge to throw something. "What happened next?" she urged instead.

"He said that he was having doubts about *us*, that maybe we were rushing into this, that he was starting to wonder if we were making a massive mistake, because marriage is forever, and what if we were tying our futures together without really knowing what we were getting into. Because being together involves *sacrifice*, and he has dreams he wants to follow for himself . . ." She trailed off into tears, her shoulders shaking. Nada held her until she calmed. "I told him we should talk about this, that I know marriage is scary and that we haven't been engaged for very long, but isn't this what our parents, and their parents before them, did? I reminded him how good we were—*are* together." Haleema turned large hazel-green eyes to Nada, beseeching. "We were happy, right?"

Nada hesitated for only a moment. "He lit up every time he saw you," she said honestly. "You were happy by his side."

Haleema nodded. "That's what I told him. Except he refused to meet me. He didn't want to talk. He said his mind was made up and the wedding was off. That's why his parents didn't show up today. They know what he did."

"But Baz was at the rehearsal dinner?" Nada said. There was no way he didn't know.

"Baz supported me. I called him when Zayn wouldn't talk to me. I told him I wasn't going to cancel the wedding. My parents had flown in the day before, and they had paid for everything. How could I tell them my fiancé jilted me three days before the *nikah*?"

Nada stayed silent. She knew her friend had a tense relationship with her parents at the best of times. Haleema had moved to Canada from Dubai when she was eighteen to attend university, and only returned to visit her parents once a year. Her parents had very high expectations of their only child, and they were highly critical of Haleema. Nothing she did was ever good enough for them.

"People get scared," Haleema said in a low voice. "Everyone gets cold feet. I know Zayn loves me. He'll come to his senses. In the meantime, I thought there was no point canceling. Our deposits were gone anyway."

"How did Firdous find out?" Nada asked, remembering the knowing smirk on Queen Bee's face.

"I told you, she's always around lately. Baz was at the office when I called him, hysterical. He told me later that Firdous was eavesdropping. She must have told that bastard Haneef too. I lost it, and now my ankle is broken and I might have a concussion." Haleema closed her eyes, and Nada hugged her tightly.

"Do you still want to marry Zayn?" Nada asked. Her mind was racing, but before she leaped into action, she needed to know what Haleema truly wanted, in her heart of hearts. "After everything he put you through, maybe he isn't the person for you. We can deal with the fallout, your parents' reaction and everything else, later. After this accident, no one will blink if you cancel or postpone the wedding. We can run away to the French Riviera or the Maldives, or to Disney World, without Zayn. #GirlsTrip."

Haleema smiled, but she was firm when she responded. "The Zayn I know was completely sure about us. I'm not letting him go that easily. If he would just talk to me, I'm sure we could figure this out together. I never wanted a giant wedding; that was all for our parents."

The curtain was pulled aside, and a familiar face in blue scrubs and a black hijab entered, clipboard in hand. Dr. Iqbal grinned at the girls. "If you're going to the Maldives, can I join? I could use a vacation." Nodding at Nada, the young doctor said, "I know you. How's your head? I hope you don't make a habit of getting in the Zaynimals' throwing path." She chuckled at her own joke, but her smile faded when she looked at Haleema, her eyes traveling from the swollen ankle to the rumpled green *lengha*. "Do you want to start at the beginning?" she asked kindly.

Nada stepped out while the doctor began her examination, and called Haleema's mother. She dialed using her friend's phone, and it rang a few times before Noor Aunty picked up. Music was blasting in the background.

"Hello? Haleema? I can't hear you, speak up," Noor shouted into the phone.

"This is Nada. Haleema is with the doctor right now."

The older woman tsk-tsked. "So long?"

"Your daughter is doing okay, but she's shaken up," Nada said pointedly.

Noor Aunty instantly sobered. "Yes, of course. Tell Haleema that everything is fine. Baz is handling it all wonderfully. The food was delicious, and we are enjoying the live entertainment she arranged." The older woman sounded pleased. "She has done a good job. I assume Zayn is with you at the hospital?"

"I'll call back when I have more news," Nada said, and hung up. The plan formulating in her mind coalesced. Once Haleema was settled, she would track Zayn down. Now that she had had some time to calm down and talk to her friend about what she wanted, she knew what she needed to do next. Call it fate or *qadr*, karma, or kismet, but Nada might be the only person in the wedding party, including the bride, who understood what Zayn was going through right now. Six years ago, she had been in a similar position: dealing with enormous pressure, facing a difficult decision, panicking because it felt as if her entire future hung in the balance if she chose wrong. It did and she had. Maybe she could stop Zayn from making the same mistake now. At the very least, she would warn him about what would happen if he chose to walk away, and in the process, threw away the best person she knew.

When Nada rejoined her friend, Dr. Iqbal was explaining what would happen next: Haleema would be taken for an X-ray, to confirm the extent of the break the doctor suspected. She had determined that Haleema had a mild concussion, and cautioned her to take it easy for the next few days. When Dr. Iqbal left to see to her next patient, an orderly took Haleema for the X-ray. Within a few hours, she was discharged from the hospital. Haleema was woozy from pain medication and sporting a new plastic boot to go along with her other gift: a compound ankle fracture.

Nada called an Uber and took her friend straight home, helped her change and get into bed.

"You're a good friend," Haleema said, drowsy from the pain medication. Nada lingered by the bedroom door as her friend started to drift into sleep. "You didn't meet the guy. Cute . . . funny . . . good for you to have someone too . . ." Her eyes closed.

"You can introduce me later," Nada said, her finger on the light switch. "At your wedding, Inshallah."

Nada locked the door behind her, and quickly texted the errant groom from the dark parking lot: This is Nada. Haleema had an accident tonight. She told me everything. We need to talk RIGHT NOW. To his credit, he responded right away with an address. Zayn, the coward, had been hiding from his rehearsal dinner and his future wife in his own house. She called another Uber to take her back to the rehearsal dinner to grab her car, and then drove to Mississauga.

It was late, and traffic was light on the 401 highway that took her to the west end of the city. Nada usually didn't have much reason to drive to Mississauga. She knew that in many ways it mirrored Scarborough in its diversity and large South Asian and Arab population. The Haq family lived on a secluded estate near Lake Ontario. A long driveway led up to a massive granite French colonial–style home set back from the main road. It looked like a new construction, and Nada was impressed despite herself. When she and Baz were together, his parents had been struggling financially, but clearly things had changed in the years since. While her parents had always been comfortably middle class, this level of wealth was eyebrow-raising. She parked in front of the three-car carriage house where Zayn lived. She wondered if Baz shared this apartment, or if he had his own suite of rooms inside the McMansion. Clearly, Deen&Dunya leaned toward the Dunya part.

Nada marched to the small door at the side of the carriage house and rapped sharply. The door opened instantly, almost as if someone had been waiting on the other side. She blinked up into Baz's face. The ice giant had returned.

"What are you doing here?" she asked.

He stepped back to let her in, gesturing toward a narrow flight of stairs that led to the upstairs apartment. "The rehearsal dinner was winding down. I thought I might be able to help here, instead."

At the top of the stairs, Nada walked directly into a small and untidy living room space, which she took in with one swift glance. Pushed up against one wall was a shoe rack overflowing with sneakers and high-end loafers, and above it were hooks on the wall for jackets. The bulk of the room was taken up by a large gray sectional sofa and a flat-screen television. Video game consoles and a sound system were lined up neatly on a low table. The walls were bare, the lighting bright white, and a narrow corridor presumably led to a bedroom and bathroom at the back of the apartment. She poked her head behind a partition wall, where a tiny kitchenette was arranged, the sink filled with dirty dishes. Nada wondered if Zayn was used to others cleaning up after him. As if confirming her suspicions, Baz started to tidy up, removing a hoodie and a pair of socks from the sofa. He awkwardly asked if she wanted tea. She nodded and took a seat, picking up a framed picture of Haleema laughing, Zayn beaming by her side.

"Their engagement," Baz said briefly. "It was a small thing at my parents' house."

Nada remembered. She had been invited but had made up some excuse last minute, terrified of bumping into Baz and ruining her friend's moment. The irony was not lost on her now. Haleema lay injured in her bed forty miles away, while Nada sat in her fiancé's living room, making small talk with her own estranged husband. Life really was bizarre on occasion.

"What did your parents have to say about Zayn's decision?" Nada asked.

Baz shrugged. "They know my brother can be unpredictable. They like Haleema a lot, but it's his decision ultimately. They're not going to force him into a marriage he doesn't want."

She thought about that. Were his parents right? Was this a fool's errand? No, she thought. Baz was here; he believed his brother was making a mistake. There was still hope for her friend and Zayn. Baz glanced significantly down the hallway.

Nada stood up. "Do you know how to make chai the long way?" she asked casually, and he nodded. Traditional masala chai was cooked slowly on the stove, to allow the cardamom pods, cinnamon sticks, milk, and black tea to intensify in flavor. It was a process that took at least twenty minutes.

Baz looked doubtfully in the direction of his brother's kitchenette.

"Pretty sure Zayn has never turned the stove on. He uses the oven to store his Air Jordans." Then, catching her eye, he started walking toward the stairs. "I'll find supplies at the big house."

She waited for the door to click shut before heading down the hall. Clearly, Baz had tried to talk to his brother already, but the situation was desperate. She knocked on the door once, before letting herself in. The room was small, better suited to staff than the Haq heir-apparent. A double bed was pushed against the wall beside a window that looked out over the curving driveway, and there was a small table heaped with clothes, a swivel chair, a dresser, and a single night table. The furniture was good quality but minimalist in design. *Haleema would hate this room*, Nada thought.

Zayn was sitting on the bed, dressed in a T-shirt and sweatpants, his head hanging low between his shoulders. He looked up when she entered and jumped to his feet.

"Is Haleema okay?" he asked. "Is she hurt?"

Nada said nothing.

Agony suffused his face, and he collapsed back onto the bed, cradling his head in his hands. "I messed up," he said. "She must hate me."

Nada pushed the miscellaneous junk piled on the chair to the floor and took a seat. "How long have you known about me and Baz?"

Zayn looked up, surprised at her question. No doubt he had expected her to jump straight to the yelling part. But Nada had had plenty of time to think on the long drive west, and she had realized a few things. First, she and Zayn had more in common than she had originally thought. Second, there must have been a catalyst for his decision, and she suspected that it was a deep and abiding fear of the future coupled with a lack of faith in what that future would bring for both him and Haleema—combined with his knowledge of what had happened between Baz and Nada.

"Almost since the beginning," he admitted.

This surprised her. "You never said anything?"

Zayn shrugged. "It was only a suspicion at first. Baz was always shy around girls. I thought maybe he was too afraid to return any of their interest over the years. The only girl he ever mentioned by name was you, the girl he met at Sunday school, and then again at camp, and finally at university. It took me until then to realize he had a thing for you. That some part of him had been waiting for you all along." He looked at her. "He was so happy for a while. Every song he wrote during that time was about you. I used to tease him about it. Then he changed, but he never talked about why. Except I know my brother— he was totally gone over you from the start, but he was also proud. When I met Haleema, and she mentioned your name, I thought if I could just get you in the same room together, the rest would sort itself out. I encouraged her to bring you to the convention. I told her it would be great if we could fix the two of you up. She had no idea."

"Except it didn't work," Nada said slowly.

Zayn nodded, miserable. "I finally confronted him about it a few days ago. He said it was over between you, that he couldn't go back."

Nada flinched, even though Baz had said the same to her.

Zayn continued. "Baz is my younger brother, but we've always had this role reversal. I look up to him. If even he can't make things work with the woman he's been in love with for half his life, what chance do I have? I'm just the screwup my parents never wanted. It's better this way, for everyone."

"It's not better for Haleema," Nada said. "She hasn't stopped crying since you called off the wedding."

Zayn looked as though her words physically hurt him. "What if I can't make her happy? I'll never forgive myself. I love her so much, but how can I be sure this is the right path for both of us?"

Nada was silent. When she had first met Zayn, hadn't the same thought crossed her mind? "Tell me why you agreed to the marriage in the first place," she said.

Zayn seemed taken aback by her question, but he answered readily. "At first it was her smile," he admitted. "Then I heard her laugh, and it just caught my heart. Of course, she's beautiful, but lots of girls are hot—attractive, I mean. Except with Haleema, it was more than that. She wasn't just smart; she was brilliant. I loved that she was good at all the things I wasn't. She's such a nerd, but not obnoxious about it, just . . . interested in learning. In a really intense way. You know?"

Nada did. It was one of the things she admired most about her friend, the way Haleema became engrossed in subjects, the way she was so good at everything, without ever making anyone else feel less. She always encouraged and cheered on the people she loved, and she was fiercely loyal and protective. Just like Baz.

"We haven't known each other for long," Nada began, looking down at her hands, at her bare left ring finger. "I won't claim to know your heart, but I've stood in your shoes, and I've faced the same decision. Take it from someone who's been there and made the wrong choice. Choose love and happiness, not fear. Have faith. Otherwise, the only comfort you'll be left with is that of loving longest, when all hope is gone."

Zayn didn't answer. There was nothing more she could say. The rest was up to him.

When Nada returned to the living room, a cup of cooling chai was waiting on the side table. Of Baz, there was no sign.

CHAPTER TWENTY-NINE

Present day

Narjis and Abbas were waiting for Nada when she returned home late that night, and they peppered her with questions the moment she opened the door.

"What happened at the rehearsal dinner? Is Haleema all right?" Abbas anxiously asked. "Those banquet halls have too many unexpected corners."

"Is it true the wedding is canceled?" Narjis demanded. "Haleema should have insisted on having the *nikah* the moment that boy agreed. Why delay for months just to plan a big party? At her age, she can't afford to wait."

Her parents were so wonderfully predictable: Narjis was single-minded, while Abbas was overly anxious.

"Haleema tripped over her own dress," Nada informed her father, leaving out the part that Haneef had played. "And the wedding is . . . on a break," she told her mother.

"On a break? I can't keep up with you young people and your slang. Is she getting married or not?" Narjis trailed after Nada as she walked over to the stairs to go up to bed.

"Inshallah," Nada replied, hoping that would satisfy her mother. Nobody could argue with "God willing"—except, of course, Narjis.

"Don't give me that Inshallah nonsense, Nada!" she called up the stairs. "And don't think that just because your friend has called off her wedding, you are off the hook too! I will set up meetings with some eligible boys for you next week."

"Nada doesn't have to get married anytime soon," her father argued. "She can stay with us for as long as she likes. Why must everything change?"

Nada closed her bedroom door behind her, blocking her parents' bickering, and a wave of exhaustion pushed down on her shoulders. She slumped at the edge of her bed, mirroring Zayn's posture from just an hour ago. A part of her worried about Haleema. Was she okay? Had the pain medication worn off? Should she send Noor Aunty a message? She didn't have the energy to reach for her phone. Instead, she lay back, still dressed in her fancy clothes, her eyes closing of their own volition. She had done what she could. Now it was up to Haleema and Zayn to find their way back to each other. And if they didn't, if they ended up like her and Baz, then they would simply learn to live with heartache and regret too.

The next day was Saturday, what would have been Haleema's wedding day. Nada woke up groggy and disoriented, her beautiful teal salwar kameez rumpled and uncomfortable against her skin. Sitting up, she reached for her phone and noticed that she had two missed calls and three texts, all from Haleema.

My sister from another mister, thanks for being there last night. Zayn came over this morning after Fajr and we talked. I'll fill you in but . . . the wedding is . . . (drum roll) . . . BACK ON!

Nada let out a loud whoop, then read the next message.

Except I don't really want to get married with a concussion, so the wedding is delayed for another two weeks. My parents are SO MAD, and the wedding planners are having a nervous breakdown. We'll have to cut the guest list and find a hall available last minute during desi wedding season. Prepare yourself for a "rustic backyard celebration." Also, we're going to get some emergency premarital counseling from Imam Abdul Bari at the Toronto Muslim Assembly. Zayn's idea.

Impressed, Nada read the final text message.

I don't know what you said to him last night, but it worked. I also don't know how we can ever repay you. I love you, babes.

Nada replied quickly with a series of smiley-face emojis and hearts.

Love you too, H. Rest up, beautiful bride-to-be!

Her parents were in the kitchen when Nada made her way downstairs. Jamal, seated at the table, was wolfing down a plate of eggs. The tremors in his right hand were more pronounced in the mornings, before he ate something, and so he drank the steaming cup of chai with his left hand, his steadier side. The sight of the tea made Nada wonder about the chai on the side table at Zayn's apartment, and what Baz might have heard.

The thought of seeing Baz again at the wedding didn't immediately fill her with dread or panic. Maybe this was progress. Maybe one day they would be able to talk civilly, without every conversation leaving them ripped to shreds. Maybe they would file for divorce and move on with their lives. The thought hurt, but the pain was bearable. Almost.

She took a seat at the table, and Narjis dropped a plate of *khageena* and toast in front of Nada, her favorite: scrambled eggs slow-cooked with heaps of onion, coriander, and green chili peppers, savory and filling. Chai slopped from the cup Narjis set down by Nada's elbow, and she realized her mother was angry. At her?

"You can tell the WhatsApp aunties that Haleema's wedding is back on," Nada said, hoping to cheer Narjis up. "It's been delayed for two weeks because of her injury, and the guest list will be a lot smaller because they have to change venues. On an unrelated note, how many people can we fit in our backyard?"

Narjis waved away Nada's words, her eyes trained on her youngest child. "Who will cook for you, once you move out?" she asked Jamal sharply, and Nada understood that she was the interloper here, interrupting an argument that had already started and which had nothing to do with her. Abbas's words from last night came back to her now: *Why must everything change?* "You think you are a grown man, now that you have a job?" her mother demanded.

Jamal grinned at his mother, his mouth full of toast and eggs. "I'll be home so often you'll get tired of cooking for me."

So Jamal had told them about his job and his wish to move out, Nada realized, slow to catch on after the events of last night. The world did not revolve around her drama or that of her friends, she realized with chagrin. Other people were allowed to drop truth bombs too. Today was Jamal's turn.

"I thought you'd be happy," Jamal said, lying cheerfully. "You can finally turn my room into a games den."

"We do not play games!" Narjis said. Beside her, Abbas silently drank his tea, but Nada knew that of the two of them, he was the most gutted.

"Great, then I can store my extra consoles and servers here. Thinking of starting a crypto farm, fam." He raised his hand to Nada for a high five, but she ignored him.

Her father looked plaintively at Jamal. "We can buy a larger home, where you can have your own separate apartment, *beta*. You do not have to leave us. Won't you be lonely?"

Jamal scraped his plate, then handily wheeled it over to the sink. "Sufyan will keep me company. He told me he's been looking for a roommate for a while, but he's picky. It's his condo, and he's giving me a break on the rent because I'll be working at his café." He turned to his sister and threw her a cheeky grin. "By the way, Nada knew about this for weeks, and she never said a word. She's the one you should be mad at, not me." With a mischievous smile, he rolled out of the kitchen.

"Did I mention Haleema's wedding is back on? Yay," Nada said weakly, but her parents were none too pleased.

"You and Haleema and *begairat* Jamal can do whatever you like. What concern is it of mine?" Narjis said, throwing the dish towel she had been using to wipe the table on the ground and stalking out of the kitchen.

"Your mother cleans when she's angry, and she cooks when she is upset. Or when we're hungry," Abbas added thoughtfully, reaching down to pick up the towel and folding it neatly. "She is worried about Jamal, *beta*." Her father turned sad eyes to his daughter. They were red-rimmed, as if he had been crying.

Nada reached over to hug him. "It will be okay, Dad," she said, awkwardly patting him on the back. "You didn't think we would stay here forever, did you?"

"The house is large enough, *nah*?" her father replied, his voice muffled against her shoulder.

"No matter where we go, our hearts will never leave your side," Nada said. She looked at her father's kind face. "Maybe you could take a cruise around the world, now that you and Mom won't have to worry about taking care of your ungrateful kids."

"Cruise ships are death traps," her father muttered darkly. Then, sighing deeply, he squeezed Nada's hand. "You're not ungrateful, and Jamal is not shameless. Perhaps you might even be right. I will see if your mother is interested in taking a trip. I hear some of these ships even serve halal meat, and we haven't taken a vacation in . . ." He paused, thinking. "Ever."

Narjis poked her head back into the kitchen, the long hose of the central vacuum cleaner drooping from her hands. "Also, if you think

I'll simply volunteer to host your friend's wedding in my backyard, you're wrong. If you are old enough to move out, then you are old enough to face the consequences of your actions. I know she broke her ankle fighting that human snake Haneef, so she can find her own backyard to marry Zayn!"

"Yes, Ammi," Nada said meekly. The WhatsApp aunties really did work fast. Why wasn't there an app that could harness their incredible powers of gossip? Nada paused, thinking, while Narjis plugged in the vacuum cleaner and attacked the meticulously clean area rug in the hallway. With a gentle tap on her forearm, Abbas motioned for Nada to follow him outside, to the always-a-backyard, never-a-wedding-venue.

Outside, the hum of the central vacuum cleaner was muted, and her father stared at nothing. While they had neighbors on either side of the house—the Chens to the left, and the Campbell clan to the right—their backyard looked over a small ravine, which had been a major selling point when her parents had purchased the lot preconstruction nearly twenty years ago. They had been so proud when they bought the house, a significant upgrade from the three-bedroom townhouse she had lived in until she was in grade three. Her brother, who had to go to high school in a new neighborhood, had been less thrilled about leaving his friends behind, but Nada had reveled in the spacious home.

"First Jamal, and soon Waqas," her father said abruptly. "You too will leave this home."

Nada ducked her head. She had given up predicting the future long ago, but she didn't deny her father's assertion. There was something in the air, and even her nervous, anxious father was powerless against its pull. Change was coming, and it was a sign of life being lived—far better than the opposite. "I don't know what I want," she said honestly.

Abbas studied his daughter, and the shrewd look in his eyes was one she rarely glimpsed on his face. "I want to invest in your company," he said.

"Why?" Nada said, startled. Her parents were in a strange mood today. "I don't have a company."

"You will. It's in your blood, more than the boys even. It has just taken you a little longer to accept this part of you." Her father smiled, and Nada thought about all that her parents had built together since arriving in Canada over three decades ago. They had their family, but also a successful accounting business and investments in other ventures.

"What would your investment mean?" Nada asked, cautious. The ideas in her notebook had been multiplying, and a few of them weren't terrible. Plus, just a moment ago, she had had a lightning strike idea while contemplating her mother's friends and their amazing ability to spread community gossip.

"Perhaps we will have an investor meeting, once a month, in our kitchen," Abbas suggested. "Perhaps you might even ask me a few questions about how to run a business. I might have a few questions for you as well. I promise not to steal your ideas, and you can promise to explain how an internet start-up works."

Nada grinned. "I accept. Thank you, Dad."

"Anything for you, *beta*."

CHAPTER THIRTY

Present day

Nada decided not to give notice at work, reasoning that until she had a viable idea and a real business plan, it would be better to keep her day job—a strategy her father approved of, despite his generous investment offer. However, she did have some vacation time, and so she took two weeks to devote to Haleema's wedding and to do some serious thinking.

The days before Haleema's rescheduled wedding were a whirlwind. The premarital counseling with Imam Abdul Bari had gone a long way to settle the couple's wedding jitters and helped them plan for the long term. The couple quickly settled on a few decisions. First, Zayn would move into Haleema's condo. They needed some space from Zayn's parents. Second, they agreed on the obvious choice of venue: the backyard of the Haq estate. Since even Zayn's parents' generously sized McMansion couldn't accommodate the original thousand-person guest list, Haleema and Zayn ruthlessly trimmed it down to an acceptable two hundred—undoubtedly sparking more than a few lifelong feuds with guests who didn't make the cut.

Luckily, Nada and her family were still on the list, and two weeks after the disastrous rehearsal dinner, they prepared to witness Haleema and Zayn's happily ever after.

For the combined *nikah* and *walima*, Haleema had chosen the mauve *gharara* with silver and gold *zari* work, forgoing the traditional bridal red, freeing Nada up to wear what she liked. As she stood in her walk-in closet a few hours before the wedding, the pretty *lengha* dress that Haleema had bought for her didn't feel right somehow. Instead, she reached behind the rack with her other fancy desi clothes and picked out the pink and gold dress with the tiny buttons on the back—the same one she had worn years ago to her own *nikah*, and then never again. She slipped into the familiar folds of satin and net and delicate gold embroidery and stared at herself in the full-length mirror.

The soft pink brought out the color in her cheeks and emphasized the darkness of her eyes. She had felt beautiful in this dress once, and remembered the way Baz had looked at her on their wedding day, the heat from his hungry, covetous gaze as he promised to love, support, and protect her. It felt right, somehow, to attend her best friend's wedding wearing this last remnant of her lost love. A final farewell, before she fully embraced her future. Her regrets still dogged her, but they felt bearable now, balanced by an understanding of her mistakes and a new determination to learn from them.

The pink dress fit her like a glove, better now than it had six years ago, when her body was too slim and girlish. The face staring back in the mirror held a knowing expression. Perhaps the prudence she had been forced into as a twenty-two-year-old could be shed, if only for one night, in favor of a more romantic memory.

Simple makeup of dramatic eyes and light pink lip gloss completed the look. She tied the shimmery cream hijab to show off her heavy gold earrings, and she was ready. When Nada joined her family in the driveway, she nodded in approval at her parents' outfits. Narjis had pulled out all the stops, resurrecting a fuchsia *benarasi* sari from her youth for the occasion and accessorizing it with an ornate *chandbali* pearl and ruby earrings and necklace set that had belonged to her nani. Abbas wore a starched black *shervani*. Meanwhile, Waqas looked dapper with his hair slicked back and wearing a dove gray three-piece suit with a purple pocket square. The twins, their foreheads adorned with tiny pearl *tika* ornaments, ran around the yard rumpling their adorable matching white and blue *lenghas*.

Waqas smiled broadly as a familiar Lexus sedan pulled up to the house. It was his plus-one, Khadijah, included in the guest list because the Syed family were particular friends of the bride. Khadijah's dress was deep purple, matching Waqas's pocket square, Nada noticed with some satisfaction. The couple would be driving to the wedding together, and the twins were thrilled to be sitting in the back of their father's new friend's car, which featured screens in the headrests, they excitedly told their aunt.

Once she waved them off, Nada joined her parents in the van, and they drove the short distance to Jamal's condo. Her little brother had moved out a few days after the rehearsal dinner, hauling his few belongings in the same van he was waiting for now, Sufyan keeping him company on the condo's circular driveway. Jamal's new roommate shook Abbas's hand and complimented Narjis on her delicate jewelry, but her mother only nodded coolly back. She hadn't entirely forgiven Sufyan for convincing her youngest child to move out. He turned to Nada now.

"I've heard that the point of a desi wedding is to produce more desi weddings," Sufyan said, a sly smile playing about his mouth. "I wish you good hunting today. Or perhaps you already have one particular prey in your sights?"

Nada shook her head. In his own way, Sufyan was just as mischievous as Jamal. No wonder they got along so well. "I heard you'll be there too—maybe you can help fend off the matchmaking aunties. How did you manage an invitation?" Nada asked.

"Kamran Uncle asked me to help with the catering. He is handling the food, while I'm in charge of the most important part of the meal."

"The chai?" she guessed with a smile.

"Now you've got it," Sufyan said.

Behind him, Jamal used the built-in ramp to settle inside the modified van. Abbas strapped the wheelchair to the stabilizing anchors, and with a final wave at Sufyan, they set off. Her parents were still not happy that he had moved out, but they were getting used to the idea. Just yesterday, Nada had overheard her mother on the phone with one of her friends, floating the idea of taking a joint Mediterranean cruise. The drive was mostly taken up by Jamal's chatter, as he shared amusing stories about the various customers at Nanima's Chai Shop.

The Haqs had wisely hired a valet service. While a uniformed attendant took the keys in exchange for a ticket, Narjis openly stared at the McMansion.

"Are you sure Zayn's family only runs the D&D convention?" she asked, none too quietly. "How can they afford all of this?" The look she threw Nada was similarly lacking in subtlety, and she knew what her mother was thinking: if they'd known the Haq family were capable of amassing this level of fortune in just a few short years, they might have had a different response to their daughter's one-time suitor.

Abbas shrugged, not as impressed as his wife. "Anyone can buy a big house. It is the content of their character that matters."

"I'd take the contents of their bank account any day," Jamal quipped, dexterously wheeling up the driveway. Another attendant ushered the family to the large backyard, where a series of connected white tents had been set up. Lake Ontario shimmered in the distance.

Considering these arrangements had been made last minute, the wedding planners had pivoted capably. Hafsa and Masood had decorated the tents with thick carpets and twinkling crystal chandeliers. The reception line was located in the first of the two smaller tents, where both Haleema's and Zayn's parents greeted guests, smiling as if the wedding hadn't been canceled just two weeks ago and hastily rerouted. Nada passed through the second tent, where white-gloved servers distributed soda and mocktails specially mixed for the occasion, as well as delicate finger foods suitable for an elegant outdoor wedding. Though Haleema had decided to merge the *nikah* and *walima* receptions, not just for the sake of economy but to embrace a new, drama-free life, Nada was pretty sure that goal wouldn't last beyond the day. Her friend lived for chaos.

When they strolled into the larger tent, Nada gasped in admiration. The venue was the height of luxury, and fresh blooms were everywhere. Heady jasmine, bold roses, and fragrant lilies adorned each of the circular tables and poured like a carpet from giant vases by the entrance. A floral wall panel formed the dramatic backdrop of the elevated stage, where two throne-like chairs were positioned. Servers helped the Syed family find their assigned seats at the very front of the room, at one of the reserved tables. They were on time, which meant they were early; the tent was half empty. The bride and groom would make their entrance once the other guests arrived. Nada texted Haleema: All good?

Haleema texted back immediately: Come to the carriage house. I could use some company.

When Nada arrived at the apartment, she was thankful that Zayn was nowhere to be found. She felt a little awkward, remembering their strangely intimate conversation. She assumed he had told Haleema about her and Baz, and she approached her friend with some trepidation, even as she paused for a moment to admire her stunning bridal outfit.

Haleema had chosen well; the mauve *gharara* with silver and gold *zari* work complemented her glowing skin and hazel eyes. Her hands were heavy with gold rings, and dark maroon henna patterns of intricate mandalas and paisleys adorned the backs of her hands. The large *tika* jewel on her forehead had been secured to her hijab and featured gold and diamond chains on either side of her head, which disap-peared underneath the heavy *dupatta* shawl draped dramatically down her back. Her makeup was glamorous with gold glitter highlighting her high cheekbones, black kohl lining her eyes, and her lips a deep maroon. Haleema glowed with happiness, and Nada hugged her, careful not to dislodge any part of her regal dress.

"I can't believe you're leaving me behind to join the married horde," Nada said lightly.

A shadow moved behind Haleema's eyes. "Is that the story you're sticking with?" she asked.

Nada knew the jig was up. "Today is about you, not me," she said firmly.

Haleema nodded. "Then expect a very angry phone call tomor-row. Why didn't you tell me the truth about you and Baz?"

Nada looked down at the gold shoe on Haleema's non-injured foot. Gold-colored footwear was a near-mandatory accessory for desi outfits, but difficult to find. "I don't know," she admitted.

"I felt like such a fool. Zayn kept insisting his brother was perfect for you, and I never stopped to wonder, *Why is he so sure about this?*" Haleema shook her head, and her eyes filled with tears.

"You'll ruin your makeup," Nada warned, quickly passing her friend a tissue.

"Bridal tears are considered good luck," Haleema said, but care-fully wiped her eyes.

"Are you happy?" Nada asked. She had reviewed escape strategies on the way over, just in case, but her friend only smiled and nodded with complete certainty.

"There's only one thing that could make this day even more per-fect, but that's out of my hands." She looked meaningfully at Nada.

"I'm afraid that request is out of my hands too," Nada said quietly. She squeezed her friend's hand. "You deserve every happiness."

Haleema squeezed back. "So do you, babes. Now be honest: Bisma knew everything from the start, didn't she?"

There was her competitive friend, hiding under all that bridal finery. Her question reminded Nada to save Bisma and Waleed, who had naturally made the guest list, a spot at their table.

She kissed Haleema on the cheek before making her way back to her seat, texting Bisma to join them as she maneuvered around the rapidly filling tables. Thankfully, she had yet to bump into Baz. Nada stopped at the appetizer buffet to fill a plate with cocktail samosas to share with her family, and placed the food in front of her parents and not Jamal, who would only eat them all. His stomach was a bottomless pit. Waqas, the twins, and Khadijah had joined them at their table, and when Bisma and Waleed arrived, Nada introduced them all. She and Bisma enjoyed a brief catch-up until Jamal complained that he was still hungry.

By the time Nada made a third trip to the appetizer line, the big tent had reached capacity, and an excited hush indicated that the bride and groom were about to make their grand entrance. It was time for Nada to take up her position. Aside from Noor and Hassan, Haleema only wanted her best friend by her side.

Haleema was serene as she stood on the expansive Haq lawn outside the tent. A photographer and videographer motioned for the small entourage to start walking as the first notes of a famous *nasheed* began to play. In keeping with South Asian tradition, the bridal party entered the venue first, and Haleema kept her head modestly lowered as she walked. Nada's hand gripped her friend's arm tightly as she helped guide her and made sure she didn't fall. Haleema had to keep her ankle boot on for another four weeks, and their progress was slow as she tried not to hobble. Once Haleema was settled on stage, Nada returned to her table.

It was time for the *baraat*, the groom's party, to make their entrance. First came the hired drummers, striking a fast and furious beat, followed by Baz, handsome in a well-fitted black suit that showed off his broad shoulders, then his parents, smiling and dressed in their usual simple style, and finally Zayn. The groom wore a cream-colored *shervani*, curly-toed shoes, a turban, and a veil of flowers over his face, which he parted to wave at the crowd, grinning in happiness. Nada's heart constricted. This joyful moment had almost not happened, all because of fear and misguided intention. As she watched Zayn make his slow procession toward his bride, who waited radiantly for the love of her life to join her, Nada's eyes met Baz's on stage. He nodded slightly at her, before turning away.

On the stage, a smiling Imam Abdul Bari presided over the brief *nikah* ceremony. Haleema's father, acting as the *wali*, clasped Zayn's hand and spoke the traditional words. Zayn repeated them. The imam made a *dua* for the couple. At her table, Nada bowed her head and echoed, "*Ameen.*"

Nada's wedding had been nothing like this. There had been no crowd of well-wishers, no crystal chandeliers, no giant vases or flower walls. There had been no music to accompany her down the aisle or drummers to entertain her guests. There hadn't been any guests at all, in fact. Only an imam, two witnesses, Bisma, and Baz. It had been enough. Her gaze drifted once more to him on stage. He had always been enough.

Something loosened in her chest in that moment, and Baz glanced over, before focusing on his brother. The ceremony concluded, and the crowd erupted into cheers, shouts of "*Takbir!*" and the answering rumble of "*Allahu Akbar!*" The happy couple posed for pictures, and Nada's heart felt full and broken at the same time. Seated beside her, Narjis sniffed and wiped her eyes.

Ever the showman, Zayn reached for the microphone and pulled Haleema up beside him. "Assalamu alaikum!" he called to the crowd. "Isn't my bride beautiful?" The guests cheered. "Some of you know that there was an unfortunate accident at our rehearsal dinner, which is why we had to reschedule the most important day of our lives. I want to take this moment to thank you all for attending, and give an extra special thank-you to Imam Abdul Bari, my brother, Bazlur Rahman, and our special friend Nada Syed. We wouldn't be here without you." The guests applauded politely, and then Zayn gestured behind him. "My brother has prepared a treat for all of you tonight. Everybody, please give a warm welcome to The Companions, featuring special guest Baz!"

The three members of The Companions each hugged Zayn and nodded respectfully at Haleema before taking up their positions. Baz took center stage, and now Nada felt free to stare. He was so beautiful. The bright sunlight streamed in from the tent entrance and cast a halo-like spotlight on his face, illuminating his chiseled features and deep-set eyes. Nada noticed that his hand shook slightly as he adjusted the microphone. Why was he nervous?

"I wrote this song for a lot of reasons," Baz said, his voice deep and raspy. He smiled at Zayn and Haleema. "This one is for my big brother and new sister, of course. But it's for me too." Then, after counting off, Baz closed his eyes and started to sing.

> *Half agony, half hope.*
> *Loving you is*
> *Half agony, half hope.*

Baz opened his eyes and stared straight at Nada, and she froze. He was singing to her, in front of everyone. A full-body flush raced through her and she started to tremble. The song continued:

> *True love like this is rare,*
> *Speak now and I'll forever swear*
> *To see all of you and be seen in turn*
> *Don't leave me lost in this*
> *Half agony, half hope.*

When he finished singing, Baz closed his eyes, allowing the silence to stretch around him. In the crowd, Nada did likewise. She knew he was praying, and she made a *dua* too, grateful for this moment. For this second chance.

Then Baz opened his eyes and thanked the audience, but Nada heard the rest of his words through a buzz. His song had been a public admission, but she didn't want the next part to be public. Her heart raced, and she stood suddenly, on legs that felt like jelly.

"Nada, are you all right?" Narjis asked, alarmed, but Nada didn't answer. She headed for the nearest exit.

Sunlight warmed her face as she stumbled outside and made her way toward the end of the backyard. No one else was around. Suddenly, Nada worried that Baz might take her flight as a sign that she was running away from him again, and she spun around, only to find him standing in front of her.

"Nada," he breathed.

Taking three giant strides, Nada went to him. And then her arms were around his neck and she was pulling him close, and she was kissing him, and he was kissing her back.

"I love you," she said. "I never stopped, not once." Tears streamed down her face, but she didn't care. Baz needed to know. No matter what he said next, he needed to hear this first.

"I know," he said, smiling. "I overheard your conversation with Zayn. I wanted to come to you right after."

Nada wiped her face, embarrassed, her mind still reeling. He had overheard their conversation, just as she had suspected. "It's been two weeks. Why did you wait?"

Baz smiled, tenderness softening his sharp features. "It was Zayn's idea. Not sure if you've noticed, but he has a flair for the dramatic." Nada laughed out loud, and Baz gathered her in his arms again, his voice urgent. "I looked for you that first year at the convention. I thought you'd come. I thought maybe we would bump into each other, maybe we could make everything right. I practiced what I would say. But you never showed up."

"I went into hiding after we broke up. Then Ask Apa failed and I think I sort of gave up. I couldn't handle losing anything else."

"I was one of your first subscribers," Baz admitted.

Nada laughed. "What was your question? *Where can I meet pretty Muslim girls who won't run away from me?*"

Baz wasn't smiling. "It was the same question, again and again: *How can I win back the love of my life?*"

Nada's smile disappeared. "What was the answer?"

"*Work on yourself, make dua, and if it is meant to happen, nothing can keep you apart.*"

Nada laughed. "Who knew Ask Apa was a hopeless romantic."

Baz gazed lovingly down at her, delicately stroking her cheek with a finger. "I remember thinking, *Maybe.* Maybe one day, we would find a way back to each other." He dipped his head as if to kiss her again, but before his lips touched hers, he paused and pulled back to look at her carefully. "I might have been stubborn, proud, and resentful, but I was never inconstant. I have loved none but you, my Nada. You have my heart, even more now than when you broke it six years ago. Can we try again?"

Nada nodded, and he kissed her. His lips were firm, and he tasted like sweet tea with a trace of cardamom. Their future unspooled in front of them, bright and hopeful once more, now that they were both finally where they were meant to be. Nothing else mattered.

"NADA! What are you DOING?" Narjis stood six feet away, staring in shock.

Nada looked from her mother to Baz. He was trying not to laugh, and she resisted the urge to bury her face in his shoulder. Or grab his hand and make a run for it. "How much should we tell our family?" she whispered to him instead.

"We got married last month, at the convention," Baz said easily. "Surprise!"

"What about the truth?" Nada pressed.

"We can share that story after our first kid is born. Our parents will be less likely to murder us knowing they'd be stuck changing all the diapers."

"Good plan," Nada said, taking a deep breath.

Baz leaned over and kissed her once more, as if to reassure himself this was real. Then, holding hands, they walked toward a sputtering Narjis, and made everything okay.

EPILOGUE

Nearly one year later...

The underground parking lot was packed with cars when Baz handily maneuvered into one of the last spots. They had opted to drive down this morning, instead of staying at the convention hotel the night before. Now that Baz was no longer running Deen&Dunya, the pressure was off, though in other ways, it had ramped way up.

Nada reached over and smoothed the furrow in his brow. "It's going to go so well," she said, smiling. She was always smiling these days. They had moved in together a few weeks after Haleema and Zayn's wedding, after securing a lease in the same condo building. Even though Nada spent every day with Baz, she had yet to tire of looking at his beautiful face.

"My parents are still so angry I quit," Baz said, almost to himself.

"Not that angry," Nada lied. But she had an ace up her sleeve, happy news she was sure would be a good distraction. She just had to share it with Baz first. "You didn't quit. You're following in their entrepreneurial footsteps. I'm so proud of you."

Baz's eyes softened when he looked at her. He leaned over and they kissed, a slow, dreamy embrace, his hand tenderly cupping her jaw. She pulled back slightly, before things got too intense.

"Maybe we should check into the hotel after all," he murmured, but Nada shook her head, laughing. They both knew they would never make it to the convention if they did. Sighing with mock disappointment, Baz kissed the back of her hand, and they got out of the car and walked to the entrance of the Metro Toronto Convention Centre, where a large crowd milled excitedly.

Haleema, who had helped Zayn with the logistics this year, had reported that the number of registrants was at nearly twenty-five thousand. Deen&Dunya was thriving under the new COO, Zayn, and under the general management of a handful of fresh hires.

Baz dug their passes, courtesy of his brother, out of his pocket, and they made their way up the escalators to the main floor of the convention. Jamal was waiting by the doors in his brand-new neon orange motorized wheelchair, alongside a serious-looking Sufyan, dressed in another black T-shirt, this one with *Nanima's Chai Shop* emblazoned across the front. In an effort to find local talent, the organizers of Deen&Dunya had asked the two young men to share their experience running a local business with global aspirations. As the newly minted manager of the chai shop, Jamal was practically bursting with pride and swagger.

"You two coming to the concert tonight?" Jamal asked his sister now. "Try to stay away from the Zaynimals, unless you're wearing a helmet."

Nada and Baz looked at each other. Zayn had finished recording his latest album recently, which he had titled *Haleema*, and the entire family had been invited to hear the new tracks live. "We'll be there," Baz said firmly. "Standing at the very back."

Nada's grip on Baz's hand tightened. "Actually, I'll be standing at the very back. Baz will be on stage. He's launching Ummah Talent at the concert."

The young men congratulated Baz, while he ducked his head, nervous and embarrassed. Baz had taken her suggestion to start a talent agency for Muslim creatives and run with it. While her in-laws hadn't been happy that their son had abandoned D&D so he could work with artists, she knew this was the right move for her creative, passionate husband.

"What about you, Nada Apa?" Sufyan asked. "When are you launching Rumor Mill? I have a few rumors I'd like to share. For instance, did you know the two very successful, very eligible bachelors who run Nanima's Chai Shop are about to franchise?"

Nada shook her head in amusement. Her latest business venture, a social media app she had named Rumor Mill as a nod to the WhatsApp aunties and their ability to spread community news at lightning speed, would be used to confirm, in real time, rumors running through neighborhoods. Nada envisioned it as a fact-checking resource targeted at microcommunities, which were often a hotbed of speculation and disinformation. Now that the Ukhti lawsuit had been settled, and Haneef's reputation lay in tatters, she was ready to launch her next venture.

Nada asked Jamal if Waqas and the twins had arrived yet, or their parents. Jamal said they hadn't, but confirmed that they were all on their way.

Waqas had moved out last fall, earlier than anyone in the family had anticipated. He was renting an apartment nearby, and taking things slowly with Khadijah, as they tried to figure out the best way to blend their families.

Haleema, rushing past them, squeezed Nada's arm, a question in her eyes: *Have you told him yet?* Nada shook her head no.

She tugged on Baz's hand, and together they strolled toward the bazaar. Nada had scoped out the venue ahead of time, and now she guided them to a particular booth. With a smile for the proprietor, she turned to Baz, holding up a tiny white onesie with the words *Bismillah Baby* on the front. Baz looked from the onesie to his wife, first with confusion and then with sudden realization. With a loud whoop that startled nearby shoppers, Baz picked Nada up and twirled her around, his face suffused with delight. He put her down and kissed her deeply, and she kissed him back, even though she knew it would get back to her mother. She was too elated to care if she was causing a scene. After so many years living her life in the shadows, she wanted the entire world to bear witness to her happiness.

She loved this man, and in a few months, their family would be growing. More love, shared and multiplied. Joy, found and lost and then found again, which made it that much sweeter. *Alhamdulillah*.

ACKNOWLEDGMENTS

Bismillah. I am so grateful to be writing the acknowledgments for my third book. While writing doesn't get any easier, one of the best parts of being a writer is the community I've met along the way.

First off, thanks to my friend and talented agent, Ann Collette. Four books later, and what an exciting ride it's been. I'm always so grateful for your encouragement, cheerleading, and spot-on advice.

Thanks also to my amazing film/TV agent, Sean Daily. It's been surreal and fun, and I can't wait for what's next!

Huge thanks to my editor Jennifer Lambert at HarperCollins Canada. Your insights make every book better, and your enthusiasm has meant everything. Thanks also to my stellar U.S. editor, Cindy Hwang, at Berkley for your continued support. Much appreciation to my U.K. family at Corvus/Atlantic Books and my editor Sarah de Souza. I am in love with this beautiful cover, for which I have Sanno Singh to thank. All the stars and appreciation to my amazing HarperCollins Canada team: Canaan Chu, Natalie Meditsky, Stacey Cameron, Alice Tibbetts, Neil Wadhwa, Brennan Frances, Kristina Jagger, Marisol Folkes, Lauren Morocco, Cory Beatty, and my publisher Iris Tupholme. Over at Berkley Books, many many thanks to

Angela Kim, Christine Legon, Rita Frangie Batour, Tiffany Estreicher, Jennifer Lynes, Jessica Mangicaro, Anika Bates, and Yazmine Hassan. I would still be writing books on an ancient laptop and mumbling to myself if it weren't for all of you.

On the home front, thank you to my large extended family in Canada, the U.S., India, and beyond. Your pride at having a writer in the family fuels me. Special thanks to my cousins Nuha, Safaa, and Sameena, the original Double Hijabis. I hope that part made you laugh.

To my sons, Mustafa and Ibrahim: I wrote this book in spite of your constant interruptions and requests for food and cookies. (Okay, I secretly enjoyed the interruptions. Now go do your homework.)

To my parents, Mohammed and Azmat, and my brother, Atif: thank you for telling all your neighbors and friends and random strangers about my books. You are the best street team a girl could ask for.

So many thanks to my writer community: Kate Hilton, Marissa Stapley, Catherine Hernandez, Sonya Lalli, Zarqa Nawaz, Sonali Dev, Huda Fahmy, Lindsay Wong, Tricia Fish, Sahar Jahani, and many others. It's been an honor to be in the writing trenches with you all. Thanks also to Shannon Chakraborty, Nalini Singh, Kate Quinn, Sarah MacLean, Emily Henry, and Alisha Rai for your kindness and blurbs. A special hug and heart emoji to my writing soul sister, Ausma Zehanat Khan. And thanks to Huda Idrees for answering my many questions!

Parts of *Much Ado About Nada* take place in a few Toronto-area institutions that are important to me. First up is the University of Toronto, St. George campus, my alma mater and the scene of many happy (and stressful) undergrad memories, especially the lobby and stacks of Robarts Library, the E.J. Pratt Library, and Hart House, which has hosted weekly *Jumah* prayers for Muslim students and staff for over fifty years. I have to pause here to give a shout-out to my sisters, my #Robarts family: our group chat and offline friendships are life-giving, and I'm so grateful to have you awesome ladies in my life.

I loved writing about the beautiful Aga Khan Museum in Toronto, a place of calm and serenity nestled outside the downtown core. If you haven't visited, put it on your bucket list!

As for the Golden Crescent neighborhood—yes, it's fictional, but it's inspired by three places where I've lived over the years: Scarborough, Malton, and Markham, each full of diversity, kind souls, and the best food in the world.

I would be remiss if I didn't acknowledge the OG social satirist and rom-com storyteller herself, Jane Austen. While *Much Ado About Nada* gets its title from pop culture and Shakespeare, the angsty meditation on second chances and regret is all Ms. Austen. Thank you for speaking beyond your time, and across cultures.

Finally, to my husband, Imtiaz. You said you like this book best—I could say the same about you. Thanks for coming up with the best title!

And a big thanks to YOU, wonderful, fun, intelligent, savvy reader. By picking up this book, you've given me the gift of your time and attention, and I am grateful. If you enjoyed the read, please consider leaving a review on the platform of your choice—it helps others find my stories. Until next time, Inshallah.

Photograph by Andrea Stenson

UZMA JALALUDDIN is the internationally bestselling author of *Ayesha at Last* and *Hana Khan Carries On*, both of which have been optioned for film, the latter by Mindy Kaling and Amazon Studios. A high school English teacher, Jalaluddin is also a contributor to the *Toronto Star* and the *Atlantic*. She lives near Toronto with her family.